"James Rollins is clearly at the top of his game."
—Steve Berry

"A master of international action and intrigue."
—*Richmond Times-Dispatch*

"Riveting. . . . Rollins gets better with each book, and his position at the top of this particular subgenre remains unshaken."

—*Publishers Weekly*

"Mind-boggling 'What if's' abound in the thrilling novels by James Rollins."

—*Sacramento Bee*

"This guy doesn't write novels—he builds roller coasters. . . . Rollins excels at combining action and history with larger-than-life characters. . . . A must for pure action fans."
—*Booklist*

By James Rollins

By James Rollins and Rebecca Cantrell

By James Rollins and Grant Blackwood

KINGDOM OF BONES

A THRILLER

JAMES ROLLINS

wm
WILLIAM MORROW
An Imprint of *HarperCollins*Publishers

First William Morrow premium printing: November 2022
First William Morrow paperback international printing: April 2022
First William Morrow hardcover printing: April 2022

Print Edition ISBN: 978-0-06-289299-7
Digital Edition ISBN: 978-0-06-289304-8

Cover art by Tony Mauro
Cover photographs © Zcetrt/Dreamstime.com (sand); © Andrei Stancu/Dreamstime.com (bones)

William Morrow and HarperCollins are registered trademarks of HarperCollins Publishers in the United States of America and other countries.

22 23 24 25 26 BVGM 10 9 8 7 6 5 4 3 2 1

To all the doctors and nurses, orderlies and janitors, to all the personnel in hospitals and clinics across this nation and the world who have worked so valiantly and heroically during the pandemic: Thank you.

ACKNOWLEDGMENTS

Laurie Anderson, one of my favorite musicians, wrote a song titled "Language Is a Virus." If she is correct, then any book must be a vector for transmission. For this novel, the language contained herein was made all the more potent via a group of first readers who helped me engineer and polish this story to its most infectious form: Chris Crowe, Lee Garrett, Matt Bishop, Matt Orr, Leonard Little, Judy Prey, Caroline Williams, Sadie Davenport, Sally Ann Barnes, Denny Grayson, and Lisa Goldkuhl. And a special thanks to Steve Prey for the Congo regional map. But I also have to single out David Sylvian for all his hard work and dedication in the digital sphere. And Cherei McCarter, who has shared with me a bevy of intriguing concepts and curiosities, several of which are found in these pages. And a special acknowledgment to moukies for his most helpful read regarding the authenticity on subject matters raised in this novel. Of course, none of this would happen without an astounding team of industry professionals who I defy anyone to surpass. To everyone at William Morrow, thank you for always having my back, especially Liate Stehlik, Heidi Richter, Kaitlin Harri, Josh Marwell, Richard Aquan, Caitlin Garing, Andrea Molitor, and Ryan Shepherd. Last, of course, a special acknowledgment to the people instrumental to all levels of production: my esteemed editor, Lyssa Keusch, and her industrious colleague Mireya Chiriboga; and for all their hard work, my agents, Russ Galen and Danny Baror (along with his daughter Heather Baror). And as always, I must stress that any and all errors of fact or detail in this book, of which hopefully there are not too many, fall squarely on my own shoulders.

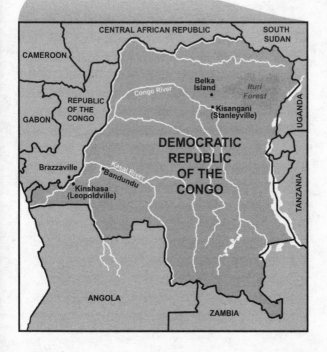

NOTES FROM THE SCIENTIFIC RECORD

This story delves into the bizarre biology of viruses—specifically how those tiny infectious specks tie all life on Earth together in a vast invisible web. I pitched this story long before "coronavirus" became part of our modern zeitgeist, before COVID-19 grew into a global pandemic. I debated whether I should even finish writing this novel while a plague swept the world. It struck me as the epitome of hubris to craft a story of a deadly virus when reality was far more frightening (and heartbreaking) than any work of fiction could be. Furthermore, it felt insensitive to tackle such a subject at this moment, to seek to entertain with "plague fiction" when the world was suffering.

Since you are holding this book in your hand, you know how my deliberation ended. Why? First, I should admit that I've tackled "pandemic" threats in past novels (*The Seventh Plague, The Sixth Extinction*). My intent with this book was not to repeat myself. The conceit of this story was less to address the *plague* as it was to look deeper into the *source*: the weird biology of viruses. It was a subject that I thought could be of interest to readers—and maybe an important one to address now.

During my research for this story, I discovered how truly strange, diverse, and ubiquitous viruses are in nature. Every day, trillions of viruses rain from the sky. Each hour, some thirty-three million viral particles cascade onto every square meter of the planet.[*] Still, despite being so abundant, viruses remain a mystery. Even today, less is known about the biology of viruses than any other life-form.[†] In addition, it is speculated that there are millions, if not trillions, of viral species yet to be discovered.

Still, what is known about viruses is how deeply they're entwined into our evolutionary history. Their genetic code is buried deep in our DNA. Scientists estimate that between 40 to 80 percent of the human genome may have come from ancient viral invasions.[‡] And it's not just us. Recently scientists have discovered how intimately viruses are woven throughout the natural world. They are the tie that binds all life together. In fact, researchers now believe that viruses could offer a clue to the origin of life; they could be the very engines of evolution, perhaps even the source of human consciousness.[§]

---

[*] "Trillions Upon Trillions of Viruses Fall from the Sky Each Day," Jim Robbins, *New York Times*, April 13, 2018.
[†] "Welcome to the Virosphere," Johnathan R. Goodman, *New Scientist*, January 11, 2020.
[‡] Robbins, op. cit.
[§] "An Ancient Virus May Be Responsible for Human Consciousness," Rafi Letzter, *Live Science*, February 2, 2018.

So, while this book is not a pandemic novel per se, I believe it's far more frightening.

Why?

Because of one last warning I heard from scientists: *Viruses—both out in nature and inside our bodies—are not done changing us, of evolving us. And it's continuing right now as you read this.*

NOTES FROM THE HISTORICAL RECORD

"The horror! The horror!"

Those are the dying words of the villain, Kurtz, in Joseph Conrad's *Heart of Darkness*. It is the moment when Kurtz recognizes the atrocities and cruelties he has inflicted upon the native peoples of the African Congo. It also serves as a warning: to beware that darkness in all of our hearts.

Conrad wrote this account (serialized in 1899) based on his captainship of a steamship along the Congo River, where he bore witness to the brutality of colonial rule of the Congo Free State, which he described as "the vilest scramble for loot that ever disfigured the history of human conscience."[*] In a little over a decade's time, ten million Congolese would be killed. As described by British explorer Ewart Grogan: "Every village has been burnt to the ground, and as I fled from the country, I saw skeletons everywhere;

---

[*] "Forever in Chains: The Tragic History of Congo," Paul Vallely, *Independent*, July 28, 2006.

and such postures—what tales of horrors they told!"[*]

So how did these atrocities come about?

Sadly, it was all due to advancements in medicine and technology. First, it was the discovery of quinine—the antimalarial compound—in the early nineteenth century that would open the heart of the continent to the world. Portuguese and Arab slavers had already been raiding the Congo, but with a treatment for malaria, a great period of European colonization began. The French grabbed a northern swath of the Congo, while King Leopold II of Belgium secured a million square miles of the southern half, roughly a third the size of the continental United States, with "cloth and trinket" treaties.[†]

Next came the technology of the "pneumatic tyre," invented by the Scottish veterinarian John Boyd Dunlop. This set up a gold rush for sources of rubber, of which the vines of the Congo were a major source. It suddenly became exceedingly profitable to exploit and enslave the Congolese villagers. King Leopold set up stringent quotas for both rubber and ivory to be produced by each village. The price for any shortfalls was the loss of a hand. In a short period of time, human hands became a form of currency throughout the Congo Free State, along with severed ears, noses, genitalia, and even heads. In addition, Belgian officers carried out a pogrom of terror,

---

[*] Robert Edgerton, *The Troubled Heart of Africa: A History of the Congo* (St. Martin's Press, 2002), p. 137.
[†] Vallely, op. cit.

involving the crucifixion and hanging of men, women, and children.[*]

These atrocities would go unreported for over a decade, leading to the eventual slaughter and starvation of half the Congolese population. While Conrad's *Heart of Darkness* served as a literary vehicle to showcase these atrocities, it was actually the work of missionaries, specifically an American, a Black Presbyterian reverend, William Henry Sheppard, who would expose the world to the true horrors suffered by the Congolese during his stint as a missionary in the region.[†]

But these atrocities were not the only "horrors" that the Reverend Sheppard experienced during this bloody time. Another account of Sheppard was buried under bones. It was a tale tied to the maps, relics, and myths of another Black Christian patriarch in Africa.

Most don't know that story.

Until now.

---

[*] Ibid.

[†] Edgerton, op.cit., p. 143.

The mind of man is capable of anything—because
everything is in it, all the past as well as the future.
—Joseph Conrad, *Heart of Darkness*

The only true villain in my story:
the oversized human brain.
—Kurt Vonnegut, *Galapagos*

The Reverend William Sheppard silently recited the Lord's Prayer as he waited for the cannibal to finish filing his teeth. The Basongye tribesman held a bone rasp in one hand and a mirror in the other as he crouched by the fire. He sharpened an incisor to a finer point, smiled admiringly at his handiwork, then finally stood.

The tribesman towered before Sheppard, standing nearly seven feet tall. The cannibal was dapperly dressed in long pants, polished boots, and a buttoned shirt. He could easily be mistaken for a fellow classmate of Sheppard's at the Southern Presbyterian Theological Seminary for Colored Men in Tuscaloosa, from which the reverend had graduated. Only, as was typical for the cannibal's tribe, the giant here had shaved his eyebrows and plucked his eyelashes, creating a frightening countenance, especially with his shark-toothed grin.

Sheppard sweated in a white linen suit and tie, and a matching pith helmet. He craned his neck to face the leader of the Zappo Zaps. The warlike tribe had allied themselves with Belgium's colonial forces and served as King Leopold's de facto army. The infamous Zappo Zaps had earned their name from the rattling blasts of their many guns. Sheppard noted the long rifle slung over the cannibal's shoulder. He wondered how many innocents had died because of that one weapon.

Upon entering the village, Sheppard had observed dozens of fly-crusted bodies. From the piles of scorched bones, it was evident many others had already been eaten. Nearby, a tribesman set about carving a fresh bloody slab from a severed thigh. Another Zappo Zap rolled leaves of tobacco inside a hollowed-out skull. Even the fire that stood between him and their group's leader served to smoke a set of severed hands, skewered on bamboo sticks above the flames.

Sheppard did his best to ignore the horrors here, even as his senses were assaulted. Clouds of black flies hummed in the air. The stench of burned flesh hung in his nostrils. To keep down his bile, he fixed his gaze on the tribesman. It would not help his cause to object or to show any squeamishness.

Sheppard spoke slowly, knowing the cannibal knew both English and French but was far from fluent in either. "M'lumba, I must speak to Captain Deprez. It is of utmost important that he hear me out."

M'lumba shrugged. "He not here. He gone."

"Then what of Collard or Remy?"

Another shrug, but the man's expression darkened. "Gone with the *capitaine*."

Sheppard frowned. Deprez, Collard, and Remy— all members of the Belgian army—led the Zappo Zaps in this region. Sheppard had come to know the trio after he had established a Christian mission along the Kasai River, a tributary of the Congo. The Belgians' absence here was unusual, especially when their group collected its "rubber tax" from a village—not that any of the officers would have stopped the atrocities committed here. In fact, the trio encouraged such brutality. Deprez even carried a bullwhip, knotted out of hippo leather, that he used to flay the flesh from his victims at the least offense. For the past few months, the captain had been leading this group in a rampage along the Kasai River, terrorizing village after village, heading inexorably north.

It was for this reason that Sheppard had left his mission in Ibanj and sought out this group. Another tribe, the Kuba, had sent an emissary from their king to plead with Sheppard, asking for the reverend to stop the murderous Zappo Zaps from entering their territory. He could not refuse this request. Two years earlier, Sheppard had been the first foreigner allowed to enter the Kuba kingdom, mostly because he had taken the time to learn their language. After proving his fluency, he was treated graciously by the royal court. He found the people to be honest and industrious, despite their beliefs in witchcraft and a king who had seven hundred wives. While he had failed to convert any of them, he had still found them to be great allies in this hostile region.

Now they need my help.

He had to at least try to make his case with Deprez, to convince the Belgian captain to spare the Kuba from the spread of this slaughter.

"Where did Deprez and the others go?" Sheppard asked.

M'lumba looked to the east, beyond the Kasai River, which flowed a sullen course nearby. He cursed in Bantu and spat in that direction. "I tell them not to go there. It is *alaaniwe*."

Sheppard knew the Bantu word for "cursed." He also knew how ingrained superstitions were among the local tribes. They believed in ghosts and spirits, in spells and magic. As a missionary, he had found it nearly impossible to break through that veil of pagan beliefs and replace it with the bright word of the Lord. Still, he had tried his best, while also chronicling the horrific acts committed here, armed with only a Bible and a Kodak box camera.

Sheppard frowned his frustration. He knew it would take something significant to draw off all three officers. "M'lumba, why did Deprez and the others leave? What were they looking for?"

"*Pango*," the tribesman muttered, using the Bantu word for "cave." Then he scowled and pantomimed digging, while looking at Sheppard for comprehension.

Sheppard squinted, then understood. "Do you mean a mine?"

M'lumba bobbed his head. "*Oui*. A mine. In a bad place. At the Mfupa Ufalme."

Sheppard stared across the river, translating the cannibal's last words.

The Kingdom of Bones.

While it was an ominous-sounding title, Sheppard paid it little heed. He knew there remained many unexplored places hidden in the trackless jungle. In fact, he had even discovered a new lake himself and had been invited by the British Royal Geographical Society to speak of this accomplishment in London in a few months. Still, more prevalent than the superstitions rampant among these lands were the countless rumors of lost treasures and hidden kingdoms. Such tales had lured many men to their doom.

And now maybe three more Belgians.

"Why were they looking for this mine?" Sheppard asked. "What were they hoping to find?"

M'lumba turned and barked to an aged tribesman, whose face was heavily tattooed, marking him as the group's *mganga*, or witch doctor. The Zappo Zaps never traveled without a shaman among them, to help ward off *visuka* and *roho*, the vengeful ghosts and spirits of those whom they had slaughtered.

The wizened elder joined them. He wore only strips of a loincloth and a necklace festooned with carved ivory and wooden charms. His lips were greasy from his recent feasting. M'lumba made some demand to the *mganga* in a Basongye dialect that Sheppard could not follow.

Finally, the shaman scowled and shifted through the tangled mass of his charms. He freed a braided loop from around his neck. A single totem hung from it. It appeared to be a metal disk, no larger than a thumbnail. The elder shook it at M'lumba, who took it and passed it to Sheppard.

"*Capitaine* Deprez found this. Around neck of another village's *mganga*. The *capitaine* whip and whip to make the peoples speak. Screams for two nights. Then *mganga* tell him where it come from."

"From Mfupa Ufalme . . ." Sheppard muttered. *The Kingdom of Bones.*

M'lumba nodded with a deep scowl, clearly angry about something.

Sheppard examined the charm. It appeared to be a coin, blackened by age, drilled through its center to hang from the braided cord. One side had been rubbed enough to reveal the sheen of gold.

Sheppard felt a sinking despair.

No wonder Deprez had been so brutal . . .

For such a depraved man, the promise of gold had to shine far brighter than any quota of ivory or rubber. Of all the rumors of secret cities and treasures hidden in the jungle, none stoked the lust of the greedy more than stories of lost gold. For ages, explorers had been scouring the jungles, searching for such caches. Legends continued to persist of mines dug out by vanished Roman legions or even by the Old Testament forces of King Solomon.

Sheppard sighed, knowing all too well how many explorers had died in such foolhardy pursuits. He started to lower the bit of gold—when a glint of sunlight revealed writing on the coin's opposite side. He lifted it again and turned it askance to reveal what was faintly inscribed there. He squinted, then his eyes widened in shock. He rubbed it clearer to be sure, revealing a name, written in Latin.

Presbyter Iohannes.

He gripped the token tighter.

It cannot be.

Though the name was in Latin, Sheppard knew this particular gold coin had not been minted by any Roman legion. Nor had the gold been mined by the forces of King Solomon. Instead, what was written here hinted at *another* story, one as fanciful as those other tales.

"Prester John," he mumbled, translating the Latin.

During his theological studies, he had learned of the formidable Christian priest-king of Africa. According to accounts dating back to the twelfth century, Prester John had ruled ancient Ethiopia for close to a century. He was said to be a descendant of Balthazar, the black Magi, one of the trio of kings who had visited the Christ child in His manger. Prester John's kingdom was believed to be one of astronomical wealth and secret knowledge. His legend was even tied to the Fountain of Youth and to the lost Ark of the Covenant. For many centuries, European rulers had sought out this illustrious personage. They sent forth emissaries, many of whom vanished into the jungle and never returned. Even Shakespeare mentioned this lost African patriarch in his play *Much Ado About Nothing*.

However, most historians of today dismissed this tale of a black Christian king who ruled over a vast swath of Africa as mere myth.

Sheppard stared down at the name written in gold. He wanted to discount what he held as some bit of fakery. Still, as the son of a slave, he could not. Instead, he felt a shiver of a kinship to this legend, to another black Christian from centuries earlier.

Could there be some truth behind all those stories?

While the promise of gold might have lured Captain Deprez into the forest, Sheppard could not dismiss his own longing—not for riches, but for the *history* hinted at by this coin.

He lowered the token and faced M'lumba. "How long have Deprez and the others been gone?"

M'lumba shook his head. "Twelve days. They take twenty men." A deep sneer of anger showed sharp teeth. "And my brother, Nzare. I tell him not to go. But *Capitaine* make him go."

Sheppard sensed that here was the root of the cannibal's ire—which offered an opportunity. "Then let us make an *mkataba*. A pact between you and me."

M'lumba's hairless brows bunched warily. "*Nini mkataba?*"

Sheppard placed a palm atop his shirt, over his heart. "I will travel to Mfupa Ufalme and fetch your brother back to you—but only if you swear that you and your men will remain here and go no farther into Kuba lands."

M'lumba stared across the ruins of the village, contemplating this offer.

"Give me three weeks," Sheppard pleaded.

M'lumba's scowl only deepened.

Sheppard waited stiffly for a response. If nothing else, those weeks would allow time for the villagers in the Kuba territory to evacuate and hide themselves within the forests. He prayed such a gambit might protect those fifty thousand souls from the barbarity on display here.

M'lumba finally held up three fingers. "*Tatu* weeks. We will stay." He stared at the sprawl of bodies. "Then I will get hungry again."

Sheppard hid a shudder of revulsion at the threat in those last words. He pictured the well-kept streets of the Kuba's royal village, lined by life-sized statues of former kings, echoing with the laughter of women and children. He imagined those happy sounds replaced by screams, the clean avenues awash in a tide of blood.

He stared past the Kasai River to the dark jungle beyond. He did not know if there was a lost gold mine out there. He doubted there was even any truth to what was written in Latin on the coin. And he definitely did not believe in any ancient curses rooted in a Kingdom of Bones.

Instead, the smoky stench of burned flesh reminded him of one certainty.

I must not fail.

FIRST

INCURSION

1

A sharp sting woke Charlotte Girard to the harsh reality of her situation. She had been dreaming of swimming naked in the bracingly cold pool at her family's country estate on the French Riviera. She slapped at her neck and sat up abruptly inside the hot, humid tent. The air stifled and swamped. Another sting struck the back of her other hand. Startled, she shook her arm, tangling it in the gauzy mosquito netting around the cot.

She cursed in French and fought her limb free. She stared down at the culprit, expecting to see one of the biting black flies that plagued the refugee camp. Instead, a red-black ant—as long as her thumbnail—perched on her wrist. Its mandibles had latched deep into her flesh.

Aghast, she knocked it away and sent the insect flying into the netting, where it scrabbled up the gauze. With her heart pounding, she pushed through the drape around her cot. Lines of crawling ants traced the dormitory tent's floor and zigzagged up the walls.

Where had they all come from?

She retrieved her sandals and donned them, knocking loose a few stray ants. She then tiptoed across the flowing map on the floor. Thankfully, she was already dressed in blue scrubs and a white vest.

She caught a peek at herself in a standing mirror, momentarily shocked by her appearance. She looked a decade older than her late twenties. She had tied her ebony hair into an efficient ponytail, but it hung askew from sleeping on it. Her eyes were still puffy and shadowed by exhaustion. Her complexion was peeling from days under the sun. Her dermatologist back in Montmartre would be aghast, but out here in the bush, she had no time for niceties like expensive sunscreens and moisturizers.

Last night, well past midnight, she had dropped, exhausted, onto her cot. She was the youngest of the four-member medical team from Médecins Sans Frontières, or Doctors Without Borders, at the camp. They were severely shorthanded with more refugees still pouring into the village camp as the jungles to the east continued to flood from the near-constant rain.

Eight days ago, she had been airlifted here via helicopter from the city of Kisangani, where she had been assisting UNICEF with their Healthy Villages program. Once here, she had quickly been overwhelmed. She had only finished her residency in pediatrics at USPC—Université Sorbonne-Paris-Cité—two years ago and had decided to give something back by applying for a one-year stint with MSF. At the time, her plan had seemed like a grand adventure, one she was determined to experience before settling into a routine at some clinic or hospital. Plus, she had spent part of her childhood in the neighboring Republic of Congo, at its capital of Brazzaville. Ever since then, she had always wanted to return to these jungles. Unfortunately, the passage of years had colored her perspective of the Congo region. It certainly had not prepared her for the hardships out in the rural bush.

Like the fact that everything here tried to eat, sting, poison, or swindle you.

She crossed to the dormitory tent flap and shouldered through to the morning's cloudy sunlight. She squinted at the brightness and shadowed her eyes with a hand. The village's thatched huts and tin-roofed shacks spread to her right. A good portion of the homes had already been swept away by the neighboring storm-swollen Tshopo River. To her left, a sprawl of tents and makeshift lean-tos spread far into the forest, occupied by refugees from other villages who had been forced to flee the rising waters.

And more people continued to flock here every day, overwhelming the area.

The smoke from a score of campfires did little to push back the smell of raw sewage. Cholera cases were already climbing, and the medical team was running low on fluids and doxycycline. Only yesterday, she had treated a dozen malaria cases, too.

It was hardly the bucolic natural world she had envisioned back in Paris.

As a further reminder, thunder rumbled ominously in the distance. Over the past two months, storm after storm had swept the area, flooding lands that were already swamps, even during the dry season. It had been the worst recorded rainfall in over a century—and more storms were forecast. Floodwaters threatened the breadth of the central Congo, and between corruption and bureaucratic red tape, relief aid was slow to keep up. She prayed for another drop-shipment of U.N. medical supplies before the situation became even more dire out here.

As she crossed toward the medical tent, she watched a young child squat and loose a wet stream of diarrhea. Ants climbed over the little girl's bare feet and mounted her legs. She cried out from their bites, until a woman, likely her mother, scooped her up by the arm and brushed at her legs and feet.

Charlotte hurried over and helped pick off the last of the ants. She pointed to the clinic tent. Her Swahili was poor at best. "*Dawa*," she said, guiding the woman and child. "Your daughter needs medicine."

Dehydration—whether from cholera or a thousand other etiologies—could kill a child in less than a day.

"*Kuza, kuza*," Charlotte urged the woman and led the way.

All around, locals scurried about. Many wielded brooms of palm leaves and fought the invading ant horde. She skirted behind a Luba native who swept a path toward the medical tent. Following in his wake, she safely reached the tarp above the clinic entrance. The smell of disinfectant and iodine wafted out, momentarily holding back the stench of the encampment.

Another of the doctors—Cort Jameson, a gray-haired pediatrician from New York—noted her arrival. "What d'ya got, Dr. Girard?" he asked in English, the de facto language among the clinicians.

"Another case of diarrhea," she answered and started to follow the woman and child inside.

"I'll handle it." He passed her a steaming tin cup of coffee instead. "Fuel up first. Looks like you barely got your eyes open. We can hold down the fort for a few minutes."

She smiled her gratitude and took the cup in both hands. She inhaled the aroma. The smell alone set her heart to beating faster. The coffee here was as thick as syrup, far from the delicate *petit café* at her favorite Parisian restaurant. The team had all grown dependent on the brew and only half-jokingly debated taking it in intravenously.

She stepped to the side to savor both this brief interlude and the dark, bitter elixir.

Her gaze fell upon the stocky figure of Benjamin Frey, a twenty-three-year-old biology postgrad from Cambridge, who was working on his doctoral thesis. The auburn-haired student wore khaki safari gear and a slouch hat. He also had on a pair of white trainers, which he inexplicably kept spotless. She suspected from his abrupt manners, along with a few tics, that he might be on the autistic spectrum, but if so, he was clearly high-functioning. The young man could also dive deep into an esoteric subject, oblivious of his audience's interest—or lack thereof.

She headed closer as he crouched near a thick trail of ants and held one up in a pair of tweezers. She was curious at this invasion, this newest plague to strike the camp.

Frey glanced over a shoulder as she joined him. "*Dorylus wilverthi,*" he explained, lifting the captured specimen higher. "The African driver ant. Also called *siafu.* One of the largest genus of army ants. Soldiers, like this one, can grow to be a half-inch long, with their queen up to two inches. They have mandibles so strong that the indigenous tribes here use their bites to suture lacerations closed."

She felt the man ramping up into one of his lengthy discourses and cut him off. "But where did they all come from?"

"Ah, they're refugees, like everyone else here." He lowered the ant to the trail, then stood. He pointed his tweezers toward the rolling flow of the Tshopo River. "Looks to me like they were flooded out of their regular nesting grounds."

It took her an extra moment to realize that the black islands floating in the current were not piles of debris, but massive rafts of dark-red ants all latched together.

"Why aren't they all drowned?" she asked.

"From a little dunk in the river? No problem for them. They can survive an entire day underwater. Ants are hardy little soldiers. They've been around since the time of dinosaurs and have colonized every continent. Except Antarctica, of course."

She felt sickened, especially as she watched one of those rafts break apart against the shore and disperse outward. The invaders all acted in unison, as if they had strategized this assault in advance.

"Smart buggers, too," Frey added, as if noting the same. "Two hundred and fifty thousand brain cells each. Makes them the smartest insects on the planet. And that's just *one* of 'em. Put forty thousand together, and they're equal to our own intelligence. And mind you, some *Dorylus* supercolonies have clocked in at more than fifty *million* ants. Can you imagine? All led by a queen who can live to be thirty years old, longer than any other insect. So don't underestimate them."

Charlotte suddenly wished she had never approached the biologist.

"Until this army moves on," Frey warned as she began to leave, "expect a lot of bite injuries. Besides being smart, driver ants have nasty tempers, along with the armament to go with it. Those jaws are as tough as steel and sharp as razors. When on the march, they've been known to consume everything in their path, even killing and stripping the flesh off of tethered horses. Or dogs trapped in houses. Sometimes infants, too."

She swallowed queasily. *Like we need more problems here.* "How long until they're gone?"

Frey frowned, setting his fists on his hips. He watched the lines flowing from the river through the camp. "That's the strange thing. Behavior like this is unusual. Typically, driver ants avoid areas of commotion like this camp, preferring to stick to the shadows of the jungle." He shrugged. "But this flooding is certainly atypical. Maybe that's what's made them extra aggressive. Regardless, they should eventually calm down and move on."

"I hope you're right."

He nodded, still watching the spreading mass with a worried pinch of his face. "Me, too."

11:02 A.M.

Charlotte flashed her penlight across the eyes of the three-month-old baby. The boy rested in his concerned mother's arms. He held a thumb in his mouth but didn't suck on it. He sat quietly, his back unusually stiff and straight. He pupils were dilated and only responded minimally to the light. Except for his breathing, he looked like a waxen doll. His skin had a feverish sheen, but his temperature was normal.

"What do you think?" Charlotte asked without turning.

Cort Jameson stood at her shoulder. She had called the American pediatrician over for a consultation. They had gathered behind a thin privacy curtain, set off from the main ward and its crowded cots.

"I saw a similar case yesterday," Jameson said. "A teenage girl. Her father said she had stopped speaking and would barely move unless prodded. She presented with swollen lymph nodes and a rash across her belly. Like this lad. I thought it might be late-stage trypanosomiasis."

"Sleeping sickness," she muttered, considering his potential diagnosis. The disease was caused by a protozoan parasite transmitted by the bite of the tsetse fly. Early signs of sickness included swollen glands, rashes, headaches, and muscle soreness. Later on, if untreated, the organism attacked the central nervous system and led to slurred speech and a sluggish difficulty in walking.

"What happened to the girl?" Charlotte asked.

Jameson shrugged. "I gave her a bag of fluid since she was dehydrated, then pumped her up with doxy and pentamidine. I covered all the bases that I could. I tried to get her father to leave her, but he refused. I heard later that the man sought out his own village's shaman."

She heard the disdain in her colleague's voice. She reached a consoling hand to Jameson. "Her father was just covering all of his bases, too."

"I suppose that's true."

Charlotte could not malign the tribesman for this choice. Many village shamans knew herbal treatments and cures for local ailments, regimens that medical science had not yet discovered or substantiated. She had studied several herself. Locals had been treating urinary infections with grapefruit long before the benefits of citrus were confirmed by Western medicine. Shamans also used *Ocimum gratissimum*—African basil—to treat diarrhea, which, if the camp ran out of supplies, their team might have to resort to.

"I don't think this boy suffers from sleeping sickness," Charlotte concluded. "Initially, from the minimal pupillary response or menace reflex, I thought it might be onchocerciasis, or river blindness. But I couldn't detect any of the parasitic worms in his eyes that cause it."

"Then what're you thinking?" Jameson pressed her.

"His mother says he was fine two days ago. If she's right, then the onset of symptoms was too fast for any parasitic disease. Protozoan or verminous. The rapidity makes me think of a viral infection."

"There are certainly enough of those out here. Yellow fever, HIV, chikungunya, dengue, Rift Valley, West Nile. Not to mention—from the pebbling rashes on the boy and the girl yesterday—all manner of pox viruses. Monkeypox, smallpox."

"I don't know. The symptoms don't match any of those. We could be dealing with something novel. Most new viruses arise from disturbances of a natural landscape. Digging new roads, deforestation, hunting exotic bush meats." She glanced back to the pediatrician. "Also from heavy rains, especially in viruses transmitted by mosquitoes or other insects."

As if summoned by this statement, a large driver ant climbed over the boy's shoulder and latched onto the child's neck. Blood dribbled as its mandibles gnashed the tender flesh. She remembered those painful bites from earlier this morning, but the boy didn't move. He never lowered the thumb from his mouth to cry out. He didn't even blink in pained startlement. He simply sat stiffly, his eyes dull.

Wincing in sympathy, she reached a gloved hand and removed the ant. She pinched it hard and tossed it away.

Jameson watched her, his brows bunched with concern. "Pray you're wrong about it being a new virus. With the overcrowding here, the displacement, the shift in population . . ."

It could be a disaster in the making.

"Until we know more, maybe we should heighten our safety protocols," Charlotte suggested. "In the meantime, I'll collect blood and urine samples."

Jameson's eyes narrowed. "I don't know if it'll do any good. With the chaos out here, it'll take weeks until we can get any samples to a proper lab."

She understood. *It might be too late by then.*

"But I know a researcher, a friend, over in Gabon," Jameson said. "A wildlife veterinarian who works for the Smithsonian's Global Health Program, specifically the new Global Virome Project. He's collecting samples, helping the group create a surveillance network for still-unidentified viruses. More important, he has his own mobile lab for testing samples. If we can radio him, convince him to come out here . . ."

He looked to Charlotte for support in such an endeavor.

Before she could respond, raised voices, full of panic, sounded from the entrance of the medical tent. They both stepped clear of the privacy curtain. Two men rushed into the tent, carrying a stretcher between them. Another of the team's doctors, a forty-year-old ob-gyn from

Melbourne, hurried forward—only to fall back in shock.

Jameson headed over, drawing Charlotte with him.

The two men who carried the stretcher were a FARDC Congolese soldier and a Swiss triage nurse who had been canvassing the outer ramble of the camp. The latter was a tall blonde, who seemed incapable of tanning. Only now his face had drained even whiter.

The nurse panted as he lowered the stretcher to the floor. "I . . . I found him at the camp's edge. There were four others. All dead. Place was overrun. He's the only one still living."

Charlotte cleared around Jameson's back to note the ravaged state of the victim on the stretcher. An elderly local man lay there, struggling weakly to sit up. Blood soaked the scraps of his clothes and ran through the shreds of his skin. Half of his face was just red muscle and peeks of white bone. He looked as if he had been mauled by a lion, but the true predators involved in this attack were far smaller.

Ants still coursed through the gore or burrowed into the raw flesh.

"We found his body weakly stirring under a mountain of ants," the nurse explained. "They were eating him alive. We used pails of water to wash off the worst of them."

"Why didn't the man simply run from the ants?" Jameson asked. "Was he passed out? Drunk, maybe?"

The pediatrician knelt closer to examine the bloody patient. The tribesman had finally managed to sit up. He opened his mouth, as if to explain what had happened to him—only a black swarm of ants boiled forth from his throat and flowed down his chin and chest. His body sagged and fell slack to the stretcher.

Jameson scooted away with a gasp.

Charlotte remembered the biologist's earlier warning: *Expect more bite cases.* She also pictured what the researcher had described, how driver ants could strip the flesh off a tethered horse. She glanced back to the privacy curtain. The mother stood there, holding her stiff son, a child too dulled to respond to an ant's bite.

She suddenly found it harder to breathe, as if the air had grown heavier. A fearful certainty welled inside her. *It's all connected somehow.* She turned and grabbed Jameson's shoulder. "Radio your friend, the virus hunter. Now."

The pediatrician frowned at her for a breath, horror dulling his understanding. Then he blinked back his shock and nodded. He gained his feet and ran out, heading for the communication tent and its array of tiny satellite dishes.

Charlotte still had her arm raised. Movement drew her eye to her wrist. Three black ants wiggled there, latched onto the gap of skin above her glove. Their pincers were dug deep. Terror grew inside her at the sight of them—not at the violation, but at a sudden realization.

She hadn't felt a single sting from those bites.

2

Deep underground, Frank Whitaker confronted the pair of red eyes reflecting the beam of his helmet's lamp. The eyes glowed down the tunnel, just above the mirror of the black stream he had been wading along. His heart clenched with a primal fear. He had been warned of the predators that lurked in this half-flooded cavern system.

Crocodiles . . .

He had spotted a few smaller ones earlier, no longer than his arm, but they had scurried away with whips of their tails. Not this one. He noted the armored drape beyond those glowing eyes. *Easily six feet long.* He also noted the orange hue to its scales, which was typical for the crocodiles trapped in this cavern system. They were members of *Osteolaemus tetraspis*, the African dwarf crocodile. Though from the length of this particular example, "dwarf" was a questionable descriptor.

The colony—or *float* as a group of swimming crocs were called—had been trapped and isolated in the Abanda caves near the coast of Gabon for three thousand years, getting caught here after the water table had dropped millennia ago. In such a harsh, sunless environment, these orange specimens were slowly diverging from their fellow brethren above, evolving in real time.

As a wildlife veterinarian, he would have been fascinated by all of this—but from a greater distance.

"They're nearly blind," Remy Engonga assured him. The Gabonese native was a pathologist with CIRMF, the International Centre for Medical Research. The facility in southeast Gabon was instrumental in evaluating emerging diseases in West Africa. "Make some noise and that little bull will shy away."

"Little?" Frank asked, his voice muffled by a paper mask.

"*Oui.* Up top, our crocodiles are many times larger."

Frank shook his head. *This one's large enough.* Still, he took the pathologist at his word about the creature being blind. He unhooked an aluminum water bottle from his hip and banged it against the karstic-stone wall and bellowed loudly. The bull croc continued to stare, unimpressed. Then finally it shrugged its bulk around and casually swam away, vanishing into the darkness.

With the way unblocked, the pair of men continued onward. In such an alien environment, Frank felt like an astronaut exploring a hostile planet, especially covered from head to toe in protective gear. He wore a MicroGuard coverall with a hood, the pant legs tucked into waterproof waders. His eyes were protected by plastic goggles, and a mask filtered both the ammonia-thick air and the clouds of gnats and midges whisking all about.

They finally left the stream and slogged through wet mud, which was mostly bat guano. The roof hung with hordes of the winged denizens, more spun and danced through the air, occasionally dive-bombing the trespassers. It was all this accumulated guano that had eventually bleached the crocodile's scales to their unique orange hue. In turn, the crocodiles, isolated in total darkness, feasted on those same bats, along with a few cave crabs, crickets, and algae.

"How far until the traps?" Frank called back to Remy.

"Nearly there. Up at the next bottleneck. I thought it was the best place to put up the netting."

Remy and a few of his team from CIRMF had been kind enough to set traps the day before. Frank wanted to collect test samples from each of the species of bats harboring here: the African fruit bat, the giant roundleaf, and a handful of others. It was bats like these that were natural reservoirs for Ebola and Marburg. Frank hoped to catalog the breadth of other viruses carried by the denizens in this cave, searching for any pathogens that could become the next great pandemic.

He had been in Africa for half a year, traveling throughout the Congo and coastal West Africa.

So far, he had collected over fifteen thousand samples.

As he headed toward the traps, he again felt an overwhelming amazement at being here. It was a strange path, from a Black foster kid living on Chicago's South Side to a wildlife veterinarian in a cavern system in Gabon. His love of the natural world had come about from his attempt to escape the freeze of Chicago winters and the swelter of its humid summers. Seeking shelter off the streets, he often found himself drawn to the Lincoln Park or Brookfield Zoos, even the Shedd Aquarium. He would spend hours reading and memorizing the information placards, dreaming of all the mysterious corners of the world described therein. It had all seemed so foreign to a Black boy huddled in a coat two sizes too large and a pair of ragged Jordans.

And look where I am now . . .

His aptitude in science and math had eventually caught the interest of a JROTC recruiter in high school—that and maybe his six-foot-four frame. He had fared well enough with the group that a glowing letter of recommendation earned him a full-ride at a community college, then he was awarded a Health Professionals Scholarship with the army that paid for his tuition at the University of Illinois College of Veterinary Medicine. Upon accepting the scholarship, he had been immediately commissioned as a second lieutenant, which had made his adopted parents nearly burst with pride.

While he had never known his biological mother and father—and never cared to after they had dumped him into the system—he was one of the lucky ones. He ran through three sets of foster families, some neglectful, others simply overwrought with the best of intentions. Then the Whitakers had taken him in, eventually adopting him. It was their loving anchor that had steadied a bitter youth, one who had been growing ever wilder, drifting further toward the streets and away from a society that had already rejected him.

When he eventually graduated from vet school—which involved additional weeks of active-duty training—he was promptly promoted to the rank of captain. He had some pre-assignment training after that, and an additional seven years of service were required of him. Those years put him into the thick of the Iraq war, where he worked on a Public Health masters and did hands-on field work with zoonotic diseases. But the war had also left him disillusioned, both with the state of the world and humanity in general.

After he returned to the States, he had tried a stint at USAMRID, the Army's biomedical research facility, but he had only lasted another year. He eventually left the service and was hired by the Smithsonian Global Health Program, a nonprofit that searched for emerging viral threats. He put together a grant to come to Africa, to catalog as much of the virosphere as possible, searching for what a fellow colleague called *dangerous viral dark matter* hidden in lost corners of the world.

"Looks like we have plenty of volunteers for your work," Remy commented as he came abreast of Frank, drawing back his attention.

The pathologist pointed to a mesh screen across a narrowing in the tunnel. Dark shapes hung there, tangled in the netting, like a swath of furry black fruit. The net across the passage had caught over two dozen bats of varying sizes. Several squirmed as they approached.

"Calm down, little ones," Frank reassured them. "We don't mean you any harm."

Once at the trap, Frank shed his backpack and knelt down. He quickly prepared a syringe with a sedative cocktail of acepromazine and butorphanol. He then donned a pair of thick rubberized gloves. He did not want to risk a bite. Syringe in hand, he started at the top and worked his way down the spread of netted bats. He eyeballed the dosages to match the sizes of the specimens, administering no more than a drop each. By the time he reached the bottom of the net, the topmost bats were already slipping into a stupor.

"Help me loosen the net?" Frank asked Remy.

Working together, they unhooked the trap and reopened the passageway. Several bats took advantage and dashed past overhead. With the netting and slumbering specimens sprawled across the cave floor, Frank returned to his pack and gathered his collection gear.

Time to get to work.

6:28 P.M.

Frank knelt amidst the orderly sprawl of sealed swabs, needles, and tiny glass pipettes. Sweat dripped down his forehead and stung his eyes, which were already burning from all of the ammonia-steaming guano.

Maybe I should've brought a respirator.

He worked as quickly as he could without risking contaminating his samples. He held the limp form of a great roundleaf bat, *Hipposideros gigas*. Remy helped him spread a wing for a blood draw. He also had a pair of swabs ready to collect samples from the bat's oropharyngeal and rectal cavities.

Frank studied the delicate creature as he worked. The bell-shaped ears were a soft velvet. Its nostrils were tiny fans of tissue. The membrane of its leathery wings was so thin that the light of Remy's helmet lamp shone through them.

Remy leaned closer as he worked. "Dr. Whitaker, if I may ask, why are you only concentrating on *bats* for your viral studies?"

Frank sat back as he used a wax pencil to catalog the sample in hand. "Basically because these little fellas are furry sacks of viruses. Not only do they naturally harbor hundreds of species, but they're also great reservoirs of environmental viruses. They pick up all sorts of arthropod viruses from the insects they eat. Even plant viruses, in fruit-eating bats. In turn, they pass those viruses to other wildlife—or even humans. Ideally, it would be great if we could survey the virosphere of *every* vertebrate, invertebrate, and plant out there. But that's not practical, if even possible. So, in the meantime, bats make excellent monitors for what lurks out there in the environment at large."

"I see," Remy said. "But I've always wondered,

with all that exposure to viruses, why don't bats get sick?"

Frank settled the roundleaf bat to the cave floor and set about untangling another, which from its shape and size was a fruit bat, *Rousettus aegyptiacus*.

"Three reasons," Frank answered. "First, bats are superstars when it comes to their unique immune systems. Research suggests they gained this ability because they're the only mammal that *flies*." He unfolded a large wing and poked a vein with a needle and sapped a few drops of blood into a pipette. "To accomplish this miraculous feat requires a metabolism that's on hyperdrive. All that metabolic heat ramps up their tiny bodies to a feverish state that helps hold back infections."

Frank set down the pipette and picked up a swab. "The second reason—and a more important one—such a boosted metabolism produces a slew of dangerous inflammatory molecules, which can be deadly. To combat this, in their evolutionary past, bats disabled ten genes. This dampened their inflammatory response and kept their immune system from overreacting—an exaggerated response called a cytokine storm, which causes the most deaths from viruses. In addition, inflammation is a major cause of aging, so dampening this process accounts for why bats live up to forty years, an extraordinary feat for such a small mammal."

Frank lifted the swab, and Remy helped him pry open the test subject's tiny jaws, exposing the needle-sharp fangs.

"You said there were *three* reasons bats are resistant to getting sick," Remy noted. "What's the third?"

"Ah, for that answer, you have to look at a bat's DNA. Most of their code—ours, too, for that matter—contains fragments of ancient viral code, bits of DNA incorporated into their genome from past exposures. Bats wield those genes in unique ways. They can split them off into their cellular cytoplasm and turn those bits into antibody factories."

"Which keeps them healthy." Remy gave a sad shake of his head. "If only we could do the same. My team is still trying to stamp out Ebola flare-ups throughout West Africa. As soon as we snuff one out, another springs up."

Frank nodded grimly. He finished with the fruit bat and searched the spread of the net. It lay limp and empty.

"It appears we've run out of volunteers," Frank said.

"Just as well. It must be close to sunset. We should head back."

Frank agreed. He had no desire to trek to his campsite in the dark. Working together, they set about clearing their site. Frank packed away the last of his samples, while Remy gathered up the net from the floor. Once finished, they set off, letting their test subjects wake and return to their roosts.

Frank glanced back as the first couple of bats took wobbly flights into the air. "Best we clear out of here before the rest take wing."

"Why's that?"

"While bats are great at keeping their viral load in check, if any of them gets too hassled or anxious, that complicated immune system breaks down. Then the viruses proliferate, making the bat all the more infective." Frank glanced over to Remy. "Always remember: a stressed bat is a dangerous one."

"I will keep that in mind."

Remy set a swifter pace away from the collection point and glanced back periodically with a worried expression. They quickly reached the flooded section of the cavern and waded back toward the exit. As they did, Frank kept a wary watch for any of those glowing red eyes in the water, but he spotted none of them. Apparently, the commotion and noise of their labors had driven the crocodiles into the deeper caves.

"What's next?" Remy asked, nodding to Frank's backpack. "What do you do now with all those samples?"

"I'll get them over to my campsite's mobile lab. I can do a preliminary analysis via PCR amplification, comparing the viral antigen sequences to a genetic database. It will help me catalog *known* viruses. I've also developed a set of reagents and nested primers to identify *unknown* viruses. It's crude, but using SISPA— single primer amplification—I can attach linker/ adaptors of a known sequence to an unknown sequence, which lets me amplify—"

Remy held up a hand. "I believe you."

Frank smiled. "Sorry. It's the best I can manage in the field. The gold standard, of course, would be to grow any of those unknown viruses in a cell culture. But that's too dangerous outside of a biocontainment unit. Like what you have at your research center in Franceville."

He envied Remy and his crew at CIRMF. They had both a primatology lab and a biosafety Level 4 containment facility. *If I had full use of that facility . . .*

Remy must have sensed his desire. "If you find anything particularly intriguing, I'm sure we can accommodate a viral isolation study. Especially for any samples collected from West Africa. Better to know what's out here before it becomes a problem."

"It's why I'm in Africa. That, and seeing how many mosquito bites it takes before a person is driven mad."

Remy cocked an eyebrow toward him. "That is one mystery you will surely solve, Dr. Whitaker. Especially with all the storms passing through the area."

"True." Frank glanced over a shoulder to the dark waters behind him. "If nothing else, maybe all that rain and flooding will eventually wash these poor crocs back into the sunlit world."

Remy pointed ahead. "Right now, I'll be happy to get *myself* out of here."

7:22 P.M.

After another half hour, Frank spotted a faint brightness in the tunnel ahead, shining across the breadth of black water.

Remy saw it, too. "*Dieu merci . . .*" he sighed out.

Drawn by the light, they splashed the last of the way to the entrance. Frank gasped with exhaustion and stood under the threshold. A rope ladder scaled up the seven yards to the bright opening above. Next to it, a thin waterfall streamed into the cavern, casting a fine mist.

Frank lifted his face to the sunlight and tugged off his goggles and mask. He took his first breath of air not fouled by ammonia. Still, the heat stifled. Even this close to sunset, the day had grown only hotter. He swore the humidity had to be a hundred and ten percent.

Remy led the way up the ladder. Frank followed, balancing his heavy pack across his shoulders as he climbed the swaying ladder. At the top, Remy helped him crawl out of the ferny grotto.

With a groan, Frank stood and faced his next challenge. A trampled path led off through dense jungle. The two of them still had a two-mile hike to reach Frank's makeshift camp. He hoped they could get there before the sun fully set. It already sat low on the horizon.

After drinking deeply from their water bottles, they set off down the path. Both were too tired to do any talking. Within a quarter mile, Frank was sweating through his coveralls. He considered stripping them off, but the effort seemed too taxing. Plus, the suit protected most of his body from the clouds of mosquitoes harassing them.

Where are all those bats when you need them?

Remy suddenly stopped ahead of him.

Frank nearly stumbled into his back. "What's wrong?"

The pathologist stepped aside and pointed to a pile of fly-crusted dung in the middle of the path. "Forest elephant. And fresh."

Frank winced. The Gabonese rain forest was home to herds of the lumbering giants. He had been schooled about their territoriality. Not that he could blame the beasts for their temperament, especially with the number of poachers out here. Over the past decade, eighty percent of Gabon's elephants had been killed for their ivory.

"Best move quietly from here," Remy cautioned and stepped past the large dung pile. The man rested a palm on a holstered sidearm, a necessary precaution in the jungle—and not just against animals. While the small pistol held out no hope of stopping a bull elephant's charge, the loud blasts might chase it away.

At least, we better pray so.

As they headed off again, Frank held his breath for long stretches, his ears piqued for any sudden trumpeting or trampling of the ground. As they continued, the forest grew ever darker, steeping the world in shadows.

Then they both heard it, coming from ahead.

A cracking of branches, the slap of leaves.

Frank froze on the path.

Remy thumbed loose the safety strap on his holster and half-pulled his weapon. He widened his stance. He whispered breathlessly, "Take off into the brush at the first sign of aggression."

Frank swallowed and nodded.

The noises grew louder—then from around a bend in the narrow track, a beast appeared. But it wasn't a forest elephant. Instead, a large dog stalked into view, half-hidden under the bower's shadow. It kept its head low, ears high. A low growl flowed from it.

A moment later, a pair of armed men strode up behind the dog. They wore jungle camo and carried long rifles.

Frank's first thought was *poachers*. But as they drew closer, he recognized the red caps and uniforms of the Gabonese Armed Forces. The pair led another figure, a tanned man with shaggy blond hair. He wore civilian clothes: a pair of scuffed boots, khaki combat trousers, and an airy, long-sleeved shirt, all topped by a ball cap.

The man pushed past the soldiers and crossed toward Frank and Remy. He held out an arm. "Dr. Whitaker, I presume."

Frank scowled at the poor joke. It was a clear attempt to imitate the famous line from the Congo explorer Henry Morton Stanley: *Dr. Livingstone, I presume*.

Frank stepped around Remy to confront the American, a man he knew well, from when Frank had served as an army veterinarian. He gripped the man's calloused hand, needing its firmness to reassure him that this sudden reunion in the middle of the Gabonese rain forest was real.

"Tucker, what're you doing here?" Frank glanced to the large dog, who sidled up alongside the man, revealing a black-and-tan ruff and tall ears. "And Kane, I see. The last time I set eyes on you two was over in Baghdad, just before you left the service."

Captain Tucker Wayne was a decorated soldier, a military war dog handler with the Army Rangers. His partner, Kane, had also earned more medals than most warriors.

Tucker shrugged. "I'm here to perform an extraction, always a specialty of ours." He patted Kane's side. "It seems someone's been frantically trying to get hold of you. When that failed, word reached your bosses at the Smithsonian. Apparently, you're a hard man to find."

"I've been underground most of the day," Frank explained. "But I don't understand, how did you get involved?"

"I know a group affiliated with the Smithsonian. Due to the urgency, they reached out to me." From Tucker's sour expression, he was not thrilled at being enlisted for this assignment. "I was already here on the continent, checking on an investment in South Africa. My business partners and I were scouting a location in northern Namibia when the call came in. And when I heard *who* they needed me to collect . . . well, I owed you a favor after all your help with Kane during the war."

"Still, why me? What am I needed for?"

"A U.N. relief camp in the DRC is experiencing an outbreak of some sort. Apparently, it's growing into a desperate situation. The request for your help came from a pediatrician working out there, someone who knows you. A man named Jameson."

It took Frank an extra moment to place the name, then he remembered the doctor he had met in Kinshasa, the capital of the DRC, a month ago. "Are you talking about Cort? Cort Jameson?"

Tucker nodded.

Frank frowned. The pediatrician had talked him into giving a speech on zoonotic diseases to a group from Doctors Without Borders. Frank had also spent the evening showing the man his operations and sampling techniques.

"Jameson called in a panicked request," Tucker explained. "Asking for you to haul your viral lab over there to evaluate the outbreak. That initial call came in eight hours ago. Then, when I landed here, I got word of a second call. It was garbled, with gunfire in the background and screams."

Frank cringed. He pictured the camp being attacked by bandits or raided by one of the warring militia out in the region.

Tucker continued, "The call cut off abruptly. Further attempts to make contact failed. The Congolese military are already being dispatched, but the U.N. has requested that you heed your colleague's appeal and help evaluate what is happening out there."

"Of course," Frank said. "I should be able to get my lab packed up within the hour."

"Good. I have a Cessna fueled and ready. We can get you to Kisangani and then by helicopter to the camp. Weather permitting, you should arrive by midnight local time."

Frank waved Tucker to lead the way, but the man stopped him with a raised arm.

"What?" Frank asked, noting the hard glint to the ranger's blue-green eyes.

"That second call. Very little could be made out. Except for your friend's final words."

"What were they?"

Tucker stared hard at him. "*'Stay away. Dear god, don't come out here.'*"

3

Charlotte gazed out the plastic window of the medical tent. Rain pattered across the ruins of the camp. Black puddles and pools reflected the few larger fires that had been abandoned and left burning.

Hordes of ants still streamed and clawed through the mud, covering nearly everything. A few winged ones—male drones—spun through the raindrops. Across the dark camp, mounds marked bodies, both those who had succumbed to the horde and a few others who had been shot.

Across the way, flashlights bobbled near a stack of supply crates as Jameson and the Swiss nurse, Byrne, worked with a trio of locals who carried rifles over their shoulders. They were loading gear into a pickup bed. The five men wore hooded white biohazard suits, along with goggles and masks. The cheap disposable suits offered the lowest level of protection, barely adequate against anything contagious. But they kept the worst of the muddy ants from finding any flesh.

Jameson called out a few final instructions to his team, readying for their group's evacuation. Only a few others still remained in the camp. Tents lay toppled, crates were strewn all about.

At least the chaos and fighting has stopped.

Throughout the day, Jameson had done his best to hold the camp together, aided by the armed ICCN team—members of Institut Congolais pour la Conservation de la Nature, also called eco-guards due to their labors at protecting the rain forest against poachers or illegal foresters. But as more ants flowed into the camp and word of an unknown illness spread, any hope of quarantining the area broke down. Desperate looting started, along with spats of gunfire as the eco-guards protected the team's medical supplies and ICCN trucks. In short order, a majority of the refugees had fled off into the jungle.

It also didn't help matters that the Tshopo River continued to steadily rise. It became evident that the medical team would also have to evacuate. Two hours ago, Jameson had tried to radio authorities and alert them that the medical team was moving to a secondary position and not to come here. But ants had overrun the innards of the camp's radio, fritzing the electronics. The pediatrician was not even sure if he'd reached anyone.

Charlotte turned her eyes to the low layer of dark clouds. A faint rumble of thunder echoed down. The rain continued at a steady drizzle, but flashes of lightning in the distance warned that the true teeth of the storm had yet to reach them.

We need to be gone before it strikes.

She turned from the window to the rows of cots. There were only a handful of patients still here, those too weak to move on their own. Fever shone from their faces. Eyes glowed with fear. Dr. Mattie Poll, the Aussie ob-gyn with the team, pulled an I.V. and capped the catheter of a frail elderly man with a crown of white hair. Mattie nodded to Charlotte.

All ready to go.

Outside, a pair of ICCN trucks stood at the edge of the camp, prepared to transport the patients to a new site, somewhere up on higher ground. A rutted trail through the jungle marked the only route away from the river.

Charlotte's eyes settled on the young mother humming softly to her three-month-old baby. The boy lay slack in her thin arms, his head lolled back, his eyes staring blankly at the roof of the tent. His chest continued to rise and fall—but for how much longer? During the earlier chaos, the mother had tried to leave with the child, but Charlotte had urged her to stay, promising she would do all she could for the boy.

Yet, what can I do? I still have no idea what afflicts him.

The tent's door unzipped, drawing Charlotte's attention. Jameson bowed his way through and tugged his mask lower, panting hard. Behind his goggles, his eyes shone with anxiety and desperation.

"We're ready. I'll have Byrne and Ndaye's men help get everyone into the trucks."

An engine coughed to life out there.

"What about Benjie?" Charlotte asked, stepping forward.

Jameson looked around the tent and sighed in exasperation. "He's not back yet?"

Charlotte didn't have to answer. The grad student had left over an hour ago, shortly after Jameson had tried to raise the local authorities. Prior to that, the biologist had spent most of the day collecting and examining ants, his brow furrowing ever deeper, fastidiously focused on his work.

Benjie had grown particularly intrigued when the camp was swarmed by the winged ants. They were so large that Charlotte had mistaken them for bees. Before leaving to investigate the swarming, Benjie had assured her that these males posed no threat, lacking the fierce mandibles of the soldier ants. Still, the drones hummed the air with a buzzing menace and inflamed the already tense situation. Before long, the camp had broken into a full panicked rout.

"We have to wait for him," Charlotte said. "We can't leave without him."

Jameson shook his head. "We'll wait for as long as it takes to load everyone into the trucks. That's it."

"But—"

Jameson turned away. "With the river rising and a storm threatening, we can't stay here. Benjie can follow us on foot—that is, if he's even still alive."

Charlotte inwardly winced. She turned to the tent's plastic window and rubbed at her wrist. The raised welts from the earlier ant bites itched, which she hoped was a good sign. She had been monitoring her own vitals, worried that whatever had afflicted the boy might have infected her, too. But so far, all seemed normal. She wanted to attribute her earlier numbness to adrenaline and tension.

Surely that's all it was.

She stared into the dark night, focusing on a more immediate worry.

Where are you, Benjie?

10:55 P.M.

Benjamin Frey hunted through the dark forest, armed with a flashlight and a fierce determination to learn the truth. He rubbed raindrops from his plastic goggles and from the lens of the GoPro camera banded atop his forehead. He followed alongside a thick trail of driver ants, heading up their stream.

Doesn't make any sense, not a bit. This is not like them at all . . .

The pockets of his coveralls clinked with small sampling test tubes. All day long, he had been plucking ant specimens and examining them under a dissecting microscope in his tent. Next to him he had kept an iPad, glowing with a digital entomology text; one of hundreds of biology-related books and journals loaded there. He had compared the anatomy of his captured specimens, noting slight variations between individuals. *The size and angular spread of mandibles, the shape of thoraxes, the joints of antennae.* These subtle distinctions differentiated the various species and subspecies of *Dorylus* ants. So far, he had identified over a dozen of them.

Their names ran like a recording in his head.

Dorylus moestus, Dorylus mandicularis, Dorylus kohli indolcilis and *militaris, Dorylus funereus pardus, Dorylus brevis . . .*

While all those species thrived in these equatorial jungles, they never ran together in the same colony. They were normally too combative. Yet, the trails throughout the camp ran with tangles from all those species. It baffled him. Still, it was not this *mystery* that drew his focus, but rather the *wrongness* of it all.

Benjie could not tolerate anything out of its proper place.

He never could.

At the age of eleven, he had been diagnosed with mild Asperger's—what was now called Level 1 Autistic Spectrum Disorder. He had been born a month premature, or as his mother often described it, *Benjie was too sodding impatient to wait the full nine.* Maybe that had something to do with his condition, but he seldom gave it much thought.

During his school years, he had been trained by a behaviorist to use his hyperfocus and nearly eidetic memory to study facial expressions and social cues. He eventually learned to cope well enough, but his most persistent difficulty was an obsessiveness when it came to problem-solving and orderliness. In secondary school, he had taught himself to solve a Rubik's Cube in under seven seconds. He had found it soothing to put right what was wrong, to return order out of chaos. But this same feature also left him with a compulsive nature, one he continually fought to temper.

Still, this nature also helped him excel in his studies. Not that he wasn't bullied at school, both for his lack of social acuity and because of a persistent tic that would set his eyes to rapidly blinking. But he was also deeply loved. He had been raised by a single mother in council housing in Hackenthorpe, in South Yorkshire. She had doted on him, encouraged him, and did her best to bolster his confidence. It was her support, more than anything, that had earned him a spot at the University of Sheffield, a public research university only sixteen minutes by bus from his house.

Now he was much farther afield, farther than he'd ever been from home. This trip to Africa was necessary to complete his doctoral thesis in evolutionary biology. His dissertation director at Sheffield had teamed him up with a colleague of his at the University of Kisangani, who in turn had embedded Benjie with the medical relief team. The refugee camp, set in the midst a local flood, offered a possible case study for Benjie's thesis, which dealt with stress-induced mutations and their inheritability.

Benjie hoped that what he discovered here with the driver ants might bear fruit. With that goal in mind, he crept alongside their trail. The earlier swarming of the winged males had suggested their mate might be somewhere nearby. A search along the fringes of the camp had revealed a trail of red-black ants that ran with daubs of white. They marked the presence of specialized workers—brood-carriers—who had fled the floodwaters, hauling along the nest's larvae and pupae.

He had already collected a few larval and pupal specimens as he followed the trail upstream. He planned, once back in Kisangani, to study the ants' DNA, especially epigenetic modifications that might have triggered this new cooperative behavior. But he still hunted for his coup de grâce, a specimen vital to any study on the inheritability of a stress-induced trait in ants.

Then he finally spotted what he had trekked out here to secure.

Ah hah . . .

At the tail end of the bobbling run of larvae and pupae, a larger ant appeared, easily two inches long. It was the colony queen. She was accompanied by a coterie of workers who escorted her away from her flooded nest.

Benjie dropped to a knee beside the river of ants and retrieved a set of long tweezers from the breast pocket of his coveralls. He used them to pluck the queen from the trail. He shook off a few escorts that clung to her, then dropped her into a test tube. He quickly plugged the top— both to keep the large ant from escaping, but also to seal away any pheromones she might exude. All driver ants were blind, guided instead by vibrations and scents. He didn't want to risk luring this army into a vain pursuit of their queen. If undisturbed, the rest of the colony should continue on their pre-programmed route, where they'd eventually either dwindle away without an egg-laying queen or a new one would arise to take over the throne.

With his prize in hand, Benjie turned and headed toward the camp. He estimated he was only a quarter mile away. As he hiked back, he eyed the neighboring river of ants for any sign of threat—then a soft grunt rose behind him. It was answered by a cough farther to his right.

He half-turned while continuing through the dark jungle. He cast his flashlight behind him. He saw nothing. Still, he set off faster. His ears strained for any other indication that something was on his trail.

He heard nothing.

But he wasn't fooled.

11:10 P.M.

"We can't wait any longer," Jameson said.

The pediatrician's words were punctuated by a loud clap of thunder. The little plastic tent window brightened with a flash of lightning. The storm was about to break upon them at any moment.

Charlotte bit her lower lip, searching for any excuse to delay their departure until Benjie could return. The tent had been emptied of most patients. One ICCN truck had already departed with Dr. Poll and the first load. The second truck waited for the last of the patients.

Only one remained in the tent.

Charlotte glanced over to the Luba mother and her son. The woman had refused to leave Charlotte's side, clearly intent on holding the doctor to her promise to help the child.

Jameson waved Byrne over to the cot. "Get these two into the truck."

The tall Swiss nurse, soaked and bedraggled in his coveralls, crossed brusquely over. The mother leaned away, shifting her child protectively to the side.

Charlotte blocked the nurse. "I'll help them. You grab anything else that we might need."

Byrne looked to Jameson for approval, which rankled Charlotte.

The pediatrician flung his arms in exasperation. "Whatever. Fine. But we're outta here in five."

Charlotte shifted over to the mother and gently coaxed her from the bed. "*Disanka, hebu tuende.* We'll get your *kitwana* somewhere safe."

The mother slid her legs off the cot, cradling her boy. She started to stand—when a flurry of commotion at the tent flap made her flinch back.

Charlotte turned as Ndaye, the leader of the ICCN team, rushed into the tent. The thin, muscular man, in his midthirties, wore a uniform of green camo, a matching cap, and black boots. He carried a rifle slung over a shoulder.

Charlotte looked hopefully at him. The only concession she had managed to get out of Jameson was to allow Ndaye and one of his men to head into the rainy jungle to search for Benjie. Another man followed Ndaye into the tent, but it wasn't the grad student. The stranger unfolded his gaunt frame, straightening with a dignity that spoke of authority. His exact age was hard to determine, but from his gray braids—swept back by a brightly beaded headband—he had to be in his late seventies or eighties. He wore loose pants and a half-buttoned shirt, exposing a thick necklace that matched his headband.

"This is Woko Bosh," Ndaye introduced. "An elder shaman of the Kuba—a people who live to the west of here."

Charlotte noted the glint of sharp intelligence in the man's eyes. His dress and demeanor were far from what she had expected of such a shaman, whom many still referred to as witch doctors. His calm gaze swept across the tent and settled on Disanka and her child. The man turned back and called sharply past the tent flap.

Ndaye explained, "I found the shaman and his apprentice headed toward our camp in a truck. He had already been en route to this region, drawn two days ago by rumors of a great sickness, one spreading through the forest, afflicting both men and the jungle itself."

"So, this must be happening in other places, too," Jameson said.

"Apparently," Ndaye confirmed. His eyes shone with worry. The ICCN leader had grown up here, but he had also been educated in England for a time, earning a degree in anthropology. He had returned with a bit of a British accent. "Despite the various tribes and warring factions out here, the jungle has an efficient means of communication. It always has. Spreading from mouth to mouth, news can travel swiftly throughout the forest."

Charlotte stepped closer. "But why did the shaman travel to our camp?"

"According to him, he sought to confirm the presence of an ancient enemy. One his people fought long ago. He claims to—"

Thunder boomed outside, cutting off the man's words. Winds kicked up, shaking the tent's fabric.

"Enough," Jameson said as the gust ended. "We don't have time for this nonsense."

Charlotte held up a hand, willing to listen— not that she necessarily believed any of this, but if it bought Benjie more time to get back to camp, all the better. "We should hear him out. The indigenous people of the Congo have lived in these forests for millennia on end. If they have any knowledge about what's happening here, we shouldn't discount it."

Ndaye concurred. "The tribes have an ageless oral tradition, going back to a time blurred between history and mythology."

Charlotte nodded. Before coming here, she had read about the Congo's past. The earliest inhabitants—the pygmy tribes—had arrived during the Upper Paleolithic Period, around forty thousand years ago.

A small shape burst into the tent, but it wasn't a pygmy native. It was a young boy, maybe twelve or thirteen. He was soaked, his boots muddy, wearing only shorts and a T-shirt, and a blue JanSport backpack. He spoke rapidly in a dialect that Charlotte didn't know. He held aloft a tarp-wrapped parcel.

"This is Faraji," Ndaye introduced. "Woko Bosh's nephew and apprentice."

The shaman took the package, knelt down, and unwrapped it. Inside was an intricately carved wooden mask, maybe a funereal object. It was elaborately decorated in shells, ivory, and painted seeds. It was also adorned with filigreed iron, and a few brighter strands that had to be gold, delineating eyebrows and eyelashes. It was a stunning masterwork of tribal craftsmanship, though the subject was unusual.

While the mask's face was similar to most African figures, done in a stylized form, the carving depicted no ceremonial headdress or crown. Instead, the bust was topped by a domed helmet, all adorned in white shells. It looked more colonial than tribal.

Before Charlotte could comment on it, Woko lifted off the mask's face, revealing the object was actually a hollow case of some sort.

Ndaye softly gasped. "It is a *ngedi mu ntey* . . ."

Charlotte glanced to him.

"A sacred Kuba Box," he explained. "Their people are known for crafting such objects, many of which adorn museums around the world. They use the boxes to preserve *tukula*, ritual pastes and powders, along with other ceremonial tools used in healing, burials, anything of high importance."

Woko reached inside and removed a carved idol, which he passed to his apprentice. Faraji held the object as if it were a deadly viper, barely letting his fingers touch it. It was a wooden figure of a man standing stiff and tall. The face had been ebonized to a dark sheen, while the stylized outfit was painted white, flecked by age. Again, the clothing did not look tribal, more like a suit and a pith helmet.

This must be the man depicted on the mask.

Ndaye nodded to it. "A *ndop* figure. Such depictions are reserved for the kings of the tribe."

"Who is it, then?" Charlotte asked.

Faraji overheard her and answered in English, proving his fluency. "He shepherd."

Charlotte frowned. *Why did the Kuba carve a figure of a shepherd?* She tipped higher on her toes to peer into the box. From its apparent age, it looked to be a relic from another century, possibly dating back to colonial times. The wood also looked unusual, maybe ebony, but veined in silver, tiny knots of which formed the figure's eyes.

Inside the box, the figurine had been holding down a stack of small squarish papers, stiff and yellowed with age. She spotted a few scribbled lines of writing on the topmost one.

As Woko rooted at one end of the box, the neat stack shifted, revealing a corner of an old black-and-white photo. The entire pile below appeared to be more of the same. Except, under the stack, a folded print of a colored map had been tucked at the bottom.

Before she could discern more, Woko stood up and blocked her view. He turned, holding aloft a stoppered glass vial filled with a grainy yellow powder.

Charlotte remembered Ndaye's description of these *ngedi mu ntey*, how such boxes preserved sacred pastes and powders.

What was it?

With strong, deft fingers, Woko twisted out the rubber stopper. He shoved through the gathered group and crossed toward Disanka and her baby. As he approached the cot, he shook a drab of powder into his palm. He spoke softly but firmly to the mother, who at first looked scared, then began to nod.

If nothing else, this witch doctor had a better bedside manner than Jameson.

"What does he think he's doing?" the pediatrician asked, looking ready to intervene.

Charlotte stopped him with a touch. "Leave them be."

She sensed Western medicine had no place here.

Disanka cupped the back of her son's head and lifted his little face higher. The child showed no sign of awareness, not even an eyelid blinked.

Woko leaned closer and blew the powder across the boy's lips and into his nose. Charlotte hoped for a sneeze, for any sign of a reaction from the child. But nothing happened. Disanka stared down at her son, clearly praying for the same, but even she grew forlorn at the lack of response.

Jameson scoffed. "We're wasting time. Let the shaman come with us if he wants, but we're leaving now."

Woko ignored him and stepped past the pediatrician. Charlotte expected the shaman to return to the box, but instead, he whispered to his apprentice and continued to the front of the tent. Faraji returned the figurine to its case and carefully replaced the lid. As the boy set about rewrapping the mask and returning it to his backpack, Woko bent down by the tent flap, which had been left open.

Trails of ants had already invaded the space, seeking refuge from the rain, exploring in all directions. Woko gathered a pinch of the powder in his fingertips, then sprinkled the grains over one of the black trails. The effect was instantaneous. The ants fled in all directions, scurrying madly to get away. A few simply curled up dead.

Woko studied his work for a breath, then nodded, as if satisfied. Still, when he straightened and turned, lines of worry etched his face.

Jameson sighed loudly, plainly done with all this. "Big deal. So it's some sort of insecticide or ant repellant. So what?"

The answer came from behind them all.

A loud bawling rose from the cot. They all turned. Disanka clutched her boy harder. The child still lay dazed and weak in her arms, but his eyes were squeezed shut and his mouth wailed, revealing a tiny curl of pink tongue.

Charlotte gasped. "The powder . . . it's waking him. Maybe it's a cure of some sort."

Jameson scowled his disdain. "We can't know that. It might just be a nasal irritant that triggered a pained response. Either way, we must—"

A loud slap of boots on mud drew them all around. A shape skidded past the flap opening— then scrambled back into the tent's pool of lamplight. A gunshot cracked in the distance as Benjie shoved inside. His coveralls were torn; a mini GoPro camera hung crookedly by his ear. Panic blanched his face. He shouted one word of warning.

"Run!"

4

From the height of thirty thousand feet, Commander Gray Pierce watched the shadowy coastline of Africa grow steadily ahead of him, lit by the glow of a small coastal town. The private jet—a Cessna Citation X+—raced across the black waters of the Atlantic toward those lights, but they wouldn't be stopping at that town.

An hour ago, they had touched down and refueled at the Cape Verde islands, the midpoint of their journey to the Democratic Republic of the Congo. They still had another five hours of flying to reach the town of Kisangani, almost smack-dab in the middle of the continent.

The literal heart of Africa . . .

A chime sounded from the digital pad propped up on the small teak table in front of his leather chair. He sighed as the encrypted satellite connection was made to Sigma command in D.C. He straightened and picked up the pad. A window opened on the screen, and an image pixelated, then settled into the familiar face of Director Painter Crowe.

Gray's boss sat behind his desk. The director had shed his usual blue suit jacket and sat with his tie pulled loose and his shirt's top button undone. He looked exasperated and combed fingers through his black hair and shifted a single white lock behind an ear, as if tucking in an eagle feather. Painter's Native American heritage shone from the burnished planes of his face, though his silver-blue eyes marked his multiracial heritage.

"Director, we're almost to the coast," Gray said. "You said to check in for any change in status with the situation on the ground."

"Good. I have a few updates. Disturbing ones, in fact. I'm waiting for Kat to loop in. In the meantime, how's our medical team faring?"

"They're boning up as quickly they can, trying to cover all their bases before we land."

Gray glanced to the pair of chairs at the cabin's front. His friend and fellow Sigma teammate, Monk Kokkalis, had his head bent across a table from Dr. Lisa Cummings, the director's wife. The woman had a background in medicine and epidemiology. If whatever was happening in that dark heart of Africa was truly a contagion, then her knowledge of diseases and patterns of transmission could prove vital.

Monk, on the other hand, was former Special Forces. Though he had shed his uniform with the Green Berets years ago, he still maintained his muscular bulk and kept his head shaved smooth. He now wore jeans, boots, and a tight-fitted T-shirt with a bulldog growling on it, a countenance not all that dissimilar to the man's own face. But that tough exterior hid a mind as sharp and quick as any chess champion. After joining Sigma, the former medic had been retrained in the biological sciences, earning a master's degree in biomedicine. He also played a mean pickup game, often besting Gray on the court, even though Monk only stood shoulder-high to Gray.

Painter glanced to the side. "Looks like Kat's ready." Another window opened on the screen, revealing the slightly freckled countenance and dark auburn coif of Kathryn Bryant, Sigma's intelligence analyst. "Maybe you'd better call Monk and Lisa over to listen to what she has to say."

"Will do."

Gray motioned to the two, who had already overheard the director's suggestion. They took the seats opposite Gray, while he shifted the pad, so they could all get a proper view.

Monk waved to Kat. The pair were married, with two young girls. "How're Harriet and Penny?"

"Missing their daddy already. I think they blame me for you leaving again."

"Duty calls," he said with an apologetic smile.

"More like the Smithsonian demands," she countered.

After a frantic call had reached D.C. from a U.N. relief camp, word of a possible viral contagion had spread throughout the Institution's network. With much of the world still recovering from the last pandemic, the scientific community had become hypervigilant. No one was going to risk another plague sweeping the world.

The director of the Smithsonian Global Health Program—a board-certified zoo veterinarian—had first sounded the alarm. Global Health was part of the Smithsonian Conservation Biology Institute, affiliated with the National Zoo. Their mission was to address the rising health crises involving humans, wildlife, and the greater environment. They named their approach One Health, recognizing how inextricably bound humans and animals were to the well-being of all. In fact, 75 percent of all emerging diseases in the past century—Ebola, HIV, COVID-19—all passed to the human population from *animals*, a method known as *zoonotic transmission*. So, it only made sense to continually monitor wildlife populations and prepare for the next threat.

Like what might be happening in the Congo.

Still, this investigation might prove to be a false alarm. For the moment, it was only a *potential* threat. Sigma had only become involved because of its own intimate ties with the Smithsonian Institution. Sigma's headquarters were buried beneath the Smithsonian Castle on the National Mall. The location was chosen due to its proximity to both the extensive research labs of the Institution and to the neighboring halls of power in D.C., which served the group well.

Sigma Force operated covertly under the auspices of DARPA, the Defense Department's research-and-development agency. They were all former Special Forces soldiers, recruited in secret by Sigma and trained in various scientific disciplines to act as field agents, protecting the United States and the globe against all manner of threats. Their name arose from the Greek letter Σ, which represented the "sum of the best," the merging of brain and brawn, of soldier and scientist. Their motto was a simple one: *Be there first.*

Following that directive, Director Crowe had rallied Sigma when word reached the Smithsonian about a possible emerging threat. He had immediately enlisted an associate who had helped them in the past—a former Army Ranger—who was already in Africa. Captain Tucker Wayne had agreed to secure the Global Health veterinarian and get him onsite until Sigma could reach the continent. Whether this threat proved to be real or not, Sigma intended to *be there first*, ready to find out.

"Any word from Captain Wayne?" Lisa asked, leaning closer. She had her blond hair tied back in a ponytail. A pair of reading glasses perched on her nose. "Was he able to find Dr. Whitaker?"

Painter nodded. "They're already en route to Kisangani. They should be landing within the hour and will airlift via helicopter to the campsite."

"Wait," Monk said. "I thought the plan was for all of us to rendezvous at the University of Kisangani and set up a base of operations there first."

"You're still five hours out," Painter explained. "And a series of thunderstorms is rolling through the area. All that lightning will ground any helicopters. To avoid any further delay, Tucker has agreed to try to duck under that storm before it hits. Especially after the latest word out of the camp."

"What word?" Gray asked.

"Two hours ago, there was another garbled radio call. From the same doctor working there. Gunfire could be heard in the background. The doctor warned against anyone going out to that camp."

"Then maybe Tucker should wait for us," Gray warned. "Who knows what mess he and that researcher might be flying into?"

"I've taken that into account. FARDC—the Congolese military—is flying in ahead of them. Everyone's rushing that storm. Only after an all-clear from the Congolese army will Tucker proceed. The FARDC team should be lifting off from Kisangani as we speak."

"They're already airborne," Kat corrected. "Heading out in two helos."

"Still, maybe Tucker should wait for us," Gray said. "We don't even know if there is any real threat. He could be endangering himself and Dr. Whitaker for no reason."

Painter remained silent for a breath. "Tell them, Kat."

She shifted in her seat, clearly reading from a screen. She was in the communication nest at Sigma. "I've been monitoring chatter and intelligence across the breadth of Africa. A WHO field camp in Uganda, near the border with the DRC, has reported strange cases coming in from the jungle, of a baffling debilitating malaise. A score of afflicted have trickled in over the past two weeks. The WHO has been slow to spread the word as there've been no deaths. Then at a hospital in Burundi, farther to the south, they have a handful of similar cases, people suddenly growing leaden and mute. And maybe more cases in South Sudan, but verification is sketchy."

"So, it's not only the U.N. camp that's afflicted," Lisa said. "Something must be spreading. But how?"

Kat shifted and brought up a map on another window. It showed a swath of central Africa. The view was overlaid with arrows and spiky arcs.

"This is a weather map," she explained. She tapped a button and set those same arrows and arcs into motion, sweeping slowly to the northeast. "This shows the direction and force of the spring monsoon that led to all the recent flooding. The wet winds off the Atlantic sweep north and east, running into the hot dry winds flowing south off the Sahara."

Lisa straightened with a grimace. "Kat, you don't think—"

"All the reported cases lay in the path of those winds," Kat warned grimly. "Uganda, Burundi, even South Sudan. Maybe it's coincidental. But I've searched for any matching reports out of Angola and Zambia to the south." She shook her head. "Nothing so far. It's all quiet in that direction."

Gray stared from Lisa to Kat. "Are you suggesting that whatever is spreading is *airborne*, being seeded by those monsoon winds?"

"At this point, it's only conjecture," Kat said.

Lisa took off her reading glasses. "It's theoretically possible for a viral contagion to spread that way. It's already been documented that millions of viruses rain out of the sky every day, sweeping down out of the upper atmosphere."

Monk frowned. "That might be true. But it's doubtful that the number of particles would be sufficient to be infectious. Sure, aerosolized transmission—from one person to another—happens, but viruses need a host. Few viruses live long in an environment outside of one, especially when exposed to sunlight and UV radiation."

"That's not entirely true," Lisa countered. "While flu viruses live only a day or so on open surfaces, cold viruses can be contagious for up to a week. And there are others that can survive longer. Still, like Kat said, this is all conjecture."

"That's why we need more intel and data," Painter said.

"And as quickly as possible," Gray added. "Something tells me I won't be leaving Africa any time soon."

Painter agreed. "I need you to delay your vacation."

For all intents and purposes, Gray had just been hitching a ride on the jet. With everything so tentative out in Africa, his original objective had been to accompany Sigma's medical team to the area, get everyone situated, then move on. His own studies with Sigma—after he had been court-martialed out of the Army Rangers—concentrated on an amalgam of physics and biology. So, he was far from a medical expert.

His plan had been to continue on from Africa and join his girlfriend, Seichan, and their young son in Hong Kong. Seichan had taken Jack to visit her mother. She had left two weeks ago, intending to spend a month there. Gray had been heading to join them for the latter half of her visit.

Now it looks like that won't be happening.

He wasn't sure how he felt about this change. He was anxious to see Seichan and Jack, but he could not discount the harder beat of his heart. Of late, there had been a lull in activity at Sigma. During the pandemic, terrorism on a global scale had waned. Regional skirmishes persisted, but the lockdown had stymied any wider reach.

But now . . .

While he loved being a father and building a home life with Seichan, he remained a warrior at the core. His ears were forever piqued for the tiny sonic booms of a bullet passing close, of the Doppler of flying shrapnel. His blood ran with gun oil. He longed for the acrid whiff of rifle fire in the air, for those moments when time slowed, and adrenaline surged. He glanced over to Monk, noting the tightening of his fist.

He feels it, too.

Still, Gray also noted the winced crinkles at the corners of his friend's eyes. Like Gray, Monk was a father. Did either of them have any right to put themselves in danger with young children at home? All soldiers struggled with this dichotomy; this pull in two different directions.

Gray had another reason for discomfort. He pictured Seichan, her leonine curves, her wry smile, her deft skill with glade and gun. She was as much a warrior as he was.

If things go south in Africa . . .

She's not going to be happy missing out.

Another passenger also expressed displeasure with this change in plans.

A groan rose behind Gray, coming from a sofa along the cabin's starboard side. The cracking of joints sounded as the last member of the team woke and stretched his limbs. Gray glanced back. Joe Kowalski shoved his six-foot-four frame into a seated position. He ran a large palm across the dark stubble crowning his skull. He cast a heavy-browed glare at the assembly ahead of him.

His graveled voice complained, "What's all this about a delay?"

Like Gray, Kowalski had no role in this mission. The former seaman was Sigma's demolitions expert, but he was currently on medical leave. He had been diagnosed with cancer four months ago. Multiple myeloma, stage 3. A cancer of plasma cells. The prognosis was grim, though his symptoms, beyond a low-grade anemia, were presently mild. He was already on a regimen of dexamethasone and a protease inhibitor. Gray had heard that his oncologist was recommending a stem cell transplant, where the man's bone marrow would be wiped out with chemotherapy, then replaced with healthy stem cells.

Ever stubborn, Kowalski had refused such a radical course—at least, for now.

Instead, Kowalski was headed to the Republic of the Congo, just north of the DRC. He was traveling to the Virunga National Park to visit his fiancée, Maria, who was checking on the pair's foster son, Baako, a young gorilla hybrid who had been released at a sanctuary there. Painter had cautioned against Kowalski traveling to Africa, especially as myelomas weakened a sufferer's immune system. Not that anyone would ever use the word *weak* in respect to the muscular brute. Still, Kowalski had insisted on coming along, pressing the matter, especially with word of some unknown threat spreading across the jungle, which could put both his fiancée and his furry son at risk. He intended to be there to protect them both.

Painter had finally relented.

How could he not?

Kowalski was not one to waste away in a sickbed. He would fight for as long as he could. Plus, no one doubted *how* the man had acquired the cancer. During a prior mission, he had been exposed to a massive dose of radiation.

So, we all owe him any accommodation he wants.

Monk answered Kowalski's query. "Looks like this trip into the jungle isn't a wild-goose chase after all. Something's definitely spreading across the jungle."

"Of course it is." Kowalski glowered and settled back to a sprawl on the sofa. "Wake me when we get there."

Gray faced Painter on the screen. "Anything else we should know about?"

"Not at the moment. I'll give you a final update before you land. Until then, maybe you all should heed Kowalski's example and get some rest. Something tells me you'll need to move fast once you land."

Gray didn't doubt this. He signed off and everyone returned to their own seats and thoughts. His heart pounded even harder now. He pictured a storm of contagion sweeping across the heart of Africa. He sensed their team was already behind the curve in getting a handle on this crisis and wished they were already landing.

But it was not to be.

That role belonged to another.

11:16 P.M. CAT
Kisangani, DRC

With a pack over his shoulder and a holstered Desert Eagle at his hip, Tucker hurried across the dark rainswept tarmac of Bangoka International Airport, a small airfield east of the city of Kisangani. Their Cessna Grand Caravan had landed a few minutes ago, piloted by his friend Christopher Nkomo. He and his brother Matthew would offload the fifteen red plastic crates that comprised Frank's mobile lab and transfer them to the University of Kisangani.

In the meantime, the weather pressed their schedule.

Tucker followed a FARDC soldier in khaki fatigues and a bright-orange vest.

Kane trotted at Tucker's side. Even so close, the Belgian Malinois's dense black-and-brown coat made him look like Tucker's shadow. The shepherd's fur was soaked from the downpour, which frequent full-body shakes did little to disperse. Kane kept watch silently, not even panting, his ears tall and pointed.

Dr. Frank Whitaker followed on Tucker's other side, carrying a backpack of sample-collection gear. The veterinarian looked like he hadn't aged a day since Tucker had left the service. Maybe a few curls of gray in his close-cropped hair. With the man's clothes sodden to the skin, he looked to have kept in lean shape. Once upon a time, the three of them had jogged together, under a sun that baked, kicking up the perpetual red sands of the base outside Baghdad.

Tucker had spent most of his service in Afghanistan, losing a partner there, Kane's littermate Abel. Afterward, distraught and nearly inconsolable, Tucker had been shipped to Iraq, where more than anyone, Frank had helped him find his center again. He had even helped Tucker steal Kane. At that time, the war dog had not completed his full tour of duty, but after losing Abel, Tucker refused to leave Kane behind. The two of them had shed enough blood. So, under the cover of night and with papers falsified by Frank, Tucker had fled. Eventually the crime had been cleared up, courtesy of Tucker's past help with Sigma. Still, he knew none of that would have been possible without his friend's help.

Tucker glanced sidelong to Frank.

I owe this man everything.

The Congolese escort led them toward a helicopter that sat atop a pad. The rotors slowly turned as the pilot kept the engine warm.

Tucker wanted to hurry. He had already heard from Director Crowe about Sigma's fear that the contagion was spreading beyond these borders. It had to be stopped. Tucker's love for this continent ran deep. It had become his home and refuge. Its natural beauty ached his heart. A couple of years ago, he had invested with the Nkomo brothers—Christopher and Matthew—in a luxury safari camp at the Spitskop Nature Preserve in South Africa. A month ago, he had returned from the States, after a sojourn through the Southwest, and joined the brothers in scouting a second location for their growing enterprise.

Until Sigma's call.

Frank sidled up closer. "Do you think we can fly in this weather?"

Tucker shrugged. "Visibility will be strained by the rain, but as long as it doesn't blow into a lightning storm, we should be able to make the forty-minute hop to the campsite."

"What do you think happened out there? Why would Dr. Jameson warn us away?"

"I don't know, but the Congolese forces should have the camp locked down before we get there. According to Crowe, a pair of military helicopters—a transport Puma and a small gunship—left a few minutes ago."

Tucker and the others finally reached the parked helicopter and ducked under the blades with their escort. The military chopper—an Aérospatiale Gazelle—was a single-engine, light utility craft, one nimble enough for quick flights in rough conditions. The escort popped the side hatch and poked his head inside, yelling over to the pilot.

After a brief exchange, the escort faced them again. He spoke English with a French accent. "Storm comes fast. You go now or not go."

Tucker turned to Frank. "The weather forecast warned that thunderstorms will be raging throughout the night. We can always wait until the skies clear up in the morning."

Frank crossed his arms, clearly unsure what to do, vacillating between urgency and caution. "With something possibly spreading already, even a day could make a huge difference." He glanced off to the dark forest. "And like you said, our Congolese friends are already en route. If we lift off now, we can follow behind them. If there's any problem ahead, the military could radio us, and we could turn back. Right?"

Tucker glanced to the escort for confirmation.

The man merely shrugged.

Frank unfolded his arms and pointed to the open hatch. "I say we go for it."

Tucker nodded and waved Frank inside. "Then that's what we'll do."

The veterinarian clambered up into the back. Tucker signaled Kane to hop in after him. The shepherd leaped atop the bench seat. Tucker followed as the pilot twisted to face them with a scowl.

"No dog!" the man shouted from under his helmet.

Tucker glared at the man. "You're right. He's *no dog*." He pointed at Kane. "He's a *soldier*."

Kane gave a low, menacing growl, confirming the same.

Frank settled back and pointed a thumb at the shepherd. "Sir, maybe you best listen to our furry friend."

The pilot swore under his breath and faced back around.

Tucker grinned at Frank. "Who knew you spoke canine?"

Frank strapped in. "Not as fluently as you. I've seen you and Kane work."

"That's more Kane than me."

Still, Tucker felt a flush of pride, both for himself and his partner. Kane had a command of a thousand words, a hundred hand signals, but that was not their truest bond. That had been forged during their years together. After all this time, the two were bound together tighter than with any leash, each capable of reading the other, a communication that went beyond any spoken word or hand signal.

He patted Kane's flank as the rotors sped up, sweeping through the rain. The engine growled into a roar. Tucker felt a tremble in his partner's body. It was not fear, but excitement. Kane was readying himself for the challenge, ramping up, clearly anxious to be underway. From the seat, Kane glanced at Tucker. The shepherd's dark brown eyes shone with flecks of gold in the cabin lights.

You ready, buddy?

Kane answered, nudging Tucker's cheek with his nose.

Of course you are.

Satisfied, Tucker snapped into his seat. He didn't know what lay ahead—only that he and Kane would face it together.

Like always.

5

Charlotte recoiled as a rifle blasted outside the tent.

The gunman appeared behind Benjie, herding the grad student farther into the tent. The shooter was one of the ICCN guards, likely the same one who had accompanied Ndaye in the search for the missing biologist. The uniformed man took up a post at the tent flap, his rifle pointing outward.

Ndaye crossed to his teammate, shadowed by the shaman and his apprentice.

Jameson closed in on Benjie. "What's going on out there?"

The student's eyes blinked rapidly in wild fright. "They're coming," he panted out.

Charlotte joined them. "Who—?"

An ululating howl cut through the rumble of thunder. A chorus answered, sounding as if coming from everywhere. All the hairs on Charlotte's body shivered in primal terror.

"We need to go," Benjie warned. "They'll rip right through this tent."

Jameson grabbed the biologist's arm. "What did you see?"

Rifle fire drew their attention. The eco-guard clutched his weapon at his shoulder, his cheek to its stock. Then something large struck him in the back, hard enough to knock him out of view. The man screamed, his body thrashing into the side of the tent. He fought something that tore into him. Dark blood suddenly sprayed the fabric.

Benjie fled, drawing them all back. Charlotte grabbed Disanka and her child and followed.

At the flap, Ndaye dropped to a knee with his rifle raised. He squeezed off a shot, then another, aiming for the fighting, which had rolled away from the tent. The guard's scream strangled to a gurgle, then went silent.

Ndaye cursed and retreated, pushing the shaman and apprentice behind him.

Woko stared past Ndaye's shoulder. "*Nyani* . . ."

Charlotte frowned. She knew that word, but it couldn't be true.

As if proving her wrong, a hulking form shoved through the flap. It stood shorter than her waist but had to weigh over fifty kilos. Its shaggy gray-green fur was soaked and matted with mud. It crouched on its back legs, balanced on one forearm. Huge eyes glowed with fury. It screamed at them, lips rippling back from its dog-like muzzle, baring pink gums and fangs as long as her fingers.

Nyani meant *baboon*.

As more savage cries echoed all around, Ndaye

fired at the beast, striking its shoulder. It spun fully around from the impact—then leaped straight at him. Backpedaling, Ndaye managed another quick shot. The baboon's head cracked backward, and its body crashed to the floor.

Ndaye leaped over the bloody remains and yanked the tent's zipper, sealing them in. Not that it would offer much protection. He knew it, too. "We can't stay here."

"I . . . I tried to warn you," Benjie gasped out.

Charlotte stared at the body on the floor. More shadowy shapes trampled all around the camp. One bounded across the tent's roof, causing her to duck. Howls and savage screams echoed everywhere. It sounded like hundreds of baboons had invaded the camp.

She still did not understand this behavior. The presence of baboons was not unusual in the camp. Over the prior days, the occasional furry thief would bound in, steal food from tables, or root through their stores. The gray furred monkeys—*Papio anubis*, or olive baboons—were prevalent throughout the Congo. But so far, they had been no more than a nuisance. Not that they couldn't be dangerous. She had read how baboons could swarm a leopard and kill it. Still, she had been assured that the shy monkeys posed little threat unless provoked, that thieves would scatter with a shout, which had proven true.

But clearly no longer.

"What do we do?" Jameson asked.

A spatter of gunfire cut through the howling outside, coming from the other side of the camp. Charlotte shared a worried look with Ndaye.

Another two of his teammates were out there. They had been guarding the last ICCN truck, readying it for the evacuation. Now they must be attempting to hold the line and protect the patients.

She pictured the beleaguered truck, their only means of escape. Still, she knew the truth.

We'd never make it that far on foot.

Ndaye looked like he had come to the same conclusion. He snapped a radio from his hip and lifted it to his lips. He spoke rapidly in French, ordering the truck to leave while it could, to follow after the first one.

Jameson overheard him and was fluent enough to understand. He grabbed Ndaye's arm. "What're you doing? Tell them to come here. To pick us up."

Ndaye shook free of his grip and remained unnervingly calm. "*Non*. They will be overrun before they could get here. It is better that they go. Plus, the noise, the motion, it might help us here."

"How?" Jameson demanded.

A truck engine roared to life, accompanied by a loud grinding of gears. Then blasts of a horn sounded, bleating out in a fading Morse code as the vehicle headed for the jungle. The message of that horn was not meant for those in the tent, but for the trampling horde outside.

Another baboon leaped to the top the tent, rattled across it, then leaped in the direction of the retreating truck. From the trail of hoots, screams, and fading howls, a majority of the troop chased after the truck.

It's trying to draw them off . . .

"We'll not have much time to seek a better shelter," Ndaye whispered.

Charlotte tightened her jaw and listened. A few shapes could still be heard scuffling about, past the front of the tent, grunting and toppling crates. Some of the baboons had remained behind.

But how many?

Charlotte shifted closer and pointed toward the back of the tent. "What about trying to reach the flooded village? Several of the structures out there have wooden walls, tin roofs."

She stared around at the others. She felt as if she had fallen into the story of "The Three Little Pigs," urging their group to vacate this flimsy shelter and make for somewhere stronger.

If only we had a brick house nearby . . .

Benjie nodded. "It's a good idea. Baboons can swim but prefer not to. Those floodwaters might discourage them from following us into the river."

"Then we hurry," Ndaye said. "Go quietly."

He stepped toward the zippered flap, but Woko grabbed him and shook his head. "*Hapana.*"

The shaman turned and headed the opposite way, to the rear of the tent. A long blade appeared in his fingers. He stabbed into the fabric and slashed downward, forming a new back door, away the noises out front. He held the torn fabric open and waved to them.

"*Endelea,*" he urged.

Jameson obeyed, hurrying to the new door. He clearly wanted out—but he did not want to be the *first* one. He grabbed Byrne and pushed the

Swiss nurse through the sliced opening. Byrne wormed his way out. Only once it appeared safe did Jameson follow.

Charlotte paused long enough to grab a scalpel off a tray table, then helped Disanka and her boy squeeze through and followed them. She tried to move as silently as possible.

Outside, Jameson and Byrne crouched near the tent. The rainswept camp lay dark, illuminated by pools of light from generator-powered lamp poles. Thunder rumbled, and distant flashes of lightning brightened the black clouds. At least, the rain had washed away the worst of the ants underfoot.

Clutching her tiny blade, she searched ahead.

Beyond the scatter of tents and crude lean-tos, shadowy outlines marked the village proper. The river reflected the growing battle in the skies, the waters briefly appearing and disappearing.

Woko and Faraji joined them. The boy gripped the straps of his backpack and its precious cargo, the Kuba mask-box. Ndaye followed Benjie out and eyed the gathered group.

Jameson shifted nervously, clearly anxious to get moving. He likely would've already taken off, except his gaze flicked to Ndaye's rifle, the only gun among them. The pediatrician intended to stick close to that weapon.

Ndaye waved them all into motion.

They set off across the camp, avoiding pools of light and sidestepping deeper puddles lest any splashing draw the attention of the baboons. The outlines of the village slowly grew ahead of them, limned against the reflected flashes of lightning.

Charlotte glanced back frequently. Her ears strained for any threat, but the constant rumble of thunder and patters of rain confounded her. She panted as silently as she could. Then a chain of lightning shattered directly overhead. The thunder pounded down at them, trembling the puddles.

In that crackling flash, movement atop a tent drew her eye to the left. A large shape rose out of a crouch, briefly illuminated. It looked huge, far bigger than any baboon. Or maybe terror made it seem so. Another shift of shadows stirred, to her right, perched atop a netted pile of crates.

Sentinels . . .

She didn't know if she and the others had been spotted in the lightning flash, but her worry became moot. A sharp cry rose from among them, rising from the tiniest throat. The blast of thunder must have frightened the child. Disanka huddled over the boy. Jameson lunged at her, his arms outstretched, looking ready to strangle the child to silence.

Disanka retreated into Charlotte.

But the damage was done.

The sentinel to the left howled. The call was carried even louder by the second baboon. They both vanished, bounding off their roosts and into the darkness. Cries erupted behind them, rising from many throats.

Too many . . .

"Run!" Ndaye shouted.

They fled, scattering apart. Charlotte stuck close to Disanka and her boy. She followed Jameson and Byrne. As they rounded a lean-to, a shape crashed into them. Byrne was struck in the side and flattened to the mud. A massive baboon battered and clawed at him. The nurse lifted a defensive arm, only to meet the beast's fangs and powerful jaws. Wrist bones crunched. With a toss of the baboon's head, the hand ripped away with a high arc of blood.

Byrne screamed.

Then two gunshots deafened Charlotte, firing past her ear. Fur flew, but the beast simply flung itself away, diving back into hiding. Charlotte glanced back around, expecting to see Ndaye, but it was another ICCN guard, a smaller man in similar attire. He ran past her. She realized the guard must have come from the truck, maybe hiding when the vehicle took off and making his way over to help them.

The guard rushed to Byrne and pulled the nurse to his feet. Byrne cradled his arm, staggering as he was half-dragged onward.

Jameson hadn't waited and was a good distance ahead. He had already reached the village's edge, but he didn't slow until he hit the water, splashing into the flooded section.

Charlotte headed after him with Disanka.

Chattering and howling chased them, closing quickly upon them.

Charlotte gasped and ran, her heart pounding.

We have to make it . . .

A terrified cry rose to her left. She glanced over. Fifteen meters away, Faraji lay facedown in the mud; two shadows tore at his form. The boy rolled and fought, more to keep his blue backpack in place than to protect himself.

She pushed Disanka toward the ICCN guard. "Get her to safety. Follow the doctor."

She then clutched her scalpel and ran toward Faraji.

Woko reached his apprentice first. The elderly shaman kicked one of the baboons away. The other rolled sideways, hissing with a baring of long fangs. More beasts closed in on the two of them, melting out of the shadows with ear-splitting howls.

As she ran, she spotted Ndaye beyond them. He had his rifle raised, but he held off shooting, clearly fearful of hitting them. Benjie crouched behind the ICCN leader.

Before Charlotte could reach the shaman, Woko flung his arm wide and spun. A yellowish powder flew from his fingertips, as if by magic. But she knew the source, picturing the tiny vial removed from the Kuba Box. Before the rain could wash the powder out of the air, a fine mist circled the pair.

The baboons tried to attack through it—only to suddenly balk and retreat, screaming even louder. Several fled fully away.

One raced straight at Charlotte. She flinched and skidded sideways, only to have it lope past her, hooting in panic and alarm.

Ahead, Woko used the momentary break to grab the back of Faraji's collar. He hauled the boy to his feet and shoved him toward Ndaye. The boy fled, still clutching the remaining strap of his pack, the other ripped to shreds.

The motion of his frantic flight drew a few strays to chase after him.

Ndaye fired, keeping the closest from the boy's heels.

Woko waited too long. The rains had cleared the powder too quickly. The surrounding baboons sniffed the air, noses high, then as if acting as one, they bounded at the shaman. The pack hit his body from all sides, climbing his torso.

A burst of lightning revealed a flash of fangs. They buried into the shaman's throat. For a moment, Woko's eyes shone at her, reflecting the storm light.

Then darkness wiped away the worst of the sight.

Without a single cry, Woko's body collapsed under the weight, under the onslaught. Something glinted in the air, passing through a pool of lamplight. It landed in the mud near Charlotte.

She snatched it up, knowing what it was.

She clutched the glass vial in one hand and her scalpel in the other. Beyond the shaman's ravaged body, Faraji crashed into Ndaye. The eco-guard caught the boy and pushed him toward Benjie. Ndaye then fired once into the air as he retreated away from Charlotte, the noise and flight drawing the baboons after him.

He shouted back to her, "Run!"

As the world thundered and howled around her, she turned and fled the other way, chasing after Jameson's group. She hated to split up, but they had no choice.

6

Benjie was never happier to be proven right.

Panting hard, he waded and pawed his way through dark waters. Ndaye and the boy flanked him, splashing fiercely to get deeper into the flooded village. Behind them, a troop of baboons screamed from the shoreline, reluctant to enter the storm-swollen river.

And for good reason.

The current was strong. It threatened to rip Benjie's legs out from under him with every step. To keep his footing, he propped one arm along the side of a wooden hovel. He reached the door but passed it by.

Not the best spot.

The small hut only had a thatched roof made of palm leaves. It would offer little protection should they be attacked. He continued onward, having already picked out his target. Ahead stood an abode with a corrugated steel roof and walls. It rose from waist-deep waters.

Perfect . . .

He hurried toward the shelter, keeping a wary watch on the river.

The strong current and riptides were not the only dangers out here. He searched for crocodiles and hippos, both equally dangerous. He prayed the storm had driven such beasts to higher ground or deeper waters.

Still, he studied the river, trying to read it like a book, watching for any telltale ripples, any blasts of expelled air.

Nothing.

Maybe my prayers were heard.

Benjie's mother certainly placed much stock on her faith, on the weekly masses at St. James Church. She swore that anything could be granted if one prayed hard enough.

Unfortunately, Benjie had not been clear enough about his wishes this night.

The howling behind him grew louder.

He glanced over a shoulder. A line of dark shapes leapt from rooftop to rooftop, crossing above the floodwaters. Clearly the baboons had devised a way to continue their pursuit without entering the river.

Ndaye realized the same. "Faster!"

Benjie kicked and batted at the river, fighting the current and his own panic. The steel-roofed structure was only a few yards ahead. He shoved and fought his body through the deepening waters.

Screams echoed across the village behind him.

He finally reached the home and edged around its side. A black doorway opened in the wall ahead.

He lunged toward it, leading the others. As he reached the threshold, he noted two disappointments. The home had no door and was open to the river. And worst of all, it was already occupied. Others had sought shelter from the storm.

Lightning flashed in the sky, bright enough to reveal a layer of slithering bodies, squirming across the water's flat surface. The long coiling lengths filled the flooded single-room structure.

Snakes . . .

11:31 P.M.

On the other side of the village, Charlotte snugged the belt around Byrne's forearm. She hoped the makeshift tourniquet would be enough to stop the blood flowing from the nurse's severed wrist.

Byrne sat leadenly atop a stool that she had found in the flooded home. His weight held it in place. His entire body shivered. His eyes showed too much white. He was in shock, close to passing out from pain and blood loss.

The ICCN guard—a man named Kendi—manned the door, which he had left cracked open enough to spy upon the shoreline. Baboons still howled out there, but the darkness and row of riverside homes kept them out of direct sight.

Jameson hovered at Kendi's shoulder. The pediatrician's hands were balled into fists. He also shook in the knee-deep water, but not from shock.

Disanka stood stiffly in the far corner. She nursed her son. But Charlotte knew the effort was less about feeding the boy than keeping him quiet.

They were still too close to the shoreline for her liking. Jameson had led them to the first structure with plank walls and a door framed in tin. She glanced up to the thatch roof, knowing it would offer little protection against a baboon's strength to rip and tear.

Still, she could not fault Jameson for his panicked pick of shelters. She kept a hand on Byrne's shoulder, which trembled under her palm. She doubted the injured nurse would've made it much farther out into the river.

She could only hope this spot was far enough.

A loud yowl rose from the shoreline. It was picked up and passed by others. It was punctuated by hooting barks. The chorus rang out for a full minute—then suddenly fell silent.

Charlotte straightened.

Disanka stared unblinking at her, her eyes glassy with terror.

Then Charlotte heard a faint pounding and slapping, along with a few grunts. The noise quickly approached. She understood, picturing shapes bounding through the air, crossing from roof to roof.

Kendi whispered from the doorway, "They're coming."

11:32 P.M.

No, no, no, no . . .

As the hunters closed in, Benjie stood at the threshold of the snake-infested chamber. He could not get himself to enter. He hated the slithering creatures. In the Congo, tens of thousands died each year from snake bites. Standing there, a list already ran through his head: *bush vipers, boomslangs, black mambas, puff adders, twig and stiletto snakes.* But what especially set his bollocks to icing was the thought of *Naja christyi*, the deadly Congo water cobra, which could grow to be seven feet long.

Still, it wasn't the fear of venom or fangs that kept him rooted in place. He simply could not tolerate the feel of slick scales across his skin. His university herpetology class had nearly unmanned him, badly enough that he had considered leaving school, abandoning his degree. Especially the practical labs, where he had to handle such creatures.

While his ASD was at the lower end of the spectrum, certain noises and sensations could set him off. The crinkle of cellophane made him want to claw at his ears. He would vomit at the smell of frying onions. And the slide of a snake over his palm—its scales somehow both bone-dry and oily—left him shaking all over.

Standing now, staring at the slithering roil, his legs refused to move.

Then he was struck from behind. "Get inside!" Ndaye shouted and shoved him into the room.

Benjie gasped and wailed. He fought to keep his footing, lifting both arms high. Snakes writhed around his waist. His vision narrowed. A ringing rose in his ears.

Ndaye waded in with his rifle, followed by the small kid with a backpack; Benjie didn't yet know his name.

"No be scared," the boy scolded him. He picked up one of the snakes, which coiled in his grip, and threw it aside. "*Chatu.*"

"Faraji's right," Ndaye assured him, crossing through the roiling mass. "They're *Calabaria reinhardtii.* The Calabar python. Nonvenomous."

Benjie didn't care and kept his hands high. He squeezed his eyes closed and fought against his terror with facts. He pulled up what he knew about the species, relying on his memory. *Calabar pythons rarely grew longer than a meter. Named after a Danish herpetologist, Johannes Reinhardt. They were found throughout the rain forest and were fossorial, which meant they lived in burrows, usually in leaf litter . . .*

He peeked his lids open enough to gaze at the stirring spread. He noted most of the snakes were juvenile and small, only as long as his forearm.

Their riverside nests must have been flooded out.

He forced his breathing to calm but refused to lower his limbs.

Still, the snakes were not the true danger here. Benjie stared toward the doorway guarded by Ndaye and his rifle. It had grown silent out there. Then something struck the corrugated steel roof with a loud bang, which made him jump.

Another shape hit.

Then another.

A soft hooting and barking rose from atop the roof.

Ndaye lifted a finger to his lips as they all stared up.

More shapes piled onto the roof, clambering about. Strong fingers pried at the corners of the corrugated steel. Then suddenly a shape swung down from above, hanging by an arm from the lintel of the doorway. It caught Ndaye off guard. Strong legs struck outward and knocked the rifle from the guard's hands. The weapon splashed into the water and sank.

The baboon—a hundred-pound male—swung back again. It bared huge canine teeth and prepared to leap at Ndaye.

Then the boy, Faraji, sidestepped the tall man. He swung his arm. A two-foot-long snake flew from his hand. It writhed through the air and struck the baboon around the neck, half-wrapping around its new purchase.

A scream ripped out of the beast, deafening in the small space.

The baboon crashed heavily into the water as Ndaye dove to the side. The male clawed at the clinging snake, its eyes round with panic. Then it seemed to recognize all the snakes surrounding it. It screeched, leaped high, then thrashed out of the room. It splashed heavily away, trailing a cry of terror.

Benjie glanced to the boy.

"*Nyani* no like snake." Faraji pointed at him. "Be scared like you."

Benjie fought against a spasm of rapid blinking.

Only now did he recall how baboons had an innate terror of snakes. With all the venomous species out in the jungle, such a fear made sense from a survival standpoint. The inbred terror was likely passed from generation to generation, imbued into their code after millennia of encounters. Behavioral research in humans attested to a similar inheritable terror. Our natural distaste for snakes and spiders was likely a survival mechanism cemented into our code from past venomous exposures.

Benjie's own thesis tangentially dealt with this subject, on the inheritability of stress-induced mutations. Only this night's stress was just beginning.

The panic of the fleeing baboon had not scared off the troop above. They screamed and ripped at the roof. A huge section of the steel bent and tore loose, raining nails down into the water. Dark shadows filled the gap.

Ndaye frantically searched the waters for his rifle. Even if he found it, the water-logged weapon would prove too little, too late.

Benjie stared up.

We're not getting out of here.

11:34 P.M.

"They're almost through . . ." Jameson moaned.

Charlotte cringed as Kendi fired blindly up at the roof. Thatch rained down on them. Not from the shooting, but from the digging above. Hooting and barks answered the rifle fire. A body splashed heavily out into the water, maybe hit by a stray shot. Still, the death did not discourage the other hunters.

Jameson had his back pressed to the door, bracing it closed. Byrne slumped atop his stool, held in place by Charlotte's hand. Disanka kept to her corner, gripping her son, who wailed at the gunfire.

Charlotte's ears rang, too.

Kendi lowered his rifle, perhaps recognizing the futility or saving his ammunition. He cocked his head, then stared up. "Listen. I think they've stopped."

Charlotte gazed toward the roof. A few strands of palm thatch fluttered down, brushing her cheek, but Kendi was right. The rustling and shaking up there had stopped.

Why did they—

Then she heard it, first in her chest, then with her ears. A low thump-thumping.

A helicopter . . .

The baboons above screeched and bounded off the thatch and clattered across the rooftops toward shore. The bell-beat of the aircraft grew louder, growing deafening.

Jameson cringed and pulled the door open a crack. She joined him, leaving Byrne balanced on his stool.

The wash of rotors swept across their village, pounding thatch from the roof as it passed overhead. A brilliant blaze of light lit the waters around them, then continued toward shore, hopefully chasing the baboons even farther away.

Jameson pulled the door wider. He still shook,

but now likely with relief. "Maybe my radio call reached someone after all."

The large-bellied helicopter looked like a shining angel, brightly lit, sweeping to a hover as it reached the shore. Its landing gear lowered toward the ground. Before it even touched down, dark shapes piled out of both sides. A taller man in a camo uniform jumped down and positioned himself in a bright spotlight. He raised a bullhorn, to be heard above the engine's roar.

He hollered in French. Just the familiarity of her native tongue welled tears in Charlotte's eyes. "Search the camp!" he bellowed out. "Secure any medical personnel. We can't stay long!"

A crackle of lightning burst across the underside of the black clouds, reminding them all of the threatening storm about to break.

Jameson hauled the door open. "Hurry," he called back to their group, then set off on his own.

Charlotte returned to Byrne and looked at Kendi. "I'm going to need help getting him to shore."

The guard obliged, shouldering up to one side of the nurse. Charlotte supported the other. Byrne tried to help, but his legs wobbled uncontrollably. He finally gave up and simply hung between them.

They exited the small hut and waded through the waters. Disanka followed with her boy. Charlotte continued to watch the rooflines for any further threat. She strained for any warning hoot or loud bark, but the helicopter's engines drowned out nearly everything.

Still, she heard Jameson shout ahead of them, already on dry land. "Over here! We're over here! We have injured and sick!"

Charlotte shook her head at his claim.

More like, I *have them*.

She slogged toward the light and noise. Even before she reached the shore, men appeared. They splashed and waded to her. They scooped Byrne, took the burden from her, and rushed away. As she followed, other soldiers escorted them, rifles raised all around.

She finally reached the shore. Though still soaked to the skin, she felt a hundred kilos lighter. She moved more swiftly with Kendi and Disanka. They cleared the edge of the village and hurried toward the waiting helicopter. It looked military, an attack helicopter, with a large rear cabin and tiny wings that supported six missiles, three to a side.

Jameson spoke to the tall soldier with the bullhorn. He was a white fellow, tanned and grizzled with clipped hair. Maybe French or Belgian. He wore the same green camo as the rest, but he clearly had an air of authority about him. He mostly ignored Jameson, who gestured as much as he talked.

As Charlotte and the others joined him, the man's dark green eyes flashed her up and down, then nodded. He turned to yell in Swahili, too fast for her to follow. Another man ducked around the camo-colored chopper and crossed over. He appeared to be Congolese, dressed like the rest. He stood shoulder to shoulder with the man holding the bullhorn. From the same gray hair and hard face, the two could have been brothers. They even shared the same green eyes. The only marked difference was the color of their skin.

They spoke with their heads bowed together, glancing occasionally at the dark skies, wincing at the spatters of lightning. Neither showed any deference to the other.

Finally, the one with the bullhorn faced their group, as the other one departed. "We cannot wait much longer. Are there any more of you?"

Jameson stammered, looking longingly at the helicopter's open door. "Maybe. I don't know if any are still—"

Charlotte shoved him aside. She wasn't about to abandon the others. She pointed in the direction where she had last seen Ndaye's group. "Another *three*. They're likely holed up in that section of the flooded village."

The leader grimaced but nodded. He barked to a cluster of men and ordered them to search that area. "And be quick about it," he finished.

Thunder boomed, reinforcing his order.

11:45 P.M.

"What are we waiting for?" Benjie asked, shivering amidst the nest of snakes.

He had clicked on a small penlight from his pocket, shadowing it with a palm. He shone his light over the roil of serpents. He wanted out of here.

The timely arrival of the helicopter had chased off the baboons with all the noise, winds, and light. He had also watched the medical team cross out of the village. They now stood illuminated by the bright lamps of the aircraft.

Ndaye had retrieved his rifle and held it warily. Though the weapon was still waterlogged, he stared through its scope.

Faraji kept near the guard's shoulder.

"They're not Congolese military," Ndaye warned, squinting through the scope. "The helicopter doesn't bear the air force's roundel. A yellow star in a blue circle."

"Then they're with another rescue group," Benjie said. "Who cares *who* hauls our arses out of here?"

Ndaye shook his head and lowered his rifle. "Something's wrong."

Thunder rumbled over the Tshopo River, but rather than fading, it persisted and grew louder. It separated into the distinct bell-beat of thumping rotors.

Another helicopter.

Their gazes all turned from shore and focused downstream. A large aircraft swept across the roiling floodwaters. It blazed with light, some steady, some blinking.

Ndaye raised his rifle's scope, swiveling his aim, then steadying it. His shoulders visibly tightened. "That's a FARDC helo. From our air force."

A second smaller helicopter followed behind the first, crossing over the riverside jungle. *They definitely sent in the cavalry.*

Relieved, Benjie turned toward shore as the

first FARDC chopper reached the village. He pointed out the door. "*Now* can we go?"

Ndaye shoved him back. "Get down!"

As Benjie stumbled from the doorway, he spotted a fiery flash near the helicopter on the ground. A smoky white trail shot outward from it, curling through the night. The newly arrived aircraft exploded into a blinding fireball. The blast rattled the corrugated steel hut. The FARDC helicopter shuddered in midair—then plummeted into the dark water.

Ndaye grabbed a fistful of Benjie's shirt and hauled him back toward the door. "We can't stay here."

The guard pointed toward the dark village. A handful of flashlights bobbled through the flooded homes, coming their way.

11:47 P.M.

Knocked to her knees by the rocket blast, Charlotte stared in shock at the burning wreckage in the river. She struggled to understand. Her chest ached from the concussion. Her hearing was muted to a muffled drone.

The others had dropped around her, too.

She turned to the soldier with the bullhorn. He raised a pistol to the back of Kendi's skull as the guard struggled to his feet. A loud crack shattered through her dull hearing. Kendi's head snapped forward, taking his body with it. He collapsed across the brightly lit mud.

The shooter shouted to his soldiers. "Get everyone on board!"

Shock kept her from reacting.

Gunfire rose from near the river. Another helicopter swept high. It was a hornet-like version of the first. Heavy cannon fire strafed the shoreline, tore into the village. Another RPG shot at the helicopter from the ground, but the swift craft dodged at the last moment. Still, the sudden maneuver threw off its own aim. A missile shot wildly from its undercarriage and blasted into the flooded village, casting up a flume of water and flame.

More rockets shot at the aircraft. It danced and spun above the river. Then a rocket-grenade slammed into its tail assembly. The blast sent the helicopter into a wild spiral. It fought against a crash, but the effort was futile. The helicopter spun, trailing smoke. Then it smashed into the shore at the edge of the village, casting up a whirlwind of flame and black smoke.

As Charlotte raised an arm across her face, someone grabbed her and shoved her toward the open door of the helicopter. Jameson did not need to be manhandled. He gaped at the threat, at the firefight, and fled inside.

The tall leader strode toward Disanka, who huddled on her hands and knees over her son. He lifted his pistol and waved the muzzle, directing another soldier. "Take the baby. We don't need the woman."

No . . .

Charlotte broke free of her captor and ran to

Disanka, blocking the men. She struggled with how to save the mother, baffled by why they wanted the child. Still, she held up both palms and used that knowledge.

"He . . . he's still nursing. If you want the boy, best take the mother, too."

The bullhorn man fixed his hard eyes on her, then nodded. "Take them both aboard." He turned. "But we don't need any more extraneous cargo."

He strode over to Byrne. The nurse was slouched on his knees, cradling his belted arm. He looked up in time to see the pistol raised at his forehead. Too dazed, maybe beyond caring, he showed no fear.

The blast knocked him backward.

Charlotte stumbled to the side, gasping, the world spinning around her. She anchored herself to Disanka as the woman was hauled to her feet. Charlotte kept with her and her boy and allowed herself to be forced into the rear cabin of the aircraft.

Once inside, she saw a strange sight.

Bodies were being shoved and rolled out the other side. The orchestration was led by the bullhorn soldier's counterpart, the tall Congolese. He ordered the dumped bodies to be hauled away in different directions. Old weapons, some wrapped in duct tape, hung from dead shoulders as the bodies were dragged along. The corpses wore a motley display of different uniforms, all in poor condition.

She began to understand.

They're framing all this on some ragtag militia force.

She was shoved into a seat and ordered to strap in. She first helped Disanka, before doing the same. Jameson already sat stiffly in a seat across from her. His face shone with sweat. His gaze was fixed and unblinking.

Outside, the tall European raised a radio to his lips. "Any sign of the others?"

Unable to hear the response, she gazed past the smoldering wreckage on the beach. Oily fires burned all around it. Flames quickly spread across the wooden structures. Thatch roofs smoked and blazed.

She willed the others to stay hidden.

The bullhorn was lifted again. "Everyone back aboard! We leave in five."

Moments later, the rain fell harder, pounding all around. Winds kicked up. Lightning chased across the belly of the clouds. One bolt crisscrossed through the air and struck the river. Thunder rattled the helicopter.

"Make that now!" the tall soldier hollered. "We're leaving now!"

11:52 P.M.

Benjie swam for the next hut. Its roof and upper quarter were still above water. The currents tore at the small structure. As he neared it, a plyboard panel ripped away and sailed across the black water. It quickly vanished into the smoky night.

Rain pelted heavily all around, pebbling the water's surface.

Behind them, fires still spread through the riverside village, too fierce for the storm to smother. The flames chased them.

Then a low roar rose behind him.

He twisted in the current. The helicopter climbed out of the smoke, wafting fiery embers toward them.

They're leaving . . .

Ndaye kicked up next to him, waving a soaking arm forward. "Go. Get out of sight."

Faraji followed in his wake.

With the others departing, Benjie didn't understand the urgency, but he knew better than to question the guard. The man had been proven right too many times this night. He swam harder, fighting the current, digging deep for the strength to reach the next shelter.

When he finally drew abreast of the tiny structure, he grabbed the planks of its walls and dragged himself through the doorway. Ndaye and Faraji joined him a few breaths later.

"What now?" Benjie panted out.

Ndaye stuck near the door. "Depends on them."

Benjie searched outside. The helicopter had risen and flew over the fires. He willed it to head off. Instead, the aircraft hovered in a slow arc across the dark half of the village. A brief spit of fire burst from its flank. Something shot forward and blasted into a row of huts with a thunderous boom. A fireball skidded across several structures, vaporizing them all.

"A Hellfire missile," Ndaye groaned. He turned to them. "They're destroying everything here."

Benjie gulped, looking up at the wooden rafters—mere poles—strung under the roof. "Maybe they'll miss this place."

Ndaye shook his head. "I spotted an armament of six missiles earlier."

Which meant they still had five more . . .

Benjie didn't like those odds, not with so much firepower spread across such a small village.

Neither did Ndaye. He leaped high and grabbed one of the poles overhead. He hung by his hands from it.

"What are you doing?" Benjie called up.

"We're leaving."

"How?"

Ndaye nodded for them both to join him on the pole. The man began to swing, kicking his feet against the far wall. Benjie understood, picturing that piece of plyboard being ripped away earlier and carried off by the current. If they could knock loose a section of the wall and use it as a raft, they could make their escape along the river.

He and Faraji boosted themselves up and hung on either side of Ndaye. They all began swinging and kicking at the wall. Another huge explosion shook the hut and the surrounding waters. More smoke rolled across the swollen river.

They all swung and kicked harder, but the wall refused to budge.

The helicopter's roar drew closer.

"We need to hit it together," Benjie gasped out. "All at the same time."

Ndaye slowed his swing and counted them off. On three, they hammered their heels into the plank walls. It gave a bit, pulling partially free of the nails holding it in place. The current began to tear at it, too.

"One more time oughta do it," Benjie said.

They swung together, only to have the pole snap overhead. They all crashed back into the water. Benjie splashed and sputtered, but he snatched a broken piece of the pole. He kicked over to the assaulted wall, shoved the section into the narrow gap, and fought to pry it wider. He braced his legs on the neighboring wall.

Faraji swam over to help him.

Ndaye retrieved another length of pole and attacked the other side of the wall. Wood groaned, but the stubborn nails refused to let go.

Then the world exploded behind them. Flames shot past the doorway. Choking smoke flooded inside. The concussion slammed into the small hut, carrying with it a huge wave of water. The river swelled into the small space.

Benjie hung onto his pole—as the surge hit the wall. The entire side of the hut fell away from him.

"Get on it!" Ndaye hollered.

As the section of wall splashed into the water, Benjie scrambled atop it with Faraji. The current immediately grabbed their makeshift raft.

Ndaye struggled to reach them. Benjie sprawled on his belly and extended his length of pole. Ndaye lunged a hand, missed it, tried again, then finally gripped it. The guard climbed along the pole as the river ripped at him and spun the raft.

With a final heave, he beached himself atop the broken section of wall. They all lay flat, limbs spread wide to hold their raft steady. The river swept them into the deeper current. Smoke covered the surface, too thick for even the rain and wind to dispel.

Benjie glanced behind him, noting the glow of the helicopter through the pall. Then the current spun them around a bend, and the sight vanished.

Thank god . . .

"We must reach shore!" Ndaye yelled over the river's churning.

"Why? How?" Benjie asked. "We have no paddles."

"We must try."

Faraji stared ahead, his eyes huge.

Then Benjie heard it. The river's roaring grew in volume, the growl of a great beast.

Oh, no . . .

He remembered that the only way into or out of the village was by air or by rutted jungle track. The river was impassable. A half mile downstream, a series of waterfalls and cataracts turned the course into a meat grinder. And the floods had only made that monster fiercer.

Benjie stared over at the dark fringe of jungle

sweeping past them, speeding ever faster. The raft bucked under them, harder and harder.

Lightning shattered the sky.

In the distance, the monster roared its fury, waiting for them.

7

"Thunder's getting worse!" Frank called out.

He leaned his cheek against the cabin window of the helicopter. The deep booms vibrated the acrylic. Far ahead, bright flashes lit the darkness. He squinted at a ruddy glow far upriver.

What's happening over there? Had a lightning strike ignited a forest fire?

The small Aérospatiale Gazelle jostled in the air as the winds picked up. The helo followed the dark river below. They crossed over a maelstrom of whitewater gnashing over black rock and crashing down steep cliffs. The helicopter's lights illuminated the heavy mists churned up by the ferocity of the cataracts.

"Storm's definitely getting worse," Tucker agreed from the other side of the aircraft, eyeing the tempest outside.

Between them, Kane lay curled on the seat, seemingly unbothered by the bumping and sudden drops in the aircraft. Then again, the

Malinois was a veteran, battle-hardened by countless sorties, firefights, and IED blasts. Still, Frank judged the canine with a clinician's eye, that of a veterinarian who had treated hundreds of military war dogs over the years. He had sutured lacerations, grafted over burns, amputated shattered limbs, and, too often, covered small bodies with a drape of flag. Few appreciated the loyalty of such four-legged soldiers. Their sacrifices and hardships were not for any political cause or national pride, but for a simpler reason, one of the heart, of a bond that could not be broken.

Frank stared over at Tucker.

Even now, the man rested a palm on his partner's flank.

That bond went both ways.

Frank reached to Kane and roughed the dog's scruff. His fingers felt a lacing of old scars under the fur, a calloused map of this soldier's past. He noted the gleam of matching scars across Tucker's cheek. They were both survivors, wounded and scarred together into one, bound to each other's heart, through loss and grief, but also joy and companionship.

Frank was glad he was considered part of that family, even if only tangentially. Back in Iraq, Tucker had readily accepted him as part of their pack—which he appreciated, especially as a Black officer. Biases and prejudices still persisted in the military. Back in World War I, there had been only *five* army veterinarians with his skin color. Today those numbers were better, but they were still far from what they should be. Then again, that was true for the veterinary profession in general. Even now, only a little over two percent of veterinarians were Black. And maybe that was part of the reason for the closeness of Frank's relationship with Tucker: they had both stood slightly apart from the rest of the forces.

The Gazelle bounced hard through the air, throwing Frank back to the present. He grabbed his shoulder strap. The belt was all that kept him in his seat. He glanced back to the window. They had cleared the last of the cataracts and sped over the Tshopo River's flat waters, easily a quarter mile across, fringed by black jungle on both sides.

Lightning flashed ahead of them, igniting the river's length for a breath. Thunder followed, booming hard enough to shake the helicopter.

Tucker leaned forward to the pilot, who hunched over his controls, leaning his nose closer to the rainswept windshield. Small blades battered back and forth across the canopy, fighting the sleeting downpour.

"Any word from the advanced team?" Tucker hollered to the beleaguered man.

The pilot simply shook his head.

The Gazelle was running twenty minutes behind the other two FARDC aircraft. So far, there had been no news—good or bad—about the status of the relief camp.

With his eyebrows knit tight, Tucker turned to Frank. The question on his face was easy to read. *Do we continue or turn back?*

The answer rose from outside.

A blinding flash of lightning burst above and

around them. Chains of crackling fire split the sky, racing across the belly of the clouds. A blazing bolt snapped down and struck the river ahead of them. The dazzle burned its image across his retinas.

Thunder followed in the next heartbeat, blasting all around, pummeling the aircraft, as if trying to slap it out of the air. The pilot struggled with his controls as the Gazelle dipped and bucked. Finally, the man swore loudly and swung the helicopter away from the storm wall growing in front of them.

Frank gripped his seat and his shoulder strap.

He did not fault the pilot's decision. They could go no farther. It would be up to the FARDC team's two helicopters to assess the situation at the camp. Having ducked under the worst of the storm, the others were likely grounded there for the night. He and Tucker would join them in the morning.

Frank readjusted the timetable in his head. Instead of collecting samples, he would use the rest of the night to set up and calibrate his mobile lab at the University of Kisangani. That way, when he collected samples from the camp in the morning, he would be ready to analyze them immediately.

Maybe I won't lose all that much time . . .

He settled back in his seat as the Gazelle made a hard turn over the fringe of jungle, preparing to return to the airfield.

Tucker lunged forward and grabbed the pilot's shoulder. "Wait!"

The man scowled over his shoulder

Tucker thrust an arm at the river. "Look! There's a light. On the water."

Whether cooperating or merely returning to their original path, the pilot rolled the aircraft back toward the dark river. Frank pressed his cheek against his window, searching ahead, to where Tucker had pointed. Without the illumination of the helicopter's lights, the water flowed black across their path.

He squinted.

I don't see any—

Then a tiny flash of light blinked, waving near the river's surface, reflected in the rainswept water.

"I see it!" Frank blurted out.

Tucker still gripped the pilot's shoulder, peering ahead. "Someone's down there."

11:52 P.M.

Benjie sagged with relief, finally letting his arm drop to the raft next to him. His tiny penlight shone in his fingertips. He shook, letting a single sob escape him.

Ndaye risked letting go of his perch atop the broken section of wall to pat Benjie's leg. Faraji lay sprawled near the front of the raft, his lips moving in a silent prayer, either of thanks or continuing supplication.

A minute ago, they had spotted the helicopter sweeping upriver, coming toward them, brightly lit in the storm gloom. Benjie had snatched his penlight from a pocket and waved it wildly, trying to signal the aircraft. He didn't know if those aboard were friend or foe, but he didn't care. The helicopter was their only hope to escape the river before the raft reached the deadly cataracts.

Still, Benjie's efforts had seemed for naught. The helicopter had sped unerringly along the river, never shifting its course or dropping lower, oblivious of his signal. He feared the aircraft's own lights were blinding those aboard to his little twinkle in the river.

Then the world had burst with a blinding cascade of lightning, accompanied by a brilliant spear that exploded into the river behind them. As thunder boomed, he had watched with despair as the helicopter turned away, sweeping wide over the jungle as it headed off.

Only now it returned, driving straight toward them, dropping swiftly.

As it reached the river, a hatch opened in the side. A ladder unfurled, its length tumbling toward the river. The storm winds whipped and tore at it. It danced and snapped like a downed power line.

How can we possibly grab that?

Benjie glanced to Ndaye for an answer.

The guard only winced. The raft bucked and rolled and spun in the current, threatening to topple at any moment. Worse, their makeshift craft raced faster and faster along the powerful current.

Faraji ignored the thrashing ladder, his gaze fixed forward.

The roaring ahead drowned out the approach of the helicopter's engines.

We're running out of time—and river.

11:53 P.M.

Tucker clutched a handgrip beside the open hatch. He stared down as the helicopter reached those trapped below. The pilot ignited the Gazelle's spotlight, pinning it to the foundering raft. Three people clung to that precarious purchase. The ladder swung wildly over them. Its end was weighted, but not heavy enough to withstand the strength of these winds.

The three below would have a difficult, if not impossible time, grabbing it.

And that's not the only problem.

Tucker glanced to the south. A billowing mist marked the maelstrom downriver.

He shook his head.

Screw it . . .

He shifted around and mounted the ladder's top rungs.

"What're you doing?" Frank hollered at him.

"We need an anchor!"

And that'll have to be me.

As he started to climb down, Kane edged across the cabin's seat. Tucker met his partner's eyes. "*STAY,*" he ordered with firm command, knowing the dog would follow him anywhere if asked.

But not this time.

Kane sat at the hatch's edge, not looking happy.

"Sorry, bud," he muttered as he descended.

Once he cleared the leeward side of the helicopter, the winds slammed into him. The length of ladder swung outward. He tightened his hold on the rough plastic rungs, waiting a breath to adjust to the motion, then set off again.

Frank yelled above, but not at him. "Steady this damn bird!"

Tucker knew the pilot was doing his best. Still, Tucker spun and swung on the ladder, but this was not his first rodeo. While he and Kane had served in various capacities during the war—search and rescue operations, covert infiltration—their main duty was exfiltration, the surgical extraction of high-value targets.

He peered down between his boots. Faces stared up at him, shining with terror. He didn't know who they were, but Tucker was their best hope, making them *high value* enough for him.

He scaled the rest of the way down the ladder. His extra weight helped stabilize the thrashing length, but it was barely enough. His lean physique was more befitting a quarterback than a linebacker. At this moment, he would've welcomed an entire defensive line to help anchor this ladder.

Still, he reached the end.

He kept a double-fisted grip on his rung and dropped his boots toward the raft. The rotor-wash had pushed the worst of the rain away and pounded the waters flat around him. His toes spun and scraped across the raft, which was just plyboard planks nailed to a couple of cross-beams. His legs danced across the backs of the three sprawled figures. He came close to kicking a boy in the face.

He heard Frank yell above, but the words were lost in the roaring.

Still, the ladder lowered enough for his boots to finally reach the raft and gain a bit of traction. A Congolese soldier in green camo grabbed Tucker's ankle with one hand, then turned to his neighbor.

"Go!" he hollered.

The closest figure, a young man in sodden white coveralls, shifted to his hands and knees. Even this maneuver looked precarious on the teetering raft. Still, the man reached a shaking arm toward the ladder's lowest rung. He grabbed it on his second attempt and hung for a moment to the lifeline.

"Keep climbing!" Tucker yelled with hard command. He knew the guy must be exhausted and terrified, but now was not the time for hesitation.

The man must've understood and lunged higher, nearly upending the raft. He scrambled up the far side of the ladder from Tucker, stepping on Tucker's fingers as he passed.

The soldier, who still gripped Tucker's ankle, turned his head to a boy of twelve or thirteen. "Faraji! Go!"

The kid scuttled over the soldier's body to reach the ladder. He stood up—only to have the raft bobble under him. Thin arms swung wildly for balance. Tucker let go of one hand and grabbed the boy's flailing wrist before he toppled backward off the raft.

As Tucker jerked him to a stop, a small shoulder pack flew down the boy's other arm. It hit the planks and plopped into the water.

The boy cried out with anguish and yanked his wrist from Tucker's grip. The kid dove after the pack as it floated away. His body splashed heavily into the swift current.

Christalmighty . . .

The Congolese soldier shoved to his hands and knees, looking ready to go after the boy, but he was clearly exhausted. Tucker grabbed the man by the collar and hauled him to the ladder.

"Up! Now!"

The soldier's hands latched onto a rung, more in survival instinct than obeying his command. Once the man had a hold, Tucker let go.

"Climb!" he said, nose to nose with the fellow.

With that last order, Tucker turned and dove headlong off the raft, aiming for the bobbing figure of the boy who had retrieved his pack and was trying to swim against the current, an impossible effort.

Tucker hit the water and immediately pushed his head clear.

He fixed on the small form flogging the black water with his limbs. Beyond the boy, the helicopter's lights illuminated a churning wall of mists. Despite the boy's struggle, he was being dragged swiftly toward the cataracts.

Tucker kicked after him. With the water's force propelling him, he reached the boy in only a few strokes. He nearly overshot him, such was the speed of the current. He snatched the boy's shirt, balled a fist in it, and dragged the wiry lad to his side.

"Grab hold!"

Tucker didn't know if the kid understood English, but small arms wrapped around Tucker's neck, nearly strangling him.

He turned and fought the current, but it was far stronger than he had imagined. The abandoned raft sped past him on the right, vanishing into the roaring mists.

The helicopter swept toward them, dragging the ladder. One figure had nearly reached the top. The other remained near the bottom—only he hung upside down, dangling from the rungs by his legs. His arms stretched toward the river, clearly intent on trying to grab them.

Why didn't I think of that?

Tucker swam hard, but he was unable to even hold his position. The helicopter pursued them, buffeted by winds. Lightning crackled behind it. If there was thunder, Tucker didn't hear it. The roaring behind him filled the world.

Then the current dragged him into the mists. He lost sight of the helicopter and the ladder. He fought even harder, only it was futile. Then the spray brightened around him. A dark shadow swept low toward him.

Tucker reached an arm toward it.

The ladder appeared. And the dangling soldier. The man's outthrust arms dragged through the water. Tucker gave up fighting the current and angled to put himself in the man's path.

They briefly locked gazes—then the two hit each other.

Tucker kicked enough to lunge up and latch his arms around the man's torso. The soldier grabbed Tucker around the waist.

The river fell away under them, both as the helicopter lifted and as the course below plummeted in a frothing cascade over rocks and cliffs.

Tucker clung tightly, locked together with the soldier, who trembled from the exertion. Tucker hollered to the boy who still hung from his neck. "Climb, kid! Up my body!"

A rung lay just above Tucker's head.

Toes dug into his back, gaining purchase on his belt. One arm loosened from his neck— then the boy scrambled nimbly upward. Once unburdened, Tucker freed an arm and quickly snatched the same rung.

In short order, he headed up after the boy. The soldier bent at the waist, and despite his exhaustion, he gripped the rungs, swung his legs around, and clambered up behind Tucker.

By now, they had risen above the mists. The ladder still swayed, buffeted by the winds, but they all made the ascent safely.

Tucker hauled himself inside, then helped the soldier. They all piled in and collapsed across the seats. The quarters were cramped. The Gazelle was normally a five-seater. With six aboard now—and a dog—they were pushing the helo's design limits, but it was an infraction he could live with.

They all could.

Tucker stared over at the boy, who hugged his backpack to his chest.

"Guess you really wanted that," he gasped out, brushing wet hair from his eyes. "What's in there? Your homework?"

The boy ignored him, or maybe didn't hear him due to the engine's roaring. The kid stared warily at Kane. "He bite?"

Tucker sighed. "Only if I tell him to."

His answer did not dim the fear in the lad's eyes.

"Don't worry." He patted the kid's knee. "He's friendly."

Until he's not, Tucker added silently.

Frank leaned over enough to yell at Tucker. He pointed to the young man who had climbed the ladder ahead of everyone else. "You need to hear what he told me! About what happened at the camp!"

"Can it wait till we get to Kisangani?"

The engine noise made any communication difficult, especially when your ears were full of river water. Besides, they should be back at the airfield in twenty minutes. Plus, if there was anything important to share, there were others coming who were better suited to handle all of this.

Frank frowned at him. "No. You need to hear this now."

SECOND

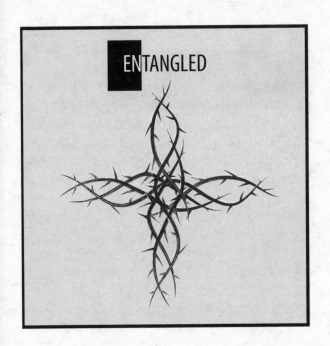

ENTANGLED

8

We're already too late . . .

A sense of impending doom spurred Gray across the campus of the University of Kisangani. During his years in the army, he had learned to trust his gut. He sensed matters were growing swiftly out of control. He searched around him, as if trying to identify what had set his nerves to jangling.

The sun rose brightly on a day swept clean by the night's storms. Heavy clouds still hung in the sky, their edges dark with rain, misting in a few places, casting up rainbows over the brown expanse of the neighboring Congo River. The forecast promised a break in the monsoon storms, at least over the next few days.

He and the others had landed at the international airport an hour ago. Director Crowe had updated him on the status overnight, about an ambush at the U.N. relief camp and the rescue by Tucker Wayne of a few survivors. To investigate the attack, a FARDC unit of Congolese soldiers had flown out before dawn, leaving just as Gray and company had landed. Painter and Kat were monitoring the situation and would send word once they knew anything.

In the meantime, Gray's team was headed to the university to establish a base of operations and to ready their group for their own investigations, both into the kidnapped medical team and into a possible contagion spreading through central Africa. He pictured that disease striking here, a city of nearly two million people, with more and more refugees arriving daily from outlying areas.

Kisangani sat at the confluence of the region's watershed. It was here that all the major rivers and tributaries—the Lualaba, the Tshopo, and Lindi—merged to form the mighty Congo, the world's deepest river, second only to the Amazon in volume. The jungle city had been established back in 1883 by the explorer Henry Morton Stanley, marking the farthest navigable point up the Congo. He named the place Stanley Fall Station, due to the huge series of waterfalls that blocked any further travel. He also chose this spot—which was later simply called Stanleyville—because anything flowing out of the vast jungle had to pass by here.

Which also meant if there was a disease spreading through this region, Kisangani was in its crosshairs.

"That should be the place," Monk said, interrupting his worries. His teammate pointed a folded campus map toward the three-story beige brick building of The Faculty of Science.

It was where the team planned to set up operations. Tucker and Dr. Whitaker had arrived last night and were prepping a lab facility on site.

"At least the place doesn't look so run-down," Kowalski groused, plainly irritated at being roused so early with no time for breakfast.

They had rushed through a traffic-jammed town of decaying colonial buildings stained with soot or graffiti-scrawled. But there was also a vibrancy and colorful verve, especially around the central market anchored by a beautiful cathedral.

Lisa shaded her eyes as she studied their destination. "Don't worry. The building was refurbished a couple years ago. Including adding a Biosafety Level 3 containment unit. Which we may need before this is over."

"Considering what we might be facing," Monk said, "I would be lots happier with a BSL-4 unit, something that can withstand the nastiest of bugs."

Lisa tucked a few loose strands of blond hair behind an ear. "Dr. Whitaker expressed confidence about the resources here. Plus, he has a colleague in Gabon who promised access to a BSL-4 unit, if it proved necessary."

Gray sighed.

That'll have to do until we know more.

Still, he remembered his earlier ruminations about Sigma's primary mission statement: *To be there first.* He considered Painter's account of the attack and abductions at the U.N. camp. It couldn't be a coincidence. Despite Sigma's best efforts—

Someone got here ahead of us.

As Gray's team reached the science building, a familiar figure opened the glass doors for them. "Looks like we're putting the band back together," Tucker said.

The Army Ranger's partner edged out to greet them, too. Kane wagged a bushy tail and nosed Kowalski in the crotch.

The big man pushed the dog back. "Happy to see you, too, bud. Just not *that* happy."

Hands were quickly shaken, and a furry flank patted.

Tucker waved them all inside. "Frank's set up on the top floor. There's a lot to catch you up on."

He quickly led their party through the thirty-thousand-square-foot building. A few students looked quizzically at their passage, especially with the group accompanied by a dog. They climbed to the third floor. It was divided into various labs and workrooms. They crossed to a door that required a code to enter.

"We have this place to ourselves," Tucker said as he tapped at the illuminated buttons. "Courtesy of the director's pull."

Tucker unlocked the door and led them into a large laboratory space with a row of windows that overlooked the river. It was clearly a biolab, equipped with centrifuges, microscopes, spectrophotometers, and chromatographs. Shelves of glassware lined three walls, except where a bank of tall stainless-steel refrigerators and freezers stood, along with a glass-fronted incubator.

Monk and Lisa studied the space with both curiosity and envy, especially the long table that split the room. Atop the worktable, a mad scientist's jumble of equipment had been spread, including supplies, labeled reagents, and a laptop that glowed with bioinformatic software depicting a spinning DNA helix.

Lisa motioned to the screen. "That's the NCBI's GenBank, their genetic sequence database."

So, clearly Dr. Whitaker's setup.

Gray glanced to the left, to where a large window peered into a neighboring room. A tiny air lock, hung with biohazard suits on pegs, led into the chamber beyond, which had to be the facility's containment unit.

Tucker led Gray's group in the opposite direction, to where two figures stood in lab coats. The pair had been bent beside a safety hood along the far wall when Gray's group had entered. Dr. Frank Whitaker nodded to them. The shorter young man next to him was Benjamin Frey, the grad student from the UK who had been working on a doctoral thesis when all hell broke loose in the jungle.

As Tucker made introductions, the student fidgeted, plainly discomfited by the presence of so many strangers.

Frank remained unfazed, though perhaps a touch wary. "We were just about to collect some test samples," the veterinarian said. "It took me most of the night to unload my lab. I think I got maybe an hour's sleep."

Lisa shifted closer. "Test samples from what?" she asked. "I thought you never reached the campsite."

Frank turned to the student. "Benjie here was able to gather a few specimens before the place was attacked. Let me show you."

Gray and the others crowded closer to the safety hood.

Benjie hugged his arms around his chest. "I . . . I lost several specimens. Dropped them, or the tubes broke, but I managed to keep a few."

Gray squinted at a trio of sampling tubes planted upright in a holder. Two looked empty, until a tiny reddish black mote scrambled up the side of one. The third held a large, segmented insect with a bulbous abdomen.

"I salvaged a few pupae, a driver soldier, and the colony queen," Benjie explained.

Monk frowned. "Ants? I heard about the camp being overrun with them, but I don't understand, what do ants have to do with the potential pathogen you're hunting?"

"Maybe nothing," Frank admitted. "But Benjie claims the ants were acting strange, overly aggressive. He also noted several different species of this genus traveling together in that raid. Which is also odd behavior. Then came the attack by the baboons. Such savagery is atypical for the species. So, it made me wonder if there could be a connection, something tying all of this together."

"Between the ants and the debilitating malaise?" Monk asked.

Lisa offered support. "Insects are often disease vectors. Mosquitoes, flies, ticks, fleas. Dr. Whitaker is right. It's certainly something to rule out."

Frank nodded. "Besides, I have nothing else to test at the moment. At least such preliminary work will help me calibrate my equipment."

Tucker interrupted, "Frank, you need to share what you told me earlier. But I don't need to hear it again. You got my skin crawling as it is. In the meantime, Kane and I'll fetch a couple others you should hear from. They're napping in a neighboring room."

Tucker headed to the door.

As the man exited, Gray faced the veterinarian. "What do you have to tell us?"

Frank frowned, his face lined with worry. "It concerns Disease X."

6:28 A.M.

Monk leaned closer to the ant queen in the tube. He knew all about Disease X, a monster that all health experts feared. It was a theoretical disease pathogen that modern science had no preventative or cure against, one capable of spreading rapidly. After the last pandemic, epidemiologists were waiting for that other shoe to fall.

Could this outbreak be it?

He remembered Kat's concern about the pattern of spread, of a pathogen possibly carried in the wind. If true, that would be a disaster unlike any other.

As Frank explained as much to the group, Monk studied the huge ant. It was as long as his thumb and looked dead. He reached a finger and tapped on the glass tube. The ant squirmed. Legs scratched and antennae waved, proving it yet lived.

Cringing with distaste, Monk closed his fist and withdrew his arm.

The student who had collected the queen noted his attention and sidled up next to him. "If . . . if I may ask," Benjie said with a clear wince of apology, "when did you lose your hand?"

Monk glanced down to his balled fist. The kid had keen eyes. Few people even noted his prosthesis. "A few years back."

The hand was a bit of high-tech DARPA engineering, crafted to be nearly indistinguishable from the real thing. Even he forgot about it most of the time. Then again, it was the latest military tech. A small dime-sized microelectrode had been wired into his somatosensory cortex, allowing him to control his new neuroprosthesis by thought alone, even "feel" what it touched. In fact, the lab-grown skin was far more sensitive than his real flesh.

And that wasn't all.

Monk reached to his wrist and unsnapped the cuff, which was held in place by magnetized contact points. He placed the prosthesis on the safety hood's tabletop. He willed the hand to lift atop its fingertips and crawl toward the kid. It was a parlor trick that unnerved most people.

Benjie simply leaned closer. "Wireless bio-feedback. Neat."

Monk reattached his prosthesis, both impressed by the young man and slightly disappointed that his trick hadn't bothered the guy in the least.

Kids these days . . .

Benjie shifted his attention back to his specimens. "Did you know the biomass of the world's ants is equal to our own? Which means they take up as much of the globe as we do."

Monk adjusted to this abrupt change in subject. "No, I didn't know that."

"And they're far craftier than most imagine. Take leaf-cutter ants, who act like little farmers. They grow mushrooms by excreting antibiotics that help spread their fungi. And most ant species can navigate the earth by using its magnetic field. In fact, insects have midbrains not unlike our own—especially large queens like this—which gives them a sense of self, including their own complex, emotional world."

"Insects have emotions?" Monk remembered the short brief that Director Crowe had passed on about the kid. Benjie was at the low end of the autistic spectrum. Monk wondered if that was the source for Benjie's interest in the emotional world around him.

"That's right," Benjie insisted. "Insects have rudimentary emotions. There's no doubt they have a fear response. And get angry." The kid glanced over. "Ever shake a hornet's nest?"

"Point taken."

"They also display a level of empathy, too."

"Empathy? Really?"

Monk studied Benjie's silhouette as the young man squinted at the ant queen. Many people believed that those with ASD lacked empathy, but that wasn't true. It was more about a difficulty in interpreting emotional responses around them. He imagined it was an ongoing hardship for the kid.

Benjie nodded. "Matabele ants—which are related to these driver ants—will carry their injured off the battlefield after a raid. They then nurse their wounded until they get better. In fact, researchers are coming to believe that such a complex inner world is one of the reasons insects developed such amazing survival strategies."

Monk sensed the kid was coming to a point.

Benjie touched the tube holding the queen. "So, don't underestimate them." He glanced to Monk. "I'm with Dr. Whitaker. They're all a part of this somehow."

Monk straightened, recognizing the roundabout way the kid had come to state his case. He glanced over to Dr. Whitaker, who was clearly struggling to do the same—with far more frustration.

From the way he was rubbing at a knot between his brows, Lisa was definitely challenging him. She could wring information out of a rock, if she thought it might help her solve a problem.

Welcome to my world, bub.

6:32 A.M.

Lisa frowned at Frank Whitaker, sensing the man had little tolerance for their interference, especially from strangers, and maybe more so from a woman. He spent too much time speaking at Gray, attending to his questions.

The wildlife veterinarian was clearly sharp, but he had his blind spots, some ingrained prejudices, likely fostered from his years in the army, which was already a boys' club—not that the academic world was much better. She had been battling such chauvinism since med school. But it was a fight she refused to give up.

It also didn't help matters that Dr. Whitaker was a field researcher, one accustomed to working solo, with little or no oversight.

Not this time.

She pressed him. "Dr. Whitaker, why are you so convinced we might be dealing with a Disease X scenario here?"

Frank sighed heavily.

She lifted a hand. "I'm not saying we're not. I'm asking for you to share your insight."

Frank turned toward the windows and waved past the Congo. "Because of that. The jungle. The world frets about biological warfare, of a weaponized strain being released or escaping a military lab. But rain forests are Mother Nature's most insidious biolabs. In such environments, the competition for resources is intense, with a near-infinite number of species—vertebrate, invertebrate, plant, and microbes—all vying to survive. This struggle fosters an ongoing chemical and biological war, one far more intense than any battlefield. To wage that war, Mother Nature experiments with evolution, playing with bodily shapes and sizes. And that's only on the surface. It occurs even more intensely at the microscopic level. There she forges her deadliest microbial weaponry. And at some point, Mother Nature will inevitably turn that arsenal on us. And when she does, the weapon she will choose will be a *virus.*"

"Why a virus?" Lisa asked.

"It's a numbers game, Dr. Cummings. Viruses are a millionfold more plentiful than all the stars in the universe. Making them the most abundant life-form on the planet. That's if you can even call them *living.*"

Gray frowned. "What do you mean?"

Frank focused back on the commander. "Can a bit of replicating DNA or RNA—one that has no energy source and is unable to multiply outside a host—even be classified as living? For many, viruses remain in the gray area between living and nonliving, between chemistry and life. I personally adhere to the opinion of another colleague, who described viruses as *a kind of borrowed life,* due to their dependency on a host cell. But their numbers are only the least of their threat."

"Why's that?" Lisa asked, drawing the man's attention back. "What's worse than a threat being everywhere?"

"One that's constantly changing," Frank answered. "Besides being so abundant, viruses are the very *engines* of evolution. They're Mother Nature's tiny powerhouses, tools that she uses to drive genetic changes. Viruses mutate at a blistering pace, millions of times faster than we do. They are constantly inventing new genes and spreading them far and wide. Genes that invade their hosts' DNA and become part of them. Including us. We're mere products of viral invasions."

"You, maybe," Kowalski growled under his breath.

"We all are. We've known for the longest time that a fair amount of our junk DNA is just bits and fragments of viral genes that entangled themselves into our own code and were carried forward."

"Inheritable mutations," Benjie added as he and Monk rejoined them.

"That's right. We once thought only a fraction of our code was so polluted. Somewhere around eight percent. Which is still a lot. But even that number keeps creeping up as we compare our code to viral sequences. In 2016, a review published in the journal *Cell* estimated the truer number could be as high as eighty percent. Still, whether eight or eighty, we now know that many of those genes acquired from archaic invasions are not junk, but vital to who we are. Without those past viral infections, humans would not exist today."

Gray frowned. "Really?"

"He's right," Lisa answered, cutting the veterinarian off. "Newest genetic research offers an explanation for why embryonic stem cells are pluripotent, meaning that they can transform into any other cell. It's due to the activity of the gene HERV-H, which came from an ancient retrovirus. So, embryo development would never have come about without this past viral invasion."

Frank stood straighter. "And if we skip ahead in our development, it was another virus that granted us the greatest gift of all. Our human consciousness."

Kowalski scoffed. "Are you saying the flu made us smart?"

Frank ignored him. "The ARC gene—which codes for the activity-related cystoskeltal-associated protein—is well documented to have arrived in four-limbed animals millennia ago, through the incorporation of a snippet of viral code. This gene is essential to the function of our synapses in storing memory, in learning. Abnormalities with this gene tend to show up in people with neurological deficits, even in people with autism."

Frank looked at Benjie, as if uncomfortable bringing the subject up. But the young man looked unfazed.

Lisa used the moment to interject. "Viral genes also play a role in our immune system. Even in fighting cancer. Following a bout of flu, leukemia patients show a dramatic drop in cancer cells."

She had been studying these findings due to Kowalski's recent diagnosis. She was hoping to discover alternate treatments for his myeloma. There had been some intriguing research in harnessing viruses to combat tumors, using them to boost our immune response to attack cancer cells.

"I didn't know that," Frank admitted, nodding at her with a measure of respect.

She accepted his bit of deference; appreciating it, even. Many men often resented being up-staged, but at least Dr. Whitaker was not one of them.

Frank pressed his case. "So again, without viruses, *none* of us would be around. In fact, some geneticists believe viruses might be the very source for life itself on this planet."

Lisa pushed him harder. "But again, *why* do you think this particular disease is viral in nature. You've not even examined a single patient."

Frank ticked off the reasons on his fingers. "From the short incubation time reported in the field. From its possible wind-borne spread. From how it can potentially harbor inside an insect or animal vector." He waved at the specimens under the hood. "It's checking all the boxes. And like I mentioned, viruses are everywhere, en-compassing hundreds of millions of species. Yet, we've only named *seven thousand* of them. So, we've barely scratched the surface of what's truly out there. It's estimated—in animals alone—that eight hundred thousand species of viruses run the risk of infecting humans."

"So, like you said before," Lisa said, "it's all a numbers game."

"Then pair those numbers with a virus's abil-ity to mutate in this hotbox called the Congo, and anything could be out there."

Benjie interjected his support, "And don't underestimate the latter. The Congo is full of evolutionary mysteries. You can see nature changing before your eyes due to environmental stressors. The tusks of African elephants are growing smaller, even vanishing, due to the threat of poaching. Generations of forest lizards have developed stickier feet to climb walls after being forced to live in cities. And if viruses mutate at a pace that's a million times faster—that's a problem, innit?"

"Which begs the question," Frank finished, "what if Mother Nature decides *we're* too much of a stressor?"

Lisa remembered the veterinarian's earlier warning.

Mother Nature will inevitably turn that arsenal on us. And when she does, the weapon she will choose will be a virus.

She glanced over to the sprawl of Frank's equipment on the center table. "Then maybe we'd all better get to work."

9

I've fallen back in time.

Charlotte studied her prison as she was marched across the central plaza of an old colonial settlement. The jungle had nearly consumed the encampment long ago. Birdsong and the hum of insects created a constant chorus all around, as if still claiming this place.

She wiped her brow with the back of her hand. The morning already sweltered. Each humid breath weighted down her lungs and tasted of rot and moldy dampness. She struggled to catch her breath, as if drowning. But it wasn't just the weather. Her heart pounded in her chest. She gazed unblinking at her surroundings.

Two dozen structures spread out from the weedy mud of the plaza. She and Jameson were marched at gunpoint along a spread of planks that crisscrossed the space to keep boots out of the muck. More men patrolled the jungle or were stationed around the collection of moldering buildings.

She ignored the latter, until another guard crossed alongside a row of planks near the forest's edge. She did a double take at the armed man's companion. A waist-high figure clomped on four jointed metal legs beside the guard. It was clearly some sort of robotic quadruped. It marched along like a tailless black dog, one stripped down to its skeletal essence. Where its head should be, a compact crystalline ring of lenses were topped by a stubby gun mount.

Jameson noted it, too. "What the hell is going on?" he muttered under his breath before they both were goaded forward at a faster pace.

Charlotte took stock of the rest of their surroundings, struggling with the same question.

All around, a century of rain and forest encroachment had exposed brick and stucco foundations of the small outpost, leaving them crumbling and encrusted with verdant moss. The roofs' old thatch had been patched with sheets of tin. Windows had been boarded up or left open, fringed by broken glass. A few buildings had been refurbished, freshly whitewashed, like the two-story guesthouse, fronted by balconies and a wide porch, where she and Jameson had been held last night. They had been locked up in a small room with bars on the windows and a row of cots along one wall.

She stared around, trying to get her bearings. She still didn't know where she was. Last night, the harried flight from the campsite amidst a raging storm had left her disoriented. The transit had been under an hour, which meant she was likely still in the Tshopo province of the Congo.

When they had finally descended toward a helipad at the end of a waterside dock, she had realized the place was a large island in a river. She had also spotted a scattering of lights to the northwest, deeper in the jungle.

She stared there now, past the impenetrable wall of green. Smoke rose from that direction, along with the distant growl of heavy machinery and faint clanking echoes.

Maybe a mining town.

Not that its presence helped pinpoint her location. The breadth of the DRC was peppered with diggings, pitheads, oil fields, and lumber mills. Even this colonial settlement was unnoteworthy. Hundreds of such abandoned places—trading posts, tiny missionaries, hunting camps—dotted the forest, long forgotten and reclaimed by the jungle.

She gazed at the centerpiece of the plaza as they passed it. An old brick church hunched at the edge. Through the open doors, she could spot pews made of cinder blocks and planks. A small bell hung in its tiny steeple.

Past the church, half-buried in the jungle were four Quonset huts, draped in camouflage netting. She and Jameson were being marched in that direction. As they crossed alongside the church, another new building appeared. It was a windowless cinder block structure with a green metal roof. From the rough mortar between the bricks, it looked hastily constructed.

When they reached the structure's door—

which had been left ajar by a red hose running into it—a cacophony of hoots, screeches, squawks, and caterwauls echoed out, accompanied by the stench of feces and urine and musk. Someone shouted angrily inside.

Both Charlotte and Jameson shied away from there, but as they circled around to the back, they came upon a stack of wooden transport crates. Creatures stirred and shuffled behind the holes drilled into the boxes' sides. The noises here were softer, fearful. She spotted a pair of leathery fingers sticking out of one hole, tugging forlornly. A fingernail bled, ripped away by the creature's efforts to escape.

Her heart ached at the cruelty here. She didn't know why the animals had been captured and brought here. The bushmeat trade was always a profitable one in the jungle, as was poaching and the trade in exotics.

Jameson expressed a grimmer assessment as he gazed back to the building's door. "It's a vivarium . . ."

She looked at him. *Could he be right? Are they conducting animal experiments here?*

"Keep moving," a gruff voice ordered them.

She glanced back to their armed escort. It was the tall Congolese soldier from last night. He forced them forward with his rifle. He had roused them at the crack of dawn, hauling them to a shower facility, ordering them to strip, tossing them a fresh pair of scrubs to change into. He had also offered a cold meal of granola bars washed down with lukewarm coffee. She had consumed everything leadenly.

During the flight here, she had eavesdropped on the conversations around her, hoping for some explanation for the attack. She had gleaned this soldier's name: Ekon. His European partner, the man with the bullhorn, was Draper.

Ekon continued with them to one of the Quonset huts. They were forced through the spring-loaded door and into a small anteroom sealed off from the space inside. Through the window, she spotted a row of modern hospital beds along one wall, while stainless-steel cabinets and workstations lined the other. Across the back appeared to be a lab facility for blood work and cytology.

What is going on?

"Get dressed," Ekon ordered them, pointing to a PPE supply of gowns, gloves, and booties.

They obeyed. She noted the masks were PAPR, battery-powered, air-purifying respirators that covered the entire face when strapped on. She donned hers, feeling like she was about to go scuba diving.

Once outfitted, Ekon pushed them into the medical ward. The soldier did not follow. Instead, they were passed off to his partner. Draper was similarly garbed inside, only he had a huge pistol holstered at his hip.

"*Bienvenue, Docteur Girard,*" he greeted her, his voice muffled by his mask, then nodded to Jameson. He waved a hand to encompass the length of the hut. "First, let me apologize for the rough evacuation from your camp, but discretion is a matter of great importance here. And I believe you'll find our facility far better equipped to investigate the mysterious illness spreading through the Congo."

Charlotte swallowed. She counted a dozen gowned and masked figures, other doctors and clinicians, all men, a mix of Europeans and Congolese. They carried themselves with a military stiffness. She was certain this hard group had not been coerced into service.

Draper led them deeper. "The Quonset across from us has a full biosafety lab, where we have a separate team working. In here, we concentrate on clinical studies. Lab work, treatment regimens, supportive care. We currently have eleven patients, all in various stages of illness, offering a time line of progression. But we're still early in our investigation. Much remains unknown."

"How . . . how long have you been here?" Jameson stuttered out.

"Three weeks."

Anger momentarily drove back Charlotte's fear. "You've known about this disease for *that* long?"

"*Non*, you misunderstand. We set up this site four weeks ago. The first case was reported to us back in March, nearly *six* weeks ago."

"Over a month?" Charlotte could not hold back her outrage. "And you've kept quiet about it?"

"As I said, *discretion* remains tantamount here. You are the first outsiders allowed to participate in our study. The consensus had been to simply shoot you two."

Jameson paled and backed up a step.

Draper lifted a palm. "But I advocated for taking advantage of your knowledge and skill.

It's not like you can escape this island. And beyond discretion, *time* is also tantamount. We can't clamp a lid on this matter forever."

"What do you expect us to do?" Charlotte asked.

Draper shrugged. "Be useful."

She understood the unspoken caveat.

Or die.

Still, she crossed her arms. She had no doubt that any cooperation would eventually end in the same place. In an unmarked grave in the jungle. She saw little reason to help here.

Then a thin arm raised from the row of beds, and a scared voice called her. She turned to see Disanka struggling to sit up. One of her wrists was cuffed to the metal railing. She cradled her boy in her other arm, her eyes shining with terror.

Charlotte took a deep breath.

I may not want to help these bastards, but I made a promise to Disanka.

She headed toward the bed, intending to keep her word. She glanced around the bustling ward. Someone had spent a lot of capital and resources to hide and secure this location.

But who? And why?

7:18 A.M.

Nolan De Coster settled behind his desk on the second floor of the refurbished colonial inn, once the former guesthouse of the Belka rubber plantation here on the island. A decade ago, he had converted the site into a rustic private fishing and hunting camp. He had hosted ambassadors, business moguls, royal family members, even African warlords.

Whatever it took to expand his influence and maintain his chokehold.

He had paneled his office in exotic African woods, a rich mix of ebony, bubinga, and zebrawood. Shelves and walls were adorned with masks, headdresses, carved bowls, and soapstone fetishes from across the continent, many of which were centuries old. Behind his desk, he had mounted a priceless Benin Bronze plaque from the royal altars of the Oba tribe in Nigeria, and under glass, a gold crown stolen from Abyssinia back in the nineteenth century.

He found it amusing to have that crown in the case behind him. When guests were seated across from him, it looked as if the gold coronet rested atop his head, crowning him some king of Africa.

Nolan's father would have disapproved of such a display—while also being secretly envious. His father had been a viscount of Belgian royalty, with a bloodline going back to kings, maybe even to Leopold II, who once owned these lands. But his family had been penniless by the time Nolan was born, most of it gambled away, leaving them rich only in title.

Besides the De Coster name, his father—a math teacher in Ghent—had also gifted Nolan with a love of numbers. Nolan had studied at ULB, the Université libre de Bruxelles, where he had completed a doctorate in applied mathematics, with an emphasis on industrial design. Thirty years later, at the age of fifty-six, he was a billionaire ten times over.

It was while working on his thesis, on the discrete mathematics of open-pit mining, he recognized an opportunity. In the late nineties, the mining industry in the DRC had fallen into disarray following the First Congo War. Identifying this, Nolan had secured scores of mining contracts throughout the Congo's copper belt at nearly no cost. Over the next decades, he leveraged those rights into interests in cobalt, tantalum, coltan, diamonds, and oil. Others had tried to rush in, but he was already well established, ensuring his dominance.

Until recently . . .

The Chinese had arrived a few years after the Second Congo War. The new fighting had left the country's infrastructure in ruins. The communist politburo came in with wheelbarrows of capital. They cleverly tied their construction of new roads, railways, and hydroelectric dams to the acquisition of mineral rights. They offered with one hand and took with the other. Backed by the might of the communist state, western companies could not compete.

Not even De Coster Mining & Industry.

Nolan had tried to negotiate with the Chinese, to work out mutually beneficial contracts, but he quickly recognized the futility. Chinese economic development was fueled by copper and cobalt—and they were ruthless in their pursuit to control those resources.

Eventually, Nolan had sought help from the

United States, who were certainly invested in stopping the Chinese takeover of Africa. But America had its hands tied, requiring democratic reforms and fiscal transparency before they would offer aid to the DRC. And in a country that was ranked 168 out of 198 on the Corruption Perceptions Index, such reforms were an impossibility.

Fortunately, De Coster Mining & Industry had no such qualms. It could not be so discerning and survive. It didn't just turn a blind eye to deforestation, wastewater pollution, and child labor—it encouraged them. The company had no choice. There was no other way to hold one's ground here. Meanwhile, Western corporations were happy to turn that blind eye, as long as the flow of cobalt, coltan, and copper continued for the production of cell phones, rechargeable batteries, and other high-tech gadgets.

But now a new opportunity beckoned.

A knock on the office door drew his attention. "Come in," he called out.

The door opened, and the tall figure of Captain Andre Draper entered, dressed in his usual green camo, black boots, and holstered Heckler & Koch pistol. The man led Nolan's personal army, a force necessary to protect his corporate interests in lands ruled more by militias and warlords than the Congolese government. Draper was a former French soldier with MONUSCO, the U.N.'s peacekeeping force established here during the Second Congo War.

"How are our guests faring?" Nolan asked, waving the man to a chair in front of his desk.

"I've situated them in the med ward." He shrugged. "We'll see how they do."

"And you still think it's wise to keep them alive?"

"For now. Beyond their medical expertise, they could prove useful as hostages. If it becomes necessary, we could always offer some proof of life to further reinforce that last night's attack was perpetrated by a militia in a kidnap-for-ransom plot. Either way, I'd like to keep our options fluid and open regarding them."

"I see."

"And who knows? Maybe their skills will prove useful. Especially with time running short. We can't keep a lid on what's happening for much longer. I think we've kept this secret for as long as we can."

Nolan nodded. The first few cases of the debilitating disease—one that left the afflicted in a dull, cattle-like state—had occurred at a corporate copper mine in the Sankuru province to the south. As isolated as it was, it had been easy to keep word from spreading. Then neighboring villages had begun showing similar symptoms. Instead of panicking, Nolan had recognized an opportunity.

The devastation of the First Congo War had opened the door for Nolan's corporate ambitions, then the strife of the Second Congo War had allowed the Chinese to elbow their way in. For De Coster Mining & Industry to prevail again, another regional disaster was needed. The spread of an unknown pathogen throughout the DRC offered a unique chance. Such a threat would undoubtedly discourage the Chinese's efforts in Africa, especially for a people who had grown so germophobic after going through so many pandemics of late.

Still, for that to work, the contagion needed to gain a firm foothold throughout Central Africa. Nolan couldn't risk a global effort being mobilized against the outbreak, not until it was too late. So, he had assigned Draper to stifle knowledge of the disease. Nolan had wanted the illness to spread silently, a smoldering fire working through the jungle. To maintain that silence, Draper's forces had firebombed clinics in the forest, razed villages, always leaving behind a false trail to militias, terrorist organizations, or tribal conflicts.

Then came the alarm from the U.N. relief camp.

At that moment, Nolan and Draper had known that their containment efforts were nearing an end. The attack last night, along with a few more today, would mark the conclusion of that agenda. It had served its purpose. From Nolan's network across the region, he knew the disease had reached its flashpoint. The smoldering forest fire was about to become a blazing inferno.

When it did, Nolan intended to take advantage of the resulting chaos and disruption to reestablish the dominance of De Coster Mining & Industry throughout Africa. To help ensure that, he had set up this research camp. He wanted as much intel as possible, about the pathogen, about the disease, about possible treatments. With a jump-start on those details, he planned on wielding such knowledge to his benefit, to prove his corporation's benevolence. Where the Chinese made inroads by literally building roads, De Coster Mining & Industry would win hearts by protecting lives.

The logistics going forward would be daunting. Still, for a former mathematician, it was all about numbers and variables.

He glanced at his laptop, which was running with algorithms and models. He had a team of statisticians crunching the necessary numbers. The mortality projections were intimidating, staggering even for him. Nolan did not consider himself to be callous. He didn't employ child labor in his mines out of cruelty. He paid families well when a son or daughter was killed or crippled.

It was simply a means to an end.

Like with this disease.

"Now that the two doctors are settled," Draper said, "I'm going to check in with the two teams who are heading out to clean up those last few hot spots."

"Of course. Keep me updated."

Draper stood, turned crisply, and headed to the door.

As Draper left, Nolan cracked a kink out of his neck. He caught a glimpse of the gold crown in its case behind him. It was a reminder that his own ambitions stretched beyond the financial stability of his company.

But that would have to wait.

He returned his attention to his laptop. He watched the graphed projections flipping through various forecast models, incorporating the information gleaned from the medical team: on prognosis, disease progression, possible treatment regimens. Everything was a variable. Still, too much remained unknown. He could collapse many of those forecasts if he could get a handle on a cure, but it wasn't vital to his plans.

He squinted at the various graphs. The wild fluctuations between them nagged him. The differences remained too large, more than could be blamed solely on a lack of a treatment.

Something was wrong.

I'm missing a variable.

There was something intrinsic to all of this that had escaped them. He came to one firm conclusion, one vital to a man holding a doctorate in mathematics.

I need more data.

7:22 A.M.

Charlotte sat on the edge of Disanka's bed. The Lubu woman wore a loose hospital gown, which was presently pulled aside, exposing a breast. Disanka struggled to get her child to latch on to her nipple, made all the more difficult with her wrist cuffed to her bed.

But being bound wasn't the real problem.

The child's head lolled backward. Tiny eyes stared at the roof. Drool ran down one cheek. Disanka murmured to the boy, shifting to try again. Plainly the child had returned to a near catatonic state.

"What do you think?" Jameson asked as he stood at Charlotte's shoulder.

She and the pediatrician had just finished examining the child. Charlotte remembered the boy's bawling last night, his tiny hands clenched into fists as he had cried.

No longer.

"I don't know . . ." she mumbled.

She scratched at the ant bites on her wrists. She had several other welts on her legs, arms, and neck. She tried to assess her own status. It felt as if a migraine threatened. She recognized the early symptoms: irritability, yawning, difficulty concentrating. She had them all, but she also knew the signs could simply be from exhaustion.

She rubbed her arms, noting both a numbness and a tingling.

I hope it's just a migraine coming on.

She stared across the medical ward, at the other patients. IVs dripped. Vitals were being checked. Monitors blipped and blinked, measuring EKGs, breath rates, oxygen saturation. Nothing appeared abnormal, but all the patients, a mix of Congolese men and women, lay slack, barely blinking, their chests rising and falling leadenly. A neurological exam was being performed a few beds down. The patient—an older man— had been propped up and remained seated there unaided, as if he were a stiff puppet that could be bent into any position.

She also noted one other detail about all the patients: the youngest among them was a girl in her late teens. *Is that why they wanted the boy, someone even younger?* Yesterday, when Jameson had radioed for aid, he had mentioned the details of the child's mysterious condition. Clearly her captors had also heard and had taken advantage of the attack to secure the boy.

Disanka tried again to get her baby to suckle but with no better success. The mother looked despondent, her face sunken with worry. She gazed imploringly at Charlotte, silently begging for help.

Jameson sighed. "Clearly the child has fallen back into a somnolent state. His rousing last night was only temporary. Plainly the shaman's powder was no cure."

A voice spoke sharply behind them. "What do you mean?"

She glanced to the foot of the bed.

The ward's head clinician, Dr. Ngoy, stood there. He had stopped after overhearing them. She had been introduced to the Congolese physician by Draper—and she already detested the doctor. His hair was a crown of gray curls with a matching beard, half-hidden by his mask. During their introductions, he had eyed her with disdain, both for her youth and likely her gender. But worse, he treated his patients roughly, callously, with little regard for their well-being.

"Did I hear you correctly?" Ngoy pressed. "Were you somehow able to stir the child before?"

Jameson waved the inquiry away. "It was nothing. A short-term reaction to some witch doctor's elixir. Nothing but snake oil."

Ngoy stepped around to the other side of

the bed. He reached out and pinched the boy's ear, pulling his slack face closer, peering down at the child. "That's still intriguing. We've not been able to get *any* response from our patients. We've tried all manner of pain stimulus with no reaction. Including electroshock. Even breaking a finger."

Charlotte inwardly cringed.

Ngoy straightened and faced Jameson. "Why didn't you tell us this before?"

The American stammered, "L-like I said, it was nothing. It's already worn off."

"Do you have any of that elixir left?"

Jameson answered, "No. The shaman kept it."

Charlotte tightened her jaw. She pictured the small vial tossed by Woko Bosh. She had hidden it back with her soiled clothes, trusting that the tiny bottle would not be noted, especially as it was empty, its contents washed away by rain and river water. She had only kept it because of the faint yellowish stain on the inside, the barest residue of powder.

"This shaman," Ngoy said. "Where was he from?"

Charlotte quickly lied. "I don't remember. It was hectic. And he was killed."

Jameson squinted and rubbed a temple with a finger.

Charlotte tried to communicate silently to the pediatrician, glaring her message.

Keep your mouth shut.

Jameson remained oblivious. "He was from Kula . . . no, Kuba. That's it."

Charlotte bit back a groan.

"Did he say what the substance was? Where it came from?"

Jameson shook his head. "He kept it in some old box, carved with a man's face."

Ngoy stared at the child. Disanka cringed back, protecting her boy, lest the doctor grab his ear again. The clinician then turned and stalked off. Charlotte watched him go, hoping that would be the end of it, but Ngoy reached the ward's guard and spoke nose to nose with the man, while pointing back at Charlotte and Jameson.

Then the guard left.

Charlotte returned her attention to Disanka. She placed her gloved palm on the woman's shoulder. "I won't let anything happen to you or your *kitwana*."

Disanka's eyes remained wide with worry, but she gave a firm nod back.

Charlotte slipped out a penlight and examined the boy's pupils. They were dilated again and showed no response to the light, not even a slight narrowing against the brightness. She had reviewed his blood work. Lymphocytes and eosinophils were low, while his c-reactive protein levels were elevated through the roof, which further supported a viral etiology.

She glanced at the clinicians working in the lab area. She had asked them earlier if they had identified any inclusion bodies in the patient's cells, which would be indicative of a virus's presence. They had ignored her, all but shoving her out of their area.

A commotion at the ward's entrance drew

her attention around. The guard had returned, drawing their earlier escort with him. Ekon spoke with Ngoy, who then barked for her and Jameson to come over.

Charlotte pocketed her penlight. She reached and squeezed Disanka's forearm, firming her promise to protect the boy at all cost. Disanka gripped her hand in turn, solidifying the pact between them.

Only then did Charlotte cross over to the pair of men.

Ngoy was already yanking off his gown and mask. He stared hard at Jameson. "You must tell Monsieur De Coster. What you told me. He will want to know."

With no choice but to obey, she and Jameson stripped back down to their scrubs and disposed of their protective gear. Ekon led them out of the Quonset hut and back across the muddy plaza. They returned to the same two-story guesthouse where she had been held. But once inside, Ekon drew them up to the second floor. At the top of the stairs stood a large set of double doors of lacquered zebrawood. An armed soldier in body armor stood guard.

Ekon nodded to the man, who then rapped on the door.

A voice called for them to enter.

Charlotte and Jameson were ushered in, followed by Ngoy and Ekon. Charlotte nearly tripped on the woven rug, taking in the handsome beauty of the office. Artifacts and dusty tomes lined shelves. A set of wood shutters led out to the guesthouse's second-story balcony, which afforded a view over the forest canopy to the river.

To the right and left, stuffed lion's heads mounted the walls, captured in midsnarl, baring long yellowed fangs. The beasts both faced the large desk between them. A figure rose from a seat. He wore a khaki linen suit, expertly tailored, with a black tie. His dark-blond hair was salted with gray at the temples. With those blue eyes, he could be mistaken for a middle-aged Chris Hemsworth, playing the role of a colonial magistrate.

"Welcome, Drs. Girard and Jameson. Please be seated. I understand you may have further information regarding the growing crisis in the Congo."

Jameson quickly took one of the leather club chairs. Charlotte did so, too, but more warily. Her heart hammered in her chest. She wanted to rail against their abduction, the callous murders, but she also wanted more information about the situation, about her captors, about everything, so she remained silent.

Her reticence earned her an immediate prize.

"I'm Nolan De Coster, CEO of De Coster Mining & Industry."

She stiffened, nearly coughed. She had thought his name had sounded familiar when Ngoy had mentioned it. She glanced over to Jameson, who seemed unaware. She faced the CEO, a billionaire known throughout the region for his wealth and philanthropy. He funded hospitals, wildlife conservation efforts, and solar installations across countless villages. He even financed the organization that had brought Charlotte here, the Congo chapter of Doctors Without Borders. He was also considered brilliant and innovative in his industry. Some called him the Elon Musk of mining.

She studied him as he sat back down. Once settled, she noted how an old African crown, filigreed in gold, was also mounted on the wall, and seemingly hovering over his head.

He waved to their guard. "Lieutenant Ekon, you can go. I can oversee matters from here."

Charlotte didn't doubt that. The man looked fit and athletic. She also noted the edges of a shoulder holster slung under his suit jacket.

Ekon snapped a respectful nod, turned on a heel, and exited, drawing the door shut behind him. Ngoy remained standing between the two club chairs, his lips set in a firm line, clearly determined to take credit for what he had pried from Jameson.

De Coster leaned forward, glancing from the clinician to them. "As I understand it, you had some success in rousing a patient after they'd passed through the refractory period of this disease and entered its somnolent state."

Charlotte remained silent, while Jameson stammered his way through his usual denials. He again insisted that Woko's powder was simply a nasal irritant. She had to fight not to roll her eyes. She refused to give herself away.

She failed.

De Coster's gaze swung to her. "But you, Dr. Girard, you do not believe that?"

It was her turn to struggle to steady her voice. "I . . . I don't know," she admitted.

"Ah, but I think you do."

He stood up again and crossed to one of his shelves. He removed an artifact and returned with it. It was an intricately carved case, adorned with a colorful geometric pattern of painted seeds, ivory, gold, and bone.

He placed it on his desk and rested a palm atop it. "This dates back to the seventeenth century. One of the earliest examples of a *ngedi mu ntey*. A sacred Kuba Box. From your description, it sounds like something similar was carried by the shaman to your camp."

She read the sharp intellect in the man's gaze. She had to remain mindful of that, recognizing that De Coster had deep roots in this region and knowledge about it.

He continued proving it. "The Kuba Kingdom flourished during the colonial era. They were a people ahead of their time. Known for their embroidered raffia and elaborate carvings. Even Picasso owed his cubist period to these people, studying an exhibit of Kuba art in Paris in 1907. And besides their art, they were already working in iron and copper long before colonists and slave traders arrived. More important, the Kuba were also renowned for their medicinal lore. Surrounding tribes often sought them out for this knowledge."

Charlotte suddenly wished she had known this history before. *Maybe I would've given Woko's expertise more attention.*

"So, I'm not ready to dismiss what the shaman brought to your camp as mere snake oil." De Coster flicked a scolding glance at Jameson. "But how do we take advantage of this knowledge? You say the elixir is gone, but what of the *ngedi mu ntey*, the Kuba Box? What became of it? Perhaps it holds some clue to all of this."

Jameson shook his head. "It's gone. Taken by the boy."

"The boy?"

"The shaman's apprentice," Charlotte mumbled before she could stop herself.

"And what became of him and the box?"

Charlotte pictured the fiery rocket attack upon the village last night as the helicopter had departed. Not a structure had been left standing. Fury grew inside her. She cast a hard look across the desk, her voice growing scathing. "Your men blew them up."

De Coster ignored her anger and returned his attention to the box. One finger tapped a corner. She could almost hear the ticking calculations in his head.

"Unfortunate . . ." he finally mumbled, then cleared his throat and looked at them. "As I said, I'm not ready to ignore history's lessons, not if we're to get a handle on this outbreak. Until we do, there will be many needless deaths."

Charlotte struggled to understand this man. He sounded concerned, but she could not ignore how she ended up seated in front of him. "What is your intent?" she challenged him. "If you're so adamant about finding a cure, why have you kept your work secret, not even divulging your knowledge of this disease for a month and a half?"

"Because you have not lived through what I have, what these people have. Years of corrupt rule, two wars that killed seven million. I've learned only to trust those close at hand. By keeping silent, I've made more progress than if a hundred nations had piled into here. The DRC is one of the poorest countries, overrun with warring militias and bloody warlords. Long ago, I learned any progress here does not come without bloodshed and an iron hand."

Charlotte faced his passion with a measure of disdain. She knew he was not telling her his entire truth.

"There is a saying about the Democratic Republic of the Congo," he continued. "Maybe you've heard it. 'The DRC is neither democratic nor a republic, but it certainly is the Congo.' And I'm doing what I think is best for this region. And yes, it would be disingenuous if I denied that it wouldn't also help my company. The fate of both are entangled by this harsh jungle, by its brutal history, by its current disarray. I intend to better all."

Charlotte scoffed, "No matter how much blood is shed."

Jameson glared at her for goading their captor.

De Coster remained unfazed. "The entire history of the Congo is written in blood, Dr. Girard. War after war, tribal genocide, ongoing slavery." He finally sighed. "You spent part of your childhood in Brazzaville, up in the Republic of the Congo, did you not?"

Charlotte glowered. She was reminded yet

again not to underestimate this man's intelligence or resources. "What of it?"

"Then maybe you remember a time when such places were less brutal." He glanced between his two captives. "You've both spent time in Kisangani, not far from here, a city of dismaying poverty, of decaying infrastructure, overrun by beggars and thieves. Yet, it wasn't always like that. During the first half of the twentieth century, it was a place of glamour and sultry exoticism. The whitewashed city drew European royalty and Hollywood stars. *The African Queen* was filmed here, with Hepburn and Bogart wandering the city's streets after a day's shoot, partaking in the town's charms through long, languorous nights."

Charlotte tried to balance that image with her disheartening experience in Kisangani.

De Coster continued, "The DRC's slow decline into anarchy and strife came about after Belgian rule ended in 1960."

"That's a simplistic view of what happened," Charlotte said. "Colonial rule of the Congo was not without its atrocities and cruelties. Millions were killed when King Leopold owned these lands."

"Of course, I'm not saying colonial rule is the answer. But for any hope of a brighter future, the region needs a *new* path. Clearly, after decades of ongoing strife, the Congolese people are not ready for self-rule. Even now, they're abdicating control to the Chinese, who will exploit them worse than Leopold."

"Then what's the answer?"

"A simple one. Economic self-rule. The DRC is a country of vast natural resources, of nearly boundless untapped wealth. To protect its interests, the country needs a CEO to lead it, to guide the country to a new future, where all boats will rise, where reforms can be made, where the DRC could be a model for the entire continent."

Charlotte leaned back in her seat. She had no doubt *who* De Coster believed should lead the country into this new era. She stared at the gold crown hovering over his head as he sat back down.

He placed his palm atop the carved box again. "Which brings us back to the lost *ngedi mu ntey*, and the cure it potentially contained; a cure that could stop countless deaths."

She did not want to help him, but she could not ignore the agony in Disanka's face as she had gazed at her stricken child, at the pleading in her eyes when she had turned to Charlotte. The entire continent needed that cure, especially one little boy.

"What can you tell us about this lost Kuba Box?" De Coster asked them. "What did it look like? What markings adorned it?"

Jameson shrugged. "The case looked like the bust of someone from colonial times. There was even a carved figure of him inside the box."

De Coster sat straighter. "A *ndop* carving."

Charlotte found herself nodding, picturing the ebony figurine veined in silver.

"Who was it?"

Charlotte remembered Faraji's description. She offered it, as the answer made no sense. "It was a shepherd."

"A shepherd . . . ?" De Coster looked confused—then his eyes widened with understanding. He sat back and smiled. "Ah, of course."

10

"Who is this Reverend William Sheppard?" Gray asked.

"Many consider him the Black Livingstone," Ndaye answered from the other side of the lab table. "He was a missionary to the people of the Congo, but also an explorer. He even discovered a lake that would eventually be named after him."

Gray squinted at the old black-and-white photo of a tall man in a white suit and matching pith helmet. The Black Presbyterian minister stood amongst a group of tribesmen, who carried spears and tall woven shields. The huts of a village could be seen in the background.

Gray compared the image to both the face on the mask and the carved figurine standing next to it.

It has to be the same guy.

A few moments ago, Tucker had returned with Kane. The ranger had escorted in two locals, Ndaye, an ICCN eco-guard, and a boy of twelve or thirteen. Painter had forwarded brief dossiers on them, after Tucker's rescue of the pair from the floodwaters of the Tshopo River.

The shaman's apprentice, Faraji, had carried in a century-old wooden case, something the boy had secured back in the camp. It was a *ngedi mu ntey*, or Kuba Box. The wooden figure had been stored inside it, along with a collection of old photos and a folded map. Monk had already left the lab to consult with Painter about the latter, recognizing that they needed additional expertise to understand it. He took Kowalski with him, though the big man was more concerned about finding something to eat.

"But what does William Sheppard have to do with the situation in the Congo now?" Gray asked.

Ndaye turned to Faraji, who shifted on his feet, glancing all around, keeping half-hidden behind the ICCN guard.

Tucker placed a palm on the boy's shoulder. "It's okay, Faraji. Tell him what you told me. You nearly got us both killed getting that damned box here."

Faraji stood straighter, maybe drawing strength from the Army Ranger. "Woko Bosh, our shaman." Faraji's voice cracked at the mention of his former mentor. He pointed to the box. "He kept for many years, pass from grandfather to father."

The boy's gaze drifted down in despair.

"And now into your hands," Tucker encouraged him.

Faraji swallowed, clearly questioning if he was

worthy of such a heritage. He glanced up again. "Only shamans know of this *ngedi mu ntey*. None other." He shook his head. "Even I know little. Only it protect against a great evil. Woko Bosh tell me some but not all."

Ndaye explained. "Back at the camp, the shaman removed a powder from the box. He claimed it could ward against the illness. He demonstrated as much with a baby at the camp—the one taken by the attackers. The powder even effected the ants that were overrunning the camp. Maybe the baboons, too."

Upon hearing this, Lisa crossed over from the lab's safety hood, where she had been observing Frank and Benjie's efforts to collect samples from the ants.

"Strange," Lisa said as she joined them. "Did the shaman believe it was a cure?"

Faraji shook his head. "No, no *tiba*. No cure. *Utetezi* . . ."

The boy winced, clearly struggling to describe what he meant. He looked to Ndaye for help.

"*Ulinzi wa virusi?*" Ndaye offered.

The boy's scowl answered him. "*Hapana*. No." Faraji scrunched his face, then finally shrugged, giving up. "Only Woko know more."

Ndaye looked apologetically at Gray and Lisa. "Whatever the substance was, it's somehow connected to William Sheppard. The man was fiercely protective of the Kuba, a tribe that was very secretive at the time. In fact, he was the first non-African to make contact with them."

Gray fanned through the seven photos, yellowed at the edges, many faded and water-spotted. Upon the backs were scribbled a few words and cryptic symbols. He spread them on the table, sensing that the reverend had been laying out a road map to some place in the jungle, but he had encrypted its location. Each photo was dated, so Gray set about putting them in order, establishing a time line.

The earliest—from October 17, 1894—showed a patch of sunlit water amidst a thick forest. Gray flipped over the photo and studied a drawing that had been hastily sketched on the backside. It depicted what appeared to be a small stream-fed pond with a stylized striped animal next to it. It looked somewhat like a zebra, with the word *Atti* scrawled below it.

It meant nothing to Gray, but Faraji pointed at the striped image. "*Atti* . . . old word. Mean *okapi*."

Gray frowned.

Ndaye explained, "The okapi is an endangered giraffid that makes its home in the Congo forests. It was once thought to be an African unicorn, more myth than real. The species was once prevalent throughout these jungles, but after centuries of hunting due to their unique hides, their numbers have dwindled. Now they can only be found in the northeast corner of the Congo."

Faraji tugged on Ndaye's sleeve and spoke rapidly in his native tongue.

After a bit of an exchange, Ndaye patted the boy's shoulder and explained. "The Kuba have tribal names for many places in the jungle. Especially old hunting grounds. Faraji says there was a watering hole once used by the okapi. They no longer gather there, but the name still stuck, used by his people, passed from generation to generation."

Gray stared at the image. *Could this be the first trail marker on Sheppard's journey through the jungle—but where was he going, and why?*

He turned to Faraji and tapped at the drawing. "Do you know where this place is? This watering hole?"

The boy nodded.

"What about these other symbols?" Gray turned over the next few photos.

Faraji studied them, then slowly shook his head.

Tucker offered a possibility. "Maybe you have to be at the first spot to find the next. To understand the clue."

Gray looked at Faraji. "And maybe you have to be Kuba to understand any of them. I have a feeling Sheppard encrypted this road map so only someone with knowledge and lore of this forest would understand it."

"But why would he keep it so secret?" Lisa asked.

"In context of the time, it makes sense," Ndaye

answered. "Sheppard distrusted the Belgian colonists and their local allies, the Zappo Zaps, a brutal cannibalistic sect of the Songye people. If there was something dangerous—what the Kuba considered evil—hidden out in the jungle, he would want to keep such information from the Belgians. Yet, if there was some *utetezi*—some *protection*—against it, he would want to preserve this knowledge, leaving behind a road map with the Kuba to keep them safe should it ever arise again."

Gray nodded. "You may be right."

"But what evil?" Lisa asked. "Is it just the illness or something else?"

Faraji stiffened and gasped, stepping away from the table. The boy had been working through the stack of photos and had reached the last in the time line.

Gray crossed to see what had so unnerved the kid. He picked up the photo. It showed a break in the forest and a pair of vine-encrusted pillars that flanked a tall crack into a fern-covered cliff. The scarp towered high, cutting a jagged line across the sky. Gray flipped it over. There was no symbol or sketch on the back, only a smudged scrawl. It was not drawn with ink, but from the darkness of the stain, maybe blood.

It formed two words.

Mfupa
Ufalme

Ndaye read over Gray's shoulder and translated what was written. "Mfupa Ufalme. It means 'Empire of Bones,' or maybe 'Kingdom of Bones.'"

Faraji pointed at the photo, while taking another step back. "Bad place. *Alaaniwe*. Cursed. All of Kuba know. Never go there."

Tucker sighed. "Well, we know Sheppard went there."

Gray nodded. "The question remains . . . what did he find there and how does it help us now?"

"If it does . . ." Lisa added.

Gray could not discount Lisa's skepticism, but with this disease spreading rapidly, they needed to consider all possibilities.

He turned to the boy. "Would you be willing to guide us to this first spot? To the okapi watering hole?"

Faraji looked scared, but he nodded. "Woko Bosh. He want me to help."

"I should go, too," Ndaye offered. "You may need someone with knowledge of the local people and region."

Gray nodded his thanks and turned to Lisa. "I'll leave you and Monk here with Dr. Whitaker, to assist him with his research. I'll take Kowalski with me. As soon as we get the all-clear from the Congolese army, we'll head to the U.N. camp first. We'll drop off Tucker and Kane and head to this watering hole."

The plan was for the Army Ranger and his furry partner to guard over Benjie, who had agreed to travel to the campsite and collect samples from the dead bodies, both human and baboon, then bring them back to the lab. Frank had wanted to go himself, but he was needed here to work on the samples being collected from the ants. His advancements in viral identification were too unique. Only he understood his proprietary techniques.

Still, there remained one detail that stymied them all. For any hope of understanding it, the team had needed to consult an expert, one with more knowledge on the subject.

A chime sounded from the door as it unlocked.

Monk shoved inside, followed by Kowalski, who clutched a half-eaten sandwich in a greasy wrapper. The big man chewed a huge mouthful. The smell of spice and barbecue accompanied his arrival.

Kowalski lifted his sandwich, his eyes nearly rolling back in his head. "Oh, man, this beats an Egg McMuffin any day of the week . . ."

Kane sniffed the air as the big man passed by, plainly wanting to test this assessment.

Monk simply headed over to the group. He propped the team's digital pad atop the table for all to see. "I've got everyone conferenced online. Took some doing."

Monk also splayed out the last piece to this puzzle.

7:47 A.M.

Tucker scooted next to the others as Monk unfolded the map that had been hidden inside the

Kuba Box. From the digital pad, two faces stared out of the screen.

The one seated behind a desk was Painter Crowe, director of Sigma. The other leaned on a table in some library, flanked by tall bookshelves. The dark-haired stranger was dressed in black with a distinctive white Roman collar.

Tucker frowned at the sight.

Why did Sigma need to consult a priest?

Gray tilted farther into view of the screen. "Father Bailey, how goes the reconstruction of Castel Gandolfo?"

The priest shrugged. "The new foundations are in place. As long as you all stay away from here, we should make good progress."

"We'll try our best," Gray said with a grin.

Tucker glanced at the others, who seemed to understand this exchange.

Clearly I've missed out on some Sigma misadventure.

Lisa offered the barest explanation, whispering over to Tucker. "Father Bailey has helped us in the past. He works with the Pontifical Institute of Christian Archaeology. Though his role with the Church is a bit more complicated than that."

Tucker lifted up a palm. "Don't need to hear anything more. You've all complicated my life well enough as it is."

Gray glanced down to the map, while addressing the priest. "What do you make of the image that Director Crowe sent you?"

Tucker shifted to get a better view of that mystery. The map was plainly old, inscribed with Latin. It looked to have been torn from an old book before being folded up and stuffed at the bottom of the Kuba Box.

Bailey scratched at his collar, as if it chafed him. "It took a little more research here at the Vatican archives to identify it, but what you have is a copy of an old map of Africa. Drawn back in 1564 by the cartographer, Abraham Ortelius. But it's less the map that's intriguing than its subject matter."

"Which is what?" Gray asked.

"The Latin in the map's legend box reads '*Presbiteri Johannis, sive, Abissinorum Imperii descriptio*,' which translates to 'A Description of the Empire of Prester John of the Abyssinians.'"

Tucker looked across to the photo of the pillars in the jungle. He remembered Ndaye's translation of the message on the back, a place called the Empire of Bones.

Gray expressed what they were all likely wondering. "Could that be what the Reverend Sheppard was searching for in the jungle? This empire of Prester John's?"

Tucker frowned. "I don't understand. Who's Prester John?"

Bailey answered, "He was a legendary Christian king of astounding wealth. He was said to have descended from the black Magi, Balthazar. His earliest stories put him in Asia, but later in Africa, making him the first Christian king of that continent. His tale grew to such prominence that, in the twelfth century, Pope Alexander III sent the fabled king a message. Only the one who carried that letter—the pope's personal physician—vanished into the jungles and was never seen again."

Tucker recalled Faraji's insistence about the kingdom being cursed.

Maybe the pope's doctor should've been forewarned about that particular detail.

"A letter *did* arrive decades later," Bailey continued. "Signed by Prester John, which further fueled his tale. Then, in the fifteenth century, Portuguese explorers who were searching for this legendary king sent back word of a Christian empire found deep in the jungle. They described the court, an elaborate city, and most detailed of all, the wealth of the empire, which they claimed was the source of gold for King Solomon's temple."

Tucker tried to picture such a place, an African Shangri-la. Even he knew this legend of Solomon's lost gold mine. Explorers had been hunting for it for ages, even up until today, convinced the vast mine lay somewhere out in the jungle.

"I dug a little deeper after Director Crowe's inquiry," Bailey said. "Prester John's story stretches beyond lost treasures. It also ties to the Ark of the Covenant, which many still believe lies hidden in Ethiopia. Just as intriguing, his tale connects to the Fountain of Youth. It was said that Ethiopians lived hundreds of years, attributable to a lake that when you washed in it, your flesh would be renewed, glossy with youth. If you drank from it, whatever ailed you would be cast off, and you would be free of illness for thirty years."

Kowalski grunted around a mouthful of sandwich. "I wouldn't mind taking a dip in that pond."

Lisa touched the man's shoulder in sympathy.

Bailey continued, "According to those stories, the properties of the lake were unique. Nothing could float on it, not wood or anything. The last anyone heard about Prester John, this priest-king of Ethiopia, it was said he was 562 years old. Then the kingdom fell silent."

"What do you mean?" Gray asked.

Bailey shrugged. "No one heard anything more about Prester John. By the late sixteenth century, explorers searching Ethiopia found a Black king, but the African lord claimed no connection to Prester John. And as geographical knowledge grew, the legend of a Christian king of Africa faded. By the seventeenth century, most dismissed his story as mere myth."

Tucker glanced at the spread of photos. "Clearly, somebody believed otherwise."

"Or at least conflated the two stories," Lisa said. "The legend of a nearly immortal priest-king and the rumors of a cursed empire hidden in the jungle."

Monk frowned down at the map. "But I don't understand how those stories could be connected. The lands of Ethiopia are on the other side of the Congo, far to the east."

Bailey offered an explanation. "You have to understand that borders were fluid over the centuries as explorers mapped and remapped the continent. While I was doing research, I found this map of Africa from 1710, by an English mapmaker."

The priest opened another window that showed that map.

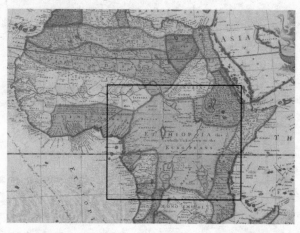

"As you can see," Bailey said, "this depicts Ethiopia as encompassing the full breadth of the Congo. So, if Prester John and his kingdom existed, it could very well be in central Africa."

Gray held up the last black-and-white photo

and tapped at the pillars shown in it. "Regardless, something *is* out there. Maybe something that could offer insight into what's happening now."

No one argued otherwise.

From the digital pad, Painter cleared his throat and lifted a hand. A few moments ago, he had been consulting with someone off-screen. He now faced forward.

"Kat just reported in," he said. "According to her intelligence sources, the Congolese army finished their canvass of the U.N. camp. Little remains there, mostly smoldering ruins and ransacked tents. A few bodies were found, wearing tattered uniforms and carrying old weapons. The consensus seems to be that the site was attacked by a militia group. Maybe the Mai-Mai, who are active in the region. Or the ADF. They're even speculating it might be Boko Haram, who have been spreading into the Congo."

Ndaye expressed his own opinion with a snort of derision. "It was not any militia. The attackers were too well armed and organized."

Tucker trusted the eco-guard's assessment. To better understand what had happened, Tucker wanted to get his own eyes—and Kane's nose—over there to investigate, which he planned to do when he escorted Benjie back to the camp. He felt a certain responsibility. Not only for the three whom he had plucked from the river, but also for the others who had been taken.

If only I'd gotten there quicker . . .

Gray also looked anxious to be underway, but he offered a few words of caution. "I agree with

Ndaye, but for now, we should let this ruse stand. Let the enemy believe their trick worked. We limit what we know to this group. We shouldn't even share our suspicions with FARDC or the Congolese government."

Ndaye nodded. "That is wise. I am proud of my country and its people, but there remains too much corruption in our government. Even FARDC soldiers have been supplementing their income of late by working with traffickers and poachers, sometimes with militias, often wearing their uniforms while doing so."

Tucker stared around their group. "Then we trust only ourselves."

Kowalski balled up his sandwich's greasy wrapper and lobbed it into a wastebasket. "So what else is new?"

11

Frank's stomach growled, reminding him it was nearly lunchtime. Still, he sat on the stool before his array of equipment. He surveyed the results being uploaded from the university's electron-microscopy lab to his laptop. As each image appeared, his heart pounded harder.

"Let this just be an artifact," he prayed aloud.

While most of the others had left for the U.N. camp, he had spent the morning prepping samples taken from the *Dorylus* queen and her soldier. He had taken fine needle aspirates, refined the collection with polyacrylamide gel electrophoresis, then plunge-froze the lot to ready them for cryo-EM. It was a delicate process.

But first things first . . .

He squinted as a final set of scans loaded onto his laptop. He spent an extra few minutes confirming what he suspected. He compared the imaging from both the queen and the soldier's sample—then sighed loudly.

"You'd better come see this," he called to Monk and Lisa.

The two DARPA scientists crossed from where they had been helping him prepare his PCR amplification of the samples, readying the search for any unique genomes that might herald an emerging new pathogen. A pair of thermocyclers ran in the background as they headed over.

"What's up?" Monk asked.

"Check out these EM scans," he said. "If what I fear is true, we may have a *big* problem. Or maybe I'd better say, a *giant* one."

"Show us," Lisa said.

The two flanked behind him. He sifted through the scans until he found the best image. He leaned back, revealing a cluster of viral particles.

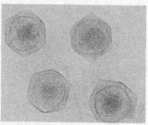

"I initially thought these were bacterial or somatic cells," he said. "Because of their large sizes. A typical virion particle ranges from fifty to a hundred nanometers in diameter."

Monk squinted at the image. "How big are these?"

Frank glanced over his shoulder at them. "*Seven* hundred. And that's just the thickness of the capsid shell. Not the *entire* virus."

He brought up another image, a more detailed scan of the viroid.

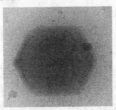

"Those fine striations radiating out from the capsid are protein filaments. If you take those into account, the virus is well over a *thousand* nanometers across."

"It's a giant virus," Lisa said.

"I'd say," Monk added. "I see why you called it a *big* problem."

Lisa glanced to her colleague. "No, I meant it's a *giant* virus. Sometimes called a *girus*. Such organisms were only identified a couple decades ago. They blur the line between viruses and bacteria."

"Dr. Cummings is right," Frank said. "The first of these jumbo viruses was isolated from inside an amoeba in 1992. Due to its size, it was initially mistaken for a bacterium. It wasn't until 2003, when it was further studied, that it was reclassified as a virus. Since then, many others have been discovered all over the place. Pithoviruses, Pandoraviruses, Mamavirus, Mollivirus."

"What about this one?" Monk asked. "Do you recognize it?"

Frank shook his head. "It bears characteristics with Mimivirus, with its icosahedral structure, like a twenty-sided die made up of triangles. But this one is far larger, nearly twice as big, putting it closer to a Pandoravirus in size—which is worrisome."

"Why is that?"

"Most viruses only carry a handful of genes. Rabies has five genes. HIV nine. Ebola seven. Even the flu only has eight genes. Pandoravirus has over *two thousand*. Even worse, *ninety percent* of those genes don't resemble anything else found on Earth." Frank frowned at the culprit on the screen. "We still know very little about them. If this virus is pathogenic, it could be like nothing we've seen before."

"But *is* it pathogenic?" Lisa said, crossing her arms. "As I understand it, giant viruses mostly prey on bacteria or amoebae. Few cause diseases in humans."

"True, but most of them—and I have to assume this one, too—are NCLDVs." Frank noted Monk's frown and explained. "Nucleo-cytoplasmic large DNA viruses. Many viruses in this same group are wildly pathogenic, including smallpox. Other examples cause diseases in both vertebrates—and invertebrates."

Lisa unfolded her arms and glanced over to the safety hood. "Like ants."

"It's speculated that these giant viruses acquired so many genes by scavenging code from their hosts and other organisms."

"Like genetic pickpockets," Monk said.

"Exactly. They carry code from all manner of different species. Vertebrates, invertebrates, microbes, even plants. Some scientists believe NCLDVs are so strange that they should be classified as a fourth domain of life, alongside Archaea, Bacteria, and Eukarya. They may even be the source for all life on Earth."

"How is that possible?" Monk asked.

"We used to believe that viruses were simply degenerate escapees from living cells, that they lost their cellular machinery and devolved into modern-day viruses. But from the recent studying of unique genes found in viruses, scientists are theorizing it might be the other way around. Take the giant Medusavirus. It has a gene coding for DNA polymerase, an enzyme necessary to synthesize DNA, but its gene is unlike any version found in modern animals or plants. Instead, it appears far more ancient, so old in fact that it might be the precursor for what's in animals and plants today. There are so many other examples like this that the Virus World Theory— the theory that all life evolved from viruses—is growing in consensus."

"But what does that have to do with the crisis we're facing now?" Lisa asked, drawing the focus back to the danger in the Congo.

Frank sighed. "Because of what my adopted mother used to threaten me with whenever I did something that really pissed her off. *I may not have brought you into this world, but I'll take you out.*"

Monk got what he was trying to convey. "You're thinking that if viruses brought us into the world—"

"Then they may take us out," Frank finished.

Lisa frowned and nodded at the screen. "Still,

we can't know if this giant virus is even pathogenic or just a normal part of the viral fauna of
Dorylus ants."

"True. But the tissues of the ants—both soldier
and queen—are flush with this organism. I've not
had a chance to sample the ant pupa, but that doesn't
much matter. I need samples from the camp, from
those who had succumbed there. I need to see if
this same virus is in those tissues, too."

Lisa checked the wall clock. "Benjie should be
back by late afternoon. Then we'll know."

Frank nodded, but he couldn't escape the feeling
that they were rapidly running out of time. As if
someone heard his silent worry, a chime sounded
from the team's sat-phone on the table. Frank
hoped it was a further update from those out at
the camp.

Monk picked up the phone and answered it.
His brows pinched as he listened to the caller.
"Got it," Monk said. "We'll check into it."

He hung up, his face tight with worry.

"What is it?" Lisa asked.

"That was Painter. Kat just got a report of a
handful of new cases of a debilitating catatonia."

"Where?" Lisa asked.

Monk faced them. "Here in Kisangani. At the
university hospital. A group of schoolchildren.
All showing the same signs."

12:07 P.M.

Lisa crossed the circular drive of the ambulance
bay under the blazing eye of the midday sun. A

sign overhead read CLINIQUES UNIVERSITAIRES DE KISANGANI. Like the university's Faculty of Science building, the hospital had been recently refurbished. It rose two stories high but stretched wide, encompassing a campus of multiple structures spread across a parklike setting bordering the Congo River.

Monk nodded to the pair of ambulances and a handful of gray-green FARDC military trucks parked at the entrance. "Looks like we're not the only ones to hear about the new patients."

Lisa hurried past the cluster of vehicles. According to Painter, eight schoolchildren from a village twenty miles into the jungle had all come down with the same deadening malaise and had been rushed here this morning. Lisa was desperate to examine them and collect samples for Frank, who remained at the lab finishing his viral assay. Monk would transport the blood and sputum samples the half mile back to the science building, while she would offer her assistance to the medical staff here.

Painter and Kat had coordinated with the hospital director to facilitate their involvement. As they neared the threshold, a tall shaven-headed African man in a white smock over blue scrubs lifted an arm at them.

"Drs. Cummings and Kokkalis," he greeted them, his English accented with French. "I'm Amir Lumbaa, hospital administrator. Thank you for your offer of assistance. If you'll follow me, I'll take you to the ward that the military has cordoned off. Both as quarantine and as security."

Lisa glanced over to the pair of uniformed soldiers sharing a cigarette near one of the parked FARDC trucks. "Why're all military here?"

He escorted them through the doors and across the empty lobby. "The militia attack on the U.N. camp has been all over the local news. Plus, word reached us two hours ago of the fire-bombing at a hospital in neighboring Burundi. Rebels claimed responsibility."

Lisa shared a look with Monk. Painter had reported that a clinic in Burundi had been one of the places where cases of the debilitating disease had been reported. Could the bombing there be related to last night's attack?

"No one has an explanation for this sudden spate of attacks on medical centers," Amir said. "Militias and rebels normally respect our facilities, even during the decades of fighting in the past."

Amir led them through the breadth of the hospital, out the back, and across a central courtyard to a neighboring building separate from the other. "We're housing the children in their own ward back here, to limit any exposure to the main hospital."

They reached the doors to the private wing and crossed through the bustle of personnel, all gowned and masked. Their group quickly donned the same in an anteroom to a ward that had been sealed behind hanging sheets of plastic and guarded by a pair of armed soldiers.

Lisa headed in with Amir, while Monk trailed. His eyes were narrowed as he surveyed every face for any signs of threat. Despite the cordon of the Congolese army at the hospital entrance, he was taking no chances. He kept one hand resting on his holstered SIG Sauer half-hidden under a fold of his gown.

While she had her own weapon—a small Beretta Nano in an ankle holster—she trusted Monk to have her back and concentrated on the row of beds along one wall, all occupied by young boys and girls ranging from eight to thirteen. Nurses and doctors whispered and worked along the beds. After hearing so much about this debilitating malaise, Lisa wanted to assess such a patient herself.

She turned to Amir. "Could I conduct my own examination of one of the children? I'd also like to collect samples for a virologist working with us."

"Of course," the administrator said. "Any assistance would be most welcome."

She nodded her thanks. She carried a plastic case of sterilized swabs, along with tiny vials to collect sputum and blood samples, all supplied to her by Frank.

Monk followed at her side. "Where exactly was the school where these children were afflicted?"

Amir stared toward the windows at the back of the ward. "Less than fifty kilometers due east of Kisangani."

Monk shared a look with Lisa. So the disease was definitely closing in on the city, the major hub for this entire region. "Maybe we should consider a quarant—"

A shatter of glass cut him off. A small black object blasted through a window near the back of the ward. Another burst through a neighboring pane. Then another to the right. The black objects rattled and bounced across the linoleum floor, then burst with sharp blasts into great gouts of acrid black smoke that swept the room in a breath.

Monk grabbed Lisa by the arm and hauled her away—only to have a spatter of gunfire erupt behind them. The two guards posted at the door shoved through the plastic sheeting and into the ward. A doctor ran toward them, only to be blown back as one of the soldiers shot him nearly point-blank in the chest.

Lisa dropped low, remembering Ndaye's warning about the duplicitous nature of some FARDC soldiers. Such apprehension had been proven all too true.

Monk already had his sidearm out. He aimed and fired two shots, striking the gunman in the chest. The other swung his rifle toward the threat and strafed wildly as he ran across the ward. Monk dropped flat and tried to return fire, but the spread of smoke quickly hid the soldier's form. Blasts and screams followed in the fleeing man's deadly wake.

Down on a knee, Lisa yanked her Beretta and swung her aim along the trail of stirred smoke. She caught the briefest muzzle flash in the pall, then fired in that direction, squeezing off four rounds. Afterward, her ears rang as she listened for any renewed rifle fire.

"C'mon," Monk said and grabbed her arm, ready to get her to safety.

She shook free. While Lisa heard no more

gun blasts, cries and moans rose all around the ward. She wasn't about to abandon those here. She waited four full breaths to make sure there was no further attack, then turned to Monk.

"I have to help the wounded."

"More gunmen could be on their way," Monk warned.

"No," she said. "I wager they'd be here by now. This was only a final gasp of whoever is trying to keep knowledge of this contagion bottled. Anyway, I don't think that was the real intent in attacking the ward."

The thumping bell beat of a helicopter passed over the hospital. The rotorwash swept through the shattered window and stirred the worst of the smoke. Through the haze, Lisa spotted the sprawled soldier and others laying on the floor or dropped into hiding.

The helicopter continued past, aiming in a concerning direction.

Lisa faced Monk. "Frank . . ."

12:22 P.M.

What the hell is that?

A strange tapping noise intruded on Frank's concentration. He had been bent over his laptop as he readied his bioinformatic software. The PCR amplification was almost complete. One final run of the thermocyclers should produce an adequate sampling of the DNA code from the giant virus. He was anxious to complete this assay before Dr. Cummings returned from the hospital ward with samples from the afflicted children.

If they bear the same viral load . . .

He prayed he was right, so the culprit was properly and swiftly identified, but he also remained fearful for all the reasons he had delineated earlier. The genetics and biology of *girus* species were poorly understood. They carried thousands of genes never seen before, let alone understood.

He glanced to the corner of his laptop screen, where an image of a lone viral particle glowed, its icosahedral shape festooned by a fringe of proteinaceous spikes. A fear had been growing. He had studied several infected cells in both the *Dorylus* queen and her soldier. He had noted the cytoplasm of those cells was full of those same spikes, like the cast-off spines of a porcupine. Most of the discarded spikes had appeared bent or oddly twisted.

A frightening suspicion had begun to take hold of him.

"Or maybe I'm just being paranoid," he whispered to himself.

He fought down his doubts, which he knew could be traced to old insecurities. Despite all he had accomplished, he could still remember the kid from the South Side in secondhand Jordans, huddled in a museum, memorizing scientific placards. Back in high school, he had seldom raised his hand in class, even when he was certain of the answer. It had been drilled into him to hide such knowledge or risk ridicule. Even his teachers would look at his six-foot-four frame and make assumptions about his intelligence. And despite his later accomplishments, he still felt too often like that high school kid who was hesitant to raise his hand.

He stared again at those misshapen proteins and pushed away those doubts.

I know I'm right.

Then the strange noise intruded again, drawing his attention away from the screen. The faint crystalline tapping was loud enough to be heard above the hum of the thermocyclers. Needing a distraction, he searched for the source. He spun his lab stool and recognized the noise was coming from the safety hood along the wall, where Benjie's samples were still stored.

He stood and crossed to the station. He bent enough to examine the tray of glass tubes. He suspected the queen must be growing agitated from her confinement and sought a means to escape. Only the two-inch-long ant lay listlessly at the bottom of the tube, looking nearly dead, except for a slight shiver of its antennae.

Then what—

The tapping came again, arising from another of the tubes. Frank lifted the culprit. It held the pupa that Benjie had collected. The brown chitinous cocoon had been the size of a pistachio shell. Only now it had cracked open and lay discarded below. Above it, clinging to the tube's glass side was a huge ant, easily an inch long. It seemed too large to have been crammed inside the pupa. Then again, maybe it was the pair of diaphanous wings across its back that added to this illusion. The wings buzzed and shook as vital fluids spread through tiny veins, further strengthening and extending their structure.

Benjie had already explained how the males of the *Dorylus* species sported such wings, but Frank hadn't imagined them this big. The tapping against the glass drew his attention to the underside of the ant. He rotated the tube to better examine it.

As he did, he stared behind the scrabbling legs. A hooked barb extended from the pointed tip of the abdomen and stabbed at the glass. Small driblets of an oily green substance spattered the glass.

Frank knew what he was staring at.

"It's a stinger."

Benjie had failed to mention that the *Dorylus* species bore such a weapon. It was a lapse that Frank knew was not due to forgetfulness. As far as Frank knew, *no* ant species bore a stinger like a wasp or bee. He squinted and shook his head. Could it be some aberrant mutation, something driven by the viral infection?

"What the hell is going on?" he muttered.

At the other end of the ant, large pincers gnashed at the glass, leaving a smear of the same greenish substance. He feared that oil carried something far worse than a painful poison. He pictured the substance full of icosahedral viral particles. He returned his attention to the large wings and remembered the pattern of disease spread through the jungle, seeming to match the direction of the winds.

Maybe the virus wasn't satisfied with simply

being airborne, of being subject to the vagaries of the wind.

He stared at the buzzing behind glass.

Maybe it grew its own wings instead.

12:23 P.M.

Monk gunned the open-air military jeep and jolted away from the entrance of the hospital. In the rearview mirror, he spotted two FARDC guardsmen standing alongside Amir Lumbaa, hospital administrator. Monk had commandeered the vehicle from the men with the fervent support of the administrator, once a former FARDC corpsman himself. As Monk fled off, the trio of men dashed back into the hospital, ready to help protect the assaulted medical ward.

Praying Lisa remained safe, Monk concentrated on the black helicopter as it swept in a tight circle over the science building and settled into a hover over the roof. While Monk ran through the hospital, he had tried to raise Frank, to warn him of the threat. But there had been no answer. Either Frank was lost in his work, or the enemy was jamming communication.

Swearing under his breath, Monk aimed the jeep in a beeline toward the science building half a mile away. He kept the accelerator floored and raced across lawns, bounced over sidewalks, and shot along a stretch of dirt road. He kept one hand on the wheel and gripped his SIG Sauer P320 in the other. He tried pointing the weapon toward the helicopter through the open roof, but the bouncing vehicle threw off any aim. He could not risk a stray bullet shattering through one of the building's windows and killing or wounding a student or faculty member.

He lowered his weapon and concentrated on reaching the doors to the science building. Movement along the flank of the helicopter drew his eye. Doors opened, and ropes were unfurled, snaking toward the side of the building where the lab was located.

Then Monk lost sight of the helicopter as he reached the school's entrance. He braked hard, skidding through grass, and leaped out before the jeep had fully stopped. He sprinted for the door but knew the truth.

I'm too late.

12:34 P.M.

"Why aren't you all answering?" Frank mumbled with the team's radio at his lips.

He had been trying to raise Benjie and the rest of the team over at the U.N. camp. He stared at the ant scratching at the sides of the specimen tube. He wanted to relate what he had witnessed: the molting of the ant pupa into this aberration of the species. *That is, if it is an aberration*, he reminded himself. He couldn't be entirely sure and wanted to consult with Benjie, who knew more about the *Dorylus* species than anyone.

He listened for any response to his call, but only heard a buzzing static. It was also hard to hear with a helicopter thumping nearby. Such aircraft—many of them tour operations—had periodically swept over the university campus, so he hadn't given it much attention, especially with his focus on his strange discovery.

But now . . .

He lowered the radio, realizing the helicopter was not passing the building. It continued to thump overhead. His heart suddenly clenched. He flashed back to Iraq, to when sirens would ring out, warning of an incoming mortar attack, sending soldiers running for cement bunkers or sandbag shelters.

He turned toward the lab's window just as shadows blackened the view. Gunfire crackled; glass burst. Kevlar-armored figures shattered through the panes, swinging into the lab on ropes. Weapons bristled. A spate of gunfire sent him ducking low behind his lab table.

He had a sidearm holstered at his hip, the weapon courtesy of his newfound allies from D.C. But he didn't even have time to thumb off the holster's restraining strap. Gunmen appeared on either side of the table where he crouched. Orders were barked in both Swahili and French. He was not fluent in either, but he understood the intent, reinforced by the assault rifles.

He lifted his arms and slowly stood up.

He was quickly surrounded, stripped of his weapon, and forced at gunpoint to a corner of the room. Another figure—a tall Congolese soldier with a ragged scar across his cheek—carried a harness toward him.

He stared at the ropes dangling outside the window and realized the intent.

They aren't here to kill me.

He was both relieved and worried. If this was a kidnapping, it meant someone already knew far too much about their operations here. Another soldier ripped Frank's laptop from its power cord, stripped its connections, and carried it off, clarifying the attacker's intent.

Someone else out there clearly values my expertise.

12:37 P.M.

Monk had heard gunfire echoing down from above as he climbed the stairs. He was not the only one. He had to shoulder his way upward against a tide of students and faculty fleeing down from above. His raised pistol and loud swearing also helped open a path ahead of him. He paused only long enough to secure what he needed from one of the fleeing teachers. As the way cleared, he took the steps two at a time and rushed for the third floor.

Upon reaching it, he leaned out into the hallway. By now, the level had emptied out. With his SIG at the ready, he did a fast check in both directions, searching for any threat. Satisfied, he ran down the hall, staying low, sticking to one wall. His ears strained for any threat.

Upon reaching the lab's door, he heard muffled shouts. He didn't know how many combatants were inside, but he dared not wait. He placed his SIG Sauer on the floor and toed it out of view.

Girding himself, he tapped in the electronic code on the lock, waited for the green light, and grabbed the door handle. With a final inhale of resolve, he shoved the way open. He burst into the room, lifting what he had stolen from one of the teachers. It was a thick folder of loose-leaf papers. He didn't know what they were. A pile of student tests? Research notes? A draft of a novel in progress?

He didn't care—it would serve his purpose well enough.

At least I hope so.

As soon as he entered the room, he studied the folder in hand. "Dr. Whitaker! I have the virology results. Shocking results! You'll want to—"

Monk then stumbled to a stop, feigning surprise at the cluster of black-clad soldiers inside. Weapons trained on Monk. He counted five armed men, confirming his earlier assessment that a one-man rescue attempt would prove futile here.

Frank stood in a corner, strapped in a harness.

A single shot fired in Monk's direction, ringing past his ear and down the hall. He yelped, ducked to the side, and threw his folder high, scattering the papers in all directions.

As he did so, he stared hard at Frank, trying to silently communicate his intent.

The man proved himself no fool, even in such dire straits.

"Don't shoot!" Frank yelled. "That's my research assistant. I need to know what he found out!"

A few of the gunmen glanced to a tall Congolese standing by a shattered window. It had to be the team leader. Past the man's shoulder, Monk spotted rooster tails of dust as military vehicles raced toward the science building. Pressed for time, the scarred man studied Monk for a breath—then barked orders.

Monk found himself manhandled toward Frank. He didn't resist, keeping his arms high. Another harness was brought forward.

As he was secured into it, Monk cast a sidelong look at Frank. The army vet frowned at him, clearly wondering what Monk was thinking. Monk answered with the slightest shrug. Granted, it wasn't the brightest plan, but he had limited options. Earlier, he had guessed that the enemy must be planning on snatching Frank, like they had done with the U.N. doctors yesterday. Otherwise, the bastards would've simply firebombed the entire top floor of the science building.

Knowing this, Monk had devised this risky gambit, heeding the wisdom of an old adage.

If you can't beat them, join them.

12

With his sat-phone pressed to his ear, Gray surveyed the ruins of the former U.N. camp. The firebombed remnants of a flooded village poked from the black waters of the swollen Tshopo River. Dark jungles surrounded on all sides, piping, croaking, and buzzing with life.

Closer at hand was only death.

Rows of bodies were lined like cord wood under canvas shrouds. He had already examined many of them. Some were villagers, a few were members of the U.N. team, and others were dressed in ragtag militia uniforms. According to Ndaye, the latter were scattered here purposefully, an attempt to cover up the true culprits behind the attack.

Gray watched Benjie as he knelt beside one of the villager's bodies. The corpse looked skinned and covered in black blood. Gray tried to picture what had transpired here before the armed assault. Benjie had related the deadening malaise that had afflicted several of the refugees, how they had not even resisted the ravages of the army ants. As the biologist worked, Benjie's face had drained of color, his eyes were fixed and unblinking. To the side, Ndaye and Faraji dragged the limp form of a dead baboon by its arms toward their group. Frank had wanted samples collected from the wildlife here, too.

As Gray listened to Painter Crowe's report over the phone, he knew the efforts here were for naught. Someone had kidnapped Frank and Monk from the university lab, firebombing everything on their way out. Gray's jaw was clamped tight. It was further proof that the enemy had far too much intel on Sigma's efforts here. Word had clearly spread to the wrong ears.

"Lisa will continue working with the doctors at the university hospital," Painter continued. "She'll try to carry on Dr. Whitaker's virology work as best she can with the resources at hand. She's also going to reach out to Dr. Remy Engonga, a pathologist with the International Centre for Medical Research who worked with Frank up in Gabon. Their institute has the closest Level 4 biosafety containment facility."

Gray took this all in, already recalibrating his own plans. "What about Monk and Frank? We have to assume they were snatched by the same ones who attacked this U.N. camp."

Kowalski overheard this and glanced up sharply from where he was kneeling beside an unusual weapon supplied to the team by Painter, a prototype rifle designed by DARPA for jungle warfare. The Shuriken—as it was nicknamed—

had a shovel-nosed barrel. It looked like a dust-buster vacuum welded to the front of an assault rifle. A large cylindrical drum magazine held its unusual ammunition.

Tucker had also been eyeballing the strange rifle with some interest. Even Kane sniffed at the weapon's case. But the ranger straightened upon hearing Gray's end of the conversation. Tucker's eyes narrowed. "What's this about Frank?"

Gray read the concern, knowing Tucker and Frank were friends going back to the Gulf War. Gray held up a palm as he listened to Painter's answer.

"That's the only good news I have," the director said.

"How is that *good*?"

"Lisa believes—and I concur—that Monk rushed over during the attack with little hope of rescuing Frank and more with the intent to be snatched along with the virologist."

Gray nodded. *Of course* . . . "And have you been able to pick up Monk's transponder?"

"Trust me. Kat is not about to lose track of her husband. The GPS unit built into his prosthesis remains active. Presently it continues to move in a northeasterly direction across the Congo."

Gray let out a soft sigh of relief. Monk's prosthetic hand—a marvel of engineering—was nearly indistinguishable from the real thing. At least from a cursory glance. He did not doubt that the enemy would have searched Monk, but in their haste to depart, they had clearly overlooked what was hidden in plain sight.

But how long would that last?

Suspicion rankled through him. He glanced over to Ndaye, remembering the eco-guard's own warning about some of his fellow soldiers' lack of loyalty to their uniforms. He lowered his voice to a whisper. "We should keep this knowledge to ourselves," he warned. "As much as I'd like to take advantage of the military's support, someone knew we were at that university. The best hope of securing Monk and Frank will be through stealth rather than a show of force. At least, for now."

Gray glanced across the ruins of the camp. They had to hope that Monk and Frank would be transported to the location where the kidnapped doctors had been taken. If so, his team would have only one chance to pull off a successful rescue. But if word again reached the wrong ears . . .

"So what's your plan?" Painter asked.

"Let me discuss it with the others, and I'll get back with you."

"Understood."

Gray signed off and lowered the phone. He appreciated Painter giving him the leeway to strategize further rather than issuing a command. Sometimes it took someone with boots on the ground to best assess a situation. Gray also trusted his gut, and thankfully the director did, too.

He waved the group into a tighter cluster, including Benjie and Faraji. He quickly related all that had happened at the university. Grim expressions met this account. No one spoke except for Kowalski, who swore under his breath, exhaling a stream of smoke from the cigar clamped between his molars.

Gray continued once the news had sunk in, "I hate to abandon the search along the trail left behind by the Reverend Sheppard. If there's a source of the contagion somewhere out in the jungle—and a possible cure—we need to find it ASAP."

A few nods acknowledged this. One only had to look at the devastation wrought here—not just from the assault by the enemy, but also from the debilitating illness that had struck the camp prior to the attack—to recognize how time was running out. Gray innately knew the entire Congo was at a tipping point. Something malevolent and ancient was smoldering out in that jungle, and it had to be stopped before it blew into a firestorm.

Tucker leaned closer. Gray could guess the ranger's next words. "Kane and I'll go after Frank and hopefully the others. You all continue into the jungle, following those clues. Just have the director keep me abreast of the tracker's signal. I'll let him know what I find."

Gray nodded his thanks. He hated to leave Monk's fate to another, but Tucker's expertise during the war—especially paired with Kane—was in search and rescue, especially exfiltration of high-value targets from behind enemy lines. If anyone could secure the others, it was this pair.

Gray turned to Ndaye. The ICCN guard had

piloted the helicopter that had ferried them all here. "Would you be willing to airlift Tucker, to get him over to that trail? I want to keep this operation limited to our group alone. I don't trust anyone else."

"*Certainement*," Ndaye answered. "I understand."

"And perhaps en route you could drop Benjie back in Kisangani with his samples."

Benjie straightened and shook his head. "No. That makes no bloody sense."

Gray fixed his gaze on the biologist.

"I wish to go with you, Commander Pierce." The student's voice was firm, but he had to swallow twice to get those words out. He also blinked rapidly, as if his body was trying to send a fearful SOS in Morse code. Still, Benjie pressed the matter further. "With cases of the afflicted already at the Kisangani hospital, I see little value in transporting my samples there. I could be of more use in the forest."

Gray wanted to argue against the young man's help, but so much remained unknown. Like how the contagion seemed to have a strange effect on jungle life. Gray dared not discount the assistance of a biologist. Still, he gave Benjie one last out.

"If you're absolutely sure," he offered. "It'll just be us, along with Kowalski and hopefully Faraji." He glanced over to the shaman's apprentice and addressed the boy. "That is, if you're still willing to help. We need someone local who might be able to interpret the clues hidden in Sheppard's old photographs."

Both Faraji and Benjie nodded their willing-
ness to continue.

"Then it's settled," Gray said.

Kowalski heaved out another cloud of cigar
smoke. "Great. We're splitting up. That always
ends well."

THIRD

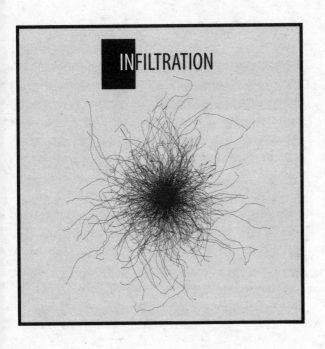

INFILTRATION

13

This is not good . . .

Charlotte continued her physical examination of Disanka inside the makeshift medical ward. The Lubu woman sat up on her cot. She must have read the worry in Charlotte's face. The patient's wide eyes reflected that same growing fear. Disanka's gaze flicked to her son. The boy was swaddled and asleep in a bedside cradle, but even in slumber, there remained a distinct lassitude. The child was not curled on his side, sucking on a thumb as he dreamed. Instead, his head was lolled backward, his tiny limbs laying slack around him, looking boneless.

The mother was not the only one concerned for the boy.

"He's getting worse," Jameson said. The American pediatrician had just completed his own examination of the baby. "His pulse ox has fallen below ninety. Likely due to his breathing growing shallower and shallower."

"We should get him on an oxygen mask."

"I'll see to it. Finish your exam on his mother. If she's also getting sick . . ." Jameson left the rest unsaid.

As Jameson departed, Charlotte cast a worried look across to a neighboring bed where a form lay sealed in a black body bag. An older patient had died, and they were readying to transport his remains to the pathology lab in the next Quonset hut over. According to his chart, the old man had arrived four days ago, already deep into the strange malaise. Whatever encephalitic condition resulted in that lassitude had progressed, slowly paralyzing the victim over time. Or maybe the sluggishness had simply become so severe that the man simply forgot how to breathe, or his heart lost its will to beat. That was a mystery for the pathologists. Not that she expected any answers to be shared with them.

She glanced to the suite of equipment at the back of the ward. She had tried repeatedly to get further information from Dr. Ngoy, who led the team of clinicians working there, only to be rebuffed again and again.

Not exactly a cooperative bunch.

Still, Charlotte had a more immediate concern. She returned her attention to Disanka. The woman had started running a low-grade fever and, with some prodding, admitted to a growing headache. It would be easy to blame all of this on fatigue and fear for her boy, but a late lunch of stew and fried bread had left Disanka nearly choking.

Charlotte picked up a tongue depressor and requested in French, "Disanka, could you please open your mouth?" She pantomimed the same by sticking out her own tongue.

As Disanka obeyed, Charlotte leaned forward. She used the tongue depressor to examine the back of the woman's mouth. The tonsils appeared slightly inflamed. Otherwise, there appeared to be no other lesions or sores. Charlotte held a breath and reached to the left tonsillar bed with her tongue depressor and brushed its wooden edge against the inflamed tissue. Normally, a patient would've jerked back and gagged. Instead, Disanka showed no acknowledgment of the violation.

Charlotte sat back and tossed the depressor into a red hazardous waste bin. She motioned Disanka to relax and patted her shoulder in reassurance. Her efforts failed to diminish the worry in the woman's eyes, but the fear was not for her own health. They both turned toward the swaddled baby in the crib.

Disanka reached over and took Charlotte's hand, reminding Charlotte of her earlier promise. To keep the child safe at any cost.

Charlotte squeezed her reassurance.

I'll do everything I can.

The fear in Disanka's eyes had dimmed, smothered by a renewed determination. They matched gazes in that moment, the meaning clear.

They *both* would do everything they could for the child.

By now Jameson had returned with a tiny pediatric mask and hooked an oxygen line to it. "Well?" he asked brusquely.

Charlotte released Disanka's hand. "It definitely appears her struggles during lunch were due to dysphagia. I don't know if it's just a lack of feeling in the back of her throat or if there's muscular paralysis, too."

"Could this be an early sign of the disease?"

She shrugged. "The fever, headaches, they could all be the signs of the onset of a viral encephalitis. But this degree of dysphagia, that's an unusual sequela."

"Not always." He glanced significantly at her.

She understood. "You're thinking of rabies."

The zoonotic disease was one she had been well versed on before coming here as part of Doctors Without Borders. The characteristic hydrophobia—or fear of water—along with the foaming at the mouth and drooling, was due to pharyngeal dysfunction as rabies triggered a deadly encephalitis.

"But this is clearly not rabies," Jameson said.

No, it's definitely not.

She found herself rubbing her own throat, trying to judge if she was experiencing such a symptom. The ant bites on her hands were still red. She had a persistent headache and felt overheated and sweaty. She wanted to blame it all on stress and being suited up from head to toe. Still, she could not escape the worry that she was infected, too.

Jameson nodded toward the back of the ward.

"Maybe we should inform Dr. Ngoy about our observation."

She turned and frowned at the head researcher and his team. The clinicians remained clustered among the serology and histology equipment at the back of the hut. To that group, she and Jameson were merely glorified interns and phlebotomists, not worthy of their time.

"Let's hold off for now," she said.

"Are you sure?"

Before she could respond, the entire Quonset hut shook as a helicopter swept over it. The rotorwash pounded the metal roof. Already on edge, she found herself ducking and staring upward. Whoever had arrived had done so with some urgency.

Curiosity drew her to a narrow window beside Disanka's bed. It sounded like the helicopter had landed close by, rather than over at the riverside helipad. Jameson shadowed her to the window.

The angle of the hut allowed her to spot the aircraft settling to its skids in the central square of the old colonial outpost. Hatches popped open on either side, and men in black armor piled out. They were more of Nolan De Coster's personal army. She spotted the tall form of Lieutenant Ekon. He led two men in civilian gear at the point of a rifle toward the guesthouse where Nolan kept his office.

Jameson stiffened next to her. "Impossible," he muttered.

She turned to him. "What is it?"

He nodded back toward the men being led away. "The one in front. That's Dr. Whitaker."

It took Charlotte another breath to recognize the name. "The virologist? The one you had tried to summon to the camp?"

"The same. But what is he doing here? *How* is he here?"

Charlotte noted the rifle threatening the pair of newcomers. "Clearly he didn't volunteer." She pointed to the stocky, bald man beside the virologist. "Do you recognize the other one with him?"

"No. But it doesn't matter. They're as trapped as we are. They won't be able to help us."

"I'm not so sure."

"What do you mean?"

"We need an experienced virologist."

She glanced over to Ngoy as the clinician bent over a microscope.

Especially one we can trust.

3:42 P.M.

Tucker knelt in shadows and readied his partner for the trek ahead.

Behind him, Ndaye remained with the helicopter as its motor cooled with metallic tinks and pings in the small clearing not far from a small river. The aircraft was the same Aérospatiale Gazelle that Tucker had ridden last night, when he had rescued Ndaye and the others from the flooded Tshopo River.

Let's pray the aircraft is up for one more high-stakes rescue.

For the past hour, Ndaye and Tucker had been tracking the GPS transponder in Monk's prosthetic. They had kept a wary distance until the moving target finally stopped—or rather the signal went dead. They'd lost the transmission about five minutes ago, requiring a swift search and landing in the clearing. The last signal had been broadcast about ten kilometers off. It was impossible to tell if the transponder had been discovered and disabled. If so, they dared approach no closer by air. They would have to continue on foot.

They being Tucker and Kane.

Ndaye would stay with the helicopter. The eco-guard needed to be ready to sweep over for an airlift if Tucker was successful in finding and securing the others. In the meantime, Tucker would maintain radio silence. He would only risk contacting Ndaye when absolutely necessary. After so many ambushes and apparent betrayals, paranoia was running high. Then again, he took heed of a quote from *Catch-22*: *Just because you're paranoid doesn't mean they aren't after you.*

Either way, for now, that meant Tucker was on his own—though not entirely on his own. He stared into Kane's dark caramel eyes, flecked with gold. It would be just the two of them from here.

Just the way I like it.

Tucker checked the shoulder and belly straps on Kane's K9 Storm tactical vest, making sure it was snug but not chaffing. The Kevlar-reinforced vest was waterproof and, more important, bullet-proof. Despite that protection, Tucker felt the old scars hidden under the black-and-tan ruff. Tucker shared the same scars, some easy to see, others just as well hidden.

As he worked, he felt his partner's heart pounding, the tremble of excitement in the dog's muscles. Kane knew it was time to get to work, to transform from furry companion to stealthy soldier. Tucker scuffled and rubbed Kane's ears, physically reinforcing their bond through touch. He then leaned closer, deepening that connection, smelling his partner's musk, appreciating the hot breath heaving through black nostrils.

In an age-old ritual, he touched noses with Kane, acknowledging what he was asking of the dog, to put himself in harm's way to save others.

"Who's a good boy?" he whispered to his best friend.

Kane licked his nose.

That's right, you are.

Tucker reached to the webbing of the vest's collar. He flipped up a camera hidden there and slipped a wireless radio plug into Kane's left ear. The gear allowed the pair to be in constant visual and audio contact with one another. Tucker positioned the camera's lens to peer over Kane's shoulder and turned it on. He then seated a pair of DARPA-designed goggles across his own eyes. He tapped a button on the side of the goggles and a live feed from Kane's camera appeared on the inside corner of the lens.

Satisfied, he slipped a wireless radio transmitter into his own mouth, fitting it behind his last tooth. The tiny radio—nicknamed a Molar Mic—allowed Tucker to communicate to Kane in whispers, while incoming transmissions reached Tucker's ear directly via bone induction through the jaw. Luckily the transmissions could be tamped down to make it less likely to be detected, though doing so limited the radio's reach. Tucker would only broadcast louder if he needed to reach Ndaye.

Testing the communication channel, Tucker mouthed breathlessly to his partner, "You ready, buddy?"

Kane wagged his tail. His partner's eyes glinted with suppressed excitement, knowing what was coming, anxious to get moving.

Then let's do this.

He straightened and swung around. Ndaye stared back, plainly guessing Tucker was ready to set off. The eco-guard offered him a thumb's up. Tucker returned it, then faced the thick jungle. The plan was to parallel the river and head toward where the signal was lost.

Tucker pointed toward the forest. Even before he whispered the command "*Scout*," Kane was already moving, anticipating the instruction.

As the dog swept into the forest, Tucker followed in his wake. Kane quickly vanished into the deeper shadows. Tucker studied the terrain both through his eyes and through the image transmitted to his goggles from Kane's camera. A bobbling view of leafy loam, bushes, and vines merged with his own. Though it was disorienting for several breaths, it quickly became second nature. Kane's panting filled his skull, coming to match his own breathing. Even the tread of his boots settled into an easy harmony with the padding of Kane's paws. In that timeless moment, the two became one, a perfect harmony of action and intent.

In another corner of his goggles, a real-time map marked his progress along the path of Monk's signal. Blip after blip vanished as he continued along that route. He kept the river on his left. He set a steady but fast pace. It was made easier by the shade-choked canopy that for long stretches reduced the undergrowth to occasional patches of thorny bushes and a scattering of bamboo thickets entwined with creepers and vines.

Otherwise, the forest climbed two hundred feet overhead, a towering colonnade of palms, rubber and mahogany trees, even small copses of red cedar. Beneath the canopy, the jungle was a damp emerald cathedral. Orchids and lilies offered bursts of nearly luminescent colors. Iridescent butterflies seemed to hover in the air, as if hung there ages ago.

Humbled and awed, he found himself holding his breath for long stretches. Even the centuries of decaying leaf litter muffled his footfalls. The silence was profound. He had expected a constant whir of insects, a cacophony of birdsong, a chattering chorus of monkeys. Instead, the place was deathly quiet, as if a great intelligence were studying him. He felt like a trespasser, an interloper who had no right to traipse this forest.

This did not apply to his companion.

Kane ran ahead, his fur blending into and out

of the dappled shadows. He moved without a sound, as much a part of the forest as any living creature. His tail flagged behind him, his ears piqued. His breathing was only a whisper in Tucker's ear.

As the pair continued, the air grew more humid, fecund and heavy. The sodden smell of rot and dampness filled his nostrils, along with the occasional sweeter brume from flowing vines. With each inhalation, it felt as if the jungle were trying to seed into his lungs. He found himself quickly growing winded, despite the steady pace. He could normally run a 10K in under an hour and barely break a sweat. With only half that distance covered, his brow already ran and dripped. His jungle camo shirt clung to his chest and back. His backpack had become a boulder over his shoulders.

Still, he kept a wary watch on the forest. He dared not let his guard down. Not just due to the unknown enemy ahead, but also from what hid in this green cathedral. Leopards and cheetahs prowled here, along with jackals and hyenas. And that only accounted for the larger denizens. Snakes of all sizes slithered about this forest, many of them poisonous: puff adders, tree cobras, mambas. Then there were the untold numbers of scorpions, spiders, and biting centipedes.

With each stride, he appreciated his waterproof hiking boots and the thickness of his khaki pants and sleeves. Still, tension built into a knot between his shoulder blades.

A scream burst through the jungle and made him jump.

A burst of color overhead revealed the angry flight of a long-beaked ibis, likely roused from its nest by his passage. He both apologized to and cursed the creature.

As he continued onward, time stretched strangely. The clock inside his goggles offered the only true assessment of his progress. He watched the blips on his live map slowly be eaten away. It took him over ninety minutes to reach the last one.

When he did, he whistled softly for Kane to stop. His partner obeyed, loping in a circle to join his side. Kane panted, his eyes bright in the shadows, as if lit by fires inside the dog. Tucker stared ahead as he offered Kane some water from his canteen. The transponder's signal had been roughly following the neighboring river. Though the trail ended here, he had to assume it continued alongside this waterway.

It must lead somewhere.

Tucker pointed ahead. "SCOUT," he whispered again to Kane. He also gripped his wrist and pulled his hand to this chest, silently adding the command STAY CLOSE.

They set off again, paralleling the river, heading downstream. Kane led the way, but only by a handful of yards. Tucker was glad he had taken the wary precaution. The jungle grew steadily thicker, less a cathedral and more like a crowded church. Visibility dropped in all directions. Even the branches lowered, threatening to brush the field hat off his head. The humidity also increased, as if the air was being crushed by the press of vegetation.

The reason for the thickening forest glinted in the distance.

Another river crossed the path ahead, likely draining into the other waterway. He slowed their pace—or rather the jungle did. With the river ahead carving a rut through the forest, the raw sunlight fueled the riotous growth at the water's edge. Vines and bushes grew into a thorny, shrouded barrier. Rotted deadfalls of tree trunks, covered in emerald moss and fronds of fungi, had to be climbed over.

Tucker noted another problem. The wireless feed from Kane's camera had begun to stutter inside his goggle, the image fritzing with pixelating dropouts. Tucker licked his lips. He could guess the reason. He glanced back along their trail, remembering where Monk's transponder had faded out.

Someone's jamming radio frequencies in this area.

It was also interfering with Kane's gear.

Tucker grimaced, but at least it confirmed he was on the right path after all. The bigger worry was that it meant he would have a hard time radioing back to Ndaye. If he was successful in freeing the others and sneaking away, he would have to get the group beyond the suppressive reach of the jammer before he could summon the helicopter. It made matters all the more difficult.

But it's not like I have much choice.

He continued forward, worming and half-crawling to the riverbank. The brighter sunlight stung his eyes, reflecting harshly off the water's flat black mirror. Blinded, he heard the warning before he saw it. A sonorous *thump-thump*ing. The noise echoed across the water. He traced the source of the noise to a large island in the middle of the confluence of the two rivers. A silver glint rose from the forests there. As Tucker blinked away the glare, he recognized a helicopter lifting off from the island.

Fearing he had already been spotted, he retreated away from the river. He buried himself farther in the jungle, but he kept watch on the aircraft. Was it the same one that had attacked the university? The chopper cleared the trees and turned in the opposite direction. It headed downriver. Tucker watched its path. It eventually swung away from the bow of the river and aimed inland. Tucker noted several columns of smoke in the distance. If he strained, he could make out a distant grinding echo. A sharp whistle also blew from that direction.

It must be a mining town. The Congo was riddled with them. He stared toward the distant plumes of smoke. Had the others been taken there? Or had they been dropped off on the island? He studied the forested silhouette in the river. He could just make out the tip of a long pier jutting downriver. Several boats were moored there. He also took into account the radio jamming of this area.

Someone's definitely set up shop there. Even if I'm wrong, I'll have to do a recon.

Which meant a swim.

He stared at the black mirror, wondering what dangers lurked below. Still, he had no choice but to risk it. With a sigh, he studied the sun, which sat low on the horizon. If there were eyes watching any approach from the river, it would be best to wait until nightfall.

With sunset only half an hour away, he settled back to wait, already strategizing in his head.

Kane did not seem happy with this plan. The dog growled deep in his throat, less a noise as a shaking of his body against Tucker's crouched form. Tucker glanced over. Kane was facing in the opposite direction—toward the shrouded forest—which looked even darker after the bright sunlight.

Kane growled again, signaling his partner.

Something's out there.

Tucker trusted Kane's instincts. He stared into the jungle. He needed eyes on whatever the dog sensed. He signaled his partner by lowering a palm before Kane's nose, then pointing a finger toward the jungle: *STAY LOW, TAKE POINT.*

Upon this command, Kane slunk off into the forest, slipping from shadow to shadow. As Tucker tracked him via the camera feed, he added a second silent command: *Be careful, buddy.*

Kane inhales the forest as he trails back into the trees. He takes in the scents to build what his eyes can't see.

Coming here, he has already memorized the spoor in the area: the bright tang of urine on a trunk, the darker musk of dung, the ammonia spatter of guano. Etched over all lingers the rot of leaf and buried bones, the ripeness of fallen fruit and maggoty decay.

On the back of his tongue, he tastes the dankness of this damp world, the sweet drifts of pollen in the air, the redolent loam stirred underfoot.

As he continues, he keeps his belly low and his ears high, tracing the unusual noise that had drawn his attention. It does not belong here. A growl of challenge builds in his throat, fueled by a hormonal fire to dominate. But he fights his own blood and holds back.

He pads forward, careful with each step. Thorns comb his ruff, but he shifts to keep those same barbs from scratching against his coarse vest and giving his position away. He is rewarded as the noise grows louder ahead.

—a squelching crunch of wet leaf, heavy, too rhythmic.

—a sharp whirring that sets his hackles high.

—a ticking, tanging of metal.

Then his nose picks up its scent, unique and separate from the forest world. It is lightning in the air, accompanied by a whiff of gun oil (of which he knows well). He also tastes burning plastic on his tongue.

The foreignness spikes his blood even hotter.

Still, he stifles any challenge.

He slows instead, shifting one paw ahead, then another. He holds his tail low. He sticks to the darkest shadows. Then he sees his target, both of them. They move with clumsy synchronicity, stalking through the forest with a dread determination, whirring with each step.

His hackles rise higher. A storm builds in his chest.

Then a command reaches his ears, urgent and forceful.

TAKE COVER!

He obeys, not out of fear, only from a loyalty that burns bright in his heart. He slips back into the deeper shadows, dropping to his belly. His haunches remain hard and tense, readying him to flee or attack.

Until then, he simply watches as the strangeness ambles closer.

Tucker gawked at the sight revealed in Kane's camera feed.

What the f . . .

A moment ago, two robotic figures had thumped into view, a matching pair of glossy black quadrupeds. They had clumped through the forest, moving in sync, like a deadly ballet of engineering and threat. He studied the closest one. It stood Kane's height at the shoulders, but it was missing its head. It had been replaced instead with a ring of camera lenses surmounted by a stub-nosed rifle assembly.

Tucker understood what he was seeing.

Guard dogs.

He had been following the development of these units for some time, having skin in the game when it came to military working dogs. They were called Quad-legged Unmanned Ground Vehicles, or Q-UGVs. They were intended to add a heightened level of security around military installations. But even the NYPD had briefly employed nonmilitary versions to assist in searching apartment complexes.

Tucker gritted his teeth.

Apparently, their deployment has expanded considerably—all the way to the Congo.

He searched beyond the pair for any sign of a handler, but he knew the robotic dogs were semi-autonomous. They were designed to patrol remote areas of a base, leaving soldiers to monitor more vital areas. The units could be controlled by a virtual reality headset worn by an operator or sent out along preprogrammed paths and assigned to react according to a set of algorithms.

He held his breath as the pair approached Kane's hiding spot. According to their specs, their ring of fourteen sensors scanned a full 360-degrees around them. They could crouch, jump, sprint, even operate at temperatures well below zero or in the most scorching desert. Then there were those rifle mounts. He hadn't heard of that addition to the robotic dogs, unless such weapons were unique to these jungle units.

The pair of Q-UGVs reached Kane's position. Tucker slipped his Desert Eagle out of its hip holster. But without missing a synchronized step, the pair stomped past Kane's hiding spot. Tucker let out his breath. He watched them vanish into the forest as they continued their patrol. He didn't know if the pair's sensors had failed to detect Kane's hiding spot, or if they had been programmed to fixate only on humans. With so much wildlife out here, it would be ineffectual for the guard dogs to be constantly shooting up the forest with every snap of a twig or flight of a bird.

Still, to be cautious, Tucker waited another three minutes before whispering a command to Kane.

"*QUIET RETURN.*"

On the video feed, Kane swung around and slunk back. Upon his arrival, Tucker gave his partner an enthusiastic rubdown.

"No one's gonna replace you, buddy."

Kane agreed with a vigorous wag of his tail.

With the greetings done, Tucker returned his attention to the river and the mysterious island at its center. If there were robotic guards patrolling here, then something was definitely wrong with that place. He was eager to get moving, but he checked the sun. It had already sunk halfway into the horizon. It wouldn't be too long of a wait.

Still, he stared across the water, knowing who was to blame for him being here.

"Frank, what goddamned mess have you gotten us into?"

14

Frank shifted uncomfortably in the deeply cushioned leather chair. Shortly after arriving at the island encampment, he and Monk had been strip searched and examined by a doctor. Only afterward had they been given a matching set of blue scrubs to don.

Monk shared the neighboring seat before a wide African mahogany desk. During the search, the captors had discovered Monk's prosthesis. He fidgeted with it now on his lap. He had been allowed to keep it, especially after feigning it to be stiff-fingered and clumsy, despite its outwardly authentic appearance.

The two of them faced the man who had orchestrated their kidnapping. Nolan De Coster, CEO of a mining conglomerate. Sadly, Frank actually knew the bastard, not personally, but the man's corporation—its philanthropic division— had partly funded Frank's own research here in Africa.

He struggled to come to terms with all that had been told to them, listening as the CEO eloquently recast his callousness and cruelty as economic necessity. Not that their attendance was voluntary. The tall Congolese soldier with the scarred face stood guard behind them.

Nolan kept his attention focused on Frank. "Dr. Whitaker, I can appreciate the hard set to your lips. You can judge me as harshly as you like. But as they say, what I've done . . . it's water under the bridge. It's a wise man who addresses the matter at hand versus wishing things to be otherwise. The viral disease is here. People are dying. More will soon be. But with your help, we can accelerate our research here. To quickly put a stop to the spread."

"So you can play the white savior of the Black man," Frank said darkly, noting the African gold crown hovering in a case behind the man's head.

The gall of this bastard.

Nolan sighed and steepled his fingers at his lips. "I've read your dossier, Dr. Whitaker. Army veterinarian turned virologist. You strike me as an impassioned but practical man. You've surely seen the best and worst of your fellow man during your years in the service. You understand progress often only comes at the cost of blood. It's more so here in the Congo. The history of Africa is written in misery and strife, measured in the number of bodies. I mean to ultimately change that for the Congo, to turn that bloody tide once and for all. And hopefully spread the same across the entire continent."

"In other words, the ends justify the means."

Nolan shrugged. "Sometimes it does. Especially if those 'ends' break the wheel of Africa's constant and escalating cycle of violence, war, and death. Consider what is happening now to be merely the final birthing pangs of a new era for Africa."

Frank sat straighter and opened his mouth, but Monk cut him off.

"What if we do help?" Monk said curtly, glancing apologetically toward Frank. Since their capture, Monk had continued playing the role of the deferential research assistant. He swallowed hard, looking nervous. "What'll become of us?"

Frank imagined a shallow grave in the jungle.

"I can assure you that no harm will come to you. I'm a man of my word. You will both, of course, remain under guard. You will be well taken care of, every luxury afforded you, your every whim met."

"But not our freedom," Frank said. "We'll be ensconced in a gilded cage for the rest of our lives. That's your offer?"

"I'm afraid so. But what is the alternative, Dr. Whitaker? You served in the army. You know something of sacrifice. Is life in a gilded cage too high a price to pay if it means thousands—possibly hundreds of thousands—of lives are saved?"

Frank sat back. He recognized the futility of trying to argue his way out of here. Maybe it was best to play along. If these assholes had a leg up on the viral disease, it would serve the world to cooperate. At least for now. Plus, Frank could not deny an aching curiosity. He wanted to know what these bastards knew, to learn what progress they had made.

He pictured the spiky giant virus isolated from the *Dorylus* ants.

"Can I count on your help?" Nolan asked with a note of finality.

Frank met the man's icy blue gaze. "Show me what you've learned, and then I'll decide."

"Fair enough." Nolan stood up. The shift of his suit jacket revealed a heavy shoulder holster and the butt of a black pistol. "I'll take you to our lab. The day's nearly over, but it's best if we start on the same page as soon as possible."

The Congolese soldier stepped forward. "I can take them, sir," he offered in French.

Frank was fluent enough to understand, but he kept such knowledge secret.

Nolan shook his head and came around the wide desk. "No, Lieutenant Ekon. I'll go along, too. I'd rather get my daily briefing from Dr. Ngoy directly."

The lieutenant nodded smartly. "*Oui, bien sûr.*"

Frank and Monk stood, sharing a look. Monk stared hard with a slight widening of his eyes. The silent message was easy to read.

Play along.

Frank knew that was the best course for now. Unable to talk freely, he didn't know if Monk had any plan. Still, he appreciated having the man at his side. They were led at gunpoint out of the office and down the stairs of what appeared to be a restored colonial guesthouse.

Once outside, Ekon marched them along a path of wooden planks past a white stone church and toward a cluster of gray Quonset huts.

Nolan played tour guide, pride bright in his voice. "I've spared no expense in expediting the installation of our research facility. We have medical wards, a pathology lab, a Level 3 biohazard unit, even a spot for animal testing."

The CEO waved at a windowless cinder block building with a metal roof that looked hastily constructed. Frank suppressed a shiver at the muffled cries and bawling that echoed through the walls.

"Ahead is our main research ward," Nolan finally said as led them to the largest of the Quonset huts.

They had to wait at the door while a form in a body bag was carried out on a stretcher by a pair of men in white biohazard suits. Nolan's cheeks reddened slightly, as if embarrassed by the sight, but he remained silent and only waved them inside once the way was clear. Frank watched the body being hauled toward a neighboring hut.

He was finally ushered inside a draped anteroom with Monk. They all donned gowns and face masks and entered the main ward. A dozen hospital beds lined one wall, almost all of them occupied. Another cordoned off area in the back was partially obscured behind translucent drapes. It looked like a clinical lab. Throughout the remaining space, other gowned and masked figures worked, barely giving their arrival any attention. Though as soon as they started across the ward, a figure broke away from a bedside and rushed forward.

"Dr. Whitaker!" the man shouted, his voice muffled by his mask.

Frank squinted, confused, then recognized the face behind the shield. "Dr. Jameson?" It was the American pediatrician, the one who had requested his help at the U.N. camp.

Nolan interceded as the man joined them. "Of course, you know each other. How fortuitous."

Frank knew it wasn't *fortuitous*. It had been orchestrated from the start.

"I'm hoping you can all work together to expedite our research." Nolan waved a hand toward a woman who approached more cautiously. "Including Dr. Charlotte Girard. She's been caring for our newest and youngest patient, who hopefully will shed further light on the disease's progress."

Frank glanced to Monk, who gave a small nod of acknowledgment. Here were the two kidnapped doctors. Both thankfully alive. It was a small blessing in an otherwise miserable circumstance.

"Let's join Dr. Ngoy." Nolan marched them all toward the clinical lab in back. "We should all listen to his briefing."

Only Frank overheard the woman at his side. "About fucking time," she muttered in French, as she scowled toward the knot of clinicians in the cordoned-off lab.

Despite everything, he could not stop a small smile. He appreciated both her attitude and her frustrated fury. He felt the same.

They reached the back of the ward and ducked through the translucent curtain into a pristine, small lab. He quickly assessed the rows of microscopes, blood analyzers, cell counters, even the polyacrylamide gel electrophoresis equipment for analyzing DNA. He also noted with a pique of anger that much of his own lab equipment had been hauled and dumped here from the university. That included his laptop that ran his customized bioinformatic software. So far, it looked like no one had bothered touching any of it.

Nolan waved to a skinny Congolese clinician. "This is Dr. Ngoy, the head of our facility."

The man joined them. He stood a head shorter than Frank, but he carried himself as if he towered over everyone. Behind his face shield, the man's lips were etched in lines of perpetual disdain. With a glance, Frank knew his type, someone with a clear Napoleon complex.

Dr. Girard crossed her arms and glared at him. Clearly Ngoy held her in no better regard, all but shoving past her to join them. The only one the clinician showed any respect toward was his boss, Nolan De Coster, but even that deference looked like it took effort.

"Sir," Ngoy said stiffly, "I think we've made some significant progress today."

"Wonderful. Perhaps you can share what you've learned with our new guests."

Ngoy glanced Frank and Monk up and down. "Of course," he said, looking none too happy.

Still, the man knew better than to disobey. He led them to a computer monitor. Tapping for a few moments, he brought up an EM image of a raft of virions.

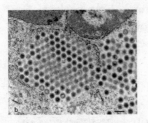

Frank stiffened, immediately recognizing the mass of octagonal structures stitched together by their spiked surfaces. He pushed closer. "I just isolated the same virus from a group of army ants. But I couldn't be certain if the virus was normal for the species or if it was pathogenic." He glanced past the edge of the monitor toward the row of cots. "I had wanted patient samples to confirm what I found."

Nolan's brows lifted. "Truly? You isolated this culprit in less than a day?"

"In under four hours," Monk corrected.

Nolan eyed Ngoy. "It took our team over a week to do the same."

This admission drew a glower from the researcher, his ire aimed at Frank. Still, Ngoy cleared his throat, his back straightening with pride. "That may be so, but today we *were* able to determine the *origin* of this virus, where it came from, specifically its original *host*."

Frank had wondered this from the beginning. The virus had to come from somewhere, spilling over from its natural host into the larger world, where it ultimately proved pathogenic. "What animal did it come from?"

Ngoy gave a small sneer of satisfaction. "It wasn't any animal."

"Then what?" Frank asked.

"It was a plant."

6:03 P.M.

Charlotte noted the shocked look on the American virologist's face. She spoke into the stunned silence. "A plant?" she asked. "Is that even possible? Are you saying this virus came from some tree or bush?"

"Or possibly a tree fungus," Ngoy acknowledged. "We finished analyzing the virus's genetic code, which took longer than we'd hoped due to its 2,236 genes."

"That many?" Frank looked concerned. "That would make this virus one of the largest giants ever discovered."

Charlotte frowned at this statement. *A giant virus?*

Ngoy ignored the American and kept his focus on his boss. "A significant swath of the virus's genome remains unknown and unclassifiable, but a large percentage—and what appears to be the oldest—is shared by both fungal species and ancient tree ferns, possibly tracing as far back as prehistoric *Cladoxylopsids*. They were a fernlike group of giant trees that went extinct millions of years ago, leaving only petrified stumps behind. They're considered by many to be the first trees."

Charlotte shook her head. "But how did you trace this virus's genome to an extinct species?"

Ngoy sighed as if exasperated. Still, his eyes shone brighter. He was clearly proud of his work and excited to elaborate. "Because *Cladoxylopsid*'s genetic descendants exist today. In modern ferns and horsetails. We were able to use recombination clocks to determine that the genes in this virus are far older than anything found in today's living species."

"So, the virus traces back to ancient trees," Nolan mumbled. "Or maybe a fungus tied to those trees."

"It appears so," Ngoy said. "But I'd like to map out a phylogenetic tree and perform a Bayesian analysis to make certain."

Charlotte interrupted. She had a more pressing question as she glanced across the ward to the row of patients. "That's all well and good. But I thought plant viruses couldn't be passed to animals, let alone humans."

"That's not necessarily true," Frank said. "We know three families of viruses—*Bunyaviridae*, *Reoviridae*, *Rhabdoviridae*—that infect humans, animals, and plants. Even the mottle virus from pepper plants can cause fevers and itching in people. Still, such instances are rare. Most plant viruses lack the biochemical key to replicate in mammalian cells. But when it comes to the ingenuity of viruses to evolve and survive, I don't put anything past them."

Charlotte's stomach churned at this thought, but Frank was not done.

"If Dr. Ngoy's team is correct in their supposition, then we have a bigger problem."

"What's that?" Jameson asked next to her, his voice squeaking with nervousness. "What do you mean?"

"I've spent most of my career studying the zoonotic spread of diseases from animals to humans. It's bad enough when a virus passes from its natural host to another. From mammal to mammal. From avian to human. Basically when it leaps from one branch of the evolutionary tree to another. But here we're talking about a virus leaping from *plants* to us. That's an entirely different story. That's a leap from one *trunk* of that evolutionary tree to another."

Frank glanced around the group, letting that sink in, then continued. "It could mark a disaster like no other. It's no wonder this virus seems capable of infecting so many species. Insects, like the ants. Mammals, like the baboons." He waved toward the medical ward. "And us, of course."

Charlotte swallowed, her blood going cold. "You're thinking it could infect nearly every living creature."

Frank shrugged. "It seems like it's already doing that."

For the first time, the implacable Nolan De Coster looked glassy-eyed and worried. He stared unblinking at the computer screen. Clearly, his plan to use this pandemic to wrest control of the Congo now appeared not just callous and risky, but possibly apocalyptic.

Charlotte refused to let this new knowledge immobilize her, to drive her into a black hole of despair. She stared over at Disanka as the woman cradled her son. She needed information that was more practical and useful.

"Dr. Ngoy, you've spent all this time figuring out where this virus came from," she said with acid in her voice, "but what is it actually *doing*? How is it pathogenic? That's more important right now than where it came from."

Ngoy scowled at being questioned, at being challenged. He turned away, as if deaf to her question.

Frank interceded. "I've had some thoughts on that, ever since I saw this bugger on my laptop's screen."

"What do you mean?" Nolan pressed, clearly ready to grasp at anything.

Frank shouldered past Ngoy to reach the computer monitor. He zoomed in and pointed to a lone virion at the edge of the raft of cells. "This virus is already huge. But note the wider spread of the protein spikes extending from its shell."

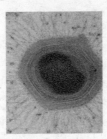

He swung to face the group. "From my scans, I noted that the cytoplasm of infected cells was littered with broken-off spikes. Most were bent and twisted in the same shape and manner. Suspiciously so."

Jameson's eyed narrowed. "Suspicious, why? What are you getting at?"

Charlotte suddenly knew, her limbs going cold. "Are you thinking those discarded spikes might be acting like prions?"

"Possibly. But I'll need to do more research."

"What are prions?" Nolan asked, looking about the group.

Frank explained, "Prions are infectious strings of misshapen protein. They're not living, per se, but they have the ability to replicate and pass their malformation on to normal proteins. They cause various diseases, mostly neurological." He glanced significantly toward the medical ward. "The most common is Creutzfeldt-Jakob disease in humans, a neurodegenerative disorder. Similarly, there's kuru, found in New Guinea, gained from the consumption of brain tissue. And rarer still, fatal insomnia, a deadly condition that doesn't allow the victim to sleep. But in this case, I'm particularly thinking about bovine spongiform encephalopathy."

"Mad cow disease?" Charlotte asked.

"Exactly. A prion disease of bovines. In humans, the symptoms present as depression, loss of coordination, headaches, difficulty swallowing."

Charlotte shared a look with Jameson at this last symptom. She pictured Disanka choking on her stew, the lack of response to the tongue depressor. "Those all sound like early symptoms of this disease."

"Perhaps," Frank said, "but keep in mind, that in cattle, the first symptoms are nervousness, aggression, even frenzy."

"Hence, *mad* cow disease," Nolan noted.

Frank nodded. "Two different presentations of the same prion disease in two different species. Stupor in us, aggression in another."

Charlotte understood. She again heard the howling of the baboons. She pictured the savage attack upon the camp. Even the ravaging floods of army ants.

Jameson pinched the bridge of his nose with his fingers. "But it makes no sense. Those degenerative diseases are slow to manifest. It takes months, if not years."

"True," Frank admitted. "Disease progression takes so long because prions don't replicate very fast on their own. But in this case, they don't have to. If I'm right, the virus here is doing the heavy lifting. The virus replicates quickly, sprouting and seeding those proteinaceous spikes at an incredible rate. We're talking about a prion disease on hyperdrive."

No one spoke for several long breaths.

"Is there any treatment for these diseases?" Nolan asked.

Frank answered with the grim truth: "Presently they can't be cured. We're talking about a chain of protein, not a living organism that can be killed with an antimicrobial. You can certainly treat the symptoms, slow down the progression, but they're all ultimately fatal."

Charlotte refused to accept this. "Still, if you're right, we're talking about a *viral* vector that seeds these particular prions. Surely if we can find a strong enough antiviral, maybe the disease could be stopped."

"We can only hope. But even if we're success-ful, it's not going to help those already infected. The prions have already been planted."

Charlotte realized he was right. She looked toward Disanka with a pang of guilt.

I promised her I'd help her child.

"And remember," Frank added, "we're talking about a virus that could theoretically infect everything in its path. It could be anywhere and everywhere."

Despite her best efforts, Charlotte felt her-self succumbing to despair. "It's like this virus is turning the natural world against us. Ramping up wildlife into a savage state, while leaving us dull and defenseless in its path."

"And that might only be the tip of the iceberg when it comes to this virus," Frank mumbled.

Nolan faced him. "How so?"

Frank shook his head. "All this hypothesizing only applies to those *spikes* on the virus's surface. We've not even begun to consider the genetic engine inside. Those two thousand genes. While many remain unknown, what's *known* seems to be far more ancient than anything found in life today."

"But what else could those genes be doing?" Jameson asked.

Frank opened his mouth as if to explain, then closed his lips again, clearly holding something back. Charlotte wasn't sure she wanted to know.

Frank's stocky assistant nudged the virologist. "Considering what's happening, Frank, if you know something, maybe you'd better share it. I think we're beyond the time for secrets."

Frank heeded this warning. "I . . . I'm not sure. But back at the university lab, an ant pupa hatched. What crawled out bore weird changes. Wings, a barbed stinger. I thought the changes could be from virus-induced mutations. But like I said, I'm not certain. I don't know enough about the *Dorylus* species to be confident of this assessment."

Upon this revelation, Nolan pulled Ngoy to the side and spoke in an urgent whisper.

Frank's shoulders slumped. "I was hoping Benjie could offer more help," he mumbled absently. "Then I would know for sure."

Shocked at hearing this familiar name, Charlotte drew closer. She lowered her voice. "Benjie? As in Benjamin Frey?"

Frank nodded.

Charlotte blinked, a joy bubbling through her. She pictured the firebombing of the village. "He survived . . . how?"

Frank tried to explain. "We rescued him from a raft in the flooded river, along with—"

His words were cut off by a touch on his elbow by his assistant. Frank didn't elaborate further. It seemed some secrets were still warranted.

Charlotte eyed the shaven-headed assistant standing next to Frank. She was suddenly sure that there was more going on here than outward appearances suggested.

Luckily, the brief exchange went unnoticed by their captors. Nolan still had his head bent with Ngoy, discussing some matter that seemed to irritate the head clinician.

"Just show them," Nolan finally snapped as he straightened back around.

"Show us what?" Frank asked.

Nolan headed across the ward with Ngoy, plainly expecting them all to follow. "It's best you see for yourselves."

6:22 P.M.

Monk kept to the rear of the group as it exited the Quonset hut.

Where is this bastard taking us?

He searched as surreptitiously as he could. With every outing, he had tried his best to get a lay of the land. He memorized buildings and tried to get a rough head count on the patrols. He had already identified an outbuilding that was an armory. Past its barred gates, crates and stacks of weapons remained under heavy guard. Another cement-block structure was festooned with antennas and a trio of satellite dishes. Probably the communication nest for this outpost.

Unfortunately, with the sun now down, evening shadowed most of everything. Only a scattering of lights dotted the place. A bonfire lit the center of the square, where a few guards stood limned against the flames. Clearly, their captors wanted this place to look like some hunting lodge from the air. Even the rows of generators humming a constant rumble were hidden under the forest canopy.

Monk rubbed at his prosthetic. He had risked much to be captured with Frank, hoping to leave a line of electronic bread crumbs for Sigma to follow. But he had no way of telling if he had been successful. He was especially suspicious of a wooden pole he had spotted from the air near the riverside pier when they had first arrived. The crownlike cluster of the rectangular plates at the top looked suspiciously like a radio-jamming tower.

For now, Monk would have to assume he was on his own. Strategies played through his head, but they all ended with his recapture. Even if he and the others could escape and cross the river, there were still miles and miles of trackless jungle.

Still, at least his captors had left him with his prosthesis. He might be sleeveless in his blue scrubs, but he still had an explosive trick or two hidden from sight. Buried under his synthetic palm was a hidden knot of C4 wired to a detonator. But it was a weapon of last resort. He only had the one charge, and it would destroy his prosthetic, leaving him with no hope of broadcasting his location.

Better hold off on that for now.

Nolan finally reached a cinder block building and escorted them all through a door. Monk kept a wary eye on the Congolese soldier still guarding them. The man followed them into what appeared to be an animal pen. Stainless-steel cages climbed the walls on either side. Birds battered against bars. Monkeys screeched. Something leonine yowled in fury. The cacophony was deafening inside the windowless space. But even worse was the stinging reek of feces and urine.

At Monk's side, Charlotte covered her mouth

and nose—likely less from the reek and more from the shock. Nolan guided them to a steel door that closed off the back section of the kennel.

"Through here!" he shouted.

He lifted a bar to open the door. They all hurried across the threshold to escape the noise and stench. The next room held only a single cage, a pen that filled the back of the space. The bars ran from concrete floor to roof. A shadowy shape lurked at the back of the pen. It pulled farther away from the light flowing through the open door.

Ngoy crossed to a wall switch and flicked it. An LED lamp ignited brightly overhead, revealing what was caged here.

Charlotte gasped, and Frank swore.

A huge cat—easily two hundred pounds—crouched in a savage hiss, its back arched, hackles high. A tail slashed back and forth. It looked like a jaguar or maybe a cheetah, but it was striped instead of spotted. Even in the bright light, its fur appeared to swirl darkly with every contraction of its muscles. But most frightening of all were its fangs. The snarled lips framed a pair of curled canines. They extended below its jaws, like those of some saber-toothed tiger.

"What is it?" Charlotte eked out.

"That's a good question," Nolan admitted.

It lunged at the sound of their voices, crashing into the bars and bouncing off. A paw slashed back in frustration, scraping bars and floor as it retreated. Hooked black claws gouged the concrete, leaving a wet crimson trail behind. At first, Monk thought the creature was bleeding, but Nolan corrected this delusion.

"Keep well back. There's poison in those claws. A neurotoxin. Similar to what's found in the venom of puff adders. We learned that the hard way."

Frank actually drew closer, cocking his head. "Is it infected with the virus?"

"Definitely," Nolan agreed. "It was trapped by a group of hunters last month. I had sent out teams, to try to discern how much of the jungle might be affected. This is not the first such aberration brought back. You were right to be concerned about what you saw in that newly hatched ant."

Frank nodded to the cat. "How old is it?"

It was a strange question considering what they were facing, but Nolan nodded. "We guess a year at best."

"So, it was likely infected while in utero, altered during embryonic development."

"Like with the ant pupa," Monk said.

Jameson kept near the door. "Still, what the hell is it?"

"It's genetically a cheetah," Nolan answered, confirming Monk's initial guess. "At least 99.8 percent the same."

"So, something changed that other 0.2 percent," Frank said.

Monk knew they all suspected the virus. Still, he gaped at how such small changes could result in this beast. Then again, the difference between the DNA of humans and chimpanzees was less than one percent.

Charlotte drew closer to Frank. "How could that be possible? Random genetic mutations should have ended up with something monstrously disfigured, not a creature so perfectly fit."

"Who says the changes had to be *random*?" Frank countered. "If Ngoy's genetic studies are correct, this virus is carrying genes going back to our earliest evolutionary history. Most of which—like in many giant viruses—we've never seen before. The virus may have honed a genetic mechanism to perfectly pair a known DNA sequence with that of another species. To know what fits. What keys fit what locks."

"And maybe how to lockpick everything else," Monk added.

Frank nodded. "With every generation, we think we understand the mechanism for evolutionary changes. Yet surprises and exceptions abound. Certainly, many changes in species occurs incrementally, one tiny step at a time. A giraffe's neck grows a little longer. A beak alters in a flycatcher. But then there are those cases where there appears to be no middle ground. As if the change occurred spontaneously out of whole cloth, a new species created in a single bound. Much still remains unknown or poorly understood. To this day, there remains no grand unifying theory for evolution."

Monk remembered Frank expressing his belief in the Virus World Theory, how viruses might not be degenerate escapees from living cells, but were far older, possibly the precursors to modern animals and plants. He had even hypothesized how viruses could be the very engines of evolution.

Is that what this virus is demonstrating?

All eyes were on Frank—even the monstrous cat in the cage glared at him. The man finally slumped under the weight of their attention.

"I don't know," he finally admitted. "It's just conjecture at this point. But I do know one thing with absolute certainty."

"What's that?" Charlotte asked.

Frank kept his gaze fixed on the cat. "No one should be out in that jungle."

15

Gray wrestled with the wheel of the huge all-terrain vehicle as it bounced and jostled down the muddy, weed-choked jungle road. Twin beams pierced the dark track ahead.

He had obtained their transportation—a Russian-made Shatun ATV 4X4—from the FARDC military who had commandeered the U.N. camp. It was the perfect jungle trekker, more of a two-ton tractor than a typical ATV. The narrow vehicle towered atop sixty-eight-inch tires. The four-wheeler could climb over tall obstacles, and even float on its giant tires, becoming an unwieldly duck to ford rivers. Also, the Shatun's front compartment articulated independently of the enclosed rear cargo bed, allowing it to navigate tight bends, even do a U-turn on the spot.

"How much farther?" Gray shouted over the rumble of the diesel engine.

Faraji rose from the passenger seat and leaned

out the windshield that had been flipped open. He searched ahead, then sat back. "Not far," he concluded.

Gray fought not to roll his eyes. That had been the kid's answer for the past several miles. They had left the camp by this jungle road four hours ago. While the ATV had a maximum speed of thirty miles per hour, Gray had never approached that limit due to the difficult terrain. Still, they had to be a good sixty miles from the camp by now.

Gray drove another painstaking mile into the night—then Faraji jerked straight and pointed. "*Ni huko!* There, there!"

Gray squinted at the spread of jungle to either side. The beams of his jostling headlamps revealed nothing but impenetrable dark walls. He slowed the ATV to a crawl.

Faraji waved toward a slight break in the forest ahead.

"That's the road to the lake we're looking for?" Gray asked. "You're sure?"

He nodded vigorously. "*Ndiyo.*"

Kowalski leaned forward from the rear bench, which he shared with the biology postgrad, Benjie Frey. The big man had been dozing on and off during the trek here, but he never relinquished his hold on his DARPA weapon, the flat-nosed Shuriken. Gray had his own weapon slung over his shoulder, a large KelTec P50 handgun. The fifteen-inch-long semi-automatic pistol held fifty rounds, each capable of piercing body armor from two hundred yards away.

Kowalski scowled as they pulled up to the

turnoff. "That don't look like any road. More like an overgrown rut."

Gray didn't disagree. If not for Faraji, he would have easily missed the gap between the two towering palms. The track was thickly over-grown, showing not even a footpath through the thick vegetation. It looked as if no one had passed through here in ages. Then again, these jungles grew at a riotous pace, quickly filling in an empty place in a frenzied competition for resources.

"That the way," Faraji insisted.

Gray had to take the kid at his word. He didn't even have satellite navigation to guide him. Shortly after leaving the camp, he had stopped and disabled the vehicle's GPS system so they couldn't be tracked. With the level of corruption here, he couldn't trust that someone in the military might alert the enemy.

Gray shifted back into drive and made a sharp turn onto the side path. The giant tires had no difficulty riding over the undergrowth. Still, their pace quickly became a slow, bumpy crawl as the way forward grew narrower. A tight squeeze between a pair of giant cedars scraped most of the paint off the sides of the ATV.

"Hope you weren't planning on getting your deposit back," Kowalski groused from the back seat, peering over his shoulder.

Gray didn't object to the big man's looming presence, not even the reek of the cigar butt smoldering between his teeth. He wanted all eyes on the trail. While the headlamps helped illuminate the way forward, that *way* became more and more difficult to discern. By now, the overgrown path looked nearly indistinguishable from the surrounding jungle. Still, Faraji assured them they were on the right trail.

Benjie squeezed forward, too. His eyelids blinked rapidly in a nervous tic. "Maybe we should stop and wait for sunrise. Make sure we don't get totally lost in the dark."

Throughout the journey, the biologist had been keeping a wary watch on the jungle. Gray understood the young man's apprehension. Benjie had to be worried about what the forest hid, especially after the events of last night: the attack by the baboon tribe, the chaos and bloodshed that followed.

"We need to keep moving," Gray said. "Another series of storms is due to hit the area. We can't risk getting bogged down if the rain becomes heavy."

Gray had other reasons for haste, too. Any delay in their search meant more lives would be lost. Plus, he was all too cognizant of the unknown enemy dogging their efforts.

With no other choice, he continued into the night. As he did, the forest awoke around them. Scores of bats flitted through the beams of their lights. Something large—maybe a boar—barreled across the brush ahead and vanished into the dark. Over the rumble of the ATV's diesel engines, sharp screeches and haunting howls reached them.

Faraji finally leaned forward and pulled the windshield back into place, sealing the vehicle.

"About time," Kowalski grumbled.

Gray forged ahead. They crossed a dozen

swollen streams and mucked their way through swampy grounds. He weighed the difficulty of the task ahead, to follow William Sheppard's historical trail to some lost kingdom, a place considered cursed by the local tribes. The effort seemed impossible. The Congo basin, with its jungles and savannas, covered over a million square miles, roughly half the size of the continental United States. It could hide almost anything. The difficulty would be *finding* what was buried here.

He remembered the last of Sheppard's photos. It showed a pair of vine-encrusted pillars that flanked a dark crack into a forested cliff. He pictured the two words scrawled on the back: Mfupa Ufalme. The Kingdom of Bones.

With each passing mile, his anxiety grew.

Even if we find the place, will it offer any answers?

He found himself pressing harder on the accelerator, setting a faster pace. The ATV rumbled and rattled through the jungle. At one point, a huge gray monitor lizard, easily seven feet long, sped away from their path, glaring back at the ATV. It looked prehistoric, reminding Gray of the agelessness of this forest. It was as if they were falling back in time.

Faraji reached over and grabbed his arm. "*Okapi ziwa!*"

The kid pointed toward a distant glint of moonlight off of water. Gray had thought it was another stream. But as he drove closer, the dark mirror grew wider and brighter. Its edges spread into the surrounding forest. The recent monsoons must have overflowed the lake's banks.

Gray slowed as he approached the shore. He

had originally imagined the place would be no more than a large pond, but the lake covered tens of acres. A haze of gnats and mosquitoes hovered over its flat surface. At their approach, a whole battalion of frogs leaped and splashed into the lake. A huge white heron took off from a nest in the reeds and swept slowly over the water.

"Is this the place?" Kowalski asked.

Faraji nodded, *"Okapi ziwa."*

Benjie shifted forward. "It's so big. Where do we even begin our search? It could take us days."

Gray knew the biologist was right. He left the ATV engine idling and pulled out the sheaf of seven photos, now protected in a waterproof sleeve. He removed the topmost picture and compared the lake in the photo to the view ahead. He searched for telltale landmarks that might confirm the two were indeed the same. In the old picture, a large boulder sat at the lake's edge. A similar rock in the shape and contour poked out of the flooded lake near the north bank.

Faraji was right. This is definitely the place.

He flipped the picture over and again studied the sketch of an okapi at that lake's edge, knowing the drawing had to be important.

Gray frowned, unable to discern its significance. Still, Sheppard must have led them to this lake for a reason. But what could it be? He suspected the answer was beyond his ability to solve. But hopefully not for another.

He twisted in his seat. "Faraji, the Reverend Sheppard tailored his clues for your people." He brought the photo higher. "Does this sketch mean anything to you? Does it offer any hint at *where* we should look for his next clue?"

Faraji bit his lower lip and squinted at the drawing. He finally simply shrugged helplessly. "Maybe Woko know more. Not me."

The boy winced with shame, maybe guilt.

Gray recognized the weight being placed on the boy's shoulders. The loss of the shaman—Faraji's mentor—clearly ate the boy's confidence.

Still, Gray refused to give up. The image of the okapi had helped identify this lake, one known only to the Kuba. It was here that the tribe had once hunted that rare giraffid. In the sketch, the okapi even had chain around a hind leg, indicating its capture.

Gray tapped a finger on that chain and closed his eyes. He tried to discern Sheppard's intent in drawing it. He pictured the tribe hunting and capturing one of the okapi, of them securing it in place, but *where* would that happen?

Then he suddenly knew.

He opened his eyes and stared hard at Faraji. "Did your people keep a *camp* here? Somewhere along the shore where they would regularly stay? Where they might bring any animals they had captured or killed?"

Faraji nodded. He turned and pointed along the curve of the southern bank, to where a snaking stream emptied into a wide cove in the lake. "We make camp over there. Good fishing and hunting. Very good."

That's gotta be the place.

Gray faced back around. "Then we'll begin our search there."

He got the ATV moving again. Rather than following the long curve of the flooded shore-line, he trundled straight into the water. Crushing through reeds, he headed through the lake's shallows. The huge tires found traction in the silty lake bed, and where it didn't, the thick treads turned the tires into paddlewheels. It did not take them long to reach the stream-fed cove.

As Gray climbed onto shore again, Faraji pointed ahead to a small fern-covered clearing. The axed stumps of trees protruded from the undergrowth. Gray also noted a trio of rock circles, likely marking old firepits.

"Kuba make camp there," Faraji confirmed.

Gray drove the ATV into the clearing and parked. He then turned to the group. "We'll split up into two teams and search the area. I'll take Faraji with me. Kowalski, you go with Benjie."

Kowalski eyed the biologist dubiously, then turned back to Gray. "What are we even looking for?"

"I don't know. Anything suspicious or out of place. Sheppard must've led us here for a reason."

They all clambered out of the ATV and stretched their legs. They were immediately beset by clouds of mosquitoes. Gray waved the photo in hand to hold them at bay. He then lifted the picture. From this position, the boulder in the lake matched the view from here. It confirmed that Sheppard must have taken this photo at the campsite over a century ago.

Satisfied they were looking in the right place, Gray called to the others. "Let's move out."

The two groups headed in opposite directions from the ATV. They set about searching their respective halves of the clearing. The rings of rocks did mark old campfires. The circles were full of thick layers of ash. Littered across the site were bits of camp detritus: a dented tin cup, a moldy coil of rope, an antelope skull with broken antlers, even a scattering of old shell casings, indicating the Kuba's hunting techniques were no longer limited to arrows and spears.

As Gray searched, he tried to imagine how this place must have once looked, when the now-endangered okapi had flourished here, when the tribe had lived more in harmony with the forest.

This group's hunt slowly spread outward from the clearing to the ring of trees. He paused at the edge and pulled out the second photo that Sheppard had taken. The picture was dated three days after the first.

He studied the image in the moonlight, hoping the context of this location would add meaning. The photo showed Sheppard in a white colonial outfit, missing only his usual helmet. He stood before a group of tribesmen who were kneeling as if in prayer. This impression was further reinforced by what was drawn on the back. He flipped it over. A cross had been sketched atop a hill with a zigzagging path to its summit.

He had shown the photo and drawing to Faraji earlier, but the youth had only given him an apologetic shake of his head. Still, this lack of knowledge further reinforced Gray's belief that Sheppard must have left behind some clue at the lake that would help guide them toward that next site pictured on the second photo.

With certainty and frustration growing in equal measures, Gray continued his search along the clearing's edge. Mosquitoes plagued them. A chorus of croaking mocked their efforts. Bats dive-bombed, bombarding them with ultrasounds that itched the ears. With every step, mud sucked at their boots. The steamy humidity glued their clothes to every crevice.

With no success, Gray began to despair, to wonder if it was fruitless search. Even if Sheppard had left a clue back then, it could be long gone by now.

Then a scream jolted Gray out of his misery. He grabbed and swung his KelTec pistol around. Across the clearing, Benjie crashed headlong to the forest floor. The hard impact silenced his panicked cry.

Kowalski rushed to his side.

Gray kept his weapon ready. "Is he okay?" he called over.

"Looks like he fell over his own feet." Kowalski extended a hand to help Benjie up, but the offer was rebuffed.

Benjie rolled around and dug through the undergrowth. He finally sat higher and lifted something muddy in his hands. He wiped at it, revealing a length of thick silvery links.

It was a chain.

7:34 P.M.

Benjie stepped back to let the others examine what he had found. While he should have been chuffed at his discovery, his cheeks instead burned with embarrassment. He felt daft for not watching where he was walking, for screaming like his mother did when she spotted a mouse in the kitchen.

He squeezed his arms around his chest, using the pressure to calm himself. While low on the autistic spectrum, he still had to contend with how a sharp jangle of his emotions took time to quell. He took deep breaths as he had been taught. He finally swallowed and let his arms relax.

Kowalski patted him on the shoulder, hard enough to almost drop him to his knees. "Good job, kid."

He nodded and backed farther out of the way, lest the man should thank him again.

Gray followed the chain back to where it had been secured around the bole of a red cedar. The growth of bark had nearly swallowed the links. It proved the chain had to be old, placed long ago.

Gray lifted the chain and stared down its length, then eyed his large partner. "Kowalski, help me with this. It's got to lead somewhere."

The two set about extracting the heavy length from where it lay buried under two centuries of mulch and mud. Despite the heavily saturated soil, it still took lots of grunting, digging, and tugging to free the chain, link by link.

Benjie left them to their work. He finally remembered what had distracted him before he fell. He had been following the ambling path of a giant moth. He had a particular affection for moths and butterflies, both for their beauty and their amazing adaptation techniques, a curiosity tied to his own studies of evolutionary pressures on inheritable traits. The moth specimen appeared to have been a *Holocerina angulate*, an African batwing. Its fiery-edged wingspan had stretched seven or eight inches. He had thought the species only grew half that size. Plus, its body had been an iridescent cerulean, which appeared to glow in the dark, though this effect was likely due to the shine of his flashlight reflecting off its carapace.

He searched the forest's edge for it again, but the specimen was long gone.

Disappointed, he returned his attention to the others. They had freed more of the chain and followed its course. Its buried length appeared to aim for the lake.

By now, Faraji had wandered ahead, peering around.

Benjie crossed over to join him. Faraji reached the water's edge and stopped. He kept one eye squinted and absently rubbed at his arms.

"Is something wrong?" Benjie asked.

Faraji stared over the water and skyward. "*Popo* gone."

"*Popo?*"

Faraji kept his gaze above the lake and pantomimed by folding his hands together, forming wings with his fingers. He fluttered his hands through the air.

"Do you mean birds?" Benjie asked.

"Not *ndege. Popo.*" He fluttered his hands again for emphasis.

Benjie frowned. Then he realized it wasn't just the sky that Faraji was studying with suspicion. It was the *night* sky. "You must mean bats," he mumbled.

Only now did Benjie realize the constant hum and quickfire flights of the bats had stopped. They were gone. Benjie wanted to dismiss their absence as just the cessation of their natural feeding time, but he knew better than to doubt Faraji, who was far more attuned to the rhythms of the jungle.

Before he could inquire further, a gruff voice shouted at them. "Out of the way, boys!"

He turned as Kowalski yanked the chain and stripped it out of the lakeside muck, bursting the links right at their heels. The two danced to either side. The huge man followed the freed chain to the water's edge, trailed by Gray. Kowalski pulled more of its length out of the water. The wet links glowed in the moonlight.

"Getting easier now," Kowalski commented and waded up to his knees to grab more of the chain.

He secured a two-handed grip, dug in his legs, and pulled hard. Still, the length fought him. It just shivered in place, its end vanishing into the black water.

"Shoulda kept my mouth shut," Kowalski said.

Gray joined him on firmer footing at the lake's edge. "You two, give us a hand. It may take all of us to free the rest."

Faraji and Benjie circled around to grab the chain.

"On three, we all pull," Gray ordered.

Benjie braced to help as best he could. Gray counted down, and they all hauled on the chain. It felt like a tug-of-war with an elephant.

No way we can move this . . .

Kowalski disagreed. "Keep going," he grunted. "It's giving way."

Benjie's palms burned, his back ached, but he fought, refusing to relent. Finally, they all went tumbling backward as whatever anchored the chain finally dislodged.

Benjie untangled himself from the pile and kicked away from the chain. The others did the same, and they all stood up. Gray grabbed the loosened chain and hauled its length hand over hand, dragging it out of the water, as if pulling in a fishing line. From the strain on the man's face, it took considerable effort. Whatever was at the end of the chain was heavy.

Finally, something crested the water, fastened to the last link. It appeared to be a sealed chest, the size of a breadbox, all bolted of the same steel as the chain.

"Is it wrong to hope it's full of gold?" Kowalski asked.

Gray scowled and dragged the crate through the shallows toward shore—unfortunately that wasn't all that the chain lured from the water.

Behind the crate, a huge form burst out of the lake with an explosion of water. It was all armor and scale and speed. It was a massive crocodile, easily a half ton. The beast shot past the box and raced toward shore, aiming straight for Gray.

The American stumbled backward, falling on his backside. He fumbled for the weapon slung over his shoulder, but there was no time.

Luckily, Kowalski reacted instantly, swinging up his own weapon. He squeezed the trigger, but rather than loud gunshots, the weapon gave off a high-pitched pneumatic whine. From the funnel-shaped barrel, a rain of silver flashed through the air. The reeds were mowed down as if cut by a scythe. Silver bounced off the crocodile's armor, but some pieces struck softer tissue and imbedded in place. One split the beast's left eye.

Under the barrage, the crocodile slammed to a stop, writhed around, and rolled back for the lake. Kowalski encouraged its flight with a few well-place single shots. The beast quickly vanished into the depths.

"Thanks," Gray said and allowed himself to be pulled up by his partner.

"No problem. I've been itching to try this out."

Faraji retrieved one of the weapon's strange silvery bits of ammunition from the shore's mud. Benjie stepped over. It was a razored disk, an inch across. It looked like a tiny Japanese throwing star, which the weapon—the Shuriken—was surely named after.

Faraji eyed the rifle with clear lust.

Kowalski noted the boy's attention. "Don't even think about it. This baby's all mine."

Gray ignored them and hauled his treasure out of the lake. He unhooked the box from the chain, picked it up, and carried it toward the ATV. They all followed, putting plenty of distance between them and what else might lurk in the water.

Gray set the box down near the ATV's open tailgate. He examined it for a breath, then worked the latch free after yanking out a locking pin. "Let's hope there's more than just gold in here."

He hauled open the lid, which appeared snug and watertight. Inside, something had been rolled and fitted in place. Gray reached with both hands and cradled it out. He lifted it up to the open cargo space of the ATV, and with great care, he unrolled it there. It appeared to be a beaded prayer rug. It looked intricately woven, made of raffia fibers, all strung with glass beads, bits of fur, tiny triangles of copper, and thousands of cowrie shells.

"What is it?" Kowalski asked.

"An example of Kuba handiwork." Gray nodded to Faraji. "His tribe is known for their fine textiles."

"So, we risked our lives for some fancy cloth," Kowalski said. "Fat lotta good that does us."

Benjie agreed with the American. He knew the Kuba were renowned for their clothwork and the intricate geometric patterns woven into them. This example, though, looked to have been hastily made. There appeared to be no rhyme or reason to its design, certainly no discernible pattern.

"It has to mean something," Gray said. "Why else would Sheppard have sunk it into the lake?"

They all knew only one of their party could help from here.

Gray leaned closer. "Faraji, does this mean anything to you?"

The boy frowned darkly. "Maybe . . . but it hides the truth."

"How do you mean? Can you show us?"

Faraji hesitated, but then stepped closer. He reached toward the tapestry's top, as if to lift it out of the cargo space. Instead, with reverent care, he rubbed his palm down its length, running from top to bottom. He gently turned beads and shells until they reached some preset stopping point. He had to do this over and over again, sometimes pressing harder, other times passing only a single finger down the cloth.

At first, there didn't seem to be any difference, but slowly as each tiny piece threaded into the raffia was spun into its proper place, an image arose within the textile. It grew clearer with each pass until finally the pattern was complete.

It wasn't geometric, but rather a mosaic made up of copper, shells, and glass beads. It looked like a cubist or pointillist painting of a small stone church with a prominent cross in front of it, all half-buried in a dark jungle.

Gray turned to Faraji. "Do you recognize this place?"

Faraji nodded. "I know. It is missionary church. The Reverend Sheppard's." He made the sign of the cross, as if seeking a blessing. "It is his first church."

"Do you know where it is?"

Faraji pointed deeper into the jungle, farther east of their position.

"Can you get us there?" Gray asked.

Faraji's shoulders slumped. "Maybe. It is old. I went only once. No trail any longer."

Kowalski groaned. "In other words, we gotta go straight through the jungle."

No one looked happy at this prospect.

Still, Gray drew out a digital pad and opened up a glowing terrain map. "Can you give us a rough estimate of where we need to go?"

Faraji joined him, clearly intending to try.

As the two murmured together, a flicker of movement drew Benjie's eye to the left. He turned in surprise. With a smattering of joy, he recognized the fluttering return of the large moth that had attracted his attention earlier. It wafted across the clearing. With each beat of its flame-edged wings, its body seemed to flash a signal of greeting at him. Like some softer version of a firefly seeking a mate.

He gaped in shock, realizing its carapace truly was glowing on its own.

Amazing . . .

Then joy turned to concern. Especially as the jungle behind it was dotted with thousands of the same moths, all glowing in the shadows, as if summoned by the first. He blinked and turned a full circle. They were everywhere, in all directions. Hundreds of them even floated overhead, while more closed in all around.

Focused on the raffia, no one had noted their silent approach. Benjie remembered Faraji's earlier concern about the vanished bats. Had they sussed out what was coming and retreated?

Something brushed Benjie's cheek. He jumped back. A moth had fallen from overhead, fluttering down like an autumn leaf. He reached to his cheek, feeling a burn setting in. As he lifted his arm, the moth alighted on the back of his hand. He stared, momently mesmerized by the beauty of its wings, all shades of black, like a shadow come to life, but its edge blazed a fiery orange.

Then his hand ignited, burning as if he had been struck by a torch.

Gasping, he shook the moth free. Where it

had roosted, his skin was bright red, already blistering; his cheek was also on fire. Panicked, he turned toward the others.

Only Kowalski seemed to have noted the moths descending on them. "What's with all the butterflies?"

Benjie's affected arm began to tremble and spasm. His vision narrowed. He feared the worst, that the chemical burn carried some neurotoxin. Before he could speak, his breathing grew constricted, labored.

Still, as the world darkened, he managed to gasp out a warning. "We're under attack . . ."

16

Tucker swam the last of the way across the dark river. The sliver of moon and mist-shrouded stars cast little light. Still, it was enough to guide him, especially with his DARPA goggles in night-vision mode. The scopes were also enhanced with thermal imaging for detecting heat signatures through dust and smoke.

He had to assume the enemy might be similarly equipped and watching the river. So, he kept his head hidden behind a log, which he had rolled into the river and kept moving downstream toward the island. The log also hid Kane, whose vest helped keep the dog afloat, enough that all his partner had to do was paddle his legs. Kane was an old pro at this, raising not even a single splash.

Tucker crossed slowly beside his partner, matching their speed with the current. He watched both the island and the river's flat surface. He didn't know if there were any crocodiles in the area, or even more worrisome, hippos. The latter were the true sharks of these waters, as dangerous as they were fast. It was for that reason he also proceeded slowly. He did not want to draw attention his way.

Finally, he let out a sigh of relief when his bare feet touched the silty, algae-covered bank of the island. The forest was a black wall before him, even under the light-intensifying surveillance of his goggles. He let go of the log and pushed it back into the current. It rolled away and continued its course downriver.

Tucker kept low, listened for a few breaths, then climbed into the dense brush. Kane followed. Before sunset, he had picked out this landing site, where the forest looked thickest on the opposite side of the island from the pier. He figured most personnel were posted on that other half of the island.

Tucker moved gingerly, careful where he stepped, what he brushed against, especially since—except for his goggles and the camo paint over his face—he wore only a pair of soaked boxers. After a minute of trekking, he found a deadfall that offered some shelter. He stopped and slipped the waterproof go-bag off his shoulder. With Kane keeping watch, he pulled back into his boots and dry clothes—though *dry* was a relative term considering their sweaty state.

He also resecured his Desert Eagle to his hip and pushed two extra magazines into his belt holster. Armed and dressed, he felt a hundredfold less vulnerable. He also double-checked the three egg crates in the bag. They held the additional armament supplied by Sigma's director: flash-bangs, smoke charges, and explosive grenades.

Satisfied, Tucker turned his attention to his partner. Kane's eyes were glued to the forest, his ears swiveling at every rustle of leaves or rattle of branches. Tucker tugged the camera stalk out of the dog's vest's zippered pouch and positioned it in place. He also fitted Kane with an external bandolier across the vest, a bit of handiwork specially designed by Tucker. He checked the bandolier's wireless antennae and made sure its battery was fully charged.

He then sat back and smiled his appreciation—not for the hardware, but for the dog underneath it all.

Who's the handsomest boy?

As if reading his mind—and maybe he did—Kane wagged his tail and butted his nose into Tucker's chest.

"You're raring to go, aren't you," he whispered.

The tail slashed faster.

"Then let's go knock on the neighbor's door."

8:02 P.M.

Charlotte stared over Frank's shoulder as he worked in the ward's clinical lab. To the side, the virologist's assistant finished setting up the customized equipment brought here with the pair. In the meantime, Frank sat before a laptop that ran bioinformatic software. A deep frown of consternation etched his face.

She kept her arms crossed, feeling useless. Jameson had retreated back to the ward, where he sat looking over a patient's chart, but from the way his head would lower, then bob back up, he was nodding off.

Charlotte didn't blame him. She, too, was exhausted. Even Disanka and her baby boy were sleeping. Still, Charlotte remained alert, intent to learn as much as she could for as long as that *bâtard* Ngoy continued to be cooperative.

Frank seemed determined to be equally supportive. They needed solutions, the whole world did. Like her, he was probably picturing the big cat penned up in the vivarium, a creature possibly altered in utero by the virus. He had asked to see the genome map of the captured cheetah, which Ngoy had transferred to Frank's laptop.

Frank had spent the past half hour studying the columns and bars that defined the beast's DNA and compared the correlating run of nucleobases—a code of A, C, G, and Ts—to a normal cheetah's genetic code. The research team had marked the locations of a small percentage of genes that were judged to be foreign.

Frank tapped a finger against his lips as he reviewed each change.

Charlotte still found it hard to believe so few alterations had resulted in such dramatic changes. She was more baffled at how these tiny genetic changes had resulted in perfectly adapted phenotypic expressions: longer canine teeth, a muscular bulk, even how the scents glands normal for a cheetah's paws had been incorporated with venom-producing cells.

It was a mystery that Frank concentrated on now.

"There has to be an answer hidden here," he mumbled to himself. "I don't understand how this virus has such deep pockets."

Charlotte shifted closer. As a physician, she knew plenty about viruses, just not to the extent of a virologist. Still, she wanted to help, if only to act as a sounding board for Frank's conjectures.

"What do you mean by deep pockets?" she asked.

Frank pointed to the marked-off sections of DNA. "These bits of altered genetic code in the cheetah are incorporated precisely into its DNA. They're stitched too perfectly in place, as if they were engineered there. Now, maybe this ancient virus has been a genetic pickpocket for millennia, gathering genes from untold number of species, tracking the evolution of life on this planet by storing some of that evolving code into its own DNA. Still, it makes no sense."

Charlotte remembered Frank mentioning something along those lines back in the vivarium. "Why?" she pressed him.

"While the Omnivirus is huge, it still only has two thousand genes."

Frank had come to calling the contagion by that name. *Omnivirus*. It seemed appropriate considering how the virus was capable of infecting all life.

"Statistically," he continued, "it seems farfetched that this bugger just happens to have those specific sets of genes at hand to fold into the cheetah's DNA. And that's just this *one* species. What about the changes in the army ants? Or the baboons? And according to De Coster, his hunters collected other altered animals over the past several weeks. How could this Omnivirus have all those perfectly adaptable genes at the ready?"

Charlotte began to understand. "You're right. It can't."

Frank sighed in exasperation.

Charlotte glanced over to Ngoy, who had his head bent with the other clinicians. She lowered her voice. "According to that bastard, his research team has already mapped the Omnivirus's two thousand genes. If the virus inserted its own genes into the cheetah's DNA, then you should be able to find those same genes in the virus. Right?"

Frank nodded. "True. Dr. Ngoy gave me the virus genome already. Let me try something using the software I developed."

His fingers flew over the keys and trackpads. Windows opened and closed. One half of the screen scrolled with streams of nucleobases, sections of which occasionally flashed in crimson or blue. He worked in silence for ten minutes— then sat back with a shake of his head.

"That makes even less sense," he muttered.

By now, his stocky assistant, Monk, had joined

them. "Frank, why do you look like someone tap-danced on your grave?"

"The new genes in the cheetah." He looked back at them. "They're not in the virus at all."

Charlotte frowned. "How can that be?"

"I did find bits and pieces of code that make up those genes, but they're scattered throughout the viral genome. They're not intact. It's almost like the Omnivirus has all the basic ingredients for those new genes—the flour, the sugar, the yeast—and somehow baked up those new ones on its own, combined those disparate parts to form genes specifically suited for the cheetah."

"Can viruses do that?" Monk asked.

"Maybe. I don't know, but a few years ago, researchers in France discovered that another giant virus—Mimivirus—had evolved its own CRISPR-like technique to defend itself."

"CRISPR?" Charlotte had heard of that tool. Geneticists used it to edit genomes. It was so precise that it could clip out a single nucleobase in a DNA code and replace it with another. "A virus could do that? Do its own gene-editing?"

"That one could. In fact, the CRISPR technique was first identified in bacteria. It was how scientists developed this method in the first place. They copied it from a bacterium."

Monk had gone pale. "So, you're thinking this Omnivirus is running its own gene-editing machine shop?"

"Like I said before, I wouldn't put anything past a virus when it came to its survival." Frank rubbed a knuckle between his eyebrows, as if working out a headache. "Especially with giant viruses. We still know so little about them. Take the Yaravirus. That giant was discovered in 2003. To this day, not a single gene in that species is recognizable. They're totally alien to anything that scientists have mapped so far."

"Which is true for much of the Omnivirus's DNA, too," Monk reminded them.

Charlotte considered this and took into account Frank's earlier description. "Maybe they're not even *genes*," she said.

Frank frowned but nodded for her to continue. "What are you getting at?"

"Maybe the Omnivirus's entire genome—or at least, its vast majority—is really just a giant pantry for those ingredients, a storehouse of raw genetic material waiting to be used."

Frank sat straighter. "Which it then cobbles together and engineers to suit its purpose."

"But what is that purpose?" Monk asked. "What is it trying to do?"

"There's little I understand about this virus, but I can answer that." Frank turned to them. "It wants to *survive*, to rid the world of threats to its existence. It certainly seems capable of turning the natural world into a more savage and deadly state."

"While weakening us by turning us dull and somnolent." Charlotte looked out across the beds of the medical ward.

"And maybe it does that on purpose," Frank said. "There are certainly other examples of pathogens that create a weird dynamic between predator and prey. Take the protozoan parasite *Toxoplasma*. It infects cats, but when it gets passed onto their prey, namely rodents, it has a strange neurological effect on them. It makes those rats and mice more docile, less fearful of predators, making them easier prey for cats."

"You're thinking something like that might be going on here," Monk said.

"Maybe those prion spikes the virus excretes were purposefully designed to shut down animals with *higher* intelligences, those with bigger brains, species that might pose the greatest risks to the virus's survival. While at the same time, making all other animals more dangerous."

Monk nodded. "Creating the perfect storm for wiping out a species that might pose the greatest threat."

"Namely us," Charlotte added.

With night setting in, she heard the howls and cries from the nocturnal jungle.

It's as if all of Nature is about to turn against us.

Frank seemed to have the same worry. "I can't begin to fathom how this dynamic came about," he said. "But Mother Nature always seeks an equilibrium, to return to a balance when it becomes unsettled. It often does this through ecological and evolutionary changes, but also through population control."

He stressed the latter with a strong look at them.

"We've seen it before," Frank continued. "It was our intrusion into stable environments—building roads through jungles, deforestation projects—that released the world's greatest plagues upon the world. Malaria, yellow fever, Ebola. Even HIV came from these very jungles in the Congo, going back to the earliest cases in the 1920s, where it first appeared, spreading along historic trade routes."

"In other words," Monk said, "don't mess with Mother Nature."

Frank nodded. "Or she'll bite you in the ass."

Charlotte stared out at the ward. She couldn't discount this possibility as to the origin of this virus, but she sensed they were missing an important piece of this puzzle. She suspected they would never discover it here. If there was an answer, it was out there in the jungle.

"For now," she said, "maybe we'd better concentrate on finding a way of helping the people here—and throughout the Congo. First thing we need to do is find a cure, and if not that, at least some treatment."

Monk shifted closer, his voice a breathless whisper. "No. The *first* thing we need to do is find a way off this island."

Charlotte knew he was right. She had little faith in Ngoy and his team, and even less when it came to their boss, Nolan De Coster. She looked over at Frank's assistant and noted the hard glint in his eyes. His facade of subservience had vanished, replaced by a steely determination. She sensed a lethality to him, as if she were standing next to a caged lion.

She suddenly knew he was no mere assistant.

Who the hell is this guy?

8:28 P.M.

Tucker lay sprawled in a nest of ferns at the edge a small colonial outpost. He studied the cluster of dilapidated buildings with rusted tin roofs and vine-encrusted stone walls. They all centered on the steeple of a white-washed church. It would be easy to dismiss the place from the air. There were probably a hundred old towns like this, abandoned and swallowed by the jungle.

Only this outpost had been recently refurbished, or at least some of the outbuildings had, like the two-story colonial guesthouse next to the church. Then there was the newer pier that jutted into the river on the far side from Tucker's position.

After making landfall, he and Kane had scouted a full circle around the place. They had to move slowly, avoiding patrols, listening for the telltale whirring and clomping of the Q-UGVs. The patrols moved in pairs, either two men, or a guard and one of those robotic dogs. The enemy had made no effort at hiding their passage, often talking, joking, laughing. Their lack of furtiveness suggested they had no fear of a covert attack. They were likely guarding against something noisier, either a raid by one of the local militias or an attack by guerrillas.

Still, this worked to Tucker's advantage. He had made a complete circuit of the outpost without being spotted. He wanted to get a proper lay of the land before attempting anything more. At the pier, he had counted five sleek watercraft, along with a handful of jet skis, even a sixty-foot yacht that looked like an armored gunboat. The fleet was guarded over by a pillbox made of sand-bags buried at the forest's edge. From that forti-fied spot, a Russian-made Kord 12.7mm heavy machine gun pointed toward the dock.

A lone guard lolled there, smoking a ciga-rette. Focused on the river, the man failed to note Tucker and Kane slipping past behind him. As Tucker suspected, most of the attention and patrols concentrated on the dockside end of the island. Once he confirmed this detail, he left Kane hidden in the forest over there, then circled back to the darker, less patrolled edge of the outpost.

Two questions remained.

Am I even at the right place? And are the others even here?

While scouting, he had continually monitored the outpost. It was poorly lit with only a scatter of sodium lamps and a bonfire in the central square. Still, his night-vision goggles pierced the shadows well enough. He had not spotted any sign of Monk or Frank. At this late hour, maybe they were locked up in some cell for the night.

Tucker kept close watch on two of the build-ings. He had noted men in white lab jackets going in and out of a Quonset hut, suggesting it was a hospital or a research station. Before Tucker had set out, Painter had told him that the kidnappers had absconded with Frank's lab equipment. If they had done that, it suggested they wanted the virologist's expertise, and if that hut was indeed a lab of some sort, maybe Frank was holed up inside.

The other building where Tucker focused his

attention was the colonial guesthouse. From all the comings and goings there, it had to be the outpost's headquarters. Unfortunately, there was no vantage point from which he could watch both places. Recognizing that, he had taken up a position closest to the guesthouse. In turn, he had instructed Kane to remain on the opposite side of the compound, where the dog's camera remained fixed on the laboratory hut. The only problem with this plan was that Kane's video feed had become patchier and more sporadic due to the local jamming. He had come to suspect the enemy must communicate on a coded frequency with their robotic guard dogs to keep them moving.

Still, for the moment, Kane's transmission fared well enough.

Now to wait . . .

As he did, he hated not having Kane at his side, but his partner still felt close. Kane's breathing whispered in his ear. He heard the occasional shift of his partner's body among the leaves. With the camera stalk raised, he even saw through Kane's eyes. It was that intimacy that gave him his first warning.

Kane growled, just a rumbling.

Tucker focused on his partner's camera feed inside his goggles. He watched a group exit the Quonset hut. They all wore matching blue scrubs, guarded over by a tall Congolese soldier with a rifle. Even from that distance, Tucker spotted the towering form of his friend Frank. Kane rumbled again, likely also recognizing the veterinarian, a man who had cared for the dog throughout his years in the army.

The group was marched away at gunpoint. They quickly disappeared out of Kane's view. Tucker held his breath. Then the group reappeared in the central square, illuminated by the bonfire. With the group closer to him, Tucker identified Monk by his shaved head glowing in the firelight. The other two in blue scrubs were a young woman, her dark hair tied in a ponytail, and an older man with gray hair and a goatee. Painter had shown Tucker photos of the two missing U.N. doctors.

That's got to be them.

The Congolese guard herded the group toward the two-story guesthouse, confirming Tucker's supposition that it was the outpost's headquarters.

Must be where they're keeping them for the night.

He waited until the group was led inside, then counted off a full three minutes. He wanted the group somewhere safe and together. His plan required perfect timing.

Once satisfied, he subvocalized his commands to Kane. "*BRAVO PATTERN. ON MY MARK.*" He counted another twenty seconds to be extra cautious. "*Go!*"

17

Monk stifled a yawn as the cell door clanked closed behind their group. He studied the cement-block cell, noting the steel bars on the windows, the row of cots along one wall.

Home sweet home.

The two U.N. doctors headed toward a set of disheveled beds. Clearly the two had spent a night here already. Frank merely scowled at their accommodations.

Monk glanced back to the scarred Congolese soldier; a former lieutenant named Ekon. "How about some dinner?" he called to the man through the barred door. "It's been a long day."

The man sneered, turning a key to lock them in.

Monk crossed closer, as if to press the matter, but he really wanted to get a better look at the hallway. He studied the pair of cameras mounted high on the wall, one pointed toward the cell door, the other down the hall. Though he failed to spot any microphones, he had to assume the cameras came equipped with them. His group would have to be cautious in speaking candidly in the cell.

As Monk turned away, a sharp blast echoed to him. It came from outside, maybe a short distance from them. Another followed. And another. Everyone froze in place. It sounded like fireworks, but from the tense posture of their guard, it wasn't the Congo's Fourth of July.

A moment later, panicked shouting reached them.

Someone's attacking this place.

Monk quickly calculated. It might be a guerrilla raid, but the timing and coincidence gave him hope. He made a snap judgment call, knowing he might be putting them all at risk.

He stepped to the door and grabbed the bars. "What's happening?" he shouted to the guard, feigning terror as another blast exploded.

Ekon crouched outside the door, his weapon raised to his shoulder, the muzzle pointed down the hallway. "Get back!" he snapped angrily.

Monk obliged, retreating from the door. Only he had detached his prosthesis and left it latched to the bars—just above the lock.

He quickly turned to the others. "Do what he says! Get back!"

He shoved Jameson toward the rear of the cell. Frank must have heard the urgency and shepherded Charlotte with him. The French doctor looked aghast at Monk's disembodied hand, likely having failed to note it was a prosthetic.

Oh, it's much more than that.

Monk tapped a code into the titanium magnetic link that normally locked his prosthetic in place. He pressed the last contact point, then waved everyone toward the floor. "Down! Now!"

The C4 pellet buried under the prosthetic's palm exploded. The blast deafened them all. The flash blinded. The concussion knocked everyone to the floor.

Except for Monk.

Anticipating the blast, he had braced his legs. He shoved back through the hot smoke and toward the door. The explosion had shattered the lock and knocked the gate off one of its hinges.

Ekon lay sprawled in the hallway, caught by the blast, possibly also struck by the door. But he proved to be a tough bastard and already stirred, struggling to his hands and knees.

Monk met his raised head with a boot heel to his nose. Bone crunched in a most satisfying way. The man went down again—this time out cold.

"Hurry!" Monk hollered to the others.

The doctors remained stunned, but Frank got them moving.

Monk retrieved the soldier's assault rifle and tossed it to Frank. It was a weapon best used by someone with two hands. Instead, he relieved Ekon of his holstered sidearm, a black-and-chrome Browning HP. He gripped it, appreciating its heft and weight.

That'll do.

Frank checked the rifle and nodded to Monk.

Monk turned to the two doctors. "Stay close. At our heels. Understood?"

Jameson simply gawked, his eyes huge. He had lost his eyeglasses during the tumult. Charlotte looked ashen, but she nodded.

They all set off down the hall.

Monk led the way.

Let's go see who came to visit.

8:37 P.M.

Under the cover of the dark forest, Tucker tossed a pair of smoke charges toward the colonial outpost. After a five-second delay, they exploded with muffled *whomp*s. Clouds of smoke welled under the canopy. The breeze flowing downriver rolled the pall into the compound.

Tucker followed, keeping under its cover.

He dared wait no longer, especially after hearing a loud blast come from the guesthouse.

What had happened?

As he headed out of the forest, he kept watch on Kane's progress. Upon his earlier command, his partner had fled a zigzag pattern through the jungle on the compound's far side. Tucker had needed Kane to draw attention in that direction, while he attempted to reach the guesthouse. To aid in that endeavor, Tucker had secured a series of flash-bangs and grenades into Kane's bandolier. The crossbody Kevlar satchel could carry a dozen explosive eggs, each individually hung along the harness, which was wirelessly connected to the device in Tucker's hand. With each press of a button, Tucker could drop one of those charges in Kane's wake. They were set on a fifteen-second delay, allowing enough time for the dog to flee before they exploded.

Kane continued through the forest on that side, spreading chaos. The bobbling view of his camera was dizzying, but Tucker trusted Kane to keep out of sight. When the dog wanted, he could become a shadow. And the patrols out there were surely searching for guerrillas or other armed men—not a fleet-footed ghost.

Tucker edged along a row of small outbuildings, keeping ensconced in the roll of smoke. The thermal imaging of his goggles revealed the bright glow of the bonfire in the square. He paused to allow a pair of gunmen to flee past his position, running toward the dockside half of the island.

Once clear, he crossed the last of the distance to the guesthouse. He kept his Desert Eagle pointed ahead, cradled in both hands. By the time he reached the guesthouse, the smoke had dissipated into a haze. Still, he was close. He ducked lower and ran the last of the distance to the steps that led up to the building's raised porch.

A shout and a spate of gunfire stopped him.

The doors burst open ahead of him. A figure—a soldier in jungle khaki—came flying backward across the porch, pummeled by a spurt of rifle fire. He tumbled down the steps and sprawled dead at Tucker's toes.

Tucker retreated as a familiar group in blue scrubs rushed out the same door.

"Frank, Monk," Tucker hissed at them before they mistook him for one of the patrols.

Monk clattered down the steps to meet him. He searched all around, clearly hoping for more than just the lone rescuer. Still, the man immediately accepted the situation at hand. "Tucker, what's the plan?"

"Get our asses out of here."

"Works for me."

Tucker turned and waved them toward the church. "This way."

8:39 P.M.

Charlotte fought her pounding heart and pushed through a threatening paralysis that had nothing to do with a viral infection. She knew she had to keep moving.

She paused long enough to grab the pistol knocked from the dead soldier at the foot of the stairs. She knew guns, going back to her earlier years here, when her family lived in the neighboring Republic of the Congo. No one traveled these jungles without protection.

Monk noted her collection of the weapons with an approving nod.

They set off after the man—Tucker—who had come to rescue them. Clearly from the explosions and shouts in the forest, he had come with others. Hopefully enough of a force to get them safely out of here.

They circled behind the tall church, sticking to shadows. Tucker tossed a strategic series of smoke bombs to help hide their path. The muffled pops and wafting pall failed to draw attention in the night. The smoke only thickened the darkness around them. Still, she felt like a leaf blown in a whirlwind. The continuing sporadic blasts out in the forest made her jump each time.

Still, they safely reached the research huts. No one was about. The scientific staff was likely hiding from the attack.

Tucker raised an arm, and the group stopped. "Stay here," he hissed and shifted forward on his own.

As she huddled with the others, she stared across at the medical ward. She pictured Disanka and her baby. She remembered her promise to the woman.

She nudged Monk and pointed. "The patients. We can't leave them here."

"No time," he answered with a pained expression. "Most of them can't even move."

She knew this to be true. By now, a majority of the patients were bedridden, lost in a viral-induced somnolence. But not all of them . . .

"If they're sick," Monk continued, "there's at least medical care here. And ultimately, their best hope is for us to reach outside help as quickly as possible."

Charlotte recognized this to be true. Still, guilt panged her. She could not stomach abandoning Disanka and her child.

Tucker returned to them. Even with the goggles covering most of his face, it was easy to read the worried set to his jaw. He nodded toward the shouts and spatter of gunfire echoing across the forest ahead of them.

"Something's wrong," he warned. "Kane should

have lured the patrols to the south by now, clearing the way for us."

Frank faced the opposite direction. "And we've got company closing in behind us."

Barked orders echoed from the central square. Boots clattered on planked walkways, all aiming toward their position.

Tucker swore, but his attention seemed focused elsewhere. He lifted a handheld device higher. "C'mon, Kane."

Charlotte frowned, staring toward the jungle.

Who all is out there?

8:41 P.M.

Kane crouches as danger closes in from three directions.

On both flanks and ahead.

Retreat is cut off by a chatter of voices, by a wall of sweat and filth. He has led those behind him, luring them in his wake. An order blazes behind his eyes, to take them farther astray.

But other hunters have noticed his trespass and block him from following that order. He holds back a growl of fury and challenge.

He can only wait.

His ears stand tall, picking out the pneumatic whir and clank of metal. Branches break, coming ever closer. His haunches tremor in readiness.

He knows his packmate is blind to the threat that comes. The other does not have his keen nose or sharp ears. It will take sight for the danger to become clear. But Kane trusts his partner with all his heart and bone.

And waits.

Finally, the first of the three stalks into view ahead. It stinks of oil and lightning. Gears hum. Gun mounts swivel for a target. Its senses are muted, dull compared to his own. But he knows that it is also deadly and swift.

Rifle fire from such hunters had chased him twice before.

Then another appears to the right, followed a breath later by a third to the left.

He stays still. He's learned movement draws their attention. Still, soon they will sense his heat, pick out his form. While he had successfully fled a few encounters, three were too many to simply run from.

So, he waits, trusting another.

Then a telltale snap bumps his sternum. A silvery object drops to the ground beneath him. His packmate has finally recognized the threat and seeks to help him.

Kane understands. He has been trained in this maneuver. He also knows he should already be running.

A command reinforces this.

MOVE. DOUBLE TIME!

He disobeys. He has learned the number of beats of his heart it takes before such objects erupt with a flash, a bang, or the shred of burning metal. He waits, trusting himself as much as the other.

The three hunters close a snare around him. One gun mount snaps in his direction, then another, and another.

Now spotted, he leaps back and away.

Gunfire tears around him, but he is gone. He jackrabbits off his hind legs and races away. The three hunters converge where he had been hidden—as an explosion brightens the forest with flame. He is too close. The blast shoves at him, driving him deeper into the forest.

A broken shape crashes through the underbrush.

Kane races onward, beyond the blast, into the embrace of shadow and concealing leaf. Free of the trap, he runs into the dark, ready at last to complete his mission, to lead more hunters astray.

Words reach him.

He hears the pride shining in them and knows them to be true.

GOOD BOY, KANE. GOOD BOY.

8:43 P.M.

Tucker sighed his relief.

That was too close.

He turned to the others. "Kane's off again. But he'll need a few minutes to lead the patrols out of our way. After that, we should be able to make it to the dock."

"I don't think we've got those extra minutes," Frank warned and punctuated it with a few spats of rifle fire directed toward the square.

Men shouted in surprise from that direction. Shadows danced out of view. But such discouragement would not last long.

Frank knew it, too. "We're outgunned and outmanned and too out in the open. We're better off taking our chances in the forest."

"Hang on," Monk said, stepping closer. "Tucker, do you have any more grenades?"

He patted his belt. "Two frags, four flash-bangs."

Monk tucked his pistol into his waistband and held out a palm. "Good. I need to blow a hole in something."

Tucker unclipped one of the tiny explosive charges from his belt and passed it over. Monk frowned at its diminutive size.

"They're meant more for distraction," Tucker explained. "But, in a pinch, they'll do some damage."

Frank fired his rifle again.

"I'd say we're in that pinch," Monk said. "What's the delay after triggering it?"

"Preset for fifteen seconds. But I—"

"That'll do." Monk groaned as he swung away. "Still, we'll have to haul ass."

Tucker watched the man sprint toward a stone-block building and kick through the door. An eruption of hoots, calls, and screams announced his trespass. Monk vanished for several breaths, then rushed back toward them, waving an arm.

"Run!" he shouted. "Get into the forest."

The others immediately took off, as if they knew what Monk had done. Tucker didn't have time to inquire and followed. Frank kept watch on the group's six, sporadically firing wildly behind them. By the time they got under the jungle canopy, Frank had emptied his weapon and scowled at it in frustration.

Then a sharp blast echoed from the cement-block structure.

"Get deeper," Monk urged.

They obeyed, burying themselves farther into the forest.

Tucker sidled up to Monk. "What did you do back there?"

The man simply shrugged. "Enlisted an ally. As they say, the enemy of your enemy is your friend."

Tucker frowned—then heard a screech that iced his blood. It was savage, full of rage, and distinctly leonine. He glanced back.

What the hell . . .

Men began to scream, both in terror and in agonized bloody cries. Gunfire erupted into a panicked firefight. Whatever Monk had freed, it was clearly tearing into the forces back there.

"I'd say that buys us some time," Frank said.

Monk pointed ahead. "Tucker, get us to the dock before our new enlistee catches our scent, too."

Tucker led the way. Despite the threat behind them, he went slowly, making sure Kane had time to draw off as many patrols as possible. Once satisfied that the way was indeed clear, he set a faster pace.

He also subvocalized to his partner. *"DISENGAGE. RETURN SILENT TO ALPHA POINT."*

They crossed the rest of the forest without incident. Lights glowed ahead, marking the riverside pier. Tucker had them hold back, while he scouted ahead. He reached the pillbox that guarded the dock. A body lay sprawled in a bloody ruin, proof that those tiny explosive charges still packed plenty of punch. Kane had planted that first egg just behind the man before running off and leading the patrols in a wild-goose chase.

Tucker searched to make sure no one else was about, then slunk to the pillbox. He crossed to a glass-and-steel case that held a line of boat keys. He used a dagger to break the case's lock, then gathered all of the fobs.

Staying low, he whistled an all-clear to the others.

They hurried out of the forest.

As Frank joined him, his friend eyed the Kord machine gun with appreciation. He tossed aside his empty rifle and set about lifting the heavy weapon from its stanchion, dragging up its belt of large cartridges. "This is more like it."

Monk grinned. "I know a big lug who would be green with envy right now."

"What are we doing?" Charlotte asked, her eyes glassy under the sodium lamp.

"Just waiting on one more," Tucker muttered.

As if summoned by his words, a form broke free of the forest and rushed to his side. "About time you got here, Kane."

The dog huffed and bumped him.

Charlotte looked aghast. "That's Kane? I thought you brought an army with you."

He patted his partner's flank. "I did."

Jameson swallowed and pointed. "Which boat do we take?"

Tucker had already picked one out. "C'mon."

He led the group to the far end of the dock, where a sleek black-and-red cigarette boat was moored. The carbon-fiber racing shell looked like a dagger floating in the dark water. Tucker wanted something swift enough to clear the jamming radius around the island as quickly as possible.

This ought to do it.

He got the two doctors aboard and followed behind them. As Monk and Frank freed the mooring lines, he rushed to the helm and fished out the proper fob, a matching black and red to the boat. He keyed the engine, earning a deafening growl from its beast of an engine.

The challenge, unfortunately, was answered from the forest.

A scream of fury drew all eyes to the foot of the dock. From the forest, a wall of shadows pushed into view. The cat was massive, all muscle and bristling fur. It howled at them, revealing a pair of scimitars for fangs.

Dear god . . .

Monk and Frank threw themselves aboard. Frank struggled to get the stolen machine gun turned toward the beast.

Kane remained on the dock, facing the cat. The shepherd lowered his front end, lips snarling with threat. His hackles were a trembling mane around his throat.

"*To me,*" Tucker ordered.

Kane ignored him, never taking his eyes off the cat, likely reacting to instincts buried in his bones.

"*Now!*" Tucker commanded with a firm shout.

That's not a battle you'll win.

Still, Kane remained planted, staring down the beast.

"Just go," Jameson urged.

Tucker refused. He would not leave Kane under any circumstances.

Luckily, the stalemate ended in a most explosive manner. A rocket-propelled grenade burst from the forest and struck the pillbox. The blast sent sandbags flying high into the air, amidst a whirlwind of smoke and flames.

The cat leaped to the side. It dove headlong into the river with a huge splash and paddled heavily for the far bank.

Unchallenged now, Kane turned with his tail high and hopped into the boat.

With all aboard, Tucker swung around and shoved the throttle forward. The black-and-red dagger shot from the dock, throwing Tucker back against the helm's seat.

Christalmighty, this is fast.

The boat sliced across the water, gaining speed. Tucker aimed downriver, using the current to propel them faster versus fighting it upstream. Once they were far enough away, he tossed the rest of the stolen key fobs overboard.

Let's see them try to follow us now.

Monk joined him, yelling to be heard over the engine. "What's next?"

Tucker pictured Ndaye leaning on the helicopter. "Time to call in the cavalry."

Monk frowned past the stern of the boat.

"What's wrong?" Tucker asked.

"I don't think it's going to be that easy." Monk faced him. "Not when it comes to the bastard who's running this outfit."

8:50 P.M.

On the second floor of the guesthouse, Nolan De Coster paced the length of his office. He tapped a hard fist against his thigh. His jaw ached from clenching for so long.

After the first volley of blasts, security measures had locked down his private room. Metal shutters had dropped across the balcony. Likewise, large sliding bolts had further reinforced the office door, which had a two-inch steel core.

Though he was closed in, a bank of monitors hidden behind a panel offered him a view of every corner of the compound. He had watched as the site had been raided. Even with so many cameras, it was still difficult to discern who led the attack or how many were out there.

Though he knew one person who was definitely involved.

The blast down on the first floor had shaken the entire guesthouse. Afterward, he had reviewed footage of the confinement cell. He had watched Dr. Whitaker's shaven-headed assistant attach his prosthetic hand to the cell door—then a blinding blast took out the cameras. Later, Nolan had watched the same man free the altered cheetah, setting it loose on Nolan's own soldiers. That "assistant" was clearly more than he appeared.

Maybe military, maybe even an intelligence operative.

Nolan shook his head, realizing how thoroughly he had been deceived by that man. The bastard had sat right across from him, feigning subservience and nervousness. Nolan had always considered himself a good judge of character.

But I was completely fooled.

That infuriated him more than anything.

He returned to the bank of monitors and stared across at the smoke, the chaos, and the sprawl of bodies. At least, the research area appeared intact. He could still carry on his work. But precautions would have to be taken.

A chime drew his attention to the camera view outside his door. A figure stood there. A scarred face glared up at the lens. Twin trails of blood flowed from a swollen, crooked nose.

"About time," he mumbled and hit the release, unlocking the door.

Lieutenant Ekon stalked into the room. Fury shone in his eyes, along with a glimmer of shame. The soldier had allowed the prisoners to escape. He clearly intended to right that wrong.

He bowed his head. "*Commandant.*"

Nolan remained silent, letting the other recognize his disappointment. He tapped another button, and the steel shutters slowly lifted across the room's French doors. He turned without a word and stepped out to the balcony.

Ekon followed.

Nolan stood at the rail and gazed across the forest canopy to the river. Its black mirror reflected the scatter of stars. Farther off, storm clouds stacked near the horizon. A distant rumble of thunder reached him.

"It appears they're headed downriver," Nolan said.

"*Oui.* In your Tirranna."

He pictured his racing boat. It was one of his favorites. "Get Draper on the horn. Right now."

He focused on the riverside glow in the distance, marking the mining town of Katwa, one of several that his company owned. Draper had left just before sunset in the helicopter, flying there to address a problem, a panic among the local miners. Nolan trusted that Draper would quickly stamp out any trouble before it grew into a full rout.

Nolan now had an additional duty for the captain.

"Order Draper to push the ore barges out into the river. Manned with artillery and floodlights. Create a blockade across the river."

"*Oui, Commandant.*"

Nolan turned to Ekon. "Also activate all the jammers. Every one of them. Shut this entire region down."

After establishing this compound, he had hidden towers along the river, even down some of its tributaries, securing the privacy of his personal fiefdom.

They won't escape my net.

He glanced back at his office, to the gold African crown shining in its glass case.

Not when I'm the master of this jungle.

18

Gray braced himself in the rear of the lumbering Shatun ATV. The vehicle rattled and jolted through the jungle at breakneck speed. The back swayed wildly, swinging from where it articulated with the front compartment.

"Slow down!" Gray yelled.

Kowalski sat behind the wheel, leaning over it, a smoldering cigar at the corner of his lips. Faraji sat next to him, trying his best to guide the determined driver. The windshield was smeared with glowing streaks, remnants of the toxic moths that had splattered against the glass or were swatted away by the wipers.

It looked like the ATV had cleared the worst of the swarm.

But the team had not escaped unscathed.

Gray returned his attention to Benjie. The student lay on his back, still addled and dazed. An oxygen mask covered his mouth and nose.

After getting Benjie back aboard, Gray had

broken out the army medkit built into the side-wall of the ATV. Not knowing the nature of the neurotoxin, Gray had treated his patient symptomatically. He had shot Benjie up with diazepam to control his quaking limbs, along with a jab of antihistamines and adrenaline to stem signs of anaphylaxis. Gray had also scrubbed the blistering spots on the student's hand and cheek, trying to remove as much toxin as possible.

"How's the kid doing?" Kowalski called back.

"Coming around I think."

Bleary-eyed, Benjie nodded at this prognosis. He tried to remove the mask, but Gray pushed his hand away. The young man was lucky only two moths had grazed him. Any more, and Benjie would not have survived.

Still, Gray knew his condition could worsen again.

Too much was unknown.

As they continued through the jungle, he weighed breaking radio silence and calling in an evac. But he feared alerting the enemy if his call reached the wrong ears. Plus, any delay would set them farther from their goal.

Still, they owed the young man. If it wasn't for Benjie's earlier warning, they'd all have succumbed to the swarm's ambush.

Faraji suddenly yelled from the passenger seat. He pointed up, while ducking low. A moth crawled along the roof above Kowalski's head, its carapace shining softly. Gray had thought they'd cleared the ATV, but one must have slipped past their hurried inspection. It dropped toward the top of Kowalski's shaved head.

Before it could land, Kowalski took out his cigar and stabbed the moth back into the roof with its smoldering stub. Wings fluttered as its body hissed and burned. When it stopped moving, Kowalski cracked open the side window and flicked the cigar and dead moth out into the jungle.

"That better be the last of 'em," Kowalski said. "If I'm going to die, it better not be because of some goddamned butterfly."

"Moth," Benjie corrected in a muffled, weak voice. He pushed his mask down, avoiding Gray's second attempt to keep it in place. "An African batwing, *Holocerina angulata*, native to the Congo."

Gray wanted to encourage Benjie to rest, but he needed his expertise. "I'm assuming they're not normally toxic."

"Not the adults," Benjie said hoarsely. "Their caterpillars have spikes that are venomous, triggering a painful sting."

"You got more than *stung*," Kowalski called back, fighting the ATV through a dense patch of undergrowth.

Benjie tried to sit up, but it took two attempts and Gray's help. "Something must've twisted the species. Like with the army ants. But I thought such alterations were just behavioral, not physiological." He stared at Gray. "It seems like something's radically changing the jungle."

Gray stared past the windows at the bobbling view of the dark forest. "You're thinking it was the virus."

"I can't say for sure, but if it is, we're heading the wrong way."

"What do you mean?"

Benjie stared at the twin beams of the headlights burrowing into the darkness. "I wager the deeper we go—the closer we get to the source—the worse it will get. And even then . . ." His voice trailed off.

Gray sensed he was holding something back. "What?"

He rubbed at his blistered cheek. "The ants, the baboons, even the moths. The changes in them had to have been recent. *New* alterations, generated at the expanding fringe of the viral spread. Where we're headed, the virus may have been active for untold millennia. There's no telling what it could produce over that length of time, what those transformations might look like."

Gray took a moment to absorb Benjie's words. Kowalski was less contemplative. He jabbed Faraji with an elbow and nodded ahead. "Tell me we don't have much farther to go."

Faraji turned to Kowalski, then back to Gray. "We here."

Gray shifted forward to peer past the windshield. As the ATV's giant wheels crawled across the terrain, he saw nothing ahead but more trackless forest. "Are you sure?"

Faraji pointed off to the side. It took a moment for Gray to make out a waist-high standing stone, topped by a crudely sculpted cross. It was so encrusted with lichen and shrouded by vines that it was nearly indiscernible from the jungle. Only then was Gray able to pick out others, on both sides of their path.

Gravestones.

The markers were clustered within a grove of trees whose trunks were considerably thinner than the surrounding forest. Gray pictured the Reverend Sheppard's missionaries cutting down a swath of the forest to make room for this cemetery. The smaller trees were younger, secondary growth filling in the space after the mission had been abandoned.

Even Kowalski recognized this. "Great, kid. You led us into a graveyard. Like that's not a bad omen."

Kowalski gunned their engine and hurried through, flattening a stone under one of the giant tires in his haste to escape the cemetery. Then a larger shadow appeared ahead, buried in the jungle. The beams of the headlamps bounced across a facade of stone, crumbling plaster, jagged broken windows, and a moss-covered tin roof. A large marble cross stood to one side, entwined in vines, as if the jungle were trying to pull it down.

"We here," Faraji repeated with a nod ahead.

Though it was far more dilapidated, it clearly was the same missionary church depicted in the raffia tapestry.

Kowalski drew the ATV to a stop near the large cross. He left the light shining toward the church's threshold. The door had rotted away long ago. The beams failed to dispel the darker shadows in the depths of the old nave. A few bats, disturbed by the brightness, cartwheeled into the night.

"You're going to make us go in there, aren't you?" Kowalski called back to him.

Gray pulled out the sleeve of old Kodak photos. He withdrew the second in the time line and held it up. It showed William Sheppard leading a prayer among a kneeling group of Kuba tribesmen. The trees behind the reverend—especially a V-shaped pair of mahogany trees—matched the view to the left of the church. Gray flipped the photo over to examine the drawing on the back. It surely had to be a clue.

Then Gray saw it. He gripped the photo tighter. Earlier, he had thought the sketch depicted a hill with a path leading up to a cross. Now he recognized his mistake.

It's a headstone . . .

"I don't think we have to go into the church," he told Kowalski and twisted to stare out the back window. "But you're not going to like the alternative any better."

"Then where—" Kowalski turned in his seat and saw where Gray was looking. He swore darkly.

Gray confirmed his guess. "We're going to have to search the graveyard."

9:13 P.M.

Benjie followed at Gray's heels. Back at the ATV, they had tried to confine him inside, but he had refused. Still, he stayed close to the man and his large pistol.

As they headed into the cemetery, Benjie swept a flashlight in all directions, keeping watch on the surrounding jungle. Though the canopy was thinner here, the night had gotten darker as a scudding of black clouds obscured the stars and moon. Thunder rumbled off in the distance, sounding like the growl of the Congo itself.

Not watching close enough, he bumped into Gray's back. The other had stopped to inspect one of the grave markers. The stone stood crookedly in the sodden muck. Gray yanked away a splay of clinging vines to examine the granite surface.

Benjie shifted around to inspect the other side.

"Anything?" Gray asked.

"No, just a name and date carved into it."

"Then let's move on."

Before leaving the ATV, Gray had shown them all the zigzag pattern sketched on the gravestone drawing. They were all searching for that symbol. Kowalski and Faraji inspected the neighboring row of stones. The two groups kept near to one another, all too cognizant of what had happened back at the lake.

Benjie's face and hand still burned from the blistering.

The group continued across the graveyard,

moving in tandem. Benjie's attention remained focused on the jungle. Mosquitoes and clouds of biting flies plagued them. Each nip made him flinch, wondering what aberrations might have been instilled in the insects out here. It also didn't help that the air smelled of rot and decaying leaf litter, especially when traversing a graveyard.

Benjie pictured the moldering bones under his feet with a shudder. The quiet of the forest compounded his edginess, as if even the jungle did not want to disturb those sleeping here. The heavy silence weighed on him. And from the way everyone else seemed to hunch and move with cautious steps, they felt it, too.

He wiped the pebbling sweat from his brow.

After another fifteen minutes, they had completed their circuit of gravestones, all twenty-two of them—even the marker that Kowalski had driven over on the way to the church. It had taken all of them to flip it over to inspect both sides.

They clustered at the cemetery's edge.

Gray's lips were a tight line of frustration. Kowalski just glared all around. Faraji hugged his arms across his chest, looking forlorn. They had failed to find the zigzag symbol on any of the gravestones.

"Maybe the one we're looking for got buried," Kowalski said. "The whole place looks like it's about to sink away."

"Or there could be other gravestones," Benjie offered. "Maybe we should search behind the church, too."

Gray nodded. "We have no other choice. It could be anywhere around here."

Kowalski sighed. "It'll be like looking for a needle in a moldy haystack."

"Or in this case . . ." Benjie slashed a zigzag through the air. "A lightning bolt in a haystack."

As if conjured by his flourish, thunder boomed. He quickly lowered his arm.

"Let's keep moving," Gray said. "We don't want to stop in one place for too long."

Benjie agreed, especially with another storm threatening. They set off again for the church— but Faraji stayed behind, rooted in place. His gaze remained on the cemetery.

Benjie drifted to his side. "What's wrong?"

Faraji unfolded an arm and mimicked Benjie's flourish in the air, tracing a zigzag. "Lightning . . ." he said, still staring at the cemetery.

"What about it?"

Faraji set off into the graveyard again, drawing Benjie with him. The others noted their path and crossed to follow. Faraji searched the stones, the same ones he and Kowalski had scrutinized earlier. Finally, he stopped and rubbed moss off the surface of one, exposing a name and date.

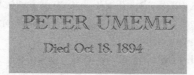

PETER UMEME

Died Oct 18. 1894

Gray read the inscription, "Peter Umeme."

It was the grave marker of a Kuba tribesman, someone who had been baptized, taking on a Christian given name while still keeping his tribal one.

Faraji pointed to the latter. "*Umeme*." He slashed his arm through the air again for emphasis. "It mean 'lightning.'"

They stared around at each other for a silent moment.

"Does that mean this is the right place?" Kowalski asked. "Maybe we shouldn't go digging up someone's grave on a hunch."

"It must be," Gray said.

"How can you be sure?" Benjie asked.

Gray reached to the collapsible shovel hung over his shoulder and snapped it open. He pointed the spade's tip at the lower line of the inscription. "October eighteenth, 1894. That's the same date as the photo."

Benjie realized he was right. "One of Sheppard's group must have died out here while they were traveling. Perhaps the prayer circle depicted in the photo was actually a eulogy."

"You may be right. But there's only one way to know for sure." Gray waved for Kowalski to help him dig. "Let's get to work."

The two men labored as a team. The wet soil helped. Fresh loam quickly piled up next to a deepening hole. Finally, Kowalski slammed his spade into the bottom and got a distinctive clank of metal on metal.

"Something's definitely here," the big man grumbled.

They continued with their hands from there, with all of them helping. A familiar steel chest emerged from the dark soil. It looked identical to the one fished out of the lake. They worked it free, revealing stout boards hidden underneath it. Benjie cringed, knowing it must be the top of Peter Umeme's coffin.

Faraji must've suspected the same. As Gray and Kowalski hauled the chest to the side, Faraji placed a palm atop the boards. The boy whispered quietly in his native tongue, perhaps thanking the man for guarding this treasure or apologizing for disturbing his rest.

Maybe both.

Benjie turned his attention to the two men as Gray pulled out a locking pin and opened the chest. He stepped closer.

"What is it?" Kowalski asked.

"Looks like another example of Kuba craftsmanship." Gray reached in and lifted free a tall hat adorned in feathers and beads, and hung with ivory charms and fetishes. "I think it's a crown of some sort."

Faraji had finished his benediction and joined them. "Yes. King's crown. *Sana takatifu*. Very sacred."

Benjie frowned. "But why bury it here? What does it mean?"

Gray stared over at the boy for help, but Faraji only shrugged. With no better guidance, Gray turned the crown around and around in his hands. He inspected its top and fingered its insides, searching for any other clue.

He finally gave a shake of his head and lowered the sacred object back into the chest. "I . . . I don't get it," he admitted.

Still, he rubbed his chin as he sat on his heels, plainly refusing to give up. He glanced from the chest to the hole they had dug. He finally shifted and pulled out the sheaf of photos. He flipped through and removed the third one in the time line, the next bread crumb on the path to Mfupa Ufalme, the Kingdom of Bones.

Gray waved everyone closer. The photo showed a picture of the Reverend Sheppard standing amidst the ruins of an old tribal village. "Faraji, you still don't recognize this place?"

"No. *Samahani*. I'm sorry."

Benjie couldn't blame him. There was nothing distinguishing about the village. The picture showed just a few rotted posts and some collapsed thatched roofs. There must be hundreds, if not thousands, of such abandoned villages throughout the Congo.

Gray flipped the photo to reveal the sketch on its back.

It looked like a tribal pattern drawn in charcoal, a patchwork hatching of diamonds and arrows, all surrounding a convoluted knot in the center. The latter reminded Benjie of an infinity symbol, the way it wound back on itself in a continual loop.

Gray eyed Faraji for help, but the teenager shrugged—then froze with his shoulders by his ears. His eyes got huge.

"What is it?" Benjie asked.

"*Samahani*," he apologized again, lowering his shoulders. He looked from the open grave to the crown, then back to the drawing. "I should know before."

"Know what?" Gray pressed.

Faraji pointed to the fringe of diamonds enclosed by arrows in the sketch. "This is *mbul bwiin*. Pattern only for *mrabaha*." He winced, clearly struggling to translate, then nodded. "Royalty, yes? Royalty."

Gray glanced to the crown.

Faraji then tapped the self-contained knot at the center of the drawing. "This *imbol*. Only for kings, yes. Each king different *imbol*."

Benjie leaned closer, beginning to understand. "So, it's like a name. Each king has his own unique pattern." He turned to Faraji. "Is that what you mean?"

He nodded his head.

Gray stared hard at Faraji. "Do you recognize this pattern? Do you know the king it represents?"

Faraji smiled with clear pride. "We learn names of all our kings. To honor them. This famous Kuba king. Big hero. *Nyim Chui*. The Leopard King."

Kowalski looked little impressed. "Great. But how does that help us?"

Gray remained silent, staring toward the open grave, then spoke. "Sheppard buried a crown in this grave for a reason, then hinted at the name of a king. Maybe he's trying to point us to the *tomb* of that same king."

"Wouldn't his grave be back at the tribe's village?" Benjie asked. "Way behind us?"

Faraji shook his head. "Kuba. We move when new king gets crown. Move to that king's village. Leave old place behind."

Benjie tried to picture this.

With each new king, the nomadic tribe shifted its main capital.

Gray turned the photo in his hand, showing the ruins of the village again. "Could this be the home of the Leopard King? Where your people left his tomb before moving on?"

They all looked to Faraji.

"Like said before, we taught all the names of our king," he said. "Much pride in them. We sing songs with their telling, what they do, where they come from."

"Does that mean you know where the Leopard King's village is?"

Faraji frowned and rocked his head back and forth in uncertainty. "I never go. But I know mostly where it was." He pointed farther east. He then cupped his hand in a scooping motion. "In a deep *bonde*. Deep valley."

Gray stood up. "We'll have to go look for it and hope we can find it."

Kowalski scowled at the cemetery. "So, we're going from a graveyard to a tomb. I guess it makes sense if we're heading toward a place called the Kingdom of Bones."

"Everyone back to the ATV," Gray ordered.

They all hurried through the cemetery. Benjie was happy to leave the last of the gravestones behind them. As they continued, the black silhouette of the old missionary church coalesced out of the darkness ahead of them. In front, the ATV sat atop its giant wheels, a smaller shadow before the larger one.

Benjie rushed toward it, anxious to get moving again.

Then a solitary howl broke the persistent silence of the jungle. The ululating call sounded both close and far at the same time. It carried a note of sadness and desolation, but the beast was not alone.

A chorus of howls answered the first, echoing all around.

The small hairs on Benjie's neck shivered with a caveman's terror.

Faraji slowed in front of him. "*Mbweha*," he warned.

As a biologist, Benjie had learned many of the Bantu words for the local animals before coming to Africa. He froze, recognizing the native name for the region's savage pack hunters.

Jackals.

9:33 P.M.

Gray swept up his KelTec handgun and gripped it with both fists. He pivoted on his back heel, searching the dark forest in all directions. Kowalski had his Shuriken raised with its stock at his cheek.

"Get to the vehicle," he warned the others.

They forged ahead in a tight group, narrowing the distance. Then movement drew his eye to the church's dark threshold. A shadow melted out from inside. Followed by another. The beasts were pitch-black, their fur bristling around their necks. Tall ears pointed high. Yellow eyes glared back at them. As the pair crept farther into view, they kept their pointed muzzles low to the ground, snarling with menace, baring upper and lower fangs.

Faraji stopped.

Benjie did, too. "Don't shoot," he warned breathlessly.

Gray and Kowalski guarded the flanks, training their weapons forward.

"What're they?" Kowalski whispered.

"Jackals," Benjie warned. "But huge ones, twice the normal size."

Gray believed him. These looked like full-grown wolves, but sleeker and built for speed. Gray wagered the jackals could be upon them in a breath. From the corners of his eyes, he saw more shadows shifting through the trees to either side.

They're likely behind us, too.

He estimated a dozen or more in the pack.

"Don't shoot," Benjie warned again.

Kowalski firmed his grip on his weapon. "Like hell I won't."

"Don't," Benjie urged. "Don't even move."

Gray noted that Faraji had been the first to freeze in place. The kid likely knew the denizens of these jungles far better than any of them.

"Do as he says," Gray ordered. Still, he kept his pistol raised and flicked a glance at Benjie. "What do we do from here?

"These buggers are smart, deviously so. They're also extremely territorial. Remember, *we* invaded *their* space. They could've attacked us at any time, but they only threatened when we tried to return to the ATV. There's got to be a reason."

Gray realized the jackals must have been hiding inside the church all along. Still, the pair had kept quiet, silently evaluating the threat, strategizing how to deal with it, even offering Gray's group an opportunity to leave unmolested.

But then we returned, closing again on their hiding place . . .

A new noise intruded into the stalemate. A hungry, plaintive mewling rose from inside the church.

"Pups," Benjie said.

Gray winced.

No wonder they're defending this place.

The shadows around them moved in closer, revealing glimpses that flashed back into hiding. They were impossibly fast.

"What do we do?" Gray repeated.

"Slow moves. Glacially slow." Benjie's voice trembled, but he tamped down his terror enough to instruct them. "Angle away from the church. Toward the rear of the ATV. And don't look them in the eye."

Benjie demonstrated, shifting one foot, then the other. He kept his gaze down, his shoulders hunched with a bowed back. "Creep low," he whispered. "As if your tail is tucked."

"I don't have a tail," Kowalski said. "But my balls are tucked plenty high."

"Good," Benjie said. "Keep them there."

The group edged toward the open rear of the ATV. Though the vehicle was only ten yards away, it seemed an impossible distance. Especially when each step raised the hackles of the guarding pair.

Gray held his breath—then one of the jackals lunged and snapped in their direction. Gray crouched lower, tightening his aim.

"Don't," Benjie whispered.

It took all of Gray's effort to loosen his finger on the trigger. He glared down his gunsight at the jackal.

The beast backed off, but not out of fear.

"It's just posturing," Benjie explained. "A display of aggression. Ignore it."

Kowalski grunted. "Tell that to my wet drawers."

"That might help actually," Benjie said. "Urine leaking is a sign of submission."

Kowalski scowled. "I'm really beginning to hate you."

They closed in on the ATV. The open rear cargo door beckoned.

Almost there.

Another step, and a sharper cry rose from inside the church. A small shape came hurdling out, passing between the adults, aiming blindly toward their group. It was one of the pups. It did not see where it was going, its head twisted to look behind.

The reason for its panic appeared.

Across the church threshold, a large snake shot out, writhing with incredible speed, chasing down its prey. Its body was as thick around as Gray's forearm.

The pup tripped over its own paws and tumbled onto its side, skidding across the wet leaves. The snake swept to it and reared high, flaring a crimson hood. It hissed and bared its fangs.

Cobra.

The larger jackals screamed in fury, but they were frozen in confusion, faced by opposing threats to their den. They surely had other pups inside, too.

Luckily, Kowalski did not have a constitution for indecision. A sharp whine discharged from his weapon, followed by a flash of silver through the air. The cobra's head flew high as a pair of razored disks severed its neck. Its body writhed in the air for a long breath, then fell in a dead slither to the ground.

The pup jerked back to its legs and, with a yelp, raced back toward the refuge of the dark church. It passed between its towering parents and vanished inside.

The adults resettled into postures of shivering hackles and snarling threat, but they came no closer. Even the shadows to either side slipped deeper into the forest.

"Keep going," Benjie urged. "Don't count on their good graces lasting for long."

They heeded this warning and crossed the last of the distance at a faster pace.

Once there, Gray let out his breath and herded everyone inside. He pulled the rear hatch closed behind him.

"Kowalski, get us moving."

"Don't have to tell me twice."

Kowalski landed heavily in the driver's seat and keyed the ignition. The Shatun's engine growled to a deafening roar. Before they could leave, a huge shape bounded in front of them, landing between the headlights. The jackal lunged up, planting its enormous paws on the windshield. Claws scratched the glass as it snarled and spit in fury.

Kowalski glared back. "You're welcome, asshole!"

He put the vehicle in reverse and shot backward. The jackal dropped down and paced before the church, its tail whipping the air.

Kowalski spun the ATV, pirouetting it in place. They were all thrown across the swinging rear compartment. Once facing east, Kowalski took off again.

Benjie regained his seat and stared back toward the church. He was trembling all over. But it wasn't the neurotoxin retaking hold, only the aftereffects of adrenaline seeping away.

Gray knew the feeling all too well. He clapped the young man on the shoulder. "You did good back there."

Benjie swallowed hard. "Just goes to prove. Respect nature, and it'll try its best to do the same."

Kowalski heard him. "Unless it tries to eat you, then all bets are off."

Gray ignored him and followed the beams of the headlights out into the darkness. The jungle filled the world. As he stared out, he remembered a canto from Lord Tennyson about the brutality of nature. The poet had described its savagery as *red in tooth and claw*.

As Gray considered this, he pictured the pair of jackals protecting their young, a species known to mate for life. Even the rest of the pack had gathered to protect the same, showing mutual cooperation.

In this regard, it seemed Benjie knew more about nature than Tennyson.

Gray decided to take that wisdom to heart.

Especially as it just saved our lives.

Still, Gray also remembered what else the young biologist had warned about this jungle, about the heart of the Congo, about the changes happening here.

The deeper we go, the worse it will get.

FOURTH

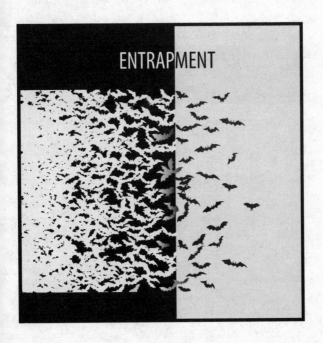

ENTRAPMENT

19

Tucker raced the cigarette boat down the dark
river. A bank of clouds obscured the stars and
moon. Despite the gloominess, he ran without
lights. Thankfully, his night-vision goggles allowed him to read the river well enough.

Without slowing, he whisked the boat smoothly
around floating logs and other obstacles. Overhead, lightning flickered within the depths of
the clouds, looking like sunbursts through his
goggles.

He was grateful for the dark night, but any
attempt at stealth was belied by the boat's
screaming engine. Tucker prayed that the noise,
echoing in all directions, would defy pinpointing
their location—at least for long enough.

"Any luck?" Tucker called over to the neighboring seat.

Monk had Tucker's radio in hand, trying to
raise Ndaye on the horn, to summon the heli-

copter for an air-evac. "Nothing but static," he reported.

Tucker bit back a curse. They had already tried the satellite phone, too. Communications continued to be suppressed. Clearly, whoever had locked down this section of the Congo had vast resources and access to advanced hardware. Then again, that was evident enough from the battalions of robotic Q-UGVs patrolling the island.

"This is bad!" Frank hollered from the bow. He had positioned his stolen machine gun atop its bipod, pointing its muzzle forward. "We should've cleared the island's jamming tower by now."

Monk lowered the phone in defeat. "De Coster must have other towers spread throughout here."

"I wouldn't doubt it," Charlotte said from the stern, where she sat with Jameson and Kane. "That bastard spared no expense in setting up shop here."

Tucker tightened his jaw. He searched the banks, looking for those other towers, but he failed to spot a single one. Tucker suspected it wasn't just the jamming that hid what was going on here. De Coster must have greased thousands of palms, encouraging the authorities to turn a blind eye to his operations.

Tucker focused his own attention forward. They were getting close to a mining town. The glow of its lights reflected off the clouds ahead, roughly marking its location in the jungle.

Maybe another half mile or so.

He intended to shoot past the town without

slowing. He eyed the fuel indicator. The racing boat sucked gas at an astonishing rate. Still, he kept the throttle fully open. If they slowed, it would put them all at risk.

He studied the river and glided the boat around a sharp bend. As he made the turn, a whistle blew. Directly ahead, the world exploded into a blinding brilliance. The goggles amplified it, burning away his vision. He gasped and instinctively slowed the boat. He toggled off the night-vision mode. As he blinked away the residual dazzle, the world collapsed into darker shades, except in front of them.

A brilliant line of lights spanned the breadth of the river. He thought it outlined a dam. But as the glare faded, he saw the blockade was actually a row of steel-hulled barges.

"Turn back!" Frank called.

Tucker angled away, tipping the starboard high. Gunfire erupted. Rounds pebbled the water all around them. Tucker careened the boat back and forth, making them a harder target in the dark. As he did, he fought their own momentum to swing around, but he was going too fast. The current swept them toward the brighter glow of the floodlights.

Frank must have recognized the danger and fired his weapon from the bow. The machine gun's chatter vibrated the entire boat. He strafed the decks of the barges. One after the other, lamps shattered and went dark.

With the collapse of those lights, Tucker spotted a gap between two of the barges. Maybe wide enough for the slim boat to race through.

He stopped trying to turn around. Where could they even go? Certainly not back toward the island.

With no choice, he straightened the boat forward.

"Hold tight!" he bellowed and shoved the throttle fully open.

The boat rocketed ahead.

A new volley of gunfire blasted the river. A few rounds struck the bow, but Frank kept his post, returning fire.

Just hold out a little longer.

The barges grew huge in front of him.

Then a new sight shot into view. With a scream of engines, a sun rose from behind the barges and climbed high. It was a helicopter, likely the same gunship he had spotted leaving the island earlier. It shot over the blockade and dove toward them.

Flames spat from its underside.

"Rockets!" Frank yelled.

Tucker cursed and yanked hard on the wheel. The boat spun wildly, skimming and hydroplaning over the river, like a stone skipping across its surface.

On the portside, the river exploded with a huge flume of water.

Another rocket blasted behind the stern.

Tucker regained control of the boat and sped away from the barges. The helicopter buzzed them and made a tight turn, its rotors going nearly vertical. It swung back toward them. They were sitting ducks on the river.

Monk grabbed Tucker's sleeve and pointed his other arm toward the shore.

Tucker didn't understand—then spotted a break in the jungle. It marked a tributary flowing into the river. Tucker didn't know where it led, only that it was off this main channel. He turned and aimed for it, not slowing. They needed to get under the cover of the forest canopy.

The helicopter gave chase, maneuvering to compensate for Tucker's sudden turn toward shore.

He ducked low over the wheel.

C'mon . . .

The boat flew across the water, catching air at times.

Then the nose reached the mouth of the tributary. It was a tight fit, but they had no choice. The boat shot into the refuge. It went immediately pitch-black under the canopy.

Tucker tapped his goggles back into night-vision mode.

Not a moment too soon.

The waterway twisted in a sharp bend ahead. Tucker pulled back on the throttle and hauled the boat around the curve. Branches along the far side battered at them. Still, he cleared the turn with a gasp of relief. His heart pounded. He wanted to throttle up, but the stream continued to narrow. Rocks scraped the keel.

He didn't slow—not with a hunter in the air.

An explosion ripped behind the boat, encouraging him to keep going.

Then he hit a submerged boulder.

The boat shot high, tilting in midair. Their vessel became a spear and shot into the forest. It crashed between giant trees and nose-dived into the brush. They were all thrown forward.

As they came to a stop, the engine coughed and died.

Monk was up first. "Everyone out! Now! Get clear of the boat."

Tucker understood the man's haste. The gunship surely had thermal sensors. Even under the canopy, the hot engine would glow like a red coal in the night.

"Help me," Charlotte gasped out.

Tucker turned to see the woman trying to get Jameson off the floor. The doctor cradled one arm to his chest. It hung crookedly, broken at the forearm. Tucker rushed to their aid and got the pair and Kane overboard. He and Charlotte half carried the dazed and moaning pediatrician. They hobbled away from the boat.

Behind them, Frank struggled to free the machine gun.

"Leave it," Monk hollered. "It's too big to haul through the jungle."

Frank accepted this and leaped down from the bow.

Monk and Frank quickly joined their group. Together, they rushed away from the crash site. They had barely gotten twenty yards when the world exploded behind them. Flames shot high. A wall of heat struck them. The deafening concussion pushed them all forward.

They kept going, not even pausing to look back at the fiery wreckage of the boat.

Tucker hoped the wash of heat would help hide their bodies until they could reach the deeper depths of the jungle. Luckily, the night also remained hot and humid, which should help mask them. But he also knew the helicopter would soon be offloading hunters into these woods.

"Where do we go?" Charlotte asked.

Tucker knew only one answer.

"Follow me."

9:55 P.M.

From a rise in the jungle, Monk spied the shine of lights through the forest. He crouched with the others. Distant grumbles of heavy machinery and rhythmic mechanical pounding reached them.

Tucker explained why he had led them to the outskirts of the mining town. "We can't keep running blindly through the jungle. We don't know how far this cone of silence stretches, or even in which direction we should go. Right now, we only have a brief window. Soon, they'll be offloading more and more men who'll scour through here. The longer we wait, the worse our odds will become."

"And they certainly won't be expecting us to walk into that town," Frank added.

Tucker nodded. "It's the only place where we can hope to reach the outside world. The town must have a communication nest, some radio tuned to a coded frequency that could breach the jamming. And right now, with the enemy focused out here—"

Monk nodded. "It offers us the best chance of reaching that radio."

"*Us* being Frank and me," Tucker added.

Monk looked sharply at the pair. "Hang on . . ."

"No offense, but you're down one hand." Tucker nodded to Charlotte who sat with Jameson. The pair struggled to use a branch to splint the man's broken arm. "Somebody's gotta stay and guard the others."

Monk sighed, knowing he was right, but he hated being sidelined.

"I'll leave Kane with you," Tucker offered. "He'll draw too much attention in town. Plus, out here, he'll give you plenty of warning if any patrols get too close. I'll also be able to keep an eye on all of you through his camera." Tucker searched through his pack and removed a compact digital pad and an earpiece. He passed them to Monk. "It's my old gear. Before DARPA upgraded my hardware. It'll allow you to use Kane's eyes and ears, too. Likewise, I can use it to radio you. Keep you updated on our progress."

Monk fitted the earpiece in place. "As long as we don't get too far away from each other."

"True." Tucker rubbed his chin and looked back at the glow of the town. "Especially as the jamming could be stronger down there."

With the matter settled, Tucker quickly showed them how to use Kane's gear. Afterward, he and Frank took off through the jungle. Monk watched as they slid down the slope toward a deserted corner of the town.

Once they were gone, Monk turned back to the others. He held the pistol he had stolen from Ekon. Jameson leaned on the bole of a tree, his eyes half-closed as he clutched his splinted arm to his chest.

Next to him, Charlotte cradled the hand-held digital transceiver tied to Kane's radio and camera. "This is amazing," she muttered.

The military dog had been sent out to patrol the immediate surroundings. Monk had worked with Kane in the past and trusted the dog to have their backs.

Still, Monk paced the area, listening for any telltale approach. He scanned the skies for the helicopter. He heard its engine rumbling out there, sometimes louder, sometimes fading, but the acoustics of the jungle made it hard to judge its exact location.

As he stared up, he heard a soft rustling through the branches and leaves. A fluttering of wings. He squinted, but he failed to spot the source. After a few breaths, it sounded as if the noisemakers had moved on.

A sharp whistle blew from the mining town, making him jump. Then another sounded, strident and urgent. Then more blasted out.

Charlotte stood and joined him. "What's happening over there?"

Monk slowly shook his head, fearing the trespassers had been discovered. "I don't—"

A siren suddenly erupted from the town,

starting low, but quickly ratcheting up into a wailing alarm.

Charlotte and Monk shared a concerned look. Even Kane loped back into view, stiff-backed with his ears high. Then the jungle lit up brightly around them. They all ducked; the dog shifted into deeper shadows. The canopy rattled and shook—then the light and disturbance swept past them.

It was the helicopter from earlier.

Monk stared toward the town as the gunship dove for a quick landing.

"Something's wrong," Charlotte said.

Monk agreed.

But what?

10:14 P.M.

Frank hid with Tucker in the shadow of a large tractor. Both wore miners' helmets and mud-encrusted coveralls, pilfered from an empty barracks near the edge of town.

All the better to look the part.

When the steam whistles had blown, they had immediately sought shelter, deciding it was best to lay low until they could figure out what was happening. Then the siren had blared a panicked klaxon, setting his heart to pounding.

What the hell's going on?

Tucker grabbed his arm and pointed toward the sky. He turned to watch a helicopter sweep over the town and drop toward a nest of cinder block buildings at the edge of an open-pit mine.

The section of stouter buildings had been

their destination all along. If the town had a communication nest, it would be found there.

The rest of the place looked disheveled and ramshackle, hastily built and spread haphazardly as the mine expanded. The workers' structures were corrugated metal shacks, all rusted over, as if the air itself sought to dissolve the place away—which maybe it was.

The cloudy air was a thick miasma of coal smoke, raw sewage, and toxic gases. The source of it all was readily apparent. The illuminated pit of the surface mine was a dark scar cut far into the jungle. A few large dozers and haulers moved sluggishly across its shelves.

Closer at hand, mountains of tailings and hillocks of overburden lay exposed to the rain and air, likely for decades, leaching heavy metals into sickly green acid ponds around their bases.

Even the light here felt toxic. Maybe it was because Frank had spent so much time on the dark river or trekking under the jungle's canopy, but the glare pained his eyes and seemed an affront to the environment.

"We should get closer," Tucker warned as the helicopter dropped out of sight and vanished within the mine's administration section.

Frank nodded.

Before they could move, the siren cut off abruptly.

"What do you think that was all about?" Frank asked.

"Only one way to find out."

Tucker headed off, leading the way through the rows of heavy equipment parked in this dark corner of the township. The machinery towered all around them, offering plenty of shelter to help hide their path toward the mine's center of operations. Unlike the rest of the town, the haulers and loaders, excavators and drill rigs, all looked pristine, in well-maintained condition. Then again, this machinery was likely the costliest expense in running this place.

Whereas workers were the cheapest—and the easiest to replace.

Frank scowled as they cleared the parking lot of heavy equipment. Ahead spread a swath of dilapidated shacks and shanties, all run through with open latrines.

It was easy to discern how De Coster had made his riches.

Off the backs and blood of the local people.

Then again, Frank knew that was the way of the world. Those in power too often abused the cheapest manpower at hand, usually those of a lower caste in society or those with a different hue of skin.

Tucker paused next to a dump truck. "Where is everyone?"

Frank shook himself back to the matter at hand. He had not paid attention to the lack of miners and workers, mostly because he and Tucker had entered through an abandoned corner of the town. But the section ahead appeared occupied. Campfires smoldered along the dark streets. Music echoed. But only a handful of figures scurried under lamps before vanishing into the dark or ducking into a shack.

Off in the distance, even the trundling dozers in the mine had stopped.

"The siren," Frank said. "Maybe it was an order to lock down the town."

"Why?"

"I don't know. Maybe they suspect we might try to sneak in here and wanted everyone off the streets to make it easier to patrol." Frank pointed toward the operation's center, which was more brightly lit. "Look."

A flurry of activity surrounded the cluster of cinder block buildings. Soldiers in black armor rushed about. Floodlights burst, spearing into the sky, sweeping all around, painting the underside of the low, dark clouds.

"Maybe you're right," Tucker said.

"How're we going to get in there now?"

"Let's get a closer look. We'll figure something out. Not like we have much choice."

Tucker set off into the murky shamble of the workers' shacks. They kept their faces hidden under their miners' helmets. Especially Tucker. Frank, at least, had the right complexion to blend in with locals. Tucker rested a palm on his Desert Eagle. Frank carried a semi-automatic at his hip. Charlotte had relieved the pistol—a Swiss-forged Sphinx S3000—from a dead gunman back on the island.

Tucker suddenly sidestepped, nearly leaping away from the corrugated wall of a barracks. A murmur of voices sounded from inside. Someone coughed. But it wasn't the presence of men nearby that had startled Tucker.

A body lay sprawled, facedown, in the muddy street.

Frank hurried past with a glance back.

What the hell?

They continued through the maze of alleyways and squeezes. They passed another body. Something was definitely wrong here. Frank paused long enough to lift a slack limb. No rigor mortis. The body even felt warm. A recent death. With a shudder, he let go.

Tucker hissed for him to keep up. He hurried after his partner. At the next corner, Tucker stopped again and waved Frank over.

He crept closer, holding his breath.

Ahead, a small communal square opened. A cold brick oven stood to one side. A scattering of black oil barrels smoldered with burning trash. In the center of the square, tarps had been draped over a row of bodies. Boots protruded from the shrouds' edges.

More dead men. A dozen or so.

A few prayer cairns had been set up, consisting of stacks of rocks and tiny personal artifacts. Several candles burned, but most had guttered out into wax puddles. The melted candles suggested the bodies had been here for at least a day. Whatever had transpired here had happened within the past twenty-four hours.

But what?

Tucker set off through the square, skirting the edges. They had both seen enough death, enough dead bodies. Still, Frank headed into the square and crossed toward the tarps.

"What're you doing?" Tucker whispered to him.

"I want to know what happened. It could be important."

Tucker cursed him but angled over. "Just be quick about it."

Frank reached down and tossed back one of the tarps. A familiar ripeness struck him, meaty and gagging. A coating of flies took wing, rising with an angry hissing. He waved them off and studied the pair of bodies. They lay on their backs, their limbs respectfully positioned.

He spotted no bullet wounds, no evidence of a mass execution or a militant attack. He dropped to a knee beside the closest body and examined a huge wound covering the man's throat and cheek. The flesh looked melted, liquefied, both the skin and muscle beneath. Bone shone through the necrotic tissue.

"What the hell caused that?" Tucker asked.

"Toxic exposure."

"To what?"

Frank shook his head. The neighboring body was similarly afflicted, though it was the flesh of the man's arm that had sloughed away. It looked like someone had dipped the limb in acid.

He gingerly lifted the arm, examining it full around. The man wore a stained white T-shirt and boxers, like he had died in his bed and been dragged here. If so, it further supported that a majority of the deaths had occurred last night. The other bodies in the street must have succumbed more recently, within the hour.

"I need more light," he told Tucker.

His partner slipped out a penlight and cupped the beam to further hide its flash of brilliance. A more discerning inspection of the body's arm revealed that the pattern of tissue liquefaction followed the major blood vessels, forming a rootlike spread of necrosis.

Frank followed those lines up the dead man's arm to the source. He pushed back the T-shirt's sleeve, exposing a pair of deep punctures at the shoulder. He examined it closely.

It can't be . . .

He recognized those marks. He had treated scores of such wounds on his own body. But this was far different. He pictured a necrolytic toxin flowing from those punctures and traveling down the vessels, burning and liquefying the flesh along the way.

"What is it?" Tucker asked.

Dizzy with the realization, Frank stood up. He stared skyward. He studied the clouds. A flash of lightning burst deep within them. The brighter spot revealed movement below the clouds' bellies. A dark river flowed in smoky streams.

He turned toward the town's operation center. Their floodlights speared the sky, revealing more of the same. A mass of shadows swirled in and out of the clouds.

He suddenly understood what the sirens had been warning about, why the town's streets were deserted.

Tucker stared up, too. "What are those?"

Frank answered, "Bats."

10:31 P.M.

Charlotte leaned against the trunk of a palm. She stared down at Kane's transceiver, which was cradled in her hands. The camera feed showed the dog stalking though the forest, making a slow arc between them and the depths of the jungle. Similarly, Monk paced the same arc, but on the opposite side. As he kept guard, he studied the mining town below.

Everyone remained on edge, especially after the town's siren suddenly went silent a few minutes ago.

Even Jameson had regained his feet, cradling his splinted arm. His eyes shone glassy with pain. Before leaving, Tucker had passed him two tabs of oxycodone from a tiny medkit in the soldier's go-bag. The pills had only taken the edge off his agony.

Monk approached.

"Any word from Tucker?" Charlotte asked.

He shook his head. "Not since they reached the town's outskirts. Just dead air. Tucker must've been right about the jamming being stronger down there."

Charlotte had already suspected the same. The view from Kane's camera had repeatedly stuttered on the transceiver.

Jameson swallowed hard. "Then what do we do?"

Monk shrugged. "We wait. Nothing else we can do."

Jameson frowned. "We should've just stayed

on the island. Fat lot of good it's done us getting away from that place."

Charlotte couldn't disagree. She pictured Disanka and her boy. Guilt still ate at her for abandoning them. *And for what?*

Under a pall of gloom, they all returned to their own thoughts. Jameson sank back to a seat, hunching sullenly over his arm. Charlotte leaned against the tree, while Monk continued his agitated pacing.

She watched Kane, the only one oblivious to defeat. His determined patrol cheered her. She could almost feel herself stalking alongside him, which helped sharpen her own senses.

She heard a soft rustling of leaves overhead, along with a slight battering of branches. She stared up, suspecting it was some bird restless in its nest, bothered by their presence. A flickering glow caught her eyes. It came and went, almost like a heartbeat. She wanted to dismiss it as an illusion. Maybe lightning shimmering through the canopy. Yet the flickering seemed too rhythmic.

What is that?

Monk suddenly rushed toward her, startling her. He held a hand over his ear. "Kane's growling," he warned.

She jerked straighter and lifted the transceiver for them both to watch. On the tiny screen, the view looked like it had frozen, perhaps another stutter in the transmission—but then a fern frond waved on the screen. She realized Kane had stopped and stood dead still.

She squinted, trying to discern what had upset the dog.

What's out there?

Monk reached to the transceiver and tapped a button on its side. The camera view dissolved into shades of green. *Night vision.* In the distance, hazily outlined figures approached cautiously through the jungle.

Six or seven of them.

"Up," Monk ordered Jameson. Then he tapped the mike taped to his throat. "*RETURN*," he radioed to Kane.

On the screen, the dog retreated backward, barely shifting a leaf.

Charlotte kept watch on the screen as the figures faded back into the dark as Kane left. Nevertheless, the patrol had been aiming in this direction. It was unclear if their group had been spotted. It could simply be dumb luck on the hunters' part. Maybe they had been heading toward town, and Charlotte's group just happened to be in their path.

Either way, she and the others couldn't stay here.

Monk pointed behind him. "Down into town," he whispered. "There'll be more places to hide. Hopefully we'll be able to reach Tucker by radio down there."

Kane rejoined them, his eyes bright—but his gaze was focused upward, into the canopy. Only Charlotte noticed this.

Monk rushed them off. "Get moving."

As they left, Charlotte heard that strange rustling again. Something took wing. It flickered a soft glow as it fled. She ignored it and hurried after the others. They reached the slope and climbed down as quietly as possible. The lights of the town grew ahead of them.

Monk knew where Tucker and Frank had entered the town and clearly intended to take them the same way. They reached the bottom of the rise and cautiously approached the forest's edge. No alarm rose behind them, so they had to assume their flight had not been detected.

Through a break in the foliage, Charlotte eyed a rusted corrugated metal shack. It was long and low, maybe a former barracks. It appeared dark and abandoned. In fact, this entire corner of the town had no lights and looked like a deserted maze.

Definitely a good place to hide.

Monk must have had the same thought. "We'll get a decent way in there, then find a place to lay low."

As a group, they set off again. Monk led with Kane. Charlotte kept close to Jameson, who stumbled more than he stepped. The pain and the drugs had clearly dizzied him.

Still, they made it safely into the warren of dark shanties.

Monk stopped and pressed a hand over his ear. His brow wrinkled as he struggled to listen. Then his arm dropped, and he turned to them. Even in the shadows, his eyes were huge.

"What?" Charlotte asked.

"Got a garbled transmission from Tucker. Then it cut off. Only made out a few words."

Jameson looked ill. "What did he say?"

"A warning."

"About what?"

"He said . . ." Monk searched around them.
". . . *whatever you do, don't come into town.*"

10:48 P.M.

As he crouched, Tucker strained for any response from Monk or the others. He finally gave a frustrated shake of his head.

"Did they get your message?" Frank asked.

"Can't say. But my radio is newer, stronger than the one I left them. They could've heard it but couldn't respond back."

"Then we'll have to hope it reached them." Frank waved him onward. "Let's keep going."

They set off again, traversing the ramshackle region of the township, aiming for the cluster of cinder block buildings. Tucker continued to watch the skies. Swarms of bats—revealed in flashes of lightning—streamed under the dark clouds. Ahead, columns of lights swept the skies.

Keep looking up there, Tucker urged their enemies.

He and Frank hoped the distraction of the airborne threat would assist them in breaching the command center. With all eyes on the skies, they had a better chance of sneaking into the site's communication nest without being detected.

Still, Tucker ran low and kept his miner's helmet guarding the back of his neck. He pictured the melted flesh and sloughing skin of the dead men. Frank had explained about the aberrations in the cheetah back at the island, about its venomous nature. He also shared how some bats carried anticoagulant compounds in their saliva to encourage bleeding after a bite. Others sported paralytic enzymes to numb their prey. Apparently, the mutagenic virus had upped this colony's game, weaponizing it with some sort of necrotizing enzyme that acted like acid in the veins, similar to the toxin found in the venom of mambas and cobras, only far more potent.

Luckily, the swarm kept to the skies so far.

Just stay there.

Tucker rounded the last of the shacks and stopped in its shadow. The cluster of multistory cinder block buildings rose before him, all surrounded by a ten-foot wall topped with coils of razor wire. Steel scaffolding rose in places, shielded by thick plates, forming guard towers. Again, Russian-made heavy machine guns had been mounted in place.

Frank looked enviously toward them.

Tucker just grimaced.

De Coster must've gotten a deal by buying in bulk from the Russians.

Additionally, catwalks linked the guard shacks. Soldiers in combat armor patrolled between the towers, carrying FN FAL battle rifles. And beyond the walls, a trio of trucks circled with additional machine gun mounts fixed in their beds.

Tucker turned to Frank with raised eyebrows.

This was going to be one tough castle to storm.

Still, whether fortunate or not, he and Frank had not come alone. The machine guns—both those in the guard towers and mounted in the trucks—all pointed up. The patrolling soldiers searched the same direction.

Tucker pulled back and motioned Frank closer. "Any thoughts?"

Before his friend could answer, a sharp keening rose from above. It started low, less heard than felt. A tingling in the ears, an itching across the scalp. Then it grew rapidly in volume. In moments, it burned through his skull, set his ears on fire. He slapped his palms to his head, trying to dampen it, but it did little good. He swore he could feel the tiny bones of his ears about to rip loose.

Back in the sandboxes of two wars, Tucker had been exposed to nonlethal countermeasures employed by the military for crowd control, acoustic weapons that cast out a wave of ultrasonics to agonize and incapacitate. This was worse, rising from thousands of tiny throats, battering those below.

Frank cringed, staring up at the sky.

Clearly, this bat colony had been upgraded with more than just a necrolytic enzyme.

Tucker noted another oddity. The dark swarm now flashed with glowing spots and streaks, as if signaling a warning or communicating with each other.

He held his breath.

By now, he and Frank suspected the town had been attacked last night. Maybe the colony was trying to drive away these interlopers, these violators of the natural world. He remembered Benjie's description of the overcrowded U.N. camp, the flowing sewage, the escalating cases of cholera. Had the campsite been attacked for the same reason?

Tucker gazed across the open pit, the haze of coal smoke, the toxic ponds.

This is surely a far worse affront.

The ultrasonic attack waned slightly, enough for Frank to shout into Tucker's assaulted ear. He pointed toward the bats. "They're trying to intimidate us!"

"Well, it's working."

Frank looked up. "Dangerous animals, especially venomous ones, prefer to ward you off, to chase you away. Using sight and sound. Coral snakes do it with their bright bands. Rattlesnakes with their warning rattles."

Tucker winced at the ongoing acoustic assault.

Maybe we'd all better heed that warning.

Unfortunately, that sentiment was not shared.

Staccato blasts of rifle fire erupted along the walls. Machine guns chattered, sending bright lines of tracer rounds arcing across the sky. Elsewhere, jets of flame shot into the sky.

The defiant challenge was noted.

In the sky, the colony suddenly went quiet and ominously dark.

The time for warnings was over.

Without a sound, the horde fell upon the town.

11:04 P.M.

Nolan De Coster leaned closer to the computer monitor. "What's the status in Katwa, Captain?"

Draper hunched before the camera at the mine

office. His face shone a ruddy crimson under a Kevlar helmet. Rivulets of sweat streamed down his face. Not from fear, but fury. Gunfire echoed behind the man, along with screams and shouts.

"The town's being attacked again," Draper said. "Like last night. Only a thousandfold worse."

Nolan sighed. He had hoped the reports from this morning had been overblown. It was why he had sent Draper over there, to quash any panic. To that end, Draper had shot a handful of deserters shortly after his arrival, to instill a greater fear.

Only, with this new attack, such scare tactics would no longer work.

The town faced a larger terror.

Nolan had two other windows open on his screen. One showed a close-up of a massive necrotizing lesion across the back and neck of a dead man. Yet more proof of new aberrations out in the jungle. He shook his head. The escalating number of affected species troubled him. They seemed to be spreading ever westward across the Congo.

And my island is in their path.

The other window on the monitor showed the mine's latest quarterly P&L. He scowled at the bottom line. The site was nearly tapped out. He would start losing money in another quarter or two.

Draper interrupted his reverie. "Sir, what would you like me to do? My scouts have still failed to track down the escapees."

That was yet another concern.

Nolan closed his eyes and steepled his fingers at his lips. He listened to the rattle of gunfire, the screams—then came to a decision.

He opened his eyes. "Perhaps we can address all our troubles in one move." He ticked off the problems at hand. "Katwa is near the end of its usefulness. The prisoners are likely still nearby. And as I understand it, most of the witnesses—or should I say, workers—are holed up on site."

"Yes, sir."

"Then it's best we clean house. Perhaps, in doing so, we can rid the world of that malignant colony at the same time."

Draper's face paled as he began to understand Nolan's intent.

"Ready the failsafe," Nolan said, confirming the captain's conjecture.

"The MOAB?"

Nolan nodded.

The full name for the GBU-43/B weapon system was officially Massive Ordnance Air Blast. Though it was better known as the Mother of All Bombs. Nolan's calculating mind always prepared for unexpected contingencies. Five years ago, he had the opportunity to purchase seven MOABs, each weighing ten tons, from a munitions company whose CEO had a gambling problem. The American military believed the bombs had been distributed among its allies. Normally each cost two hundred thousand U.S. dollars. Nolan had paid three times that much to secure each one, and another hundred thousand to make them vanish.

Afterward, he had buried them in bunkers at strategic areas of his operations.

As a failsafe.

In case he ever needed a site erased.

Like now.

The MOAB had been designed to be a bunker buster, to destroy tunnels and other buried facilities. Its yield was equivalent to that of a small tactical nuclear weapon, with a blast radius of a mile in every direction.

Nolan planned on blaming the explosion on an industrial accident. Any further inquiry would be quashed by those in his employ within the DRC government. Plus, he would collect a hefty payout from the mine's insurance policy, far more money than he could ever hope to earn from the failing mine.

All in all, a win-win.

Satisfied, Nolan addressed the question shining in Draper's face. "Your men," Nolan said. "How long will it take you to gather them and evacuate?"

"Forty minutes," he said, plainly anticipating this inquiry, proof that he was a good man and a better soldier.

"Maybe we'd better allow you a bit more leeway, Captain. To make sure you get well clear of there."

Draper straightened, ready to carry out his order. "Yes, sir."

Nolan nodded to him. "I'll set the failsafe's timer for midnight."

20

Positioned at the back of the ATV, Gray stood guard over Kowalski. The big man splashed through calf-deep water, tugging each boot out of the muck. He reached the last of the ATV's four tires, uncapped its stem, and slowly let air out.

Shortly after entering the swamp, the wheels had mired up to their axles in the mud of the swamp. They were stuck. The plan was to partially deflate the tires and hope the greater surface area of tread would give them the extra traction to pull free.

"About done?" Gray called over as he watched the flat water. He had a flashlight clutched next to the length of his KelTec handgun. His heart pounded in his throat, knowing the risk they were taking being out of the ATV.

The night was pitch-black. The little glimpses of sky through breaks in the canopy were cloaked in clouds. A heavy mist, nearly drizzle, hung in the air. All around, mosquitoes whined. Frogs croaked. Birds and monkeys called across the swamps, objecting to their trespass.

"Almost finished," Kowalski grunted.

"Don't let out too much air and give us a flat."

"I know what I'm doing, Pierce. It's not the first time I've gone mudding." Kowalski grumbled under his breath, then resecured the cap on the tire stem. He straightened and slapped the nearly six-foot-tall tire. "See? Still plenty of cushion."

"Then back inside. Let's get moving again."

Kowalski waded to the open rear gate, and the two clambered into the ATV. Benjie shifted aside to let Kowalski pass and return to the driver's seat. Faraji kept watch up front, ready to guide them onward to the village of the Leopard King. It marked the next goalpost along the trail left by the Reverend William Sheppard.

Gray sighed.

That's if we get moving.

They had been trekking for nearly two hours. He estimated that by now the team had crossed out of Tshopo Province and had entered neighboring Ituri, a more remote and heavily forested section of the Congo. They had to be nearing that abandoned Kuba village.

Kowalski started the engine, gunned it, then set about rocking the ATV back and forth, fighting to pry their tires out of the mud. Water and muck fountained all around them.

A pack of small monkeys fled from the display, sweeping across the canopy. A few landed on the roof with loud bangs, then bounded away. One hung around long enough to scream through a window at them, its tiny face scrunched in fury, baring needle-like teeth.

"*Allenopithecus nigroviridis*," Benjie said. He craned near the window as the monkey fled, following the rest of its troop. "Also known as Allen's swamp monkeys."

"Did that one look normal to you?" Gray asked.

Benjie shrugged. "I . . . I think so."

Faraji added his own assessment. "Very tasty, yes. Good eating."

Kowalski grunted. "I'll take your word for it, kid."

He continued to rock the ATV, heaving his body back and forth in the seat, as if his extra mass would make the difference.

And maybe it did.

One last shove and the ATV broke free. Trundling once again, they were tossed about the compartment for a few breaths. Then the vehicle found its proper footing and sped onward across the deepening swamp.

"See? Piece of cake," Kowalski noted with satisfied triumph.

"Yes, cake," Faraji commented. "Very tasty, too."

Kowalski patted the youth on the shoulder. "That I'll agree with. But you can keep that roasted monkey all to yourself."

Faraji nodded seriously. "Thank you."

"Don't slow," Gray warned. "Keep a steady pace. We don't want to get mired again."

"Enough with your backseat driving already." Kowalski twisted to glare at him. "You want to take the wheel? I'm happy to take a goddamned nap."

Gray waved forward, knowing they were all on edge. The oppressive darkness, the press of the jungle, the lack of sleep, all wore at their nerves.

"Sorry," Gray said. "Just keep going. Listen to Faraji."

As they forged ahead, Gray returned his attention to the glowing topo map on his digital pad. He had been roughly tracking their progress, pinging a GPS reading once every half hour, then turning it off again. He didn't want to risk exposing their progress, but they were deep in the weeds out here. Even Faraji looked skeptically out at the drowned jungle.

Gray compared the map to the landscape around them. Since leaving Sheppard's old missionary station, the elevation had been steadily dropping. He suspected this section of the jungle was not normally a swamp. The heavy monsoons had likely flooded these lowland forests.

With every passing mile, Gray grew more worried. Before long, the bouncing and jolting of the ATV smoothed out into a gentle rocking. The floodwaters of these drowned lands had gotten so deep that the vehicle had turned back into a duck. The spinning tires became paddlewheels, propelling them along. Their pace slowed considerably.

The jungle grew even denser. Clusters of raffia palms crowded with groves of cedar. Orchids hung all about. Drapes of vines tried to snag them in their nets. Twice—with much cussing from Kowalski—they had to use machetes to break themselves free.

Despite the flooding, the dark forest stirred with life. Pythons languidly shifted their loops away from their passage. Rabbits fled in all directions, leaping from mossy hillocks to brambly thickets. Countless troops of monkeys wailed at them. Gray even spotted one of the rare striped okapi as it splashed across their headlights.

With each new sighting, Gray looked to Benjie. The biologist shrugged.

From a distance, there was no telling if any of the animals were altered. Still, Gray remembered Benjie's warning. The danger would grow as they neared the source.

Kowalski was no happier to continue deeper into the dark heart of the Congo. "Kid, how much farther to that dead king's village?"

Faraji pressed his nose against the side window, then the windshield. "This look all wrong. Should be at the *bonde*, the valley. But not here."

Lightning crackled through the cloud layer. Thunder boomed, loud enough to rattle the ATV's windows. As if on this signal, the constant hanging drizzle turned into a heavy shower. The drops pelted the water, pebbling the black surface.

Benjie nudged Gray and pointed out his window. "Look."

Gray shifted over and squinted outside. All he saw was a rain-swept jungle. The entire forest vibrated under the storm's assault. "What?"

Benjie searched the cabin and picked up his flashlight. He ignited it, momentarily blinding everyone. He twisted and pointed its beam out the window. He splashed the light across the dancing water, aiming it slightly behind the ATV. He fixed his beam on a grassy raft that looked stuck in place, undisturbed by the wake of their passage.

"We passed another a moment ago," Benjie said. "I didn't pay attention."

"What is it?"

Benjie kept the flashlight pointed but turned to Gray. "I think that's *thatch*."

Gray understood and grabbed Kowalski's shoulder. "Hold up."

Kowalski braked the spinning tires but kept the engine idling. He glanced back. "Why?"

"I think Faraji's suspicions were right all along. We did reach the valley." Gray scooted over and turned on his own flashlight, sweeping the beam along the other side of the ATV. More of the thatched rafts dotted the pebbling waters. "Those are roofs. We're at the king's village. Only the valley's been entirely flooded over."

Now focused, Gray picked out several beams and poles poking out of the water, further evidence that a large village once stood here.

Kowalski groaned. "No way we're finding any clue hidden here."

"Not without scuba gear," Benjie added.

Gray's heart sank, recognizing this truth. If there was a king's tomb somewhere below them, it would be hard to find it, especially in the dark. And even then, trying to excavate any answer out of it would be impossible. They would have to wait for these floodwaters to recede.

And that could take months.

Gray turned to the front passenger seat, grasping at straws. "Faraji, do you have any suggestions?"

The boy cast his gaze down and shook his head. "*Samahani*," he mumbled. "I'm sorry."

"So, it's the end of the road," Kowalski concluded, sounding almost relieved.

11:22 P.M.

Ten minutes later, Gray worried that Kowalski might be right. Still, he refused to give up—at least, not yet. They'd come all this way.

He had collected his digital pad and briefly pinged the GPS to mark this location.

It appeared as a red diamond on the glowing topo map.

One more bread crumb left by Sheppard.

He shifted the sheaf of photos to his lap. He took out all seven, hoping for some answers. Three photos led to this place: the okapi lake, the missionary church, and now this drowned village. Three more photos extended the path to the very last picture, which showed a crack in a jagged cliff, flanked by stone pillars, marking the possible entrance to Mfupa Ufalme, the Kingdom of Bones.

But how can we reach that place?

He fanned through the next three photos, three more bread crumbs. Could their team skip over the clue lost here and move forward? He studied the next picture. It simply showed a dagger stuck into the trunk of a palm. Faraji had previously studied it and remained clueless. If there was any further meaning to it, that answer was drowned under them. The other two black-and-white photos offered no better direction. In one, Sheppard stood in front of two slabs of stone, as tall as him, that leaned against one another, forming a shelter beneath where a fire burned. In the other, the reverend filled a canteen at the confluence of two streams. The sketches drawn on the photos' backs didn't help either: a scrawled compass rose and a collection of stick figures, all carrying spears taller than the hunters themselves.

Gray wondered if the latter might represent pygmies. Such tribes still made their home in the Ituri forests. Though their population, along with their tribal lands, had dwindled to a fraction of their size from Sheppard's time. Still, even if Gray was right about this assumption, it didn't help. It offered no clue to their path forward.

He picked up the topo map and zoomed out, studying their route backward. Two more red diamonds marked the site of the okapi lake and the missionary church. He noted that the three diamonds formed a relatively straight line across this corner of the Congo, as if Sheppard had trekked a beeline through the jungle.

Gray frowned. That didn't seem likely, considering the stubborn terrain. Then again, Sheppard buried these bread crumbs and left the photos with the Kuba *after* he had returned. Had the reverend chosen these locations less to mark his own original path and more to guide others in the future along a straighter route?

He closed his eyes, trying to put himself in the boots of William Sheppard. The man was an excellent cartographer and explorer, even discovering a lake that had been named after him. From the beginning, they had all supposed that Sheppard had left these clues in case a great danger should ever threaten the Congo again, a peril tied to Prester John's lost Kingdom of Bones. If so, in such a dire emergency, the reverend would not want those future hunters led on a wild-goose chase, running hither and yon.

He wouldn't do that.

Gray opened his eyes. "He would've drawn a straight arrow, pointing to the lost kingdom."

Benjie overheard him. "What are you talking about?"

Gray shook his head. He wanted further reassurance. "Faraji, can you hop back here?"

The kid scrambled over the seat, nearly kicking Kowalski in the head. The big man had lit a new cigar, puffing a stream of foul smoke toward the window which he'd cracked open. The smell of diesel flowed in, rising from the exhaust snorkel, as the engine idled.

Faraji joined him, waving a palm by his nose, looking grateful to escape the cigar stench up front. His eyes glowed with curiosity.

Gray lifted the topo map. "Can you pinpoint the location of the village that Sheppard visited when he first met your people?"

"Yes. Easy. Village is my home. King now is same as king from Sheppard time."

Which meant the village hadn't moved as the monarchs changed.

The Kuba Box, the one that held Sheppard's clues, had been left at Faraji's hometown. If so, it had to mark the true starting point of this journey.

Faraji scooted closer to study the digital pad. He used a finger to trace some rivers, then tapped a spot on the map. Pride filled his voice. "Here. Here where I live."

Gray converted the location to a red diamond and let out a sigh of relief. The additional mark was in direct line with the other three. Gray drew a blue line connecting all four.

Even Benjie saw it now, too. "They're all in a row."

And if this was indeed a straight arrow . . .

Gray extended the line eastward, broken now into dashes. The first three clues had led them into lands that sunk ever lower, ending at this drowned valley. The continuing line crossed terrain that climbed again, stretching toward the broken highlands at the eastern edge of the Ituri forest.

Benjie leaned closer to the glowing pad. "Is that where we're supposed to go? Up into those mountains?"

"We'd better hope so."

Benjie sat back with a sigh. "That's a lot of hard terrain. On the topo, it looks like some angry god hit that area with a hammer, shattering it apart.

Even if you're right, it would take us months, if not longer, to search through there."

"Maybe not," Gray said.

He reached to his pack and retrieved his sat-phone. He replaced its battery. He had disabled the device at the start of this journey, fearing someone might use it to track them. With the U.N. camp ambushed and the university attacked, the enemy had proven themselves resourceful. To orchestrate those strikes, they must have deep pockets throughout this region.

Kowalski noted what he was doing and exhaled a stream of smoke. "What're you up to, Pierce?"

"Possibly making a mistake."

The call was a gamble, but a necessary one. Still, he needed to keep it brief. While the sat-phone could scramble the transmission, make it impossible for anyone to eavesdrop, the signal could still be traced. After a brief pause, weighing whether this was a smart move, he tapped in the code for Sigma headquarters.

The connection was made immediately. "Commander Pierce," Painter answered, speaking curtly. "What's your status?"

Gray debriefed him on their situation, speaking rapidly, trying to keep this call as short as possible.

Painter also updated him. "The situation in Kisangani is growing worse by the hour. Lisa reports that there are hundreds of cases now. Many already dead. More flowing into the city. Panic has set in. Looting and chaos. There are also reports of outlying villages being overrun with wild animals—although those are sketchy."

Gray looked at Benjie. "Those animals may be more than just *wild*." He shared their concerns about what else the virus might be doing to the Congo. "If we could consult Dr. Whitaker, the virologist . . ."

"Can't expect that anytime soon. There's still no word from Tucker. So, if there are any answers to be found out in that jungle, we need them ASAP."

"That's why I broke radio silence. I need help." He explained about their dilemma and the hope of skipping over Sheppard's last clue and driving straight to the end. He transmitted a copy of his marked-up map, along with the reverend's last photo. "That cliff. Its jagged escarpment against the sky. It wasn't unique enough before, not when we had the entire Congo as a possible location. But if we focused our search, narrowed it down—"

"Along the line you drew into those mountains," Painter said, immediately understanding.

"Exactly. With satellite mapping, maybe that cliff could be pinpointed, or at least, other areas ruled out."

"We can try. I'll get Kat right on it. But it will still take hours to complete such a detailed scan."

"Understood. Until then, we'll continue along the path I transmitted. I'll go radio silent and reach out again when we get there."

"Very good."

Gray signed off and cut the connection. He snapped the battery out of the phone and returned them both to his pack.

Kowalski frowned at him. "So, we're continuing blind from here."

"Better than just sitting on our asses."

Kowalski turned back around and gunned the engine. "I wouldn't be so sure about that."

11:36 P.M.

Seated in the back, Benjie tugged at his ear as he studied the topographic map shining on the screen. He hunched over the pad on his knee. He zoomed in and out on the map. His other hand continued to yank on his earlobe. Hyper-focused on the map, it took him several minutes to realize what he was doing. He forced his hand away from his head.

His ear still ached from the persistent attention.

Hadn't done that since I was at uni.

He licked his lips, accepting the repetitive tic—the tugging at his ear—as part of his autistic behavior. Likely triggered by stress. That, and his focus on the map. He had often hurt his ear back at uni, when he was lost in his studies, especially if a difficult test was coming up.

He stared out at the passing swamplands.

This certainly counts as that.

He turned off the digital pad, fearing to waste the battery needlessly. His efforts had failed to glean any further insight. Then again, they had plenty of time to chew on the problem. It looked like it would take most of the night to reach the highlands.

He leaned back, knowing he should try to

sleep, but recognizing that would never happen. Instead, he listened to the rumble of the engine and the patter of rain. Thunder boomed in the distance. He rocked with the sway of the ATV as the giant tires churned the waters.

How much longer will we be in these swamps?

From the map, he knew the terrain rose ahead. They should be onto drier land before long. Confirming that, he spotted rocks in the water. They hadn't been there earlier. The granite boulders offered some hope that the ground was rising under them. He set about counting those he could see, to distract himself from his anxiety.

Fourteen to the left, maybe another eight on the right.

He kept searching for more—then one of them moved, rising higher, lifting a set of ears that flapped in agitation.

Those weren't rocks.

He sat upright. "Mates! We need to be careful."

Gray had been leaning forward, talking to his partner in the front seat, likely strategizing. "What's wrong?"

"We're entering a bloat of hippos."

Kowalski scowled. "A what?"

"A group, a nest, whatever." Benjie pointed forward. "Those gray humps are hippopotamuses. Probably even more submerged."

As if summoned by his words, another handful of backs lifted into view. Steamy fountains of exhalations marked their rising.

So many of them . . .

"Can we go around?" Gray asked.

Kowalski turned the wheel. "I can try, but this vessel ain't no speedboat."

The ATV lumbered to the side, moving at a snail's pace. Hippos floated in every direction. By now, the beasts had noted their presence and began gliding toward them. Some vanished away, likely sweeping faster underwater toward the trespassers. Hippos might look slow and ponderous on land, but in water, they were swift killers.

Gray turned to Benjie. "Could they be altered, like the jackals?"

"I don't think so. The genetic alteration must occur in utero, after an adult is infected. Which means a full generation would have to be born and grow." He shook his head. "A hippo's gestation is over eight months. And their calves are slow to mature."

"Which is too long."

Benjie nodded. "Not enough time has passed since the virus had begun to spread. These hippos couldn't be corrupted already."

Gray looked behind them. "But what about the changes in the jackals?"

Benjie gulped down his fear, leaning on his studies to temper his panic. "Their gestation is only *two* months. By eight months, they're full grown. Plus, jackals have a wide territorial range. They normally inhabit the Congo's grasslands and savannas. But not always. The pack we encountered could have drifted from the source of the virus, where it could've been brewing for who knows how long. But hippos—they stick to their own territories."

Gray understood. "So, those beasts out there can't be corrupted."

"But they can still be *infected*. If they are, the virus might make them hyperaggressive. Like what happened with the baboons, who are normally timid. Though, in this case, hippos are already naturally combative."

"Great," Kowalski said. "So super-angry hippos. Then we'd better—"

A wave of water burst across the windshield. A massive bull reared up, jaws wide, exposing its throat and two-foot-long tusks. It slammed those teeth into the glass, shattering through, sending a web of cracks across the windshield. The entire ATV jolted backward. As the bull dropped away, its two-ton bulk ripped the windshield clean off.

Benjie searched around.

Hippos closed in from all directions, ready to challenge the intruder.

Kowalski struggled to get his weapon to his shoulder. "Get ready! We're about to play the worst game of Hungry Hungry Hippos."

Gray yanked Faraji from the front seat and shoved the boy toward Benjie. "Both of you get to the back."

Benjie wasn't sure it was any safer there, but he obeyed.

Gray lowered the windows to either side. The openings were too small for a hippo to breach through, but they offered the man more room to fire. Gray clutched his long-barreled handgun in both fists, glancing right and left. He darted one way, then the other, firing at those gray humps if they approached too close. The blasts were deafening in the enclosed cabin.

Hippos sank away from the assault, looking little fazed.

In front, Kowalski kept the ATV moving, one hand on the wheel, the other pointing and firing his unusual weapon. The whining *zing*s escalated into a buzzsaw as he shifted into automatic fire. Silver flashed across the headlights. Sharp disks imbedded into arched backs or sliced through ears.

Still, all their efforts only seemed to roil the bloat.

Benjie gasped as another bull exploded out of the water to the right. It ripped into one of the massive tires. The ATV lurched as the hippo tried to drag that corner underwater. Benjie and Faraji tumbled forward. Then rubber tore as the bull broke free, nearly taking the tire with it.

The ATV bobbed back up.

The shredded tire spun and frothed the water. The only benefit was that the ripped tire gained more traction in the water on that side. It started turning the ATV all on its own.

Kowalski fought the wheel to compensate—but he was too slow.

Another hippo butted hard on the other side, sending the ATV into a dizzying spin. It was only stopped when another slammed the opposite side. Gray fired wildly, trying to discourage further assaults. Only the blasts seemed to attract the hippos.

Thrown about, Benjie felt like a pinball in

an arcade. His head rang, his body was bashed. Still, he crawled toward Gray.

"Stop it!" he hollered.

Gray kept his gun pointed. "What? Why?"

Benjie pointed to the left rear wheel. "Get them to shred that tire, too." He read the confusion on Gray's face. "To help balance the torn one on the opposite side. Together, they might drive us faster in a straight line."

Gray considered the idea for a beat, then crabbed toward the tailgate. "Get clear!" he ordered.

Benjie and Faraji crowded away.

Gray shouldered the tailgate open, enough for him to lean out. Hanging from a handgrip, he pointed his pistol past the rear of the giant tire. He fired potshots at a large hippo, a massive bull, far bulkier than the others, maybe the leader of this bloat. It sank away, as if shrugging off the attack.

Gray frowned in frustration.

Then water flumed, framing the four-foot-wide jaws of the bull. It slammed into the ATV's side, catching the tire and a chunk of sidewall. Gray got tossed out the open tailgate. The bull crashed back into the swamp, dragging the ATV down with it. Water flooded into the cabin.

Benjie fought the flow to reach the tailgate.

Gray sputtered up.

"Over here!" Benjie hollered, reaching out an arm.

Gray lunged with a hard kick. He slapped out a hand and snagged Benjie's forearm. Benjie grabbed the man's wrist and yanked backward, falling, using his bodyweight as leverage.

It wasn't enough against the tide.

Past Gray's kicking legs, another hippo rose, sweeping toward him, impossibly swift. Water surged ahead of it. Benjie held tight, not letting go.

Then arms hugged him from behind.

It was Faraji. He helped Benjie pull.

It was just enough to yank Gray back into the cabin. The hippo behind him struck the rear, slamming the tailgate closed. The other bull finally tore free of the tire, letting the ATV go. The vehicle bobbed back up, sloshing everyone around.

Benjie pushed up enough to see the assaulted tire spinning, loose rubber slapping at the water. With two shredded tires offering better traction now, the ATV treaded faster across the swamp.

Gray nodded to Benjie. "Smart."

He took the compliment as Gray sidled forward. The man had somehow kept hold of his pistol, though it was surely waterlogged.

Ahead, Kowalski glowered at the rainswept swamps.

Other humps lay out there, but whether it was the flailing tires or their greater speed—now heading away—the hippos hung back. The bloat closed slowly behind them, discouraging their return, then vanished into the dark.

Soaked to the skin, Benjie sat in a few inches of water.

He couldn't be more relieved.

The ATV continued its frothing passage across the swamp. They continued unmolested.

Finally, tires caught hold of mud. The ATV crawled out of the water, pushing through a fringe of reeds. It limped along with two intact tires and two torn ones.

Still, Gray ordered Kowalski to carry them a good distance away from the swamp before calling for a stop. He faced the group.

"We'll need to swap out the tires. There are two spares, deflated and stored under the cargo deck and a powered air compressor to fill them. But keep in mind, we have no more spares after this. That's it."

"Then I'd better watch out for loose nails," Kowalski said sourly.

Gray ignored him. "We should also top off the gas tanks while we can. We've still got a long way to go."

Benjie pictured the blue line drawn across the topo map. He stared into the dark jungle as rain flowed out of clouds rumbling with thunder.

But where will it lead us?

21

Tucker straightened over the soldier's limp body. He shifted the Kevlar vest to settle the armor's weight over his shoulders, then swapped his miner's helmet for a combat one. It had been a long time since he'd worn such gear, flashing back to sandstorm-swept streets and crumbling stone walls.

He shook his head to clear the memory.

Not the time.

Frank looked at him, as if sensing his momentary lapse. His friend was similarly attired and dragged a second body deeper into the concrete bunker. "You good?"

Tucker gave him a thumb's up. Despite his distaste for his new outfit, he appreciated both its added protection and its aid in blending them among the other combatants at the mine. Still, he felt only half-dressed. Without Kane at his side or sharing the dog's sight, Tucker felt exposed, vulnerable.

In the corner of his goggles, he caught occasional snatches of garbled transmissions, flickers of camera feed. Still, the local jamming thwarted any true connection to his partner.

"Let's keep going," Tucker said, firming his grip on the ParaFAL rifle he had pilfered from the dead soldier. It was fitted with a fifty-round box magazine, along with a steel bayonet at its tip.

Frank released the other body and shouldered a matching weapon.

They crossed to the bunker's door. Outside, the war with the sky continued. Screams and shouts echoed into the bunker. Gunfire chattered all around. Flamethrowers roared.

Twenty minutes ago, the horde of bats had swept down upon the city, attacking anything in sight. Tucker and Frank had ducked into the shelter of one of the worker's shanties. Luckily the worst of the aerial attack was aimed at the cinder block administration center, where the gunfire and flames drew the bats.

From the shelter, Tucker had watched a guard tower fall to the bats. A body tumbled from its machine gun nest; the figure writhed in midair, covered in black leathery wings. Taking advantage, they had raced out of hiding with a sheet of corrugated metal shielding their heads. It still had old boards nailed to it.

Once at the wall, they propped the metal shield against it and used the boards as a makeshift ladder. They both bore deep cuts from rolling over the razor wire at the top of the wall and dropping into the fortified compound. With all eyes on the sky or battling on the ground, Frank and Tucker were able to duck into the nearest shelter, a concrete bunker at the base of the barricade. Two gunshots had dropped the soldiers who had been hiding inside.

Prepared to continue on, Frank gripped the door handle. "Ready?"

"No, but that can't stop us."

Frank shoved the door open, and Tucker dashed out, running low. No one paid them any heed. They looked like any of the other dozens of men in armor and helmets. Automatic fire rattled all around them. Tucker ran past a man down on a knee with a flamethrower aimed at the sky, sweeping a fiery swath through the air.

Bodies sprawled everywhere, some still covered in bats, others with limbs tremoring in poisonous agony.

A burning bat tumbled out of the air and landed ahead of Tucker. It flopped and smoked, a slight glow rose from its chest fur, looking like a smear of phosphorescent algae—and maybe it was, acquired from some viral-induced symbiotic relationship.

Tucker leaped over it, leaving such mysteries for later.

Frank gasped, drawing attention. A dark shadow flapped atop his helmet, struggling to reach flesh. Tucker stabbed it with his bayonet and flung the bat away.

Without comment, they rushed into an alleyway between two squat buildings. Tucker had already identified their goal, using his scope's binocular features. In the center of the administration sector rose a four-story tower, the roof festooned with satellite dishes and antennas, along with a taller pole ringed in radio-jamming plates. It had to mark the communication center for the mine.

As they reached the end of the alley, winds buffeted them, trying to push them back. The source was a familiar helicopter, the gunship that had been plaguing their group from the start. Men in combat gear loaded crates into the back; others climbed into the crew hold.

Frank leaned toward Tucker's ear. "They're evacuating."

He nodded and couldn't blame them. Even now, bats dive-bombed the enemy's efforts. Bodies dotted the open square. A soldier had collapsed nearby. His face was a blackened mass, weeping with blood. Worst of all were his intact eyes staring upward.

Tucker ducked lower. The fierce rotorwash from the parked helicopter kept Frank and Tucker momentarily protected. Frank motioned around the edges of the square and toward the open door into the communication building. There was plenty of activity over there, but that might serve them.

Tucker led the way, running low, rifle in front of him. Frank followed at his heels. They circled the square, ducking periodically under metal awnings. Bats pelted all around, either blown by the helicopter's chop or flying under their own volition. Glass rained on them as windows shattered under the assault.

Tucker felt a blow to his shoulder, hard enough to almost knock his rifle loose. A bat clung there, teeth gnashing at the Kevlar shoulder pads. Tucker lunged sideways and smashed its body into the nearby wall, crushing it. He felt a twinge of guilt, knowing there was no malice in the tiny creature's attack, only instinct and fury.

Still, he had others to protect. Not just Monk and his team, but everyone who was threatened throughout the Congo.

He continued around and reached the open door. The helicopter roared behind him. Rotorwash shoved him across the threshold. He shouldered through other soldiers, but even their entry was ignored amidst the terror, chaos, and rush to evacuate.

Tucker hurried down a hallway, searching right and left for any space that looked like a radio room. It would take them time to canvass each floor. Frank suddenly grabbed him and shoved him through an open office door.

Tucker frowned at him.

Frank edged back to the doorway and pointed toward a stairwell at the end of the hall. Two figures stood in agitated conversation. Frank indicated the taller of the two, with grizzled features and close-cropped gray hair. He carried himself with stiff-backed authority.

"That's Captain Draper," Frank whispered.

Tucker recognized the name of De Coster's righthand man. He must be the one overseeing operations and leading the evacuation. Draper waved an arm toward the exit, shouted something in Swahili, then turned away. He hiked up the steps, taking them two at a time.

"Follow him," Tucker urged and headed back out.

From the urgency of the captain's departure, Tucker sensed he might be reporting in. If not, they could always waylay him and force him to reveal the location of the radio room.

Tucker hurried to the stairwell and mounted the steps, staying well back from their target. He didn't want to raise the suspicions of the man they were tailing. Draper climbed to the top floor, further reinforcing that he was headed to report to someone in authority. If there was a radio room, it made sense that it might be under a rooftop covered in dishes and antenna.

Reaching the fourth floor, Tucker proceeded more cautiously. It appeared deserted. Still, he heard voices coming from a double set of doors to the right. He and Frank edged forward to eavesdrop. They slipped into a dark office across the hall that allowed them a partial view into the other room.

Draper stood before a bank of satellite equipment and monitors. He leaned over a radio technician, a Congolese soldier, and barked orders, this time in French. Tucker knew a smattering of the language, but not enough to follow the hurried conversation.

He glanced to Frank, who Tucker knew was more fluent.

Frank's eyes grew huge.

Tucker leaned close. "What's wrong?"

11:42 P.M.

Frank held up a palm.

I need to hear this, make sure I'm not mistaken.

Draper leaned over the tech and passed him a thumb drive. "Call up De Coster. We only have another eighteen minutes until this whole place becomes a smoking pit."

"Yes, sir."

Frank glanced to his wristwatch.

That timetable's set for midnight.

The tech plugged in the thumb drive and tapped a few keys. A moment later, the monitor in the room bloomed open a screen, showing Nolan De Coster seated at his desk. He had shed his suit jacket and had rolled up his sleeves. "Captain Draper, what are you still doing at the mine?"

"The attack is far worse than I anticipated, sir. Took much longer to secure and load everything and rally my men. We already lost a fifth of my personal contingent."

"You need more time?"

"No, sir. Everything is loaded, and we'll be airborne in two."

"If there's a problem, I can reset the timer on the MOAB. The bomb can be delayed if necessary."

Frank winced at the mention of a MOAB. *It can't be . . .* Still, he remembered Draper's description a moment ago, about leaving this place a smoking pit. If that bomb set to go off at midnight truly was a MOAB, its pit would consume the entire mine and a good portion of the surrounding jungle.

Draper shook his head. "There's no problem, sir. It's handled. And the quicker this place is wiped off the face of the earth, the better."

"Understood."

Draper stepped back from the monitor. "I'm headed out now."

"Good. Considering the escalation of events, I think it's best if we clean house at the island, too. I'll start orchestrating an evacuation. Set the research team to collating and collecting all the data. We should be ready by dawn. A few hellfire rockets should take care of the rest, yes?"

Frank clenched a fist, picturing the ward of patients.

"*Oui, Commandant.*"

"Then get moving."

The connection ended, and Draper straightened. He ripped the thumb drive out of the radio and pointed it at the tech's nose. "Send a final rally order to our men, then get your ass down to the chopper."

Frank pushed Tucker farther into the office as Draper stormed past and headed toward the stairwell. He waited for the man to vanish and the clatter of his boots to fade. Frank didn't have time to explain to Tucker.

He rushed across the hall and burst into the radio room. The tech jolted, shocked by the sudden intrusion. Frank put the point of his bayonet against the man's throat. "Do you speak English?"

The man tried to nod, slicing his neck in the process. "*Oui* . . . yes."

"Then you're going to help us." Frank turned

to Tucker and gave him a thumbnail account of the conversation. "The bastard has a MOAB buried somewhere at the mine. The bomb's set to explode in—" He checked his watch. "Fifteen more minutes. We need to be at least a mile away from here before then."

Tucker pointed to the tech. "Deactivate it."

The tech stammered, "I . . . I can't. It's not controlled from here."

"De Coster has his finger on the button," Frank explained.

"What about Monk and the others? They're still in the jungle, directly in the blast zone."

Frank nudged the tech with his bayonet. "Turn off the jammer. You should be able to do that from here."

He gulped and gave a small nod. Sweat ran down his face. He had to know the only threat was not Frank's gun, but also the timer ticking ever downward. They all needed to get out of here.

The tech returned to his console and swept through windows on his monitor. A final tap, and a big red button turned green. "Done."

Frank looked to Tucker for confirmation.

Tucker stepped back and firmed his goggles in place. His gaze shifted high as if he were staring off to nowhere. His mouth opened in shock at whatever he saw, viewed through Kane's camera. This was confirmed with his next words, radioed out to the others.

"Monk, what the hell are you doing in town?"

11:45 P.M.

Monk heard the panic in Tucker's voice.

He could understand why.

He leaned by a greasy window in the abandoned barracks. Charlotte stood guard with him, one hand resting atop Kane's head. Jameson sat well away from the window, with his splinted arm cradled to his chest. The man rocked in place, his eyes glassy with pain and terror.

Outside, four bodies lay strewn along the street, lit by the sheen of their own lights. They were members of the patrol that had nearly caught Monk's team in the jungle earlier. He had spied their approach through the deserted corner of the mine. They had spread out with flashlights affixed to their rifles. They kicked in door after door, searching each shack.

Then the sky had fallen upon them. It looked like shredded bits of shadow raining out of the clouds. It took several breaths for Monk to even recognize them as bats. They appeared drawn by the patrol's lights. The panicked gunfire only exasperated matters. Monk hadn't expected the bats to be more than a nuisance, but he took their arrival as a blessing. He prayed for the swarm to batter the patrol out of the area.

Then the screaming had started.

One of the soldiers had run past the window, a bat clinging to his cheek. Another was latched to his wrist. He fell only steps away from their door. His body flopped and writhed in plain agony. He clawed at his face and throat. When he finally lay still—which took considerable time—his neck and the side of his face were blistered with boils, torn by his clawing.

Out on the deserted streets now, bats had settled all around the barracks: under eaves, scrabbling along rooftops, scaling walls. A few still winged through the air. The scraping of their claws on the tin roof overhead set his teeth on edge. Most eerie of all was the winking glow that flowed through the bats, as if they were silently communicating to one another.

"Stay put," Tucker radioed. "We'll come to you. With the local jamming down, I can follow Kane's homing beacon. Just be ready to go. We need to be out of here in fifteen."

Monk was happy for the extraction, especially considering the circumstances, but he didn't understand the urgency. "Why fifteen?"

Tucker's answer set his heart to thudding harder. "There's a massive bomb set to detonate at midnight."

Monk closed his eyes.

Of course there is. Because poisonous bats aren't enough.

But Tucker wasn't done with the bad news. "The blast radius could extend a mile out from ground zero."

Monk shook his head. "No way we can clear that in time."

"We're gonna try."

Monk stared at the horde outside. "How?"

"Just be ready."

11:47 P.M.

Tucker paced the small communication nest as he signed off with Monk. He turned to Frank. "Any luck?"

Frank still guarded over the tech with his rifle. In his other hand, he clutched Tucker's sat-phone, trying to reach Ndaye at the helicopter. "Still nothing but dead air. I can't get any connection."

Tucker glared at the tech, wanting to blame him, but he suspected the small local tower on the roof only locked down radio communication across the mine itself. De Coster must have a whole network of more sophisticated blockers dampening longer-range communication.

Tucker stepped toward the array of radios. "You were able to connect to De Coster before. Employing some jam-breaking code, I'm guessing."

"Yes, but I don't have it. I swear. It's on a drive that only Captain Draper carries."

Tucker grimaced, remembering the thumb drive the bastard had given the tech. He glanced to the window, knowing there was no time to commandeer it. The helicopter had begun to roar out in the square, readying for liftoff.

"We can't wait any longer," Tucker decided.

"What do we do?"

"We're getting out of here."

Frank frowned. They both knew Ndaye could not fly here in time to evacuate them. The ecoguard would only get himself blown up, too.

The intent of the failed call had been to alert the world of Nolan De Coster's involvement, to get Sigma command focused on the man. But neither was happening now.

Which means we're on our own.

Tucker turned to the tech. "I saw trucks patrolling earlier. Where's your motor pool? Your garage?"

The soldier stood and pointed out the window to a neighboring building. "In the basement."

"Keys?"

"Kept in the vehicles."

Tucker waved to Frank and pointed to the tech. "Shoot him and c'mon."

The man stumbled back into his console, lifting his palms.

Frank leveled his weapon. "Or do you want to live?"

"Anything. What? Tell me."

Tucker had approved this plan already. Neither he nor Frank wanted to leave without giving the mine workers a fighting chance to escape.

Frank jabbed the bayonet at the tech's chest. "The siren earlier. It sounded a lockdown, yes?"

The man nodded vigorously.

"There must be another that signals an evacuation," Frank said.

"Yes, in case of an emergency."

"I think this situation counts." Tucker pointed to the communication array. "Sound it or die."

The tech whipped around and popped open a protective case over a toggle. He flipped it. An alarm immediately rose from above their heads and spread outward, growing into a deafening klaxon roar.

Tucker could only hope that as many workers as possible would flee, chancing the bats to reach the jungle. Otherwise, it was certain death to stay. Everyone in the room also knew that. The tech's eyes were huge with terror—more so when the helicopter rose from the square, likely driven off by the alarm. Draper must've suspected something was amiss when the siren blew and had ordered his team to flee.

Tucker sneered at the tech. "Your ride's leaving, bub. Looks like we're all in the same boat now." He pushed Frank toward the door. "Let's go."

The two turned and fled out of the radio room.

Confident of his own internal clock, Tucker still double-checked his diver's watch. *Eleven minutes to go.*

"We're cutting this close," Frank said, grinning hard at him. "Just like the old days."

"Old. As in the past. Where they belong."

They rushed down the steps and out the front door. The square was deserted and windswept by the departed helicopter. Even the bats had mostly gone, maybe in pursuit of the gunship.

Still, Tucker ran low, trying to shield as much of his exposed flesh behind armor. Frank kept at his side and pointed toward the building that the tech had indicated. An open garage door led to a ramp heading down, hopefully to the promised motor pool.

They dashed for it—when an ear-piercing

whistle, followed by an abrupt explosion, knocked them both to their knees. Tucker initially thought the bomb had prematurely blown, but he craned his neck back. A rocket had struck the roof of the communication nest, silencing the siren. Shattered bricks and glass cascaded down, falling through smoke and fire to pelt the square.

A chopper sped high above the carnage and swept away.

Tucker scowled at it. *A parting shot from Captain Draper.* De Coster's man must have clearly been suspicious of that sudden klaxon, guessing something was wrong.

They regained their feet and sprinted the last of the distance.

Tucker reached the sheltering darkness, glad to be out of sight, and rushed down the ramp. They slowed at the foot of it. A few bare bulbs lit the garage ahead. The scatter of light did little to cast back the shadows. The motor pool looked ransacked. The space was large enough to garage a dozen trucks, but there was only one left, sitting sullenly in a pool of light at the back: an old Land Rover that looked more rust than truck and was missing its front bumper.

But beggars couldn't be choosers.

Tucker led the way toward it, when Frank grabbed his arm and pulled him lower. He pointed up. Tucker suspected what he was going to see and wasn't disappointed. The roof of the garage stirred with shadows and flapping wings. A mass of bats crawled and hung there, turning the motor pool into its personal cave. Amidst the darkness, flickering glows and phosphorescent streaks flashed down at the trespassers.

Tucker remembered Frank's earlier ruminations, how the display was likely a warning, the visual equivalent of the shake of a rattler's tail.

"Move slow," Frank whispered to him. "We gotta make it to that Rover."

Tucker knew he was right. All instinct told Tucker to turn and run, but the bats weren't the only danger here.

A shout rose behind them, coming from the top of the ramp. "We're taking that truck!"

Tucker dropped even lower, leaning a hand on the floor. He recognized the voice of the radio tech, proving no good deed goes unpunished.

Should've shot him after all.

Especially as the bastard hadn't come alone. A crowd of armed men backed him up. He must've gathered them on his way out and led them here, knowing that commandeering a vehicle was the best chance to escape the blast zone.

The men headed down the ramp.

Tucker waved for Frank to keep going, then flicked his thumb toward the approaching group.

Just need fifteen seconds.

By now, the soldiers had entered the motor pool. Rifles bristled. One even hauled forward a machine gun.

To distract them, Tucker pointed a hand up. "Don't shoot," he warned softly.

Gazes flicked to the ceiling. Many of the men did double takes or dropped into wary squats. They all knew the danger above their heads. But that wasn't what they should've been watching for. A tiny silver sphere—the one Tucker had flicked toward them a moment ago—bounced and rolled under their feet.

Tucker counted in his head.

. . . twelve, thirteen, fourteen . . .

He shoved Frank forward, all but lifting the man off his legs. "Go!"

They rushed the Rover when the count reached fifteen.

The flash-bang exploded behind Tucker, blinding even with his back turned. The blast pounded his head. Still, Tucker didn't slow. Screams rose from behind him as the bats crashed upon the noisome threat.

He and Frank slammed into the Rover. Frank got the door open and slid across to the passenger seat. Tucker climbed in and dropped behind the wheel. He searched for the keys in the ignition.

Not there.

Frank reached over and flipped the visor above Tucker's head. A fob dropped. Tucker caught it with a prayer of thanks. He keyed the engine, only to have it cough and die.

Gunfire erupted across the garage. Rounds ricocheted and sparked in the dark. Men continued to bellow. Several ran for the ramp, only to fall under the onslaught of the bats.

Tucker pumped the gas pedal, turned the key, and begged for the slightest bit of mercy. It was granted as the stubborn Rover coughed again, then growled to life. He popped into gear and jammed the accelerator to the floor. Though the

Rover was mostly rust on the outside, its old diesel engine still had some life in her.

The Rover barreled through the chaos, choking a cloud of oily smoke behind it. The grill knocked bodies aside. Tires pummeled over others.

Both bats and men.

Tucker aimed for the ramp, shot up it, and skidded across the square. He headed for the compound's gates, which had been left open as others heeded the evacuation siren. He did not slow. He kept one eye on the road, the other on the tiny compass spinning at a corner of the goggles, guiding him back to Kane.

He counted the seconds until they were reunited—while another timer ticked down in his head.

Eight minutes to go.

11:52 P.M.

With the siren gone silent again, Charlotte watched the mass of bats settle and return to their wary perches. She felt like Tippi Hedren in Hitchcock's *The Birds*, waiting for the winged flock to attack.

Just keep calm, she warned both herself and the horde.

During her vigil, a handful of men had furtively passed through the area, either singly or in small groups. They weren't patrols, but miners in dirt-caked clothes. They edged through the deserted warren, moving silently, trying not to disturb the lurkers above them. Once free, they all sprinted for the forest and disappeared into its shelter.

They must know what's coming . . .

"We're running out of time," Jameson said at her shoulder. "We should've followed those men into the jungle."

Charlotte stayed silent. Monk had explained the danger. The blast zone would be huge, stretching a mile from the bomb in all directions. If they'd wanted to escape on foot, they should've left long ago, especially with Jameson compromised by his broken arm.

Her group's only hope lay with Tucker and Frank.

Still, how could we possibly clear such a blast in time?

"Someone's coming," Monk hissed.

Charlotte glanced over. Monk stood by the entrance to the barracks. He had cracked the door open enough to peek out and watch the rutted streets. He cupped his earpiece, then nodded at Charlotte and Jameson. "It's them. They say they'll be coming in fast."

They'd better be.

"Tucker wants us at the door. He'll pull in close."

Charlotte searched out her window. A short ways off, a truck's headlights bounced toward them, careening through the shantytown. The vehicle bulldozed a corner off of one shack, leaving it in ruins behind them. The reason for such haste was not just the shrinking timetable. A dark cloud pursued and battered at the truck. Its rumbling engine and dancing lights had stirred and attracted the bats, drawing the colony in its wake.

Outside, the nearby bats stirred from their roosts. Several took wing and headed toward the tumult, ready to aid their brethren in the assault.

Monk lifted a flashlight and briefly flashed it through the opening in the door, signaling and confirming their location. He then turned to them.

"Everyone gather up," he warned. "As soon as they stop, we're all piling in the back."

Charlotte swallowed her fear and nodded. She pushed Kane ahead of her. Jameson crowded in with them. He braced his splinted arm tight to his chest.

Through the crack in the door, Charlotte caught fractured glimpses of the vehicle's wild approach. Once in full view, it raced toward them. She stepped back, remembering the truck sideswiping one of the shacks. But the driver fishtailed at the last second, swinging the tailgate toward the door. The rear bumper came to a stop only a few feet from the threshold.

"Now," Monk whispered to them.

He shouldered the door open and led the way. He rushed to the tailgate and yanked it open with a screech of old hinges.

Charlotte followed, but there were bats everywhere. Something struck her head. Claws scrabbled, momentarily tangled in her knotted ponytail. Someone ripped the bat off of her. She turned, expecting Monk to have come to her aid, but he had only one hand—and it was still holding the door latch.

Jameson clutched the bat with his good arm, looking as surprised as her by his action. The shocked moment was all it took for the bat to strike and dig fangs into the meat of his thumb. He gasped, tried to shake it off, but it had locked deep. In his panicked eyes, she saw the pain strike.

She tried to help him, but he shoved her with his shoulder, knocking her into the back bumper.

"Get the fuck in there!" he yelled, sounding angrier with himself than her.

Before she could move on her own, hands grabbed her from behind. Frank yanked her into the rear.

Jameson finally freed his hand by smacking the bat into the side of the Land Rover. Agony etched his face, but he knocked away another bat that flew at his head. He flung around, grabbed Monk with his bleeding hand, and pushed him after Charlotte.

"Go already, goddamn it!"

Next to him, Kane struggled with a bat riding his back and lashing at his vest. The dog snapped and tried to grab it. Jameson came to his rescue, too, and snatched the bat away. This earned him another bite, this time to his wrist.

Jameson staggered back, either from pain or certain knowledge. As Kane leaped to safety, he slammed the tailgate behind them all and slapped his palm against the glass outside.

"Go . . ." he gasped loudly.

Charlotte strained to help him, but the driver—Tucker—was coldly practical. The engine revved, and the Rover took off. She stared out the window. Jameson remained stiff-backed, not even trying to run. Bats fell upon him. Still, he stood longer than she imagined was possible.

Monk pulled her from the view. "The guy knew he was a goner."

"I know, but if I'd only—"

"*If only*s do no good. He gave us room to survive—and that's what we need to do."

She struggled to accept that and swung toward the front. Tucker leaned over the wheel, racing the Rover across the last of the deserted warren. The jungle stretched ahead of them. It looked like a solid wall. Then Tucker yanked the vehicle into a hard turn, following the forest's edge.

She sat straighter.

Where is he going?

11:55 P.M.

Tucker didn't have time to explain.

Only five minutes left.

There was no way they could traverse a mile of jungle to escape the blast. He had recognized that from the start. Instead, they all needed to find a bunker, one far enough away and strong enough to protect them.

Tucker clutched to one hope.

A slim chance courtesy of that bastard De Coster.

He reached the southern edge of the town and spotted a road heading off. It was deeply rutted from regular use. He turned and sped along it. The Rover leaped and bobbled, jerked and bounced, acting like a furious bronco trying to buck them off. Still, he kept the accelerator pressed to the floor.

At least the bats had given up their pursuit. Perhaps because the harrying horde had accomplished its mission—to chase them off.

The road ended faster than he had hoped. He would've preferred more distance from the mine. But the dark expanse of the river blocked the way forward. Their path ended at the working dock for the mine.

He let out a sigh of relief at the sight stretching away from the piers.

The row of barges still blockaded the river, anchored in place from earlier. Their wheelhouses stood tall, a few glowing with lights. Tires hung along their flanks.

Monk patted Tucker's shoulder. "Smart."

"We'll see about that."

His internal clock counted down.

Three minutes.

Tucker squinted, readjusted his trajectory, and sped toward the last pier, the one closest to the nearest barge. A gangway led straight to an open hatch in the hull's side. The ramp was wide, lined by tracks, meant for hauling in ore carts.

He raced down the pier, hit the gangway, and shot up its length. The Rover rattled but held together long enough to reach the end and barrel into the barge's hold.

Two minutes . . .

He didn't stop. The headlights revealed giant piles of coal and metalliferous ore. He raced around the hillocks, swerving back and forth, trying to put as much of it between them and the mine.

He finally braked hard and turned to the others. "Brace yourself. Cover your ears. Mouths open. You're about to have the worst ride of your lives."

And hopefully it won't be the death of us.

The last minute stretched painfully. He crawled over the seatback to join Kane. He huddled with his buddy, inhaling his panted breath, feeling his warmth. A tongue licked him; a cold nose nudged his chin.

"I know. We're in this together."

To the very end.

He checked his watch and saw the last second tick away.

De Coster was nothing if not punctual.

The blast sounded like the end of the world. It felt strong enough to flatten them on its own. For a beat, Tucker thought they might have escaped the worst of it—then the concussive wave hit. The barge got shoved hard, rolling sideways. Rockslides from the piles flowed toward them. Seams broke in the hull as the force crimped its length. Collisions with other barges shattered plates inward.

The Rover tried to ride it out, sliding and skidding, but eventually it toppled end over end. Ore and coal rattled around them, over them.

They all clung to seatbacks, to one another. Still, it was like being dumped into a paint shaker set on high. They tumbled over each other, elbowed and kicked one another. It felt like forever, but Tucker knew all too well how terror slowed time to an infinite moment.

Finally, the world resettled around them.

Ore still fell and shifted. Metal groaned under stress. The Rover sat ass-down in a pile of rock, sunk to its sidewalls.

Frank climbed to the windshield that was mostly shattered and kicked it the rest of the way free. They gathered weapons and gear, then clambered out and slid down a pile of coal. It looked like the barge had landed on its side.

"We'd better get out before it sinks," Monk warned.

Tucker had recovered an intact flashlight and used it to guide them. In the dark cavernous space, as they climbed over sliding rock and shale, he felt like the expedition leader of a group of cave explorers—accompanied by one hearty dog.

They all limped and hobbled, deeply bruised and concussed, bleeding all over, but surprisingly there appeared to be no broken bones.

Finally, Tucker reached a metal ladder that sloped horizontally to the toppled wheelhouse. They followed along its length until they could climb into the barge's helm. All the glass had been shattered or blown out of it. They crossed as a group to get their first view of the damage.

Frank groaned. "I don't think we need to worry about sinking."

Tucker stared out across the dark jungle. It surrounded them on all sides. Barges lay crashed across the forest, looking like the wreckage of a train derailment. The entire blockade had been shoved from the river into the jungle—including their barge.

Beyond them, past the fringe of jungle, a massive crater smoked. Fires burned at its heart, glowing through the cloud of dust. Its breadth was impossible to fully fathom, especially in the dark.

"What do we do now?" Charlotte asked.

Tucker shared a glance with Frank. They had already discussed the matter, with the foolish optimism that they might survive.

And just look at us now.

Tucker pointed upriver. "That bastard De Coster is planning something similar at his island. We overheard him. *Cleaning house*, he called it. At dawn. We intend to make sure it stays messy."

Charlotte looked aghast. "You're going back there?"

"It's our best chance to reach a radio. Especially now that we know how to make it work." He pictured Draper's encoded thumb drive. "Plus, we might get a little payback along the way."

Monk nodded at this plan.

Kane wagged a tail.

"I'm going with you," Charlotte said. She seemed to sense an objection building and stepped forward against it. "I have patients there. They're still my responsibility."

"It'll be a long walk back," Frank warned.

Charlotte's spine straightened. "I'm not giving up on them."

Monk gave her a small smile. "With that attitude, can you be my doctor, too?"

22

Gray fought the ATV up a difficult terrain of lichen-scribed boulders and mossy rocks. The vehicle's headlights speared through the darkness under the heavy canopy. The beams bounced all about. Massive tires chewed across the landscape, riding over obstacles like a rampaging monster truck. The cabin tilted one way, then crashed down on the other, jarring everyone side to side.

Benjie and Faraji rode in the back. Though strapped to their seats, they still braced their arms and legs in all directions, looking like a pair of squirrel monkeys struggling to keep their perches in a storm-swept tree.

Next to Gray, Kowalski snored, competing with the rumble of the engine. His head snapped back and forth, but failed to wake him, proving there was likely nothing inside his skull that could be rattled.

Gray had taken over the wheel two hours ago, just as the night's storm had finally ended. Still, the humid jungle continued to weep and drip all around. He searched the eastern skies for any sign of dawn, praying for some hint that this interminable night would come to an end.

Unfortunately, the world ahead rose in a wall of forested mountains, cliffs, and volcanic cones. Some of the peaks rose to over fifteen thousand feet. Their path climbed from the western half of the continent, topographically known as Low Africa, to the high plateaus and mountain ranges of High Africa. Splitting the two regions was the great Eastern African Rift. It stretched four thousand miles long, cracking down its length into many smaller pieces. According to the topo map, directly ahead of them was the most inhospitable section of all, called the Albertine Rift.

The blue line that Gray had drawn on the topo map headed straight into the heart of that broken landscape, where the Somali tectonic plate shoved high, forming an impenetrable barrier of sheer cliffs and jagged mountains.

As they climbed toward it, Gray hoped that the forest would thin, but instead it only grew taller and thicker, as if the jungle were trying to push those highlands back down by the sheer weight of the vegetation.

The trunks of palms and red cedars grew to gargantuan sizes. Ropy lianas netted them all together, while stands of bamboo formed impenetrable barriers that had to be skirted around. The entire landscape—shrouded with moss, entangled with vines, and festooned with giant ferns—looked prehistoric, like some Jurassic holdover.

The jungle tried to push into the cabin through the missing windshield. It smelled of a rotting sweetness. Leaves slapped at them. Mosquitoes and black flies swarmed inside, plaguing them with stings and bites. The only reprieve came when they slowed enough to allow the diesel fumes from the ATV's exhaust snorkel to drive off the haranguing hordes. But as soon as their vehicle started moving again, the clouds would swamp back inside.

But such tiny nuisances were the least of the threats. Gray constantly searched the jungles for any bigger dangers. Back a mile ago, a herd of wild hogs, curl-tusked beasts, had trampled around their ATV, skirting them like a boulder in a river. But the hogs had moved onward, ignoring them, leaving them unmolested.

Gray found himself holding his breath for long stretches. Tension tightened the muscles between his shoulder blades. He felt exposed with the window missing. They had not been attacked in hours, so he expected another assault at any moment. He glanced all around as he forced the ATV up the next steep incline.

When he reached the top, the terrain finally leveled out for a stretch. He followed a swollen stream, where a recent flash flood had cleared much of the undergrowth and brush from along its banks. Able to travel faster, he felt more hopeful.

Still, the dark jungle around them remained

daunting. The Ituri rain forest covered over twenty-five thousand square miles. A fifth of it was preserved and managed under a conservancy, but the rest was wild and untamed. Especially this remote eastern corner, where the land was a confounding maze, all buried under thick forest.

Anything could be hidden here.

The same worry must have drawn Benjie to release his vicelike hold on his armrests and lean forward. "I've been thinking about the source of this virus," he said.

Gray looked back to him. "What about it?"

"If it truly lies somewhere ahead of us, it must have remained dormant for ages, possibly for millennia."

"At least going back to the time of Prester John and his lost kingdom," Gray agreed.

"Exactly. But what set this virus off *now*? After so long? Something had to trigger it. That's what I've been struggling with."

Gray frowned at the biologist. "I thought we believed it was the recent flooding, that it flushed that virus loose into the greater world."

"I have no doubt that the heavy monsoons exacerbated the spread of the virus. But I think its initial release *predated* the storms. By several months. Probably longer. Especially after what we've seen."

"How do you mean?"

"I keep thinking about those jackals. The rains and flooding must have forced them to migrate from their normal territory. Wherever the pack had come from, the virus must have been smoldering for at least a year in order to generate those biological changes."

Gray considered this. According to Benjie's earlier discourse, a jackal's gestation period, followed by the time it took for a pup to grow to maturity, spanned nearly a year.

Benjie continued, "But if that jackal pack had *always* lived within the scope of the virus, I would've expected more divergence from their normal appearance, especially after so many generations of exposure. They wouldn't be just bigger versions of themselves."

"So, you think the animals were exposed within the past year, causing them to be only mildly altered. Then the floods drove them farther afield."

He nodded. "If I had to guess, I would say the virus began its spread abruptly, but it only reached a limited area at first, effecting local species. After that, it slowly spread outward. Passing from species to species."

"Until the storms came."

Benjie nodded. "The flooding would've triggered a mass migration, a huge shift in the environment, leading the virus to eventually spill over into the human population."

"Which we know was a recent event. But you're thinking the virus was brewing out there for far longer."

"I do. Which worries me."

"Why?"

"We've been focused on trying to figure out *where* the virus originally came from, but I think it's equally important to know *what* triggered its initial spread, after millennia of being dormant."

Gray suspected he was right. "Do you have any thoughts on that?"

"Maybe . . ."

Gray heard the hesitancy in the biologist's voice. The young man was clearly gifted, able to work out puzzles, maybe as well as Gray could. Benjie was a kindred spirit in this regard.

"What are you thinking?" Gray pressed him.

Benjie stared off into the jungle. "Right now, we seem to be the main target of the virus. It makes us dull and unresponsive, while ramping up the environment into a more hostile state. Though, perhaps I may be placing too much intelligence and forethought into a virus. Instead, all of this might simply be due to man's encroachment into the virus's normal biosphere. Through roads, construction, deforestation."

Gray pointed ahead. "On the map, it shows a major mining enterprise—Kilo-Moto—at the northeast corner of the DRC, right on the border. It's only a couple hundred miles from where we are now. I read that its operations have been slowly spreading deeper into the jungle."

The mine had also caught Gray's attention for another reason. It was a major gold-mining operation, established when nuggets were discovered along the Ituri River in 1903. Considering Gray's team was hunting for a mythic kingdom tied to legends of King Solomon's famous gold mine, he thought the current operation might further support an historical basis for a lost mine being established in this region.

Benjie stared off in the direction where Gray had pointed. "Maybe the uptick in local mining upset the virus's natural environment, allowing it to break loose. But I don't know." He rubbed at the peach-fuzz scruff of beard over his jawline. "I'm not buying it. I still think we're missing a main *catalyst*. Something more dramatic that *immediately* impacted the environment and loosed the virus on the world."

"Like what?"

Benjie shrugged. "I have no idea. But if there's an answer, it lies somewhere ahead of us."

Gray returned his full attention forward.

Then we'd better find it.

5:02 A.M.

Forty minutes later, Gray rubbed the sweat from his eyes. The stream they had been following had grown steamy, heated to a near boil. It raised the humidity in the area and added a sulfurous stink to the air.

He was relieved when the waterway finally vanished underground. As he rode past the hot spring, its presence served as reminder that this entire rift area was geologically active, prone to frequent earthquakes, and home to volcanoes both dormant and active.

Unfortunately, while he was happy to escape the spring's sulfurous heat, the jungle quickly closed in on both sides. To make matters worse, the terrain climbed yet again.

Gray slowed the ATV. Through breaks in the

canopy—and with the clouds momentarily thinning to allow the moon to shine—he spotted the dark silhouette of peaks and cliffs cutting the sky in half ahead. He tried to judge the distance.

We must be close.

Gray drew to a stop and nudged Kowalski, who still snored next to him. When there was no response, he tried once more, with more fervor. After still nothing, he tried to elbow him in the ribs—only to have his arm caught in a large mitt.

"Hit me again," Kowalski said, shoving Gray away, "and I'll return the favor—only a lot harder."

Gray ignored the threat. "Just grab my pack. It's time we checked in. Maybe Painter and Kat are having better luck than us."

Kowalski grumbled, retrieved the sat-phone from his bag, and resecured its battery. He handed it over to Gray. "I'd bet my left nut that Sigma's as lost as we are."

Gray placed more confidence in the others. He called up Sigma command. The connection was immediately picked up. Both Painter and Kat were on the line, clearly waiting for this call.

"We reached the highlands," Gray reported in. "Any luck at your end?"

"I'll let Kat answer that," Painter said.

Gray heard the strain in her voice when she came on the line. "We weren't able to pinpoint any single site with certainty," she admitted. "Then again, the photo was taken over a century ago. Between erosion and landslides, the topography has likely changed significantly."

Gray closed his eyes, his heart sinking in his chest.

Kat continued, "Jason and I were able to do some extrapolations. We searched for those areas that most closely matched the silhouette in the photo. We came up with eighteen possible sites. I'm transmitting them to you now."

Cradling the phone at his ear, Gray pulled out his digital pad and brought up the topo map. As he watched, tiny blue squares appeared on the screen, dotting the highlands.

So many . . .

"You weren't able to narrow them any further?" Gray asked.

"We've been a tad busy," she said sharply.

He could guess the source of her irritability and tension. "Any word on Monk and the others?"

"Not yet," she answered curtly.

Painter cut in. "Between the chaos spreading with the virus and a less-than-efficient chain of command in the DRC, it's been difficult to get cooperation. Plus, the entire area is being pounded by thunderstorms. We're hoping by dawn to be able to mount a more determined effort."

Gray could only imagine Kat's fear. "I have no doubt Monk will hold his own until then."

"He damned well better," she answered.

Gray studied the spread of blue dots on his map. Despite his own worries for his best friend, he set aside those fears, compartmentalizing them away. There was nothing he could do out here, and he had his own daunting task ahead.

Fearing to keep this connection open any

longer, he signed off. He gave the others a brief account of the call. He passed the topo map around to show them the challenge ahead.

Kowalski returned the pad to him with a scowl. "Doesn't give us much to go on."

"No, it doesn't."

Kowalski settled back to his seat. "Well, at least I get to keep my left nut."

Benjie stared out at the jungle. "Where do we go from here? Where do we even start?"

Gray got the ATV moving again. "We'll head to the closest spot on the map—then search each site after that."

Benjie leaned back. "We could be out here for weeks. Do we have provisions for that long?"

"No," Gray admitted.

Still, with no other guidance, they had to continue. He aimed the ATV up the next ridge and set off across the jungle. The forest thickened with every mile, and the terrain grew ever steeper and more treacherous. Their pace became slower than a man could walk.

Gray became convinced that Benjie's judgment of their timetable was a vast underestimate. *It could take months, rather than weeks, to search all eighteen sites.*

He grunted in exasperation as he reached a challenging ridge. The tires slipped, and dug, then slipped again. Their passage left a deep scar behind them. Still, considering how quickly the jungle filled in any open space, he knew their path would vanish in mere days.

That thought only unnerved him.

As he rattled and rolled deeper into this maze

of rock and forest, he remembered the story told by Father Bailey, how back in the twelfth century, the personal physician of Pope Alexander III had vanished into this jungle, searching for the lost kingdom of Prester John, never to be seen again.

No wonder.

Gray glanced at the rearview mirror. He swore he could see the path closing up behind them. Maybe it was a trick of the vehicle's jostling light, but it looked as if vines had snaked across the ruts and tears. On either side, ferns draped their fronds across their trail. He rubbed at his eyes and squinted, but he was focused the wrong way.

"Look out!" Benjie yelled.

He shifted his attention forward—then braked hard.

Kowalski was thrown against his seat restraints. "What the hell?"

Something shot through the open windshield and imbedded into the seatback between Gray and Kowalski. It was a spear. The shaft vibrated in place next to them.

Swearing loudly, Kowalski snapped off his seat belt and raised his Shuriken, shouldering it at his cheek.

Gray reached over and pushed the muzzle down. "Hold on."

Ahead of them, lit by the headlights' beams, stood a cluster of small figures. They were naked, except for loincloths, and armed with spears and bows. Gray was certain there were more hunters hidden in the forest, too.

He flashed to the stick figures sketched on the second-to-last photo in Sheppard's collection. It had depicted a similar scenario.

Pygmies.

He held up his palms and shoved his arms out the windshield. He suspected the impaled spear next to him was a warning shot, encouraging them to turn back. But he also hoped for more than peace. He needed this local tribe's cooperation. If anyone knew this area, it would be this group who had hunted these lands for millennia.

Was that the message sketched on the back of Sheppard's photo?

To seek the tribe's help.

For now, the hunters showed no further aggression, yet they also didn't move out of the way.

"What do we do?" Kowalski asked.

"We need to end this stalemate." Gray kept his hands up but glanced behind him. "We need an ambassador."

5:20 A.M.

Benjie hung back with Gray and Kowalski. The three of them stood next to the ATV. Benjie cringed with worry. Across the way, illuminated by the glow of the headlights, Faraji closed upon the group of pygmies. The boy kept his arms high and his palms empty.

As he reached the group of hunters, spears were lowered toward his chest. Bows were drawn tighter.

"Maybe this wasn't such a great idea," Benjie murmured.

Gray looked worried, too, but he acknowledged the obvious. "Faraji is the only one who might speak their language. We need to find out if they'd be willing to help us."

Benjie swallowed down his nervousness. He hoped Faraji could get the hunters to understand, to earn their trust.

It would not be easy.

Before traveling here, Benjie had read up on the pygmy tribes who inhabited the Congo. Many of them were Bantu-speaking, like Faraji, but other tribes spoke their own dialects. Long ago, pygmies had once been a cohesive people, sharing the same ancestral population—until three thousand years ago, when farmers had swept through the area and divided their tribes. Today, many tribes didn't even know others existed.

Still, pygmies had been living in central Africa for over ninety thousand years. Their origins remained a mystery, which intrigued Benjie.

Even the reason for their short stature was unknown. Some believed it due to a vitamin D deficiency from living under a shaded canopy all their lives, leading to poor calcium uptake. Others claimed it was from a lack of protein and a limited diet. There were other theories, too. But no matter the reason, it ultimately changed their genetics. While their children developed at a normal rate, the last growth spurt of adolescence was suppressed, keeping them forever short.

Benjie found this genetic uniqueness fascinating, as it dovetailed into his own studies on stress-induced inheritable traits.

Unfortunately, such knowledge did not help them.

Across the way, Faraji gestured with his arms. Snatches of conversation in Bantu reached them. A few of the hunters clearly spoke this language. Not that it seemed to do any good. Heads shook and spears continued to threaten.

Benjie could guess the reason for such wariness. A little over a decade ago, rebel forces in the DRC had started a pogrom of genocide, targeting the indigenous pygmy tribes. The operational name was *Effacer le tableau*, French for "erasing the board." In a matter of a year, the rebels slaughtered over seventy thousand pygmies.

It's no wonder they look upon us as a threat.

Spears stabbed toward Faraji's chest, driving him back. He stumbled away, his shoulders slumped in defeat.

"Don't look like diplomacy's gonna work," Kowalski noted.

Benjie refused to give up. He considered their options, running them through his head, testing them against what he knew about these tribal people. He had read how the pygmies maintained a lengthy oral history, one shared in song and stories.

Could they have retained knowledge from a century ago?

Benjie turned to Gray. "Show them Sheppard's photos. We know he passed through here. Maybe they'll recognize him."

Gray considered this for a breath, then nodded. "Why not? It's worth a shot."

As Gray returned to the cabin to collect the black-and-white photos, Benjie hurried to the tailgate. He popped it open and shifted through their gear until he found Faraji's backpack. He fingered it open and slipped out the shaman's *ngedi mu ntey*, the tribe's precious Kuba Box. He removed its wooden cover and grabbed another object that might jog the hunters' memories. He lifted out the *ndop* figurine, a detailed totem carved in the likeness of William Sheppard.

He quickly joined Gray. "We should take everything. Hope they understand."

Gray pointed to Kowalski. "Stay with the ATV."

Kowalski shrugged, looking happy to stand guard. Though Benjie suspected Gray's order had less to do with protecting their vehicle and more about avoiding any impolitic outbursts by the big man.

Gray and Benjie headed over to join Faraji. Their approach did not go unnoticed. More hunters shed from the forest's shadows, flanking and closing behind them.

Faraji turned as they arrived. He looked aghast at what Gray and Benjie carried, maybe fearing his precious artifacts were about to be bartered away as gifts.

Benjie explained. "We want to check if these hunters know anything about the Reverend Sheppard. We know he came through—"

One of the pygmies stepped forward. He was clearly old, with gray hair and sagging skin over wiry muscles. Still, he looked vital, his eyes bright.

"Shep. Perd," he said, pronouncing the name as if it were two words.

Still, it appeared the man recognized the reverend.

Benjie looked to Gray, who stepped forward and fanned out the photos. He held them toward the elder. His efforts only earned a scowl. A spear knocked the pictures from Gray's hand. They fluttered to the ground.

Faraji gasped and ducked to gather them up.

The elder shifted his spearpoint toward Benjie. He indicated the carving clutched in Benjie's hands. With a nervous gulp, Benjie lifted it higher.

The elder stepped forward and snatched it away. The old hunter studied the figurine, even sniffing at it. A finger traced from the colonial hat down to the face under it, the delicate features carved of an ebony veined in silver. He finally handed it back with great reverence. The pygmy planted the butt of his spear and stared over at them expectantly.

When Faraji rejoined them with the photos, Gray placed a hand on the boy's shoulder. "Tell them of the danger in the forest. Of how we're seeking where Sheppard went. To a lost city hidden in these jungles."

Faraji waved an arm. "I told them. Not about the Reverend Sheppard. But the rest, yes."

Gray frowned in frustration. "If there's some cure hidden out here, we need to find it."

Benjie noted how the elder had followed this brief exchange, his eyes narrowing slightly as if he understood. The man's attention then settled again on the *ndop* figurine, his expression softening into sorrow, maybe disappointment.

Before Faraji could press further, the old hunter turned away. He lifted an arm and whistled a haunting note, ordering his people to leave, clearly done with these trespassers.

Gray feared the same and stepped forward. "Wait."

But Benjie was mistaken. The elder wasn't whistling for the hunters to leave—he was summoning others.

From the jungle, shadows broke free and stalked into the glow of the headlights. They closed in all around. The beasts approached with heads low, their blunted muzzles bristled with long whiskers. Ears stood stiff and tall, tufted at their tips. A shivering line of hackles rode across short, arched necks, looking more like spines than fur. Dark amber eyes reflected the lights.

Once stopped, the beasts' backs stood as high as the hunters' shoulders.

Despite their large size, Benjie recognized the species.

Or at least, what they once were.

He studied them closer to hold back his fear. He focused on picking out other identifying features.

The striped fur helped firm his classification. Only these beasts' coats shimmered in a way that challenged the eye, as if those markings sought to blend the animals back into their surroundings. It was no wonder the pack's presence had gone unnoticed until now. In the jungle, they would be more shadow than substance.

"*Fisi ndogo*," Faraji whispered, also identifying the animals, even in their altered state, using the Bantu word.

Gray glanced over to Faraji, then to Benjie.

"*Proteles cristata*," Benjie explained. "Aard-wolves."

Gray frowned his lack of recognition. "Those are wolves?"

"Actually, the species is more related to hyenas than wolves," Benjie said. "But these are massive."

Benjie never took his gaze from those normally reclusive creatures. They typically subsisted on termites and other insects. But that was their smaller selves, not these two-hundred-pound brutes. Lips snarled, showing teeth meant for more than chewing on bugs.

All the while, the pack remained eerily silent.

The elder faced the largest of the group, a huge male. He offered a palm. The aardwolf edged forward and bumped a nose into that hand; then it shifted closer to brush a greeting. A thick bushy tail swept back and forth—but those unblinking eyes never left Benjie and the others.

The elder leaned to the beast. His lips moved silently. It reminded Benjie of Tucker with Kane, but he sensed something more intimate here, a bond far deeper and older. The beast bobbed its head once, gave a final graze of cheek to shoulder, then swung away. In a single bound, it vanished into the forest.

The old hunter followed after the aardwolf, drawing the rest of the party with him, both beasts and men. Benjie and the others remained standing in place—until the elder frowned back at them, clearly scolding them to keep up.

"He wants us to go with him," Benjie realized.

Gray turned and waved Kowalski over. "Then that's what we'll do."

Benjie briefly matched gazes with the elder. The small hairs on his neck shivered under the intensity of those dark eyes. In that moment, Benjie felt as if the entire jungle were staring back at him.

Worst of all, he suspected the truth.

Maybe it was.

6:04 A.M.

Gray hiked behind the hunters. Despite their diminutive size, the tribesmen moved swiftly through the forest, following a path known only to them. After a half hour, Gray was thoroughly lost.

Before abandoning the ATV, he had taken the precaution of pinging their location to mark the spot on his digital map. Still, as he searched behind them, he was uncertain if he could find his way back.

Benjie and Faraji—both sweating heavily—followed at his heels.

Kowalski hung farther off. He rested his Shuriken on his shoulder as he climbed through the jungle. The pygmies had not objected to them bringing their weapons or their packs. Then again, the tribespeople had plenty of protection. The wolves flanked to either side, invisible in the forest, only revealing themselves for the briefest snatches.

Despite the threat of those beasts, Gray took cold comfort in their presence. If the tribe worked alongside those altered wolves—especially a species so radically altered—they must have a history tied to the source of the virus.

Gray was counting on that.

They continued through a forest crowded by cliffs on all sides. Pinnacles of rock rose high enough to pierce the canopy. Boulders had to be vaulted over. What little of the skies could be seen had begun to brighten. The sun had yet to rise, but dawn approached.

As they hiked deeper, the forest remained hushed. There was no piping or screaming at their passage. Even the whine of mosquitoes had died away. The silence weighed on him. Each footfall felt like a trespass. He found himself holding his breath, afraid to further disturb the solitude.

Finally, they followed a dry stream bed that ran along the bottom of a deep ravine. Bluffs rose to either side, their sheer faces enshrouded by jungle. The bed of polished stone led them toward a towering cliff, one draped in wet ferns. It was only then that Gray realized the rock underfoot was not a dry stream, but the remains of an old road, broken by the passing centuries into a tumbled trail.

It ended at a huge crack in the rock face. The

small hunters stopped and gathered between two familiar stone pillars that framed the entrance.

Benjie gasped at the sight, relief shining on his face as he stumbled forward. "We made it."

Faraji's features remained dour, turning a name into a curse. "Mfupa Ufalme."

"This had better be worth all the blisters on my feet," Kowalski griped.

Before they could approach closer, a dark shape burst out of the shadowy ravine. It was the huge aardwolf who had fled earlier. The beast rushed to the tribal elder and circled his form once, brushing close in greeting. There was no servility or deference to this gesture, only cold acknowledgment of the man's return.

All eyes turned toward the entrance.

The aardwolf had not come alone. Drawn in his wake, another appeared. Taller by a foot, shaggy with age. The beast's fur was gray, striped in darker shades, its muzzle snow-white. It padded from the shadows and stood guard.

A tall man appeared next, his skin dark, his cropped hair graying in age like the aardwolf. He carried a staff of polished white wood. He was Congolese, though Gray suspected the man bore no nationality or allegiances to borders or governments. Despite his age, his eyes shone clear as he gazed over the hunters to the new-comers.

He stepped past the aardwolf, thumping forward with his staff. He wore sandals and a simple brown robe embroidered in black, in a pattern of diamonds encased in arrows. Gray recognized the design. Faraji had called it *mbul bwiin*, a pattern limited to Kuba royalty. Across the man's chest, an embroidered double knot folded in on itself, so intricate that it threatened to capture one's gaze. Its curves and convolutions seemed to move on their own as the man shifted out of the shadows and stepped into the first light of a new day.

Gray knew this symbol, too, taught to them by Faraji. An *imbol*. It marked the presence of a king. This was reinforced by the circlet of gold atop the man's head.

The hunters bowed, showing respect, but Gray sensed no subservience.

The king lifted an arm in greeting, his voice firm. Surprisingly, he spoke English with a slight British accent. "If you seek answers, follow me." He turned around, but not before adding an admonition. "Yet, know this. You may be refused. She is angry—and most merciless."

He headed off.

Gray glanced at the others. He had a thousand questions, but one burned the brightest now.

Who the hell is he talking about?

FIFTH

INVASION

23

Gray followed behind the tall figure bearing the gold circlet, trying to comprehend who led them. The man's bearing was regal, even when leaning on his staff. His gray curls formed a nimbus that supported his simple crown. The pattern on his robe shifted with each step, looking more like a dappling of shadows than embroidered thread.

As they continued along the chasm that cut between high cliffs, the king conversed softly with the older pygmy who had guided Gray's group here.

To either side, the pair's aardwolves paced them, brushing through the ferns fringing the gravel path, often vanishing completely out of sight. More wolves and the remaining pygmy hunters followed behind their group.

As they hiked, the cliffs to either side had slowly pulled back, allowing a thick forest to grow between them. A canopy crested over the trail, turning the path into a tunnel. Still, the fo-

liage was thin enough to show peeks of a bright-
ening morning. Occasionally the loose stones
underfoot became solid rock cut into steps. The
trail climbed slowly higher, leading them deeper
into the labyrinth of this mountainous region.
More pillars dotted the path, like ancient road
markers. They grew taller as the march continued, looking quarried from the same rock as the
cliffs.

"I think those were once the bases for arches,"
Benjie whispered. He pointed to the next set of
pillars. Their tops did seem to bend toward one
another, but the spans between them had long
crumbled away.

Gray nodded. He glanced back to where
Kowalski and Faraji trailed them. He tried to
picture a road of stone arches leading through
this chasm.

As he faced back around, Benjie nodded to
the taller man ahead of them. "If this trail truly
does lead to some lost kingdom, do you think he
could actually be a descendant of Prester John?"

Gray had wondered the same.

The king heard this inquiry and drifted back
to them, allowing the old hunter to take the lead.
"I am not," he answered crisply. "The lineage of
Prester John faded centuries ago, long before my
time. If there's any of that bloodline still flowing, it would be found in Molimbo's people."
He gestured toward the pygmy leading them.
"They've lived in these forests and mountains
for thousands of years. They've protected its
secrets, acting as caretakers, while also being
nurtured in turn."

"But what about you?" Gray asked, glancing up and down his tall form. "You're clearly not of this tribe."

"I am not so lucky, though they took me in long ago, welcomed me into their fold." He looked behind them. His eyes, slightly clouded by cataracts, stared off into a distance that wasn't just measured in miles. "I was not born here, but in Muxenge."

Faraji gasped, stepping closer. "That's where I live. That's my home."

The man smiled a bit sadly. "Of course, I can tell you are Bakuba." He placed two fingers to his forehead, then touched the same to his chest, a traditional Kuba greeting. "My name is Tyende. Joseph Tyende."

Gray looked between boy and elder, recognizing the tribal resemblance now. The old man could be Faraji's grandfather. He also noted how this supposed king had used the older term for the Kuba people.

"How did you come to be here?" Gray asked.

"The same as you, it would seem. By following the Reverend Sheppard."

Gray's brows rose. He wondered if the man had once been a tribal shaman, someone with access to the sacred *ngedi mu ntey* and the secrets it held. "You were able to decipher Sheppard's clues and found this place, too."

"No, you misunderstand. I came here *with* the Reverend Sheppard."

Gray stumbled a step.

Tyende sighed, his expression sorrowful. "The reverend was my friend and teacher. It was he who taught me English, or rather finished my education after a few years at a British colonial school."

Gray struggled to digest this information. According to the dates on the photos, William Sheppard had come on his quest in 1894. Even if Tyende was only a boy back then, it would still make him well over a hundred today.

"That's impossible," Gray muttered.

Even Kowalski snorted dismissively.

Tyende shrugged and gestured to the small hunter leading them. "Molimbo was already old when I first came here with the Reverend Sheppard. He claims Bala is his third blood-bonded *fisi ndogo*."

As if summoned by her name, the aardwolf shifted out of the brush to trot several steps alongside the pygmy—then vanished away.

"Such proud beasts live only a century or so." Tyende smiled at the old wolf shadowing them, his white fur nearly glowing, as if he were already a ghost. "Mbe is near the end of his life with me. He was only a pup when I first came here. I could cradle him in both palms back then."

Gray frowned toward the old pygmy, who looked younger than Tyende, but according to this account, Molimbo was many times older. He remembered the myths surrounding Prester John, attesting to a miraculous longevity. According to those stories, the last recorded age of the lost Christian king was 562.

Gray studied Molimbo more closely. If all of this were true—and not some exaggeration or lie—then he understood why Tyende believed the bloodline of Prester John still flowed through the veins of this pygmy tribe.

Gray turned to Tyende. "If you came with the Reverend Sheppard, why did you stay? Why did you remain behind?"

"I consider it an honor now," Tyende said. "And I do venture outward in rare occasions, even once returning to Muxenge. But after so many years, I felt a stranger there." He swept his staff around him. "Here is my truest home. Where I took a wife, who sadly passed, but who gave me two strong sons—who themselves had children and grandchildren. So, you see, I've had a good life, better than I deserved."

"What do you mean?" Gray asked.

Tyende shook his head, his gaze downcast. "You asked me *why* I remained behind. I've not truly answered it. Even now shame weighs down my tongue."

"Then what kept you here?" Gray pressed again.

Tyende looked over, his expression pained. "Penance."

Gray wanted to know more, but the Kuba elder thumped forward with his staff, leaving them behind.

Tyende offered only one last comment, tossed back at them. "You will understand better soon."

The hike reached another staircase, cut into switchbacks that climbed a tall ridge. They continued in silence, each lost in their own thoughts. Gray struggled to put all the pieces together in his head. By the time, they reached the top of the rise, he had more questions than when he had started up.

Tyende waited for them at the summit, leaning on his staff, bathed in sunlight as the trail crested over an open spine of rock. He looked exhausted, then again, he was over a hundred years old. He lifted an arm as Gray and the others reached him.

Gray looked out from the high vantage point. A wide forested basin opened ahead, circled by peaks and ridges. Their jagged outlines were barely discernible above the thick jungle that filled the valley to the brim. From this height, the canopy looked dense and impenetrable, its dark emerald nearly black.

"Here is what you came to find," Tyende said. "Molimbo's people call it *Utoto wa Maisha*. The Cradle of Life. The Kuba named it Mfupa Ufalme."

"The Kingdom of Bones," Gray said.

Tyende stared across the expanse. "Both names are equally true. As you will see."

The man set off again, descending into the valley along another steep staircase.

Gray followed, passing out of sunlight and back into shadows. He stared down the steps that vanished into the darkness below. If there were any answers, they'd be found down there.

But can we discover them in time?

7:45 A.M.

After nearly an hour of descending the ridge, Benjie wondered if the stairs would ever end.

The course zigged and zagged, delving ever downward, proving the valley was far deeper than he had imagined. By the time they reached the last step, he estimated they had traveled a mile down into the valley.

During their descent, the jungle had continued to grow taller around them. Massive trunks—some a dozen feet in diameter, many even larger—marched off into the darkness. The trees formed a colonnade that held up a multilayered canopy. Only a few emerald-hued slivers of light reached the valley floor.

It was so dark that Gray finally broke out his flashlight.

Benjie was happy for the additional light.

Two of the pygmies also gathered up torches from a neat stack at the base of the stairs. They lit the oily brands with strikes of flint. One was passed to Molimbo to help guide them. Benjie suspected the torches were more for the new-comers' benefit.

"It is not far from here," Tyende promised.

"Where are you taking us?" Benjie asked.

"First to the scourge," the man answered cryptically. "To understand, you must know the temptation that lured so many to their doom."

Kowalski grumbled, "I'm more than happy to skip the doom part of this tour."

Tyende ignored him and set off. Molimbo once again took the lead, holding aloft his torch. The other pygmies drifted to either side. Their aardwolves dispersed wider, vanishing into the gloom.

The group set off across the valley. The darkness had smothered most of the undergrowth. All around, the valley's black loam looked rich and fecund, formed by centuries of leaf rot and decomposition. The air was cool and damp, almost clammy. It smelled of wet foliage and a moldy sweetness, all undercut by a musky rot.

Still, nature took advantage of this sunless world. Rafts of fungi climbed the massive tree trunks. Pale mushrooms sprouted everywhere. Some rose waist high, with caps stretching a yard across, their undersides frilled by gills. Elsewhere, basketball-sized puffballs littered the dark floor.

"It's like we're in the world's largest root cellar," Benjie whispered. "One long abandoned and left fallow. I've never seen such huge examples of *Psilocybe congolensis*." He pointed to a swath of knee-high yellowish mushrooms. "They normally only grow as big as my palm. They're notoriously rich in psilocybins and baeocystin, powerful hallucinogenics."

Kowalski drew closer. "So, African magic mushrooms?" He gazed around. "Don't think we need them. Feels like I'm already high. Like I fell into Alice's Wonderland."

Benjie stared around. He found himself jabbering away nervously. "Did you know, a couple years ago, the fossils of the world's *oldest* mushrooms were found in the Congo, not far from here?"

Gray glanced to him.

Kowalski simply shrugged.

Benjie nodded his head. "The fossils date back some eight-hundred million years. It's believed that ancient fungi played a critical role in forming the first primordial soil, laying the groundwork, so to speak, for the first plants and later animals to colonize land." He turned to Gray. "In fact, the oldest living organism is found in your country, in Oregon. *Armillaria ostoyae*, or the honey mushroom. It's over eight thousand years old. It's hyphae network extends three square miles, forming *one* organism, weighing thirty-five thousand tons. Making it also the world's largest organism."

Benjie forced himself to quiet down, knowing he was prattling on. His spectrum made it too easy to fall into a state of hyperfocus, to fixate on a single topic. Still, maybe this diatribe wasn't entirely unwarranted. The team had come here searching for the source of a virus unlike any other, one that seemed capable of manipulating DNA, maybe of steering evolution.

Perhaps such details could prove important.

He was certainly right about another topic.

The group approached a tall stone arch that spanned the path, proving that the hundreds of pillars were indeed the remnants of ancient archways.

Similarly, as they had continued across the valley, the gravel underfoot had become flat cobbles set in an intricate pattern. The path was occasionally broken by roots of the surrounding trees, but there was no mistaking it.

Definitely an ancient road.

Benjie studied the archway as he passed under it. The rough-hewn bricks were black with age and covered in layers of moss, but a glinting caught his eye. Overhead, the centermost key brick was not stone. Unable to help himself, he reached over and guided Gray's flashlight up.

Kowalski whistled appreciatively, recognizing it now, too.

It was a massive wedge of gold.

Benjie stared back along their trail, picturing the other hundreds of pillars. He tried to calculate the value of such a path, lined by arches topped in gold. Was this proof of Prester John's wealth and maybe a connection to the legends of King Solomon's mine?

Tyende turned to them, noting them lagging behind. His form was limned in torchlight, his gold circlet shining bright. "We are here," he said.

8:03 A.M.

Gray hurried forward with the others.

Tyende stood at a Y in the road, where it split and diverged into two paths. Their guide took the fork to the right. As Gray followed, he glanced down the other trail. It vanished into the darkness, but he thought he caught a vague glimmer in the distance, nearly illusory. He rubbed his eyes, trying to discern its source. But it quickly dimmed as he continued after Tyende and Molimbo.

Gray focused forward again. They didn't have far to go. The road ran for another hundred yards and ended at a cliff face. They came upon it abruptly as the forest abutted right against it, hiding the bluff nearly completely. The sheer rock was further masked by thick mats of damp moss, which served as the bed for a riotous growth of mushrooms and fungi.

Gray searched around, realizing that their trek had curved to meet the base of the valley wall. The cliff's heights stretched to the right and left, disappearing into the darkness. He had no doubt it was an unbroken barrier. He frowned, unsure why Tyende had brought them here.

The old man must have guessed this question. He removed his circlet and examined it with a forlorn expression. "I am the last king of *Utoto wa Maisha*. Of Mfupa Ufalme." He returned the crown to his head. "It is my burden. My penance to bear."

Gray did not understand.

Tyende nodded to Molimbo, who turned and spoke to one of his tribesmen, the one carrying the second torch. The pygmy ran forward toward the cliff, clearly wanting to dispatch his duty quickly. Gray noted a few of the other hunters had reappeared but none drew any closer. Even the aardwolves hung back.

Faraji grabbed Gray's sleeve and tugged hard. The boy pointed to the left, to a patch of mushrooms and a reef of fungi. Gray failed to spot what alarmed him and swung his flashlight in that direction. Only then did he spot the white glint among the pale growth.

"*Mfupa*," Faraji warned.

Bones . . .

A skull glowed in his flashlight's beam. Gray

moved closer, recognizing that a skeleton lay buried among the mushrooms.

A gasp rose from Benjie, but the biologist was staring toward the cliff. The pygmy with the torch had come running back, but he no longer carried a flaming brand. He dashed past to join his brethren.

Back at the cliff, a fire glowed within it. As Gray watched, it swiftly spread outward, running along channels both inside and outside, pooling brighter for stretches, then extending again. Gray imagined thin troughs and gutters of oil fueling this fire.

As the flames spread, they revealed the truth hidden behind the moss and fungi. What appeared to be a sheer cliff was in fact a cityscape carved into the rock. The flames rose higher and to either side, revealing the true breadth of the place. It climbed tens of stories and stretched far to the right and left.

The firelight soon revealed how Gray had been mistaken a moment ago. The ancient city wasn't cut into ordinary *stone*. Instead, the surfaces glinted and shone with a ruddy brightness. Gray took a step back, struggling to take in the scope hidden here. The city had been mined out of a giant vein of *gold*.

Kowalski swore, his face aglow with lust in the firelight. Gray couldn't blame him. Even he had to fight down a twinge of avarice. Entire countries would be financed by what lay before them. The wealth here was incomprehensible.

Benjie pointed higher up the cliff. "Is that what I think it is?"

By now, the flames had crested higher, outlining a giant gold cross glowing above the city. Gray considered its presence here. Was the shape purely happenstance, or did it further support the myths of Prester John, a Christian king who founded an empire here?

Unfortunately, there was no way of knowing for sure.

Tyende noted their attention. "The Reverend Sheppard was equally disappointed to discover there was no lost kingdom still thriving here. It was as empty as you see it now, left to the ghosts of the past, those who only left their bones behind."

Only now did Gray see the tumble of skeletons strewn about the base, as if washed against the cliff. He searched around and saw more skulls and jumbles of rib cages, leg bones, clawed hands. Some were yellowed by age, others polished white. Now spotted, more and more revealed themselves, all around them. They spread far and wide throughout the forest. Even more were likely layered under centuries of rotting leaves.

No wonder this place was considered cursed.

Even the pygmies knew to keep their distance.

"Over the decades," Tyende said, "I tried to count the remains. I finally stopped when I reached fifty thousand."

"What happened here?" Benjie asked.

"The Reverend Sheppard believed we're looking at all that's left of Prester John's kingdom. I've had long conversations with Molimbo. The kingdom had fallen into ruin before he was born, but the tribe carries forward stories of that time. I've tried to piece together that history. As best I can tell, some six or seven centuries ago the kingdom was overtaken by interlopers, who came with crossbows and lances and war hammers."

Tyende swept his staff toward the forest. "I've found a few metal bolts, broken pikes, and rusted chainmail, confirming such a story. From sigils on the armor, I'm guessing they were Portuguese conquerors, who came searching for Prester John's gold."

Gray remembered Father Bailey's story of a group of Portuguese explorers from the fifteenth century who had returned from Africa, claiming to have discovered Prester John's kingdom. Maybe they had, but clearly only a few of them had made it back.

Tyende frowned at the spread of bone. "But it wasn't just the kingdom that the Portuguese discovered here, what they had to contend with. They woke what had been slumbering for ages. They tried to take what was not offered and were punished for it. For such an affront, they were afflicted with the disease that threatens now, falling into a deadly lassitude."

Gray tried to picture those forces succumbing to such an illness.

No wonder those Portuguese explorers never came back.

Tyende continued, "Still, the damage was done. The kingdom was so decimated that it never recovered."

Benjie nodded to Molimbo. "What about them?"

"Ah, his people have lived in this valley for thousands of years. Long before Prester John. They taught that future king and his people how to live in harmony here. Even gifting Prester John with his first aardwolf. And after the kingdom fell—as all empires do—Molimbo's people abided, carrying on as they've always done."

Tyende smiled sadly at the old hunter. "I've come to believe that it is *here*, in this valley, that the pygmy people originated. Possibly they were forged by Her, gifted by Her graces, until eventually tribes and families spread outward, forgetting where they had come from."

Gray pictured the jackals, the other altered animals. Had the people here been equally changed, manipulated at the genetic level? Could that explain the claims of extreme longevity, their resistance to the disease? Questions tumbled through his mind, but one remained foremost.

"Tyende, *who* are you talking about?" Gray asked. "Who do you think forged them?"

Tyende appeared deaf to his question and headed toward the city. Molimbo and his hunters didn't follow. "There is one more bit of history you should know."

Gray hurried to catch up. "What history?"

Tyende glanced over. "My own."

They crossed toward the edge of the firelit city. The heat grew intense. The brightness stung the eye. Finally, Tyende drew them off of the cobbled path. They waded through fields of mushrooms.

Kowalski brushed a puffball, and it blasted a

powdery fluff around him. He choked and spit and stumbled away. "That better not be poisonous."

Benjie studied the growth more closely as he passed it.

Kowalski looked to the biologist for reassurance, but Benjie straightened with a shrug, clearly failing to identify it.

Kowalski stalked away with a scowl. "This jungle seems determined to kill me."

Tyende led them a short distance, then stopped, leaning heavily on his staff. A group of bodies lay sprawled all around, half-buried in the loam. They looked mummified, with mushrooms growing from their corpses. This set of remains was clearly a newer addition to this boneyard. One body still had a spear jammed through its chest.

"Who are they?" Gray asked.

Tyende lifted and pointed his staff at one mummified corpse, then the next. "Collard and Remy. Two Belgian colonists. They came here looking for gold but found only death." He moved his staff to another body. The corpse's mouth gaped open, showing teeth filed to points. "This is Nzare, brother to the cannibal Mlumba, head of the Zappo Zaps who wiped out many villages."

Tyende turned to Gray. "The Reverend Sheppard came searching for the Belgian colonists."

"Is that how he discovered this valley?" Gray asked.

"Yes, but he came too late. Days late. The

colonists arrived with twenty men, armed with rifles and axes. They slaughtered many of Molimbo's tribe, along with dozens of their bonded *fisi nyongo*. Once again, She lashed out in fury, driving them into a poisonous slumber."

"Like with the Portuguese," Gray said, reminded that history is too prone to repeating itself.

"When Sheppard and our group arrived, the others were already as you see them. Weak and dying."

Gray noted one piece of this morbid tableaux that did not match Tyende's story. "And the spear impaled in that body?"

Tyende stared down at one of his palms. "I was furious. The valley ran with blood. The cries of the dying echoed. I had heard that song too many times, in too many villages. So many had been slain, slaughtered, brutalized. And many of those deaths were ordered by one man's tongue."

Gray stared at the body. He noted the rifle buried in the growth, a knotted bullwhip coiled on a hip. "Who is he?"

"Captain Deprez. He led the Belgian contingent in his region. He drove the Zappo Zaps to kill and feast on our bodies. He himself beat many of my tribesmen, whipping them to death by his own hand. Often laughing as he did so."

"So, you killed him," Gray said.

"I could not stop myself. Though the captain's eyes were glazed, I wanted him to see who took his life. To know it was the son of the Kuba king."

Faraji glanced hard at Tyende, his eyes wide with shock. "You . . . you are son of Kot aMweeky, king of Sheppard's time."

Tyende bowed his head, one hand rising to the circlet. "A son who now rules an empty kingdom."

Gray remembered Tyende's earlier assertion concerning why he stayed here. "Your penance . . ."

"The Reverend Sheppard was angry, disappointed. I stole a life that was not mine to take. Death was already coming for the captain, yet I still killed him. Sheppard said it was a mortal sin—and maybe our group was punished for it. Or maybe the sickness was still in the air."

"You all became infected, too," Benjie said.

"We would've died, except Sheppard interceded. The reverend sought absolution for the crimes committed here. The purity of his heart was found worthy of salvation. We were saved."

"You were given a cure?" Gray asked, hope spiking through him.

"She was merciful. Afterward, the Reverend Sheppard tasked me to remain here, to be ready if the world ever needed salvation again. I was left as a sentinel and guardian. Molimbo's people honored this duty, especially as Sheppard had treated and saved many of those wounded by Deprez's men. Likewise, She accepted me, too, granting me the years until I was needed again."

Gray had his fill of the history lesson. If there was a cure here, he knew who held it. "Enough," he said curtly. "Who exactly are you talking about?"

Tyende turned his back on the golden city, the firelight already fading as the fuel was used up. He headed away, while pointing back to the trail. "She awaits you," he said. "Only She can judge you worthy from here."

8:17 A.M.

Benjie trotted along the cobbled path to keep up with the party. Tyende had reached the crossroads and took the other fork. It led deeper, toward the heart of the valley. The way grew darker, or maybe it was only his own misgivings that made it seem that way.

Still, as they continued, a glow slowly rose ahead of them, silhouetting the huge boles of the trees into dark columns that held up the canopy. The crown of the forest climbed higher as the woods grew taller.

And not just the trees.

The rafts of fungi spread into huge shelves along the trunks, looking wide enough to park a car atop. Elsewhere, across the valley floor, the mushrooms now hung their caps higher than Kowalski's head. Many of the growths also shone with a bioluminescence, in hues of crimson, azure, and yellow. The foxfire, as it was termed, was due an oxidative enzyme, luciferase, which emitted light.

Kowalski rubbed an eye with a knuckle. "I think those hallucinogens are kicking in."

Benji appreciated this sentiment. "It's like we're stepping into Tolkien's Middle-earth."

Kowalski pointed a thumb toward the tiny hunters. "And we've brought hobbits."

Benjie sighed and shook his head. He reached toward a wide span of fungus that extended over the path. As his fingers brushed along its underbelly, the glow brightened.

Amazing . . .

Kowalski tried to do the same with the shining gills under a mushroom cap. But as he touched it, the frills went dark, and the mushroom stalk pulled its top away. Startled by the movement, Kowalski shied back with a grimace.

"What the hell . . ." he muttered.

Benjie was just as shocked. He knew some plants could move, could respond to touch or shift toward sunlight. He searched the forest, noting the gentle breeze stirring the leaves of the canopy, rustling branches. He blinked and stumbled a step, looking all around. He lifted a palm.

No wind.

The air remained still, heavy with moisture. He studied the movement through the canopy. The shivering of leaves extended ahead of them, the branches waving in the same direction. Behind their group, the forest lay quiet.

It's responding to our passage. Almost like it's sending a warning ahead.

Benjie drew closer to the others, fearful of who the forest was alerting.

Gray also noted the movement around them as the forest seemed to wake. "Have you seen anything like this?"

Benjie shook his head. "Venus flytraps and bladderworts can close on prey. *Mimosa pudica*, a tiny fernlike plant, will curl its leaves if touched.

Even flowers open and close on their own." He waved a hand. "But all this . . . maybe the virus infects plants, too. Maybe what grows here has been equally altered."

Kowalski pointed to the left. The loam rose and fell, as if snakes were burrowing through there. The ground split at one point, opening enough to show something woody tunneling underground.

"I think that's a root," Benjie said. "Or maybe a subterranean vine of some sort."

Benjie followed its trajectory. It looked like something was retracting it back, pulling it toward its source, which lay ahead of them.

"She knows you're here," Tyende said.

None of this motion seemed to faze the pygmies or their four-legged companions. They continued through the forest on either side, flowing with it.

Benjie studied the phenomenon around him. His initial terror subsided to a wary fascination. "I read somewhere that plants should be considered more like slow-moving animals. Ones that operate on a time frame alien to us, a slower dimension that spans years, centuries, even millennia."

Kowalski waved at a patch of mushrooms that withdrew from their passage, like a woman pulling back a skirt. "Those don't look slow to me."

Benjie conceded this. "Bear in mind that plants are not passive spectators to life. In fact, they're highly responsive. They're attuned to magnetism, to gravity, to both sunlight and starlight, to insects that chew on them, to toxins that harm them.

Even sound. One study recorded the munching of a caterpillar and played it near a plant. The leaves responded by producing a surge of chemicals to ward off those supposed attackers. And you can see that everywhere in the plant world. Biochemical cascades that combat or mitigate threats. And though you might not see it, they are responding. They compete for territory, search out food and water. They can also evade predators or even capture prey. So, again, don't consider plants to be inert or even docile."

Benjie recognized that he was prattling on again, hyperfocusing on a topic.

Gray, though, encouraged him. "Could any of this tie into the virus? Could it be this forest's way of reacting to a threat?"

Benjie shrugged, but he enjoyed the speculation. "Maybe. Plants do harbor viruses of all sorts. But could something have weaponized one of them? I don't know. The natural world is full of innovative survival strategies, especially when it comes to dealing with threats. And *we* certainly count as that. We wreak all manner of damage. From pollution, to deforestation, to wanton destruction of habitats."

The discourse was cut short as the path took a sharp turn to the left.

Tyende stopped there and pointed his staff toward a dense section of the woods ahead. It looked like an impenetrable wall, a natural fortification that split the forest. The curving road tunneled through the barrier. A brighter glow flowed back at them from the far side, illuminating the cobbles.

Benjie caught a heady whiff of a flowery perfume, redolent with an undertone of a richer musk. He couldn't say why, but he sensed an ancientness to that scent, as if the prehistoric world had exhaled toward him. Something primal in him responded, a warning that chilled through him.

We don't belong here.

But it was too late. There was no turning back.

Tyende made sure of that. He urged them to continue down this road. "She waits for you." As Gray passed, he offered one final warning. "But know this. If you are found wanting, you will not leave here."

24

Tucker crouched once again under a deadfall at the north end of De Coster's private island. Only this time, he and Kane weren't alone. Frank, Monk, and Charlotte huddled alongside them. The group looked like the survivors of a shipwreck, soaked to the skin, bone-tired—which he realized was actually true. He pictured the barge crashed on its side in the jungle.

It had taken them all night to follow the river back to Belka Island. The jungle fought them every step of the way, as did their exhaustion. Still, they had forged on, determined to thwart De Coster before he erased all evidence of his involvement and disappeared.

Through breaks in the forest, the skies to the east shone dully. The sun had risen an hour ago, though remained hidden. A pall of thick smoke from the bomb blast had spread and covered the area. It hung as low as the treetops, smelling of oil and burned wood. It cast the first light of dawn into a hellish dark orange.

Thankfully, De Coster's plan to have the island bombed at dawn was clearly running behind schedule. Tucker didn't know the source of the delay, but he imagined the thick smoke had something to do with it. The wind had changed direction overnight, blowing upriver from the mine. Helicopter engines did not fare well in air choked heavily with dust and dirt. De Coster and his men were likely waiting for the worst of the smoke to clear.

Tucker stared up at the sky, perturbed. By now, he would've expected some response to the blast. News helicopters, a military response. Then again, the mine was hundreds of miles into the heart of the Congo, a territory run by De Coster and his billions. The bastard certainly had the resources to quash any inquiries, especially in a poor region already contending with a spreading plague.

If anyone hoped to stop him, it would have to be Tucker and the others.

Accepting that, Tucker opened his waterproof go-bag and distributed their weapons. He holstered his Desert Eagle and passed Monk the smaller Browning that the man had stolen. He turned to Charlotte and held out the Sphinx S3000, a blued steel 9mm she had lifted from a dead soldier on this very island.

When she reached for it, he pulled it back. "Dr. Girard, are you certain you want to continue from here? It might be better if you remain hidden in the forest."

"Better for whom?" She snatched the weapon, snapped open the slide, and inspected the weapon with a ready familiarity. She then resecured the pistol. Her eyes narrowed on him. "We already had this discussion on the other side of the river. I've not changed my mind after the swim."

By now, Frank had finished cleaning and drying their two FN FAL battle rifles. The weapons hadn't fit into his go-bag. He pushed one into Tucker's arms. "I think the lady has made up her mind."

Tucker frowned.

I had to try one last time.

While trekking to the island, the team had discussed skipping past it and heading straight to Ndaye and the helicopter. But as exhausted as they all were, it would take them the rest of the morning, maybe until the afternoon, to reach that site. That's if they could even find it, especially without GPS to guide them. By then, De Coster would have burned the island to the ground and been long gone, ready to deny any involvement or culpability. And what could their team do afterward? It would be their word against his billions of dollars.

Tucker knew how that would end.

But beyond holding the man accountable, they had to consider the innocents trapped on the island, who would surely be slaughtered if left behind. None of their group could stomach turning their backs on those patients.

Plus, Frank also intended to secure the data that De Coster's research team had gathered before it was whisked away, likely to vanish forever.

To replicate that work would take weeks, if not longer.

It was time the world did not have.

With matters settled, Tucker got them all moving toward the colonial outpost. He led the way, while Kane trotted ahead, extending Tucker's eyes and ears. They moved quietly but swiftly. They encountered no patrols, neither human nor robotic. De Coster must have drawn his forces in tighter as he readied for a final evacuation.

As they continued through the forest, the morning grew steadily brighter, much too quickly. The fickle wind had changed direction yet again. The smoke was rapidly clearing away from the island.

We're running out of time.

Shouts and the roaring of engines confirmed this. From the frantic nature of it all, it sounded as if De Coster's forces were rushing to leave.

Tucker led the others to the fringe of forest and called a halt. Kane rejoined him. Past the trees, glimpses of the outpost confirmed the worst. Armed men bustled about. Small electric ATVs sped throughout the compound. Two helicopters idled in the square, rotors spinning, keeping the engines warm. The larger of the two was Draper's gunship.

But that was not what stopped Tucker's breath.

The second helicopter was equally familiar. It was Ndaye's small Gazelle. Tucker zoomed his goggles for a closer inspection. Men loaded crates into the Gazelle's cargo hold.

Tucker clenched a fist.

Had Ndaye betrayed us? Had he been a mole all along?

Searching around the chopper, he spotted the eco-guard. He was down on his knees, his hands secured behind his back, his face beaten, swollen and bloody.

Tucker cringed at the sight, ashamed of his momentary suspicion. He remembered Ndaye hanging upside down and plucking him out of the raging river.

Of course, the man's not a traitor.

Seeing Ndaye here, Tucker was relieved that his team hadn't set off directly for the Gazelle after all. They would have been stranded in the jungle, if not eventually captured.

De Coster's forces must have discovered the FARDC helicopter in the forest after they had all escaped. Tucker felt a twinge of guilt, guessing what had happened. Nolan must have extended a search parameter around the island, suspecting Tucker had come from somewhere in the jungle. Once captured, Ndaye had clearly been brutally interrogated. That beating explained why the eco-guard still lived. De Coster must've wanted to learn what the man knew and who had sent him.

Still, Ndaye's reprieve would not last for long.

Tucker turned to the others. He quickly adjusted their plan to accommodate this new variable. "Frank and I'll go for Ndaye, then Draper. Afterward, we'll deal with that gunship."

Tucker recalled De Coster's earlier threat, to destroy the outpost using Hellfire missiles. Six rockets—three to a side—graced the stubby wings of the helicopter's launch airframe. Draper must have restocked his gunship. It was enough firepower to turn the island into a smoking cinder.

He faced Monk and Charlotte. "You two take Kane as planned. Secure the medical ward. If necessary, move the patients into the forest. Get them as far from the compound as possible if the bombing starts."

Monk shifted closer. He pointed to an outbuilding between the church and guesthouse. "That's the armory."

Tucker nodded. It was another goal. Before swimming here, Monk had sketched a rough map of the place in the mud. While a prisoner, Monk had identified the island's weapons depot. For the assault to come, their team would need more than two rifles, a trio of pistols, and a handful of flash-bangs and grenades still secured to Kane's bandolier. Unfortunately, there was no way of telling if the armory been cleared out or not.

Setting that concern aside, Tucker studied their ultimate target.

On the far side of the square from the guesthouse stood a squat cement-block building. Its roof sprouted with antennas and satellite dishes, marking the outpost's communication shack. Still, commandeering the radio would do no good. He pictured the small thumb drive in Draper's possession. It held the code to break through the jamming across this region.

We need that first.

Tucker shifted a few steps forward and swept his gaze around the square, searching closely with his goggles' binoculars. He failed to spot Draper. Tucker's survey ended at the guesthouse.

If he's anywhere, he's in there.

Tucker sidled back to the others. He firmed his lips, asking a silent question. *We ready?* He got nods all around. He then leaned down to Kane, touching noses with his partner in a tradition that went back years.

"Who's the best boy," he whispered.

Kane licked his chin.

That's right.

Tucker pointed to Monk and Charlotte. "CLOSE GUARD," he ordered.

Ever the soldier, Kane shifted over to them, but his eyes glowed back at Tucker. Tucker felt a stab of misgiving, an uneasy premonition. Maybe it was the strange cast to the light, maybe it was simply the PTSD that haunted them both. Still, in that moment, a shiver passed through him.

Kane took a step toward him, then back again.

As if he felt it, too.

With time ticking down, Tucker shook it off. They both had a mission to do. He motioned to the right, and Monk and Charlotte headed off. The pair would circle through the woods to reach the back of the medical ward's Quonset hut.

Kane lingered a moment longer, his eyes bright—then he turned and vanished.

"C'mon," Frank said, drawing his attention, and set off in the opposite direction.

Tucker followed. They would circle to the left and try to reach the armory first. Still, he glanced back toward where the others had vanished. At the corner of this goggles, the jostling view from Kane's camera feed stuttered, blacking out for several long seconds before continuing again.

Another twinge of dread rankled through Tucker.

Be careful, buddy.

8:32 A.M.

Charlotte kept close to Monk as they headed through the forest. She clutched her pistol in an iron grip. She searched every shadow and shift of leaf. The air reeked and stung her eyes. Her head pounded.

She swallowed down a threatening surge of bile—or tried to. She rubbed her throat. The back of her tongue was numb. Her fingers felt cold. It was why she held so tight to her weapon. She struggled with a truth that had been building throughout the night.

I'm getting sick.

She had told no one, fearing they would force her to stay behind. She couldn't let that happen. She would defend her patients with her last breath. She remembered her promise to Disanka. She pictured the baby boy's delicate features, the pink purse of his mouth.

"Almost there," Monk said. "Anything from Kane?"

She lifted the dog's transceiver. Armed with his pistol, Monk had no free hand to carry it. The tiny screen showed a view between two palms, obscured by the fronds of a fern. "Kane's stopped. So far, the back of the medical ward looks clear."

"Then let's go." Monk hurried the last of the distance to the forest's edge.

They found Kane nestled under bushes. His gaze remained on the windowless rear of the Quonset hut. The entrance lay on the far side.

She and Monk crouched next to the dog. An open stretch of ten yards separated them from their goal. Trash and piles of debris, including red bags of medical waste, covered the ground. She and Monk shared a look, both ready to move closer.

Before Charlotte could step out of hiding, a shout rose from beyond the hut. She recognized the curt, irritated voice of Ngoy.

"Get moving, you *imbéciles*! We have no more time!"

A moment later, a cluster of lab-coated figures hurried into view. Two of them pushed gurneys, with stacks of CPUs and file boxes precariously piled on top. As the wheels rattled along the wooden plankways, one of the boxes tumbled off and hit the ground hard, spilling papers.

"Be careful!" Ngoy yelled. "That's all my hard work!"

Charlotte silently cursed the bastard. Even now, it was all about him. One of the techs hastily gathered the papers back into the box and set off after the others.

"We're running out of time," Monk said.

She nodded. Still, they waited until Ngoy's group had vanished out of view. Once all was quiet again, they set off through the trash piles.

Kane kept alongside them. They reached the hut and circled the side that was farthest from the bustling central square.

Once around, Charlotte stopped at the corner and studied the entrance, lit by a single caged bulb. They waited for three breaths. No one else exited the medical ward. Across the way stood the dark Quonset hut that served as a morgue and pathology lab. She pictured the dead bodies stacked inside there.

With a small shudder, she returned her focus to the medical ward.

Is anyone still alive in there? Or had it been turned into another morgue?

Her ears strained to hear beyond the hum of the generators. The small windows on this side glowed, but she spotted no movement inside.

Monk set off again, drawing her and Kane onward. They ran low along the wall, keeping clear of the windows. Steps from the entrance, the sharp crack of a gunshot froze them all in place. It came from inside the ward. Then a moment again, another blast.

Charlotte knew there could be only one reason for the gunfire.

Now that the researchers had fled . . .

Someone's slaughtering the patients.

8:34 A.M.

Frank shook his head with despair. He gripped the barred gate of the armory. The place had been ransacked. Except for a handful of loose rounds scattered across the concrete floor, the weapons cache had been emptied.

"No wonder they left it unguarded," he mumbled. He turned to Tucker, who kept his face low, his weapon slung loosely at his shoulder. "What now?"

Tucker nodded toward the neighboring stone church. They retreated as discreetly as possible amidst the tumult of the square. They were still in the combat gear obtained at the mine, both the Kevlar body armor and the gray-green helmets. While not exactly the outfit worn by Draper's forces, it was close enough, especially amidst the chaos of the evacuation.

In the deeper shadows alongside the church, Tucker pointed to Ndaye. The eco-guard still knelt between the two helicopters. His hands had been zip-tied behind his back. His head hung low, blood dripping off his chin and from a broken nose.

"We need to free him," Tucker said. "Get him out of harm's way. Plus, I need to get a closer look at that gunship. Make sure Draper isn't aboard there."

They had yet to spot the captain. Frank scowled at the helicopter. Its rumbling could be felt in his chest. Compared to the tinier Gazelle, it looked like a massive lion sitting on its haunches, waiting to attack. Frank identified the craft as an older Russian Mi-24 Hind, what the Soviets called a flying tank. Gear continued to be loaded inside.

Frank tightened his jaw. "What's the plan?"

Tucker straightened and stepped toward where Ndaye was guarded over by a Congolese soldier with a rifle. "We pretend like we belong here."

Frank hurried after him, drawing alongside. "Then you'd better let me do the talking. I've got the right complexion." He motioned to his face. "Plus, I heard you try to speak French. Just your pronunciation alone will expose us. And your grammar will get us killed."

"That's exactly what my high school French teacher said."

Frank pushed forward to lead the way. "Keep that pale face of yours down."

They strode with a purposeful step. Tucker elbowed aside a soldier struggling with a handcart piled with crates. Frank tried to mimic Tucker's confidence, but sweat ran down his back, and his fingers fidgeted with his rifle. They sidled and sidestepped through the flurry of activity and closed upon Ndaye and the guard. The soldier ignored their approach, more focused on dragging deeply on a cigarette.

He didn't give Frank or Tucker a second glance until Frank pointed at Ndaye. Frank cleared his throat, yelling to be heard over the helicopter's engines. "*Capitaine* Draper sent us to take the prisoner. He's done with the *bâtard* and wants him dispatched."

The guard finally stirred, slipping the cigarette from his lips and leaning closer so he could be heard. "I thought the captain wanted to take him with us, to finish the *interrogatoire*."

"The man . . . he is no longer important."

The guard must have heard the hesitation in his voice and squinted harder at Frank's face, as if struggling to recognize him.

Frank turned aside to make that more difficult. He gestured vaguely behind him. "Check with *Capitaine* Draper, but he is in a foul mood. More than usual."

The soldier rocked his head, acknowledging the universal truth held by subordinates for their superiors.

Tucker pressed another truth. He kept his head low and held out a palm and motioned with his fingers. "Let me bum one of your cigarettes," he managed in passable French. Luckily the rumbling engines and low whomping of the rotors masked his terrible accent.

The soldier retreated a step, clearly not willing to forgo what was likely in limited supply. Tucker must have assumed it was a request that the man would refuse.

The soldier obliged, waving them away. "Take the *bâtard* and be gone."

Before anyone interceded, Frank and Tucker grabbed Ndaye by the shoulders and pulled him up roughly. Throughout this exchange, the eco-guard hadn't lifted his head, clearly resigned to his fate. Ndaye struggled for balance as they got him on his feet, dazed and bleary from his beating.

Half-dragging Ndaye between them, they carried him away from the helicopters. Once clear, Tucker leaned to the eco-guard's ear. "Thanks for saving my life back at the river. About time I returned the favor."

Ndaye stiffened and tilted his head toward Tucker. His body jolted with recognition. His footing grew more solid. Shock cleared the glaze from his eyes.

"Tucker . . ."

"Let's get you out of here." They carried him a few more yards, heading toward the shelter of the church. Before they reached it, Tucker pushed Ndaye toward Frank. "Send him after Monk and Charlotte. I'm going to make a fast canvass of the gunship. Make sure Draper isn't aboard. I'll meet you back at the church."

Tucker drew the brim of his helmet lower, further shadowing his features, and set off toward the tumult around the flying tank.

Frank turned and hurried with Ndaye to the back of the church. Once there, Frank cut the zip ties off the man's wrist and pointed through the trees toward the cluster of Quonset huts that constituted the compound's research lab. He indicated the largest of them.

"Monk and Charlotte—Dr. Girard—are trying to secure a group of patients over there."

Ndaye clearly struggled to follow his sudden change of circumstances, especially with the players involved. "*Docteur Girard . . . comment cela est-il possible?*"

Frank didn't have time to explain and pushed him toward the tree line. "We'll rendezvous there. Get moving but be careful."

Ndaye stumbled off, but he quickly steadied and vanished into the woods.

Frank edged back around the corner of the church. He returned his attention to the square.

He looked for Tucker among the rush of men but failed to spot him. Time stretched—or maybe it only seemed that way.

Where are—

A hand grabbed his shoulder from behind.

He flinched and jerked around. Tucker stood there, his face sheened with sweat, his eyes bright. He must have circled the other side of the church and come up from behind.

Tucker gave a shake of his head. "Not there."

Frank sighed.

So, Draper is still MIA.

Tucker turned and brought around what he had hidden behind his back. "But I did find this," he said with a savage grin.

He lifted up a rocket launcher, already fitted with an RPG. Frank knew exactly where Tucker planned to aim it. They both eyed the gunship.

"You can't take it out yet," Frank warned. "Not until we find that bastard and secure the code key. At the moment, we have the advantage of surprise. Blow that gunship up, and they'll lock this place up tighter than a duck's ass in a cold lake."

"Not the plan." Tucker nodded toward the guesthouse. "Draper has to be in there, likely finalizing the evacuation with the head honcho. We jump him, grab that thumb drive—then we'll deal with that helicopter."

Tucker set off toward the guesthouse, circling behind the empty armory. Once they neared the steps leading up to the front porch, Tucker sidestepped to a cluster of bushes flanking the stairs. He hid the rocket launcher there, but not too deeply, making it an easy grab.

Tucker straightened. "Backup," he explained. "Just in case."

Frank nodded and herded Tucker toward the stairs. The quicker they were through the door and out of sight, all the better. Tucker must've thought the same, clattering up the steps.

Before they could reach the porch, the door slammed open ahead of them.

A familiar figure barged out of the guest-house, flanked by two soldiers.

Draper.

The man's gaze immediately noted their up-turned faces. He recognized Frank in a flash. Without any hesitation, Draper snatched a pistol from his holster, his motion a blur.

Tucker got his rifle up, but he was a touch too slow.

Draper fired.

Tucker was hit in the chest and flew backward from the impact. He crashed hard at the bottom of the stairs.

Draper leveled his gun at Frank's head. All Frank could do was lift his arms. The two soldiers pounded down the steps and centered their rifles on Tucker as he sat back up, gasping, the wind knocked out of him. His body armor had saved his life.

Draper crossed to the edge of the porch and glared down at Frank. "Welcome back, Dr. Whitaker."

8:38 A.M.

Another muffled gunshot cracked inside the medical ward.

Monk cringed, fearing the worst.

Goddamn it . . .

He hurried to the entrance but stopped at the threshold long enough to raise a palm toward Charlotte. "Stay with Kane," he quietly urged her.

Fury shone in her eyes, along with determination. She crowded behind him and lifted her 9mm higher, clearly not intending to hang back.

He hoped another was more obedient. "STAY AND GUARD," he ordered Kane, reinforcing the command with a hand signal taught to him by Tucker.

The Belgian Malinois settled forward, drawing closer to the wall.

Satisfied, Monk slipped to the door and glanced back at Charlotte. "Stay low. Let me take the lead."

Another gunshot covered the creak of the door as Monk pulled it open. He rushed low into the sealed anteroom. He kept below the observation window that looked out into the ward. He nearly had to crawl to stay hidden. A quick glance around the enclosed anteroom showed that most of the protective gear—gowns and respirators—had already been cleared out. Not that it mattered. Isolation protocols had been abandoned. Even the door into the ward hung crookedly by one hinge.

Charlotte scooted next to Monk, leaning a palm and cradling her weapon near her chin.

The door clapped quietly closed behind her as the pistol blasted yet again.

Monk edged up enough to peek over the window's sill.

The ward looked like a storm had blown through it. Carts lay toppled. Drawers had been pulled out of cabinets and dumped haphazardly. Glass pipettes and flasks littered the floor, broken and trampled over in the haste to evacuate.

But not everything had been cleared out.

Patients still lay atop the cots. A figure in body armor and helmet stood in the middle of the hut. He held a smoking pistol in hand. Monk scowled with recognition. *Ekon.* The lieutenant stepped over to the next bed, leveled his weapon at an old man who stared unblinking at the ceiling, oblivious of the threat. The blast snapped the elder's head back, exploding gore across the pillow.

Beyond the cot, the other beds were equally bloody. Closer at hand, another half-dozen patients cowered in their cots, staring in terror at their executioner.

Charlotte gasped and tried to push past Monk, but he stopped her with a raised arm. He needed a moment to assess the situation. It looked as if Ekon had taken out the patients in the deepest throes of the disease, those nearly comatose and immobile. The bastard had likely chosen the order of targets out of a sadistic maliciousness, savoring the remaining patients' terror, those who were still in various stages of responsiveness. A teenage boy sobbed, covering his face. Others clutched sheets to their chins. Lips moved in prayers or begged for mercy. A mother guarded a child, shielding the baby with her body.

One of them must have tried to run for the exit earlier. A young woman lay facedown, her knee shattered by a round, her face cratered by a large exit wound.

Ekon moved on to the next bed, where the young mother turned her back, trying to further protect her baby.

Charlotte responded before Monk could stop her. She rose and fired through the window. The round punched through the plexiglass, but in doing so, it ruined her aim. Ekon smoothly ducked behind the cot, his cold expression never changing. He grabbed a fistful of the woman's hair and used her as a shield.

"Disanka . . ." Charlotte moaned.

Cursing, Monk dove out of the anteroom. He slid on his shoulder across the broken glass and debris. He fired one-handed at Ekon—less in an attempt to strike him, and more in the hopes of chasing the bastard away from the woman.

His efforts failed.

Ekon simply pressed the hot muzzle of his pistol to the back of the woman's head, dragging them both lower. As he did, he whispered in her ear.

Monk rolled behind a steel cabinet that had been toppled on its side. He sheltered there, gritting his teeth in frustration. He knew Ekon's whispering wasn't some threat to his captive. Monk had noted the microphone at the man's chin.

He's radioing for reinforcements.

By now, Charlotte had dropped back down.

She looked guiltily toward Monk, but he couldn't blame her. Her instincts had been to protect the innocent. Even now the woman—Disanka—clutched her baby to her bosom, a palm supporting his tiny head.

"Go," Monk called to Charlotte. She could still back out the door and seek shelter with Kane in the woods.

She shook her head, refusing.

"Get to the others," he pressed. "I'll do what I can here."

She visibly gulped, her eyes narrowing with pain. With a wince of guilt, she backed low toward the door. As she reached it, Kane growled in Monk's earpiece.

"Wait," he warned.

Through Kane's microphone, Monk heard a pounding of boots on boards—then a moment later, a burst of automatic fire. Rounds pinged against the outside of the hut. A few breeched the door, forcing Charlotte to her belly.

In his earpiece, a sharp canine yelp reached him.

Monk winced.

Still sprawled on the floor, Charlotte stared back at him. They both knew the truth.

We're trapped.

8:48 A.M.

Over the span of his career, Nolan De Coster learned to appreciate his victories, those both large and small. He came to savor each triumph with a grateful heart.

Like now.

Captain Draper had radioed a moment ago from the porch, reporting on the recapture of Dr. Whitaker and another interloper, likely the one who had freed the prisoners earlier. Then Lieutenant Ekon had called in, summoning support to ensnare two more who were pinned down in the medical ward. The audacity of that group to return here, especially after miraculously surviving events at the Katwa Mine.

Still, Nolan had to respect such an effort— not that he wouldn't dispatch them all once he had squeezed all he could out of them. But that would have to wait.

Standing behind his desk, he stared around his office. All his treasures had been carefully boxed and loaded into the gunship's hold. All that remained was the Abyssinian gold crown. It had been removed from its glass case and now nestled in a bed of straw within a wooden crate. He crossed and let his palm rest possessively atop it.

As much as he appreciated the good fortune of the last few minutes, a worry nagged at him. The recapture of the escapees allowed him to extrapolate a future course with less ambiguity, eliminating variables from the equation. Still, he sensed he was missing something critical. It kept him edgy, even irritable.

His computer chimed with an incoming video call. He crossed over to it, expecting it was Ekon, sharing the conclusion of the matters at the medical ward. Instead, another face appeared on the screen.

A young Belgian military engineer wore headphones with a microphone pulled aside. The tech manned the outpost's communication station, part of an extensive network throughout the Congo. The engineer had reported in periodically throughout the night following the bomb blast. He had been monitoring chatter across the region and shared any concerns that required Nolan's intervention.

Nolan leaned on his palms before the monitor. "What is it now, Corporal Willem?"

The man grimaced. "I don't know if this is worth bothering you about at this critical juncture. But you said to bring any anomalies to your attention."

"Go on. If it's concerning you, it's well worth bringing to my attention. I trust your judgment."

"Thank you, sir. The tracking program has been monitoring and evaluating all transmissions in the local region. It collates a list of anomalous broadcasts or communications. I found one result puzzling, strange enough that I thought you should know about it."

"Strange how?"

"The program detected a series of GPS pings in a remote corner of the Congo, working slowly eastward. Initially, I thought it might be rebel forces or guerrillas, but the intermittent regularity of it struck me as atypical for such forces."

"Understood."

"I looked closer at the program's logs. Three hours ago, a short satellite burst registered along that trail. I almost missed it. It lasted only six minutes, carrying a scrambled and encrypted call. One far too sophisticated for any militia forces."

Nolan didn't like this. He recalled his earlier concern about Dr. Whitaker's assistant, the man with an advanced—likely militarized—prosthetic.

And now this . . .

"You were right to bring this to my attention, Willem. Were you able to pinpoint the location of that transmission?"

"Yes, sir, it came from a dense, inhospitable region, a couple hundred miles southwest of the Kilo-Moto mine."

Nolan frowned, holding back a growl of aggravation. He didn't own that mine near the border, but he had invested heavily in it, financing an independent enterprise near there—until a mishap with a fracking unit had resulted in thousands of deaths at an isolated lake. He had spent a small fortune shifting the blame, attributing the tragedy to an unfortunate earthquake.

"Were you able to decrypt any of that transmission?" Nolan asked.

"No, it's quite confounding. I've never seen anything like it. But if you'd like, I can keep working on it. I know some Chinese hackers who could help."

Nolan hated to enlist the Chinese. They were his main competitors in the region, but he knew better than to let his personal pride stand in the way of learning the truth.

"Do it. And keep monitoring for any repeat of that signal. Let me know immediately if you spot it again."

"Yes, sir."

After the call ended, Nolan remained standing behind his desk. That nagging grew inside him again. He recalled his earlier sense that he had been missing a variable in the equation, something just out of sight.

A certainty grew in him.

Whoever sent that call—they're the true threat.

He felt better simply knowing that. He tapped his knuckles on his desk. It was the unknown variables that were always problematic. Once they were known, they could be dealt with.

As he calculated in his head, he grew more confident, more assured. He knew what he needed to do and set about arranging it.

To solve this equation—

The last variable must be eliminated.

25

Gray crossed down the cobbled path toward the dense wall of jungle. Ahead, massive trunks of mahogany and cedar trees crowded against one another. Their branches were knitted together, drawing their canopies lower, creating a leafy green shield. Even their roots—kneeing high out of the loam—tangled into a tall blockade.

The stone road passed through that barrier. A bright glow flowed back at them, coming from the far side. As they approached the tunnel, Gray flicked off his flashlight and packed it away. It was no longer needed.

He ducked his head low to pass under the leafy, vine-strewn arbor. Tyende accompanied him, thumping with his staff. The old man came by himself. Molimbo and his hunters remained outside.

Behind them, Benjie kept at their heels, with Kowalski trailing alongside Faraji.

As they continued deeper, the tunnel stirred

around them. Wide splays of wet leaves curled away from their passage, forming green fists, as if angered by their presence. Thorn-encrusted vines snaked and writhed, their barbs scraping like claws through the foliage. The thorns wept and leaked a crimson sap.

A drop fell on Gray's cheek. It burned like a bee sting. He used his shirt cuff to wipe it away, fearing it might be poison.

Tyende noted his concern. "Keep your faces down. Don't let any get in your mouths, and you'll be fine."

"Trust me," Kowalski grumbled, ducking lower. "I wasn't planning on licking those thorns."

Benjie rubbed as his wrist, wincing, likely struck, too. "Feels like the burn from a stinging nettle," he said, sounding more amazed than concerned. "Their venom is a witch's brew of histamines and various acids. Formic, tartaric, and oxalic."

Gray wondered again if the virus loosed upon the world had altered the flora in this valley, tweaking its genetics after so many millennia of exposure.

Benjie tugged on the back of Gray's shirt. "Look . . ."

Gray glanced around. Benjie pointed behind them. The tunnel slowly squeezed closed. Branches tilted lower, fanning leaves wide. Those spiky vines wove into a tangled net, sealing them in.

Gray eyed Tyende, remembering the man's warning. *If you are found wanting, you will not leave here.* Apparently, he meant that literally.

With no other choice, Gray continued down

the last of the tunnel. The glow grew ahead of him, not blinding, more like the soft luminosity of dawn. He wondered if the cast of this light contained some photosynthesizing energy that fueled the thick growth around them, like a tiny sun buried in this dark jungle.

Gray finally reached the end. He gaped as the view opened ahead of him. A vast wonderland, dotted with ponds, spread for hundreds of acres, encircled by those denser woods, roofed by a canopy as equally dark.

Benjie gasped, stumbling alongside Gray and Tyende. His gaze swept everywhere. "It's like a forest inside a forest."

Gray agreed. Preserved within the impenetrable dark emerald pocket, another forest abided. Countless trunks, all a snowy white, rose a hundred feet into the air. They could be mistaken for a spread of giant birches, only with barks less papery and more fleshy, like the skin on mushroom stalks. Their branches formed perfect domes of gold-green fronds, none touching another, as if this groove had been groomed or planted purposefully.

The glow here rose from the forest floor. The rolling landscape was festooned with phosphorescent fungi and swaths of shining mushrooms. Tiny ponds also cast forth a shimmering sheen, their waters radiant with some bioluminescent algae.

The air reinforced this conceit, smelling of mold and decay, along with a heavy fecund sweetness, like rotting fruits. At the same time, the scent felt old, as if it had seeped into every pore of this place over untold ages.

"What now?" Benjie whispered, hushed in awe.

"We go on," Gray answered.

He got a confirming nod from Tyende, who also added a warning. "Do not stray from the path."

The road led across this undulating terrain, wending this way and that to pass through the forest. Gray set off again, leading the others with Tyende. The road was only wide enough for two to walk abreast.

The odor grew stronger as they progressed, as the grove surrounded them. The strange forest also noted their passage. The hillocks of mushrooms stirred as roots tunneled through the soil, churning and occasionally revealing their pale woody lengths. One thigh-thick rhizome kneed out of the ground to the right of the path. As it did, sharp spines lifted from its surface, then flattened as it dove away again.

Kowalski stared after it. "Yeah, I'm definitely sticking to the road."

Benjie didn't seem to note this eruption and threat. His gaze remained on the forest. "I don't think this place is made up of individual trees. They're all too uniform. It reminds me of Pando."

"Who's Pando?" Kowalski asked.

"It's not a *who*, but a *what*," Benjie answered absently, still staring all around. "It's a forest. In Utah. Also dubbed the Trembling Giant. It's a stand of *Populus tremuloides*, or quaking aspens. While it outwardly looks like a forest of forty thousand trunks spread over miles, it's actually all one organism, a single tree connected by its roots that casts off clones of itself. It's believed to be eighty thousand years old, maybe as old as a million."

"You think we're looking at something like that here?" Gray pressed him.

"Maybe. Especially as I think I recognize these trees."

"You do?"

"Maybe. But only from the fossil record. Their wide bases, their tapering trunks. I'm almost certain their akin to prehistoric *Cladoxylopsids*, a class of giant trees related to ferns. They're considered to be the first true trees, appearing nearly four hundred million years ago. See those splits in their skins. I spotted a big tear back a ways, big enough to show the trunk was hollow inside. And notice how those splits are refilling with fresh xylem, repairing itself. It's how early trees once grew."

Benjie glanced over to Gray. "Remember when I told you about the oldest fungi found in the Congo, how it's believed to have prepared the primordial soil for future trees to root?" He waved to one of the trees. "This is what grew first. While it's definitely a tree, it still bears characteristics of mushrooms and fungi. That's why I think these woods are all *one* clonal complex, similar to many mushroom species. In fact, this forest, its composition, it should really be considered half tree, half fungus."

Gray swallowed, gazing at the forest with new eyes. The trees' domed tops even looked like mushroom caps, only formed of giant fern-like fronds instead of frilly gills.

Benji pointed higher up a neighboring trunk, clearly not quite done making his case. "And look at those rounded protrusions. They're primitive spore sacs, like those puffballs we saw earlier." He shifted to one that appeared to be smoking from a score of tiny holes across its surface. "Look, that one's already expelling spores out of its ostioles."

Gray grimaced at the sight. "So, half tree, half fungus . . ."

Kowalski looked no happier. "I think these buggers are more than that." He shied from another eruption of a spiky root. "I think it's got some animal in there, too."

"It might," Benjie conceded with a shrug. "Something is definitely playing a game of mix and match along evolution's pathway."

Gray pondered this. Could the virus have altered everything here, even this primitive life-form?

He searched ahead, seeking answers. The cobbled road wended deeper into this strange grove, clearly heading to the heart of the forest.

But what awaits us there?

8:53 A.M.

Benjie lagged behind the others, focused on the mystery at hand. Ahead, Gray plied Tyende with questions, but the old man merely pointed down the path, refusing to say more. Kowalski followed with them, looking none too happy.

Benjie tuned out the others, more interested

in what lay around him. By now, the tiny shimmering ponds at the outer edges of the forest had grown steadily larger. Arched bridges spanned a couple of them.

As Benjie forded a third one, he stared down into the water's depths, fascinated by its rusty, yellowish sheen. He had already discerned that all these ponds were fringed by an ochre-colored slime mold, the source of the luminosity. The phosphorescent growth stained the waters the same color, like a weak tea that glowed.

He studied those depths, careful to keep a wary distance from the bridge's edge as there were no rails. From this height, he discovered something new. The bottom of the pond looked like a pale white net had been strewn across its bottom. He squinted, studying the pattern. He noted the tiny nodules that held the threadlike net together. With a sharp inhalation, he realized what he could be looking at.

"Hyphae," he mumbled.

If he was right, it further supported his theory.

Hyphae were the branching, vegetative filaments that composed the mycelium—the veiny structure—of a fungus. They connected everything into a whole. He didn't know if this hyphae network was part of the organism here, or in some symbiotic relationship with it. Many trees formed a mutual beneficial relationship with soil fungi. Some even considered such mycorrhizal networks to be the brains of a forest, mimicking a neural network. They even flowed with neurotransmitters, including glutamate, one of the main transmitters in human brains.

Benjie stared to the pond's shore and beyond, imagining that same net spreading underground, traveling everywhere, forming a vast complex that spanned hundreds of acres. He shivered at the thought of some cold, vast intelligence staring back at him.

He hurried after the others, wanting to share his theories.

But one of their group remained on the bridge, staring down at the pond.

Benjie crossed to Faraji. "C'mon. We should catch up."

When Benjie tried to pass, Faraji remained rooted in place, with a hand clutched at his throat.

"What's wrong?" Benjie asked.

Faraji pointed down into the pond. "*Utetezi . . .*"

Benjie frowned. He had a nearly eidetic memory, which had allowed him to fill his head with so many facts from his years of studies. Still, it took him a moment to recognize the Bantu word. He had only heard it a couple times, back in the lab at the University of Kisangani. *Utetezi* meant "protection." Faraji had used it in context to the vials of powder his shaman had deployed back at the U.N. camp.

Benjie flashed back to the frantic night of their escape, of the ambush by the baboons. He pictured Woko Bosh spinning in place, casting the fine dust toward the beasts, driving them off.

Time slowed as he focused on that moment.

The powder in the air . . .

Benjie stared down at the pond. It had been the same rusty yellow hue. He grabbed Faraji's shoulder and called for the others to come back.

They looked none too happy but obliged. Too anxious to wait, Benjie rushed to meet them near the end of the bridge.

He pointed back at the pond and shared what both he and Faraji suspected. "The mold," he gasped out. "Or maybe something else in the water. I think this is the source of Woko Bosh's warding powder. They must have distilled it from a pond like this."

Gray looked at Tyende. "Is that true? Did Sheppard get it from here?"

"Molimbo's people gave it to him as a gift, to protect him on his journey back home." Tyende set off again, encouraging them to follow. "But, yes, it came from these ponds."

"Still, it's not a cure, right?" Gray asked. "Only a means to ward off the infected."

Tyende bowed his head, admitting as much, but he would say no more.

Benji kept next to Gray as they continued. He briefly shared what he also found at the bottom of the pond. "It's all got to be connected. The fungal hyphae network, this massive clonal complex of primitive trees. And now we know the forest is capable of distilling a counteractant to that virus. If that's true . . ."

He quailed at the thought.

Gray forced him to voice it aloud. Benjie sensed the man had already come to the same conclusion, maybe even before he had. "Go on," Gray urged.

Benjie passed another tree. The large cysts along its trunk smoked into air.

"The forest isn't *infected* by the virus," Benjie said. "It's the *source*."

Gray nodded with a grim set to his lips. He set a harder pace for them, clearly sensing time was running short.

Benjie understood.

We could all be infected by now.

The road approached a towering boulder with a slanted top. The rock was larger than a two-story house, covered in moss and mushrooms, scribed in lichen elsewhere. A single tree had taken root atop its skewed surface. It was a sapling, its trunk no wider than Benjie's forearm. Most of its roots had burrowed into the thin mulch, but a few were exposed. Some of the rhizomes at the higher edge shifted and dug, as if the tree were struggling to keep its foothold. Lower down, other roots extended past the base of the boulder and vanished, likely to join the greater body hidden below.

Benjie studied this effort, remembering how mushrooms had laid the foundation for plants to move onto land. The tableau atop the boulder looked like a microcosm of that first colonization.

As they continued around the rock, a tall hill could be seen rising behind it. Though only the crowns of the trees atop it were visible, marking a more successful colonization of those heights.

Gray led them to the far side of the boulder and drew to a hard stop. Benjie almost bumped into him and quickly scooted past—only to stumble back in shock.

He instantly recognized his mistake.

It wasn't a *hill* hidden behind the boulder— but a single massive *tree*.

Kowalski swore at the sheer size of it.

Faraji gasped.

The dozen treetops Benjie had spotted a moment ago actually made up the crown of the single beast, which arched hundreds of feet high. Its trunk alone was twenty meters wide, all scarred and gnarled. The upper sections were pale, like the rest of the forest, but it grew darker down below, turning black at the base, as if petrified by age, yet still living.

It sat amidst an acre-wide apron of gnarled and spiked roots. Some were as thick around as Kowalski's chest. The tangled mass rose in nodules and knots to encircle it completely, rising at least twenty feet all around.

Benjie found his voice. "It's . . . it's the mother tree."

8:58 A.M.

He's gotta be right . . .

Gray gaped at the enormity of the massive tree, his mind struggling with the sheer size of it. Here was the heart of the entire forest, ancient and eternal, something that had survived for millennia, maybe epochs of time.

He sensed it wasn't just a mother tree that rooted here.

But Nature herself.

Tyende had another name. "Here stands your judge. She will decide if you're worthy."

Tyende led them forward again. Dragged in his wake, they followed down the last of the road. As they approached, the tree filled the world ahead. Its ring of spiked roots looked sculpted of solid ebony, appearing more stone-like than wood. Once they drew closer, veins of silver could be seen streaking across the black surface.

Tyende stopped before the barricade. The road could be seen continuing, coursing under that tangle. They would have to crawl from here. No one looked willing to do so, not with all those daggered spikes lining the narrow path. Despite the petrified appearance to the roots, the mass creaked and groaned ahead of them.

It's still alive. It knows we're here.

Gray pictured the other woodland tunnel closing up behind them when they first entered this grove.

If that happened here, while we're still in there . . .

Kowalski scowled at Tyende. "You want us to go scooting through there. Do I look like a goddamned pygmy?"

Tyende waited, stating simply, "You will be tested."

Benjie edged closer, cocking his head, studying the roots. "Hmm . . ."

"What is it?" Gray asked.

The biologist stepped back. He twisted and squirmed, finally freeing something from the side pocket of his cargo pants. He held it aloft. It was the *ndop* figurine, carved in the likeness of

William Sheppard. Benjie still had it after showing it to Molimbo last night.

Benjie lifted it toward a curve of root. He glanced back with an eyebrow raised. Gray saw it now, too. The ebony carving was veined in silver, matching the root.

Gray turned to Tyende. "It's the same wood."

The old man nodded. "Another gift from Molimbo. It is a rare honor for them to share even such a small part of Her with another. A sign of how much they revered Reverend Sheppard. He saved many of their lives."

Gray hoped his team would be found equally worthy. He stared past the threatening circle of roots to the vast crown of leaves. There was only one way to find out.

Tyende pointed his staff toward the passage. "It is time."

Gray accepted this. He shifted forward and dropped to all fours. "I'll go first."

No one objected.

Gray moved the sling of his weapon to his chest and crawled into the tunnel. He kept low, shimmying and sliding to avoid those spikes. Still, there was no escaping all of them. They poked everywhere. It was like squeezing through a broken glass bottle. Spines nicked him: on the shoulder, the crown of his head, along one cheek. He flinched each time, not from the pain, but from the fear of what those spikes might be harboring.

The others fared no better. Squeaks and gasps and a litany of curses rose behind him as the team followed. Gray expected those fangs to

close on them at any moment. He scra
faster, earning more cuts and stabs. The len
of the tunnel seemed interminable, though i.
reality, it was only fifty or sixty yards.

He finally reached the end and crawled the
last of the distance while holding his breath.
Once clear, he stood up and moved to the side.
The sheer breadth of the mother tree forced him
back a step.

With the tree only thirty yards away, the
trunk rose as a dark wall before him. Even cran-
ing his neck, he could not spot the tree's crown
any longer. But under its lowermost branches,
and extending out along them, were hundreds, if
not thousands, of those sporulating cysts. They
crowded together, growing over one another,
looking like macabre grape clusters. The smallest
of them were the size of basketballs, the largest
ten times as big.

As he watched, scores of them steamed and
smoked.

By now, the rest of his group had clambered out
of the tunnel and joined him. They all gawked at
the sight, at the majesty before them. Between
them and the trunk, the ground was rock, but
it was not barren. Another lower wall of roots
writhed and stirred. It stood between them and
the tree. Only these were a pale white—younger,
more volatile and agitated by their presence.

Beyond the roots, directly ahead of them, the
black trunk was split by a tall crack, revealing a
hollow interior.

Only it wasn't empty.

Past the dark threshold, a large pool glowed

inside the tree, illuminating its heart. The surface shimmered softly, like all the other ponds, but here the waters shone *silver*, as if a bright moon were glowing in its depths.

Inside the trunk, the black walls of the tree ran with bright veins, matching the sheen of the water. It was as if the tree's very essence flowed into that small lake.

"*Mzazi Maziwa*," Tyende said, joining them, leaning on his staff.

So focused forward, Gray hadn't even known the man had followed them.

"It means 'mother's milk,'" Tyende explained.

Gray gave him a hard look. He appreciated the man's help, but he bristled at Tyende's stubborn lack of candor. Gray needed answers—though he believed he had figured out the most critical elements.

"Mother's milk," Gray said. "From such a nurturing name, I can only assume that if there's a cure, it's harbored in that pool." He pointed up toward the smoking cysts. "A cure against that."

Tyende's shoulders sagged with resignation. "For the longest time, She has remained quiet, slumbering throughout the years. Until eighteen months ago. She reacted to something that had changed, something She considered a threat. She expelled her poison for weeks on end—the entire forest did—before all eventually went quiet again."

Gray pictured a smoky cloud rising from this valley, roiling with that deadly virus, seeding the pathogen across this area.

Tyende continued, "I had hoped that the

damage would be limited to this region. And that it, too, would eventually subside. As it had in the past."

Gray glanced to Benjie. The biologist had hypothesized that the first outbreak of the virus was limited in scope, confined to a smaller region. But then matters had abruptly changed.

"The monsoons, the months of flooding," Gray said. "It washed the infection far wider than usual, allowing it to establish itself across a greater swath, to gain a firmer foothold, to give it the breadth to blow into a firestorm."

Tyende nodded.

Gray frowned. "Still, I don't understand. What set the tree off to begin with?" He waved to encompass the valley. "No one has invaded here or threatened this grove."

"Maybe not directly. But you learn Her moods over time. She has grown more temperamental these past several decades. Possibly due to a rise in pollution. The foulness to the air, the acid in the rain, the toxins in the watershed, the summers that grow hotter and longer. Even the encroachment by man into her neighboring areas. All of this has left her tense and edgy."

Gray glanced to Benjie, remembering the biologist's discourse about the sensitivity of plants, of their reactivity to the world around them, of their ability to sense the smallest changes to their environment—especially when it came to threats.

Gray focused back on Tyende. "But what actually lit that match eighteen months ago? What finally pushed the tree over that edge?"

Tyende sighed. "It took me too long to learn the truth. The threat She detected, it came from the northeast, near the Kilo-Moto mine."

Gray remembered spotting that operation on his digital map. "Did it encroach too closely on her territory?"

"No, it was something far more dramatic," Tyende said. "A lake in that region exploded. Thousands living around its shores were killed, suffocated to death."

"What caused the explosion?" Gray asked. "Was it an accident at the mine?"

"They claim it was an earthquake." Tyende scowled. "But I traveled there myself, heard from those who live in the area. It was not a quake, at least not a natural one. Someone had moved in heavy equipment. Blasts were heard, shaking the ground violently."

"Sounds like fracking," Kowalski said.

Tyende shrugged. "Villagers tried to warn the ones running the operation. Local superstitions warned against disturbing the lake, of the deadly ghosts that would rise from its waters if woken. Their pleas were ignored. Afterward, that same outfit covered everything up, blaming an earthquake."

"But I still don't understand," Gray said. "How did a quake—natural or otherwise—cause a lake to explode and suffocate all those villagers?"

The answer came from a surprising source. Benjie's eyes had gotten huge. "I remember reading about that incident. Before I came to the Congo. It was a methane burst."

"Methane?" Gray asked. "From where?"

"It was an unusual source," Benjie explained. "But one not all that rare in this tectonically active region. There's a whole chain of lakes between the DRC and Rwanda. A few are fed by volcanic hot springs. They're so deep that the methane released from those springs remains dissolved, trapped at the bottom, due to all that water pressure above. It's a precarious situation, an unstable stratification. An earthquake—or anything that gives those lakes a good shake—can break that stratification and cause the trapped methane to be released all at once. It's happened before, in 1986, at Lake Nyos in Cameron, where it killed two thousand people."

Gray pictured the villagers around that place waking to that quake, only to have the nearby lake boil wildly, releasing so much toxic methane that it became impossible to breathe.

Benjie continued, "It's a huge worry for one of the largest lakes in that chain. Lake Kivu. It's equally unstable. And far more populated. If it should ever blow, it would kill millions."

Gray began to understand what happened here. "That methane cloud. It must've swept down from that mine area. And the mother tree detected that toxic spike."

Tyende nodded. "She considered it an immediate threat—and reacted violently."

Gray rubbed his forehead at this tragic chain of events. He also recognized a hard truth. If it hadn't been that methane burst, something else would've triggered the tree eventually, especially when it was already so stressed by the degradation of the environment.

He stared up at the mother tree, which still smoked in threat.

Nature was clearly growing fed up with mankind's negligent stewardship. The Anthropocene era—the time of humans on this planet—was but a blink of an eye. The natural world has existed far longer, developing survival strategies over hundreds of millions of years.

How could we hope to compete?

Still, such a question would have to wait. He had a more immediate concern. He pointed to the silvery pond glowing at the heart of the tree. He didn't know what curative powers those waters possessed, but it was the world's best hope.

"Will She share her gift with us?" Gray asked.

"As I said before, if She finds you worthy." Tyende waved back to the barbed tunnel. "You've already been tested."

"What do I have to do from here?" Gray asked.

Tyende nodded forward. "You merely approach. She will let you know her answer."

Gray stared at the writhing roots snaking across the bare rock. Spines rose and fell as their lengths wound around and through each other. He suspected those razored spikes could shred him to ribbons, strip the muscle off his bones, before he could take more than a few steps.

Still, I have to try.

He took a deep breath, prayed for some manner of mercy—not just for himself, but the world. He headed across the rock toward the churning threat. Each step, he expected to be bashed away or impaled by a hundred spikes. The writhing grew more furious, reacting to his approach.

He stopped at the edge of the barrier.

Apparently, he was still too close.

A root lashed out, quicker than his eye could follow. It struck him across the chest. It felt like being hit by a truck. He flew backward, landed hard. He sat back up, gasping, the breath knocked out of him. He rubbed at his ribs.

At least, I wasn't stabbed.

Still, the truth was worse. He glanced back to Tyende, whose expression was easy to read.

I've been rejected.

Gray coughed and rolled to his feet. "It might just be me. You'll all have to try. We have no other choice."

With clear misgivings, Benjie headed over next—only to meet the same fate, rolling back to them. Faraji fared no better.

"To hell with this." Kowalski swung the Shuriken from his shoulder to his hands. He stalked forward, pointing its muzzle at the mass of roots. "I have my own way of knocking."

Gray lunged after him. "Don't—"

Before Kowalski could take another two steps, a root cracked out and whacked the weapon from his grip. The impact bent the steel and sent the rifle flying into the spiked barrier behind them.

"Hey!" Kowalski yelped out.

But it wasn't being disarmed that had so alarmed him. Another root had whipped out and latched to the man's wrist. Before he could move, a third shot between his legs and wrapped around his upper thigh.

Kowalski was yanked forward toward the churning mass of spikes. He lifted an arm to protect his face. His legs stumbled and fought against that pull, but this was one battle he could not win.

Gray ran to help him.

"No!" Tyende shouted. "Do not interfere!"

Gray respected the old man, but he could not abandon his partner. Still, he paused a fraction too long. Kowalski was lifted off his feet and jerked forward. The big man shouted as he hit the coil of roots—only to have them part and pull him inside. His huge form vanished into the twisting mass.

Gray skidded to a stop.

Too late . . .

He expected screams of agony, but only a stream of frustrated curses echoed out. Gray backed a few steps and lifted to his toes. Kowalski reappeared on the other side. Roots still shrouded him, but he was alive.

Kowalski struggled to free himself.

Tyende drew alongside Gray. "He has been chosen. Found worthy."

He stared at Tyende in dismay. "Kowalski?"

Tyende frowned at him. "Does he not have a good heart?"

Gray stammered, unsure how to answer that.

"Then is he perhaps ill?" Tyende offered.

The question so surprised Gray that it took him a breath to answer. As tough and hardheaded as Kowalski was, it was easy to forget that he was fighting malignant myeloma, another battle he might not win.

"Y . . . yes," Gray admitted. "He has cancer."

"Ah." Tyende stared back at the barrier of black roots behind them, at the barbed tunnel that they had all crawled through. "She must have sensed it."

Gray stiffened with the realization. He pictured those spines and spikes, cutting and poking. He had worried back then about them inflicting poison—when, in fact, the thorns must have been sampling them, drawing blood purposefully, to better understand who approached.

He again recalled Benjie's assertion about the highly attuned nature of plants. He also remembered Tyende's words: *You've already been tested.*

Again, he meant that literally.

"She does Her best to heal," Tyende explained. "Though She is a hard Mother, merciless in Her anger, She is also kind in many ways."

Gray stepped forward. No matter the reason, they had to take advantage of the situation. He cupped his mouth to yell. "Kowalski! Don't fight. Let the tree do what it needs to do. Just make sure you fill your canteen with some of that water!"

Kowalski continued to struggle, while yelling back, "Why am I always the goddamn guinea pig?"

His body was hauled inexorably toward the tree, passed from root to root. His boots skidded and kicked. It did no good. A new set of roots snaked out from inside the hollow trunk and snagged him, running tendrils across his face, through his clothes.

He hollered, wriggling, clearly outraged, "Poke up there again, and I'll burn you to the ground!"

Despite his protests, he got dragged across the threshold. He passed through the crack and into the heart of the tree. The roots pulled him to the water's edge—then gently drew him into the glowing pool.

As Gray watched, he considered Tyende's inquiry a moment ago.

Does he not have a good heart?

Gray remembered when Kowalski took another swim, through a radioactive pond, risking all to save others. It was why he got sick, how he acquired bone marrow cancer. Had the mother tree somehow sensed this sacrifice, too? Was it more than just his cancer? Was that why he had truly been chosen?

Across the way, Kowalski was pulled fully underwater, as if partaking of some vernal baptism. Gray prayed that this ritual might help—but a larger concern weighed.

Even if the cure could be secured, they still needed to get it out of here—and quickly. Recognizing that urgency, Gray didn't intend to stand idle. He shifted his pack and pulled out his sat-phone, ready to break radio silence one last time.

I must reach Painter.

And hopefully no one else.

26

This definitely wasn't the plan.

Tucker knelt at the base of the porch steps. He had his fingers folded atop his head, gripping tightly, his heart pounding. The muzzle of a rifle stabbed his back. His Desert Eagle had been stripped from him by the guard behind him and shoved into the soldier's belt.

Frank fared even worse. He shared the mud next to Tucker, on his knees, but sporting a split lip and a swollen eye. Another soldier held a handgun to the back of Frank's head. His friend, at least, had put up a decent fight.

Tucker's sternum still throbbed. Draper had proven his skill, catching Tucker square in the chest. The Kevlar body armor was the only reason he wasn't already dead.

Not that such a fate isn't far off.

Draper lorded over his victory from atop the porch of the guesthouse. He had a radio at his lips, coordinating the final evacuation. All the while, he glared down at them, refusing to lower his guard.

The door opened behind him. Two figures strode out: a Congolese doctor in a lab coat and a taller man, early sixties, wearing a crisp linen suit and black tie, his dark-blond hair oiled and neatly combed.

Tucker guessed the first had to be the head of the compound's research team. The sneer on Frank's face confirmed this. The second was clearly Nolan De Coster. Frank had described him, but the man's identification was evident enough from the deference that the doctor and the soldier showed him.

De Coster had clearly come out to gloat, perhaps summoned by Draper on the radio. The CEO's gaze settled on Tucker. "So, this is the fellow who caused us so much trouble. But no matter, we'll soon find out how he came to be here."

Tucker lifted a hand slowly from the top of his head, as if to ask a question. Instead, he raised a middle finger toward the man.

De Coster rolled his eyes and turned to Draper, who leaned in closer.

Good enough . . .

With the captain momentarily distracted, Tucker slapped his raised hand down to his hip pocket. He might be unarmed, but that didn't mean he had come unprepared. His palm struck the button on the tiny transceiver in his pocket.

The small grenade he had planted blasted behind him.

Earlier, when canvassing Draper's gunship,

Tucker had lodged the last of his frag charges near the propellant tank of a Hellfire rocket's engine.

Always good to have a backup plan.

He had no hope that such a small grenade would ignite the rocket's warhead, but the effect was dramatic enough. Gas shot out of the propellant tank, screaming like a banshee.

Tucker, however, was already in motion when the grenade exploded. He burst to his feet, catching his guard by surprise. He yanked the rifle under his arm and got a finger on the trigger. He strafed the porch. His aim was wild, striking the side of the building, the roof above the porch. Still, it was enough to force Draper to shelter the two new arrivals behind him— mainly De Coster.

The captain returned fire but had no better aim. He concentrated instead on getting his charges through the door and into the guesthouse.

Draper didn't linger—especially as Frank had gained a weapon and added to the barrage. His own guard lay sprawled at his feet, groaning and dazed, clearly coldcocked.

Under the combined assault, Draper ducked away and slammed the door.

Tucker let go of his captured rifle and twisted hard. He snatched his Desert Eagle from the soldier's belt, lifted the gun under the man's chin, and fired. The guard's helmet kept his skull in place, not that it helped. The body slumped to the ground.

Another gunshot caught Tucker in his armored

shoulder and spun him around. The firefight
had drawn the attention of the forces around the
helicopters. He dove to the right of the steps.
Frank took shelter on the left.

Tucker reached to the bushes next to him.

Back to Plan A.

He lifted his stolen rocket launcher.

9:04 A.M.

Monk lay on his side in broken glass. Blood
poured into his right eye, blinding him on that
side. His head rang from being pistol whipped.

Ekon loomed over him.

A muffled blast a moment ago had drawn the
lieutenant's attention toward the door. The four
soldiers—the reinforcements who Ekon had
called in earlier—had also looked in that direction. One of them had propped open the door
for a better view. A flurry of gunfire had echoed
to them.

Monk hadn't known the source of the commotion, only that he needed to take advantage
of it. He leaped at Ekon, determined to grab his
weapon. But the lieutenant was no slouch—and
damned quick. He struck Monk hard with the
butt of his pistol. The world had gone dark for
several seconds.

Now as his vision cleared—at least in the
one eye—Monk rolled to his seat. Ekon crossed
closer, kicking Charlotte to the side. He raised
his pistol, preparing to club Monk again.

Monk lifted an arm against the attack, eyeing the pistol. He wondered if he'd had both hands, if he could've secured that weapon. He really needed to talk to DARPA about innovating a new prosthesis, one that didn't require him blowing it up all the time.

Of course, I need to live first.

Ekon growled down at him, swinging his weapon high.

Monk winced, knowing what was coming.

He was wrong.

A massive blast shook the Quonset hut, rattling the metal walls and windows. Ekon backed up a step, never letting his focus drift from Monk.

Monk smiled.

Big mistake, you misogynistic bastard.

9:05 A.M.

Charlotte lunged from the floor.

The blast had turned the metal hut into an echo chamber. She counted on the deafening reverberations to cover her effort. That, and the lieutenant's clear lack of concern that she posed any threat. Like all women, she was accustomed to slights, oversights, and the lack of presumed value.

She took advantage of it now.

She leaped at Ekon's blind side. In her hand, she gripped a broken flask by its neck. She swung hard and stabbed its jagged end into his neck, aiming for the carotid. Before she could rip it free, he smashed an elbow into her side. A rib snapped with a lance of agony. She flew far and crashed hard, sliding through more glass.

Monk tried to follow up on her attack, but Ekon stumbled away, falling to a seat on one of the beds. He left the broken flask in place, smart enough to know not to yank it out. He shifted his pistol toward Monk and fired. He missed, but it forced Monk to dive aside.

Ekon recentered his aim, intent not to miss a second time.

Unfortunately, the lieutenant had failed to learn his lesson about women. The bed he had fallen on was not empty. Fingers reached up from behind him. They grabbed the impaled flask and slashed its sharp edge across his throat.

The pistol clattered to the floor. Ekon used both hands to try to stop the flood of blood. He coughed and choked as his life spurted from both carotids. He finally tipped sideways off the bed, revealing his slayer.

Disanka crawled back to where her baby lay nestled on a pillow.

Charlotte recognized a fundamental truth.

Never threaten a mother's child.

Monk had already retrieved Ekon's fallen pistol, catching it on its first bounce. He fired at the door, forcing the other soldiers to a huddle in the anteroom. One lifted a rifle and strafed the room blindly.

"Everyone down!" Monk hollered. He waved a teenaged boy to the floor, then shouldered the cot up on its side. "Find cover!"

Charlotte rushed low to Disanka and helped

her off the bed, along with her baby. Once they were down, she followed Monk's example, tipping the cot over as a shield. But the thin mattress and scant frame offered little protection.

Rounds punched through, proving this fact.

She flattened lower with Disanka.

With the armed soldiers guarding the only exit, they were trapped. A fresh barrage of gunfire erupted. Charlotte tried her best to shelter Disanka and her boy under her.

Then sharp screams rose—coming from the doorway.

Perplexed, she rolled enough to peek out.

A soldier came tumbling into view, firing wildly at the doorway. She spotted another pair of legs, unmoving and still, sticking out from the anteroom. Return fire pelted the retreating soldier, blasting through the open door. Rounds ricocheted off the soldier's armor and helmet.

Then a shadow leaped high and struck the soldier in the neck.

Kane . . .

The dog brought the man down and savaged his throat until his target lay still.

The firefight ended. All was quiet, except for the ringing in her ears. She held her breath. Another figure dashed into the room, sticking below the anteroom window.

"It's all clear!" Monk shouted to their rescuer and stood up.

Charlotte did the same, woozy, but determined. She expected Tucker to show himself, but as the shooter cleared the anteroom and straightened, she recognized her mistake.

Ndaye crossed over and patted Kane's side. "Good boy."

Where had the eco-guard come from?

She didn't know, but she couldn't be more grateful. She turned and offered Disanka a hand up. Instead, Disanka rose on her own, her strength likely fueled by adrenaline. *But how long would that last?* Charlotte stared around at the other patients. Six were still alive. She had to accept that as a win.

Monk noted her attention. "We need to get everyone into the woods. We can't get trapped in here again."

She didn't argue. Though the gun battle had ended in the ward, weapons fire still echoed from the square. If that war should shift in this direction, they needed to be gone.

The three of them did their best to get the patients moving. The worst afflicted had to be carried by Monk and Ndaye. The others managed only a little better, struggling with debilitation and weakness.

"Wait!" Charlotte called out.

She ran to the far end of the hut, to the ransacked clinical area. She grabbed what Ngoy had left behind, what that vainglorious bastard had considered useless, as it wasn't his own work. While being held captive, she had noted it abandoned on the floor, half-buried in debris.

She fished out Frank's laptop and headed back.

"Good thinking," Monk said. He grabbed a pack off of a dead soldier, emptied it one-handed, and secured the laptop inside. He hooked the pack over her shoulder. "Keep it safe."

She nodded.

They gathered everyone and headed to the door. Once outside the hut, Monk guided them away from the fighting toward the less traveled woods.

Before leaving, Charlotte had also recovered one of the rifles. She kept next to Disanka. The young mother staggered alongside her, clutching her child. The woman's condition was clearly worsening. All Charlotte could do was steady Disanka with a free hand.

They finally reached the woods and slipped into the deeper shadows.

"Keep going," Monk warned.

Charlotte knew they had no other choice. She clutched hard to the stolen rifle. It was the only way she knew she still held it. Her hands had gone entirely numb. She couldn't feel her feet. Her head pounded with a pain that narrowed her vision. The tension and terror exacerbated her symptoms.

Still, she forged on, goaded by the firefight behind her.

9:09 A.M.

Wreathed in oily smoke, Frank crouched on the porch with Tucker. The compound's main square choked with a thicker pall. The wreck of the two helicopters smoldered at its heart. Bodies lay strewn all around. Many were burned, either by the initial RPG strike or by the explosion of two fuel tanks.

Still, many combatants had survived, too many. Soldiers fired at them through the flames and smoke. Rounds peppered the planked sides of the guesthouse, tore through wooden posts, and pinged off the steel bistro table that Tucker had knocked on its side. They sheltered behind it and fired at any shadow that approached too close.

"Ready?" Tucker asked, his upper face hidden behind his goggles. They had recovered their helmets, too.

Frank gripped the tiny silver egg in his palm and nodded.

The ferocity of the firefight had ebbed over the last minute. A majority of the remaining soldiers must have decided caution was the better part of valor and retreated out of harm's way, waiting to see how matters resolved. But a stubborn contingent remained, firing sporadically at the porch.

It was a stalemate that Tucker and Frank couldn't wait out. They were running low on ammunition, and they had to worry about Draper slipping away, too. They couldn't let him escape with that decryption key.

That's if he hasn't already.

"Find out if he's in there," Tucker said. "And keep him there. I'll hold the fort and join you when I can."

Frank nodded.

Tucker lifted and strafed with the rifle. "Go."

Under the cover of that barrage, Frank ran low for the door. He edged it open and tossed the smoke bomb inside. He heard its muffled pop, waited two heartbeats, then shouldered across the threshold and dove low.

Fresh gunfire erupted outside as the skirmish renewed once again.

Inside, a double blast of a pistol answered two questions. Draper was still inside—and he was a damned good shot. Frank gasped and rolled. A round had grazed the meat of his thigh, burning a fiery line across it.

If not for the smoke, Frank knew he would've suffered far worse than a graze.

He rolled behind a mahogany credenza near the door. More rounds chipped the thick wood. The shots had come from the upper landing at the top of the stairs ahead of him. He lifted Tucker's Desert Eagle and fired blindly through the smoke—which was rapidly thinning.

He peeked enough to see the shadowy form of Draper running low along the railing of the upper arcade, holding the higher ground. The man kept tucked into his Kevlar, turning himself into an armored turtle.

Frank squeezed off two more rounds. Both missed, but one struck the entrance to De Coster's office. It rang loudly enough to suggest the door was reinforced with steel. Draper must have already secured Ngoy and Nolan inside.

Another pistol blast forced Frank down. Splinters stung his face.

Guy's good . . .

Frank weighed his options, his thigh burning like a motherfucker. He only had to keep Draper pinned down, keep him from leaving. Once Tucker secured the front of the guesthouse, they could both go after him, flank him, and get that damned key.

Already it sounded like the firefight outside had ended.

Just need to hold out a little longer.

He willed Draper to stay up there, to keep guarding De Coster.

The creak of a wooden stair warned Frank that the captain was not so agreeable to this plan. Draper intended to bring the fight down here.

Why is he giving up the high ground, exposing himself?

Frank lifted his Desert Eagle, ready to drive the man back up. He tilted out and spotted Draper edging down the top stairs, going for a better vantage on Frank's hiding spot. The man carried a black ballistic shield in front of him. Frank grimaced. He knew such shields could stop even armor-piercing rounds.

Once Draper secured his position, a weapon appeared. The captain had abandoned his pistol and rearmed himself with a bullpup rifle. A larger barrel sat below its usual muzzle.

Grenade launcher.

Crap . . .

Sensing the inevitable, Frank dove out of hiding and rolled across the room—and not a moment too soon. A loud blast was followed by an explosive boom. The massive mahogany credenza shattered apart behind him. Shards pelted his armor and impaled any exposed flesh. The concussion of the blast shoved him even farther.

With his head ringing, he rolled onto his

back, skidding to a stop. He had managed to keep his pistol and aimed it past his legs toward the top of the stairs.

He fired wildly.

The rounds ricocheted off of Draper's shield. The captain braced against the assault and brought his bullpup around, centering his shot.

Frank was exposed on the open floor.

Then glass shattered from a window on the opposite end of the landing. A form came hurdling through, firing a rifle.

Tucker . . .

His partner must've heard the ongoing battle inside the guesthouse, after his own skirmish had ended, and sought to outflank Draper by scaling the building. Unfortunately, the captain had heard the tinkling of glass in time to swing his shield around and block Tucker's assault.

Still, in turning aside, Draper left himself momentarily exposed. Frank aimed for that damned turtle's soft spot—and fired twice. The first round hit the meat of the captain's thigh, payback for Frank's own injury. The other shattered the man's knee.

The leg collapsed under Draper, sending him tumbling down the staircase. His shield clattered from his arm.

Tucker chased after him, rifle at his shoulder.

Frank gained his feet and came at the man from the other side.

Draper crashed to the floor between them, sprawled facedown. As Tucker and Frank reached him, the man rolled over with a groan. Blood poured from his leg, pumping out in a strong jet. Frank's first shot must have severed a femoral artery.

"Back!" Tucker hollered.

Focused on the leg, it took Frank a fraction too long to react, to see the grenade roll from Draper's fingers and land in the spreading pool of blood.

Frank shoved around and ran for the door.

Not going to make it.

The blast deafened and caught him. He was lifted off his legs and slammed into the door, cracking its frame. Dazed, addled, he twisted back around, shocked to be alive and not shredded by shrapnel.

He turned to see Tucker come tumbling down through the smoke, clutching hard to the ballistic shield. He must've grabbed the armored buffer from the foot of the steps and smothered it over Draper and the grenade.

Tucker crashed back to the floor at the side of the blast crater. He bounced and rolled farther away.

Frank rushed over and helped him up. They hobbled away together. Frank supported Tucker under an arm. Tucker limped on one leg, his ankle clearly broken, his face bleeding profusely.

Tucker mumbled, but Frank was still deaf and only shook his head as they reached the door.

Tucker coughed and tried again, gasping louder to be heard. He waved weakly toward the smoky ruins behind them, at the bone and gore blasted across the space.

"Don't think we're gonna get that thumb drive now."

9:12 A.M.

Charlotte slumped down the trunk of a palm. She shivered, chilled, despite the exertion and the growing morning heat. She gratefully sank to her seat, leaning her back against the tree, and positioned her rifle across her knees.

Monk remained on his feet and gently lowered an older woman, a patient of fifty or sixty, to the ground. The woman's head lolled back. She then slipped onto her side, unable to hold herself up on her own.

Monk looked on with concern, then faced the forest. "We should be deep enough in the woods by now."

Good. It's not like we can go any farther.

Disanka had collapsed nearby when the stop was called. Her legs had been trembling; her arms could barely hold the limp boy in her lap. She sat now, hunched over him, sheltering him with her entire body. The baby was nonresponsive, barely breathing. He did not have long to live.

Charlotte leaned her head back. It pounded, and she had difficulty swallowing. She wiped at her lips, which felt fat and numb, like after a novocaine injection.

I've failed him, failed them all.

Ndaye settled his own patient to the forest

floor, a gangly young man of twenty or so. He shivered like Charlotte. He sat with his head hanging between his knees. Snot ran from his nose, but he made no effort to wipe it away.

The eco-guard shifted over and offered a water bottle to a pair of adolescents, a boy and girl. They shied from him, maybe fearful of his swollen, beaten face. From the way they clung to each other, supporting one another, she wondered if they might be brother and sister, or maybe simply two frightened children who needed a measure of closeness to hold back their terror.

Monk crouched next to her, but his eyes looked off toward the outpost. They had all heard the explosions a few moments ago. "Someone's still engaging De Coster's forces."

"Tucker and Frank . . ." she mumbled.

Who else could it be?

Monk nodded and glanced around the group, all slumped under the canopy. He gripped his pistol higher. "We're as hidden as we can be."

She understood what he was hesitant to ask. "Go help them. Take Ndaye." She lifted her rifle and nodded to Kane. "We'll keep watch here."

He nodded his thanks, then quickly spoke to Ndaye. A spatter of gunfire echoed through the forest. Monk glanced one last time toward her, clearly checking if she wanted to change her mind.

She waved them away. "Go."

They took off.

Charlotte listened until she could no longer hear the soft crunch of their boots. She rubbed at her sore eyes and shifted higher against the trunk. It took more effort than she had imagined. She steadied the rifle on her knees, but her hands trembled on the weapon's stock.

She didn't know if it was the disease or simply exhaustion. At this point, she couldn't remember the last time she had slept.

The others all settled into various degrees of slumber or lassitude.

As she kept guard over them, she fought against the drooping of her eyelids. Despite her terror, she caught herself drifting off, her chin hitting her sternum. She bobbed her head back up, which set her skull to pounding again. She stared at her hands. They were empty. The rifle sat at her toes. Her numb fingers had dropped it.

She collected the weapon back up.

Maybe I should've had Ndaye stay with us.

She turned to the other guard on duty. Kane kept close, still standing, with his ears tall. She reached and patted him.

We've got this.

As she touched him, she felt his sides vibrating. A low growl flowed. His hackles rose under her palms. His gaze was fixed to the darker woods, away from the compound. His growl became a low snarl of warning.

Someone's out there.

She firmed her hold on the rifle, but her fingers refused to obey. The weapon slipped and slid, feeling oily in her numb grip. She tried to stand, only to discover any effort left her limbs trembling.

She turned to the only weapon she could trust.

"Kane . . ."

He glanced once to her—then back out to the woods.

She lifted an arm, which took all her effort, and pointed. She used the command that Tucker had taught them in case of emergency.

"*PROTECT.*"

27

Ensconced in his barricaded office, Nolan studied the bank of security monitors. He leaned on his fists, his face so heated it felt sunburned. He surveyed the status of the compound. Only a few cameras still operated, offering him a sketchy view of the camp.

The feed from the top of the church steeple showed the smoldering wreckage of the two helicopters, his planned exit from the island. Spatters of gunfire still reached him, mostly centered around the square, but the two earlier grenade blasts also echoed in his head. The explosions had shaken the entire guesthouse.

Afterward, Nolan had been unable to raise Draper.

"What are we going to do?" a nasally voice begged behind him.

He glanced over to Ngoy. The researcher paced before the steel shutters across the balcony.

His eyes shone with fear as he hugged his arms around his belly.

"We're getting out of here," Nolan said.

"How?"

Nolan turned to a monitor running feed from an active camera. It showed a shimmer of the river, a long dock, and his armored personal yacht. The ship's sixty-foot length was plated in steel, all of its windows bulletproof. He had ferried dignitaries aboard it, even a U.S. president. In such a volatile region, the yacht's fortifications were a necessity. He had once survived a rocket attack by rebel forces aboard that craft while piloting the vessel himself.

And now it will keep me safe yet again.

He hit a button on the monitoring station. A panel of steel-reinforced zebrawood slid aside behind his desk, revealing a secret stair. The steps led down to a camouflaged garage at the back of the building, where an electric ATV was parked. It would whisk them to the dock, avoiding the battle around the main square.

Ngoy rushed over, his eyes huge, his face hopeful.

Only a handful of people knew about the secret exit. Like the armor on the yacht, securing a covert escape was an equally smart precaution.

Nolan intended to survive, to right this listing ship. He could still turn this plague to his advantage. He hadn't become CEO because of needless panic. He adhered to Baron Rothschild's adage: *Buy when there's blood on the street.*

He glanced to the wreckage in the square, the broken bodies around it. Though the equation had become more difficult, he was determined to solve it.

He straightened, ready to head off.

As he stepped away, his computer chimed behind him. Both surprised and curious, he crossed to his desk to answer the video call. He tapped the keyboard, and the familiar face of Corporal Willem, the Belgian military engineer, appeared on the screen. The young man hunched low, his face running with sweat, but he hadn't abandoned his post. Then again, the communication shack was built of concrete blocks, practically its own fortress.

"What is it, Corporal?"

"Sir," Willem gasped out. "You instructed me to inform you if I detected another aberrant transmission."

It took Nolan a full breath to remember. "That satellite communication from the jungle."

"It was picked up again. Farther to the east. I ran it through the decryption program. The one the Chinese hackers sold to us."

"And?"

"It failed."

Nolan wasn't surprised. *The Chinese couldn't be trusted.*

"But that initial decryption broke it enough for my own hack to discern a single word."

"And what was that?"

"The word was 'cure.'"

Nolan stiffened, clenching a fist. He had been convinced that the forces directed against him were far more sophisticated than mere mercenaries. Likewise, he suspected that aberrant signal coming from the deep jungle was tied to the attack here. That unknown variable needed to be eliminated.

Especially now.

He couldn't let another party get the upper hand. He didn't know if that single word—*cure*— was as important as it sounded, but Nolan never took chances, not when he could hedge his bet.

"Sir, what should I do?" Willem asked.

"Send me the coordinates of that signal."

"Right away."

A moment later the latitude and longitude designations appeared on his screen.

"Thank you, Willem. Hold pat until I get confirmation."

"Understood."

With grim satisfaction, Nolan tapped rapidly at his keyboard. After Willem's earlier alert, Nolan had set up a contingency plan, in case it was needed. He had a large drone—a Russian S-70 Okhotnik—prepped and waiting on a camouflaged airstrip. Two years ago, he had it stripped of its armaments, all to serve as the delivery platform for a single bomb.

In the past, Nolan had secured seven MOABs, but he only buried *six*. The seventh he had built into that drone. Nolan had wanted the leeway to be able to deliver destruction whenever and wherever it was best needed.

Like now.

He passed the coordinates to the drone operators at the airstrip. Once finished, he had to wait. His finger tapped impatiently on the desk.

Willem had been monitoring Nolan's communication with the on-site team. In fact, the engineer had helped coordinate this contingency. Now that it was happening, the man's face grew stoic, his lips drawn tighter. But he was young, not as hardened by necessity as Nolan. With time, that would change. Willem would be a strong asset to the corporation.

Finally, a new screen bloomed with the confirmation from the airstrip. It also came with a projected schedule, an estimation of launch and travel time. In the corner of the screen, a countdown began running.

Content, Nolan shifted his attention to the other screen. "Thank you, Willem. Now get yourself to safety. Try to make it to my yacht."

"Yes, sir. Thank you, sir."

After the video call ended, Nolan watched the timer wind down.

Twenty-two more minutes.

Then that unknown variable would be eliminated from the equation.

9:22 A.M.

Tucker hunched to the right of the steel door to the communication shack. Smoke choked the area but also helped hide them. A few soldiers still threatened, but all the fighting had stopped for the moment.

Tucker leaned a shoulder against the wall, trying to keep his weight off of his broken ankle.

Earlier, using an entire roll of duct tape from Tucker's pack, Frank had fashioned a relatively stiff splint.

Frank now huddled with his rifle on the other side of the locked door.

A narrow window had allowed them to peek inside. A single tech—a young man in a radio helmet—manned the bank of equipment. While they couldn't enter, they were able to eavesdrop on snatches of the conversation. It involved something about an encrypted communication from the deep jungle and maybe a possible cure.

Tucker whispered across to Frank. "That's gotta be Gray and the others."

De Coster was clearly plotting some recourse.

"Get back," Frank warned.

Through the window, Tucker spotted the tech rushing toward the door. The man carried a duffel and had grabbed a combat shotgun from beside the console.

Frank flattened to the side. Tucker did the same. A bolt scraped, and the door pulled open. The tech poked his head out. Tucker slammed the butt of his rifle into the man's face, knocking him back inside. Frank followed with the Desert Eagle at the tech's chest. The man dropped his duffel and weapon and lifted both arms.

"*Niet schieten . . .*" he pleaded.

Limping on his splinted leg, Tucker forced the tech back with his rifle, while Frank secured the door.

"Do you speak English?" Tucker asked.

The man nodded vigorously. "*Ja . . .* yes."

"What's your name?"

"Willem . . . Jan Willem."

Tucker pointed to the monitors which still glowed. In the tech's haste to leave, he had left everything running, maybe to keep the jamming going. One monitor showed a screen with a digital map, a set of crosshairs, and a small blinking dot in the shape of a tiny plane.

"Your communication with De Coster," Tucker demanded. "What's being planned?"

Willem hesitated, but Frank encouraged his cooperation with the muzzle of his huge pistol. "Tell us," he demanded.

Willem swallowed and nodded. He quickly recounted the events of the past few hours, ending with De Coster's contingency. "The bomber will strike the coordinates in"—the tech glanced to a timer counting down—"eighteen minutes."

On the screen, the tiny plane icon had begun to move.

Frank checked his watch. "That's roughly nine forty-five."

Tucker pictured the smoking crater back at the mine. He shoved Willem toward the equipment. "Shut down all the jamming towers in the area."

"I can't. Not from here."

Tucker scowled with frustration. "Then power off the one on the island."

Maybe it would be enough.

Willem turned to the console and hit a toggle. "It's done."

Tucker tugged out his sat-phone. Gray needed to be warned. He lifted his phone, searching for a signal. He shifted the stubby antenna in all directions, but he couldn't get even a single blip of satellite contact.

Tucker swore loudly.

"Wait." Frank leaned toward the monitor. He pointed a finger at the red plane icon as it slowly moved across the glowing map. "That's a real-time feed, isn't it? Same with the countdown."

Willem nodded.

Frank pointed the pistol at the tech's face. "Which means you have an outside line. You have the decryption to break through this jam."

Willem seemed surprised this was even a question. "*Natuurlijk*. I'm the head engineer."

Frank turned to Tucker with wide eyes. "That means we can radio out."

Tucker froze in place—but not because of Frank's revelation. He steadied his goggles with the edge of his phone. When the local jamming had dropped, the feed from Kane's camera had stopped its erratic frazzling and long dropouts. The video had turned crisp and clear. His heart clenched at the sight revealed.

Oh, god . . .

"Tucker?" Frank stepped closer. "What's—"

Tucker punched the speed dial for Sigma command and shoved the sat-phone at Frank. "This number. Director Crowe. Tell him everything." He turned toward the door. "Get the FARDC military out here. Get him to warn Gray."

"Tucker!" Frank called after him.

He had no time to explain.

He tossed his rifle aside and grabbed the tech's

shotgun—a Mossberg 930 tactical. The 12-gauge semiautomatic carried eight shotshells.

Better be enough.

Limping on his leg, panic numbing the pain, he dashed out the door—straight into a firefight.

He ducked low from a barrage that erupted outside, cutting across his path. A trio of soldiers, likely the last still around, strafed the woods. Return fire came from the forest. One soldier dropped, hit in the face. The other two turned tail and ran.

From the woods, a pair of figures emerged.

Monk and Ndaye . . .

Tucker rushed toward them. "Over here!" He reached the pair and passed them. He waved back at the communication shack. "Protect Frank!"

"Where are you going?" Monk yelled after him.

No time . . .

9:25 A.M.

Kane runs through the woods. He dares not stop. Gunfire pursues him, shredding through leaves, and shattering bark. An order continues to blaze behind his eyes, burned into his will.

Protect.

He intends to do that.

The others, huddled and weak, are far behind him by now. Earlier, he had heard the telltale whir and muffled clank, caught the scent of gun oil and lightning strike. He recognized that danger. To draw it away, he had set off into the forest.

Even now, he uses his body, his heat, his growls to keep the hunters on his trail. They are everywhere. And many. He has zigged and zagged, backtracked and circled, gathering all in his wake, luring the threat away.

Now he is trapped in his own snare.

They close all around, coming from every direction.

He finally clears the gunfire, races into deeper shadows, skids on his paws. He searches, extending his senses. He smells spoor and wet loam, damp leaf and rotted wood. Still, over all wafts the scent of burning oil. It hangs everywhere. The whirring fills the world around him.

He is a seasoned soldier.

He recognizes the truth.

To run again is death.

Exhausted, he pants heavily. Blood seeps hot from a graze to his flank. He settles to a wary crouch. He must stand his ground, keep the danger drawn here, away from those he must protect.

The hunters close upon him, bringing lightning and firepower.

His hackles rise against that threat.

But he will not be moved.

9:27 A.M.

In a haze of agony, Tucker sprinted through the forest, carrying the shotgun in both hands. He limped on his bad leg and propelled himself forward with the other. Pain flared with each step, like a fiery heartbeat matching his own pounding heart.

He bashed through low branches and bounced off of tree trunks. He kept one focus on the path and the other on the spinning needle of Kane's homing beacon. A moment ago, he had watched Kane come to a halt after a mad flight through the trees, pursued and shot at the entire way. The thermal mode of his partner's camera had showed a score of overheated Q-UGVs pursuing Kane. It was difficult to determine the exact number. They were everywhere around the dog, coming from every direction.

So many . . .

During the evacuation, the soldiers must have gathered all of the robotic dogs in one place, readying them to leave. Once the firefight had started, they had clearly released that entire pack into the forest, maybe to help cover their own escape.

Tucker watched the dark orange glows closing on Kane's position.

I'll never make it in time.

Still, Tucker had to help. He fumbled out his transceiver and found the series of buttons that controlled Kane's bandolier. He found and pressed the proper button and released a frag grenade. He prayed it would be enough to give Kane the advantage to escape that noose.

Like last time.

Kane notes the jolt under his sternum. His ears pick out the snap of the release. The tumble of the silvery charge brushes his inner leg and lands in the wet leaves under him.

It assures Kane that his partner is with him. The

thought calms him, reminding him of a life shared. He tastes the scrap of meat tossed from a plate. Feels the huddle of a warm body next to him. Sees the toss of a red ball through bright sunshine. Smells the sweaty musk that is as familiar as his own.

At the back of his skull, he notes the passing of each heartbeat, marking time until the fire and blast.

He knows what he must do.

The order still blazes bright.

Protect.

He can't let a single hunter drift away, to return and threaten the others. He must hold his post. Knowing this, he settles atop that silvery egg.

He accepts what's coming. Off in the distance, he hears the deep blast of a large gun. Still, he does not move.

He's a good soldier.

And more important . . .

He's a good boy.

Through his goggle's thermal scopes, Tucker spotted the boxy orange glow to his right. He aimed his Mossberg and fired. The Q-UGV shattered into pieces. Tucker didn't slow. As he charged through the woods, a countdown ran in his head.

Ten seconds . . .

Other glows lit the forest, marking more of the robotic Q-UGVs. They were everywhere. Easily a dozen or more. And he was down to six rounds.

Nine seconds . . .

Tucker radioed through his Molar Mic. "Move, Kane. Now!"

But like before, the dog remained in position, refusing the order, clearly still adhering to another command. Kane had been taught to prioritize, to trust his own instincts, not to follow blindly.

The dog could also be damned stubborn.

Eight . . .

Tucker limped and hopped, refusing to give up on Kane. A blast of gunfire ripped through the woods. Rounds slammed into his body armor. He twisted and aimed as one of the Q-UGVs appeared.

Tucker fired the Mossberg. The slug shattered the leg off of the robotic dog. The impact sent it crashing away. Its gun turret continued to fire blindly, shredding the canopy overhead.

Seven . . .

He hobbled fast, his body now a torch of pain. Leaves slapped his face; branches tore at his bare skin. He kept going.

Six . . .

He fired again, blasting another Q-UGV aside, clearing a path in front of him.

Five . . .

"Kane, buddy, move it. Please . . ."

Four . . .

Out of the smoky gloom, a new glow rose ahead, softer edged. He knew that shape. It meant home, like a lamp in the night.

Three . . .

Other shapes closed to the right and left. Rounds fired at him, chugging from the automatons' turrets. But he ducked lower, not bothering to return fire. He didn't have time.

Two . . .

He shoved aside the heavy leaves of a fern. There was Kane, half-buried in another bush. The dog's dark eyes shone toward him. A tail wagged in a last greeting.

One . . .

Tucker leaped headlong. Time slowed to a standstill. He wished this moment could last forever. Still, he would take what he could.

To be together—to the very end.

Tucker hit Kane as the grenade exploded.

9:29 A.M.

Inside the com shack, Frank winced as the loud blast echoed out of the forest.

What the hell?

He and Monk had just finished the frantic call to Sigma command. They had kept it brief, giving Director Crowe as much time as possible to warn Gray of the coming threat. The director had also promised to alert the FARDC military and get them to dispatch helicopters to the island.

Frank crossed to Ndaye, who guarded the door. Monk kept his weapon on Willem. They had all heard the earlier shotgun blasts. Frank pointed to a billowing curl of smoke to the southeast.

It had to mark Tucker's location.

"Is that anywhere near where you left Charlotte and the others?" he asked Ndaye.

Had Tucker gone to help them?

"No." The eco-guard waved due south. "We left them over that way."

Frank frowned.

Then what was the meaning of that blast?

9:27 A.M.

Tucker heaved off of Kane but held tightly to his buddy. The world had become a pinched knot. His skull ached. His hearing had flatlined to a single tone. Blood ran down his face, down his throat. He tasted it, breathed it.

He raised a palm to his face, felt the jagged bits of shrapnel imbedded there. A finger fell through a hole in his cheek.

Still . . .

I'm alive.

He ran his palm over Kane's Kevlar vest.

Please . . .

He reached a soft ear, felt a whiskered muzzle. Then a tongue licked the blood from his fingers.

Thank god . . .

He rolled to a seat, gasping, cradling Kane, who panted hard. A low whine from his buddy pierced the storm in his skull.

I know . . . but we made it.

Still, they weren't out of danger. He searched the blast area. Leaves were shredded from trees and bushes; branches hung crookedly. He had managed to roll off of the grenade at the last moment. His body armor—shielded around Kane—had spared their lives.

The four Q-UGVs that had been closing in

on them had caught the brunt of the blast. They lay smoking and sparking. One had been tossed into the branches of a cedar and hung there.

Tucker searched for any others, unsure if there were more, or if the explosion had overwhelmed their sensors.

All he knew for sure—

"We need to get out of here."

Kane whined again, sounding louder now that Tucker's hearing had cleared a bit. Tucker shifted to help his buddy up, to start them moving. He couldn't trust that those robotic dogs might not come sniffing around again.

Tucker got to his knees, but Kane remained sprawled on his side, panting hard, tongue lolling. His eyes shone with pain, staring off into a glazed distance.

"Kane . . ."

Then Tucker's heart clenched.

Oh, god, no . . .

Blood poured from the dog's front leg, soaking the ground. Kane's forearm was shattered, showing bone, hanging by only skin and tendon.

Tucker clamped the dog's elbow, squeezing off the flow, trying to hold Kane's life in place by sheer will. He lifted his partner with his other arm, finding strength that he didn't know he still possessed. He shambled away from the blast zone. Though he had lost his goggles, he knew the way back.

He fought through the woods, trying to go faster. His ankle screamed, he bled from a thousand cuts, and shrapnel cut deeper into his thigh and shoulder with each step. He panted and choked. His vision tunneled to a point aimed toward the camp.

His gait wobbled. He tripped, almost dropping Kane. He lost hold of the broken limb. Blood sprayed until he could resecure his hold. He cursed himself for not finding something better than his weakening grip to serve as a tourniquet, but he didn't know if Kane had the time to spare.

He stumbled on, the forest stretching endlessly before him.

Did I get turned around?

Then something shone ahead. He prayed it was a sign of the compound nearby. Instead, one of the robotic dogs clambered into view—then pounded swiftly toward them. Its turret swiveled for the kill.

Tucker turned his back, still trying to protect Kane. The gunfire was deafening. He waited for the pummeling of rounds.

It never came.

He glanced over a shoulder and saw Frank and Monk come charging toward him, rifles smoking. The Q-UGV lay on its side, punched with holes, legs stirring the air.

Tucker turned and rushed to meet the men. He slammed into Frank, passing him Kane.

Tucker fell to his knees. "Save him . . ."

Frank caught the dog in his arms. The army veterinarian immediately spotted the macerated limb and clamped hard to the leg. "He's lost so much blood."

Not just him . . .

Tucker slipped sideways, toppling in slow

motion. The world darkened as he fell. Still, his gaze never left Kane. Only now did he recognize how slack the dog hung in Frank's arms. Those dark eyes stared unblinking; a tongue draped too long, too blue.

Kane . . .

Frank's last words followed him into oblivion. "He's not breathing."

28

"Did that sodding tree drown your friend?" Benjie asked.

Gray knew this was a reasonable question. Kowalski had not surfaced for over ten minutes. His partner had big lungs, but not that big. Gray tilted higher on his toes, trying to get a better view past the churning pale roots, the shivering thorns and spines.

Across the way, the hollow of the mother tree glowed a shimmering silver. The pool's water had settled to a flat mirror. Gray couldn't tell if Kowalski had surfaced elsewhere in the pond and was allowed to take a breath. The pool's sides stretched beyond his view, hidden by the curve of the tree's trunk.

He glanced to Tyende with concern. The Kuba tribesman simply leaned on his staff. Faraji kept him company. The elder's eyelids hung at half-mast. Clearly the morning's exertion had taxed the man, someone who claimed to be over a hundred years old.

Still, Tyende noted Gray's attention. "If She chose him, She will care for him."

As if summoned by his words, the glowing waters surged up into a shining fountain. Kowalski was carried along with it, thrust high by a tangle of roots. He struggled in their grip. He sputtered and coughed, choking out water. It poured from his nose and lips.

The snare of roots carried him to the pool's edge and deposited him at the entrance to the tree. Kowalski fell on his hands and knees and vomited more water.

"She is done with him," Tyende said.

Clearly . . .

Kowalski sat back, gasped a few more times, then swore loudly. He gained his feet. "I'm *never* doing that again."

Gray called over to him. "Are you okay?"

Benjie shouted, too. "How do you feel?"

Kowalski scowled. "Like a friggin' drowned cat. How do you think I feel?" He grunted and spit. "Stuff tastes like antifreeze mixed with mildew. Stings my cuts like a mother, too."

Kowalski stumbled toward them.

Gray lifted an arm and pointed back. "Your canteen! We need a sample of that water!"

The big man heaved an exasperated sigh, looking none too happy to return to that pond. Still, he swung around, struggling to free his canteen from his belt.

Unfortunately, another was done with this whole affair.

As Kowalski attempted to reenter the tree, the roots inside reared up like angry cobras, flaring sharp thorns, blocking the way.

Kowalski balked. "Yeah, I don't think that's happening."

"You have to try!" Gray shouted.

Kowalski glared at him. "Then *you* come over and do it."

Gray turned to Tyende, ready to plead for the man's help.

Before Gray could speak, his sat-phone buzzed and rattled in his pocket. He slipped it out. He had left the battery in place after his last call with Painter. The director was coordinating a helicopter evac once they obtained the cure. The rally point was the bare ridge of rock overlooking the valley. It offered the only break in the forest for countless miles.

Gray was relieved that the director was checking in. He glanced over at Kowalski, who still stood with his canteen in hand. It looked like that evac would have to be pushed back.

Gray lifted the phone and opened the connection. "Director Crowe, we have a—"

Painter cut him off, his voice sharp with urgency. "Gray, you need to clear out of there. Right now. There's a drone bomber winging your way, set to your current coordinates, carrying a MOAB payload. The blast will destroy everything for miles around."

Gray clutched the phone harder. "When will it get here?"

"Fifteen minutes, maybe less."

Gray stared over at Kowalski, at his empty canteen. "But we don't have the cure."

"Doesn't matter. Get off this line and haul ass."

The connection went dead.

Kowalski glared his way. "What now?"

Gray waved for him to return. They had no time to argue with a tree that had lived for millennia. "Forget it!" he shouted. "Run!"

Kowalski was happy to obey that order. Still, he hollered as he pounded toward them. "Why? What's the rush?"

"A bomb! Headed our way. In fifteen minutes!"

Kowalski swore and sped faster. The outer tangle of roots parted to let him through, then closed behind him. He skidded to a stop and jabbed Benjie's chest with a finger.

"You owe me fifty bucks."

Benjie looked sheepishly at Gray. "He bet me someone would try to blow us up before this was all over."

"You shouldn't have taken that bet." Gray shoved Benjie and Faraji toward the outer barrier of black roots and sharp thorns.

He waved for Tyende to follow, casting the old man an apologetic look.

The tribesman looked distraught, but also resigned.

Gray got them all moving. The low passage under the briar proved less of a gauntlet than before. The woody daggers and spines had retracted into the dark mass, allowing them to travel faster.

As they crawled, a countdown ran in his head.

The blast radius from a MOAB stretched a full mile from ground zero—maybe farther with the explosion trapped within the valley's high cliffs.

There was no way the team could clear that distance in the time remaining.

At least, not all of us.

Still, he refused to abandon any others. They would *all* make it out or none would. He intended to reach that golden kingdom, a city mined into a vein of precious ore. He prayed it would offer them enough shelter.

But first we have to get there.

Gray reached the end of the thorny briar and climbed back up, facing the rolling wonderland of glowing ponds and golden-green forest. A mist hung over the glade, cast forth by those sporulating cysts.

He waved everyone onward. "Keep going. As fast as you can manage."

He set a hard pace, trotting, running, slowing when Benjie or Tyende were left gasping for air, then pushing them again when they faltered too long.

As they fled, the ground stirred across the breadth of landscape. It was a reminder that the true bulk of the forest lay beneath their feet, in a vast interconnected network of roots and fungal hyphae, forming an intelligence far older than anything on Earth.

Knowing what was coming, what would be destroyed, Gray gritted his teeth with frustration.

We should never have come here.

What had it gained them?

Kowalski's empty canteen bounced at his hip.

Gray held out a slim hope that perhaps whatever curative powers had been gifted to the big man could be distilled back out of his blood, used to stop the spreading contagion.

They finally reached the edge of the ancient forest. The fringe of darker woods beckoned. Benjie slowed—less due to his gasping breath and more for Tyende's sake. The flight had left the man wheezing, his face gaunt and running with sweat. He had lost his staff along the way. Kowalski now supported the elder, with Faraji trying to help on the other side.

Gray took the boy's place. "Keep going."

They set off again, forging through the dense barricade of dark forest until the main woods opened around them.

Gray checked his watch.

9:38 A.M.

They had only another seven minutes—if even that.

Benjie noted the problem first, slowing down and searching around. "Where are the others?" he huffed out.

Gray looked, too, and realized that Molimbo and the rest of the pygmies had left, taking their bonded aardwolves with them. They were nowhere in sight.

Gray shook his head. "We'll have to hope they got far enough away."

"Maybe they sensed what was about to happen," Benjie offered. "Maybe they're already sheltering at the city."

"Maybe," Gray muttered, but he doubted it,

not after the way the hunters had shunned the ancient place, a dead kingdom ringed in bones.

Still, they had no time for debate.

Gray got them all moving. "Keep going."

As they set off, a lone sentinel appeared on the road, materializing like a ghost out of the woods. The snowy-furred aardwolf stopped ahead of them, his old eyes staring back, welcoming the return of his partner.

"Mbe . . ." Tyende gasped.

The wolf flowed like silver down the cobbles to meet the tribesman. He drew abreast of Tyende and paced alongside him. His presence reinvigorated the elder. Tyende shook free of Gray and Kowalski and ran a hand along the beast's flank, as if drawing strength from that furry body.

They set a faster pace, rushing down the winding path. Still, by the time they reached the fork in the trail, Tyende needed help again. He hobbled and stumbled, falling behind. Gray dropped back and supported an arm under him. The elder's limbs trembled. Gray felt the pounding flutter of his heart through his thin ribs.

Though far younger than Molimbo, the Kuba tribesman was still well over a hundred, maybe as old as a hundred and fifty. Gray wondered if it took generations of exposure—millennia of living here—to achieve the pygmies' extreme longevity. In that respect, Tyende was still a relative newcomer, more susceptible to the ravages of age.

Kowalski came up on the elder's left side,

looking ready to carry Tyende if need be. The big man tried to get the aardwolf out of the way.

Mbe growled, plainly not willing to give up his post. Even still, the old aardwolf panted heavily. His eyes rolled with the stress of the run. A reminder that, like Tyende, the century-old beast could not hold back time forever.

"Almost there!" Benjie called back, pointing ahead.

The city lay dark, shrouded by forest. The flames that had lit the place had guttered out. Gray understood why the pygmies avoided the place. It wasn't just the bones. A haunted quality hung over it.

Still, the team had no time for superstitions.

He checked the glowing face of his watch.

9:42 A.M.

"Three more minutes," Gray shouted.

Benjie cringed, running faster toward the dark facade.

Would that be enough time?

Gray rushed everyone faster. "Get as far back as you can in there! As deep as you can go!"

Benjie and Faraji reached a curve in the road. They took a more direct route, abandoning the path and crashing through the underbrush and across fields of mushrooms. A puffball blasted at his heels, startling him. Old skulls and ribs shattered under the pound of his boots, making for treacherous footing.

He prayed that their own bones wouldn't be added to this ancient mausoleum.

He and Faraji reached the dark threshold. Kowalski ignited a flashlight behind them, casting their shadows deeper inside. Benjie balked at the entrance, but Kowalski bowled into him, shoving him forward.

"Move it!" he bellowed.

Benjie tripped, caught himself, then ran after Faraji. Kowalski crowded behind them. The beam of his flashlight bobbed all around. The shining walls warmed that light into a golden hue. Benjie ran a palm along one surface, feeling how smooth it was. But his reach was more to keep his balance.

Bones were strewn everywhere underfoot. Most of the skeletons were still intact, macabrely so, as if untouched since the bodies dropped. A few still had scraps of clothing adhering to them. A couple wore aged-black chainmail. Steel weapons—pikes, hammers, swords—lay scattered all around, further proof of the invasion into the valley that Tyende had described.

As they continued, Benjie followed Faraji's example and tried sidestepping and dancing through the skeletons to avoid disturbing their rest.

Kowalski was not so courteous. He crushed and cursed his way down the subterranean alley.

To either side, golden homes spread out in stacks of sharp-edged blocks, climbing higher and higher. Bridges and archways spanned everywhere.

Benjie gawked about him, trying to picture how the place must have once looked. In his mind's eye, he hung lamps and lanterns across the city. He imagined people chattering and bartering, kids running and laughing, aardwolves loping and playing.

He glanced back, recognizing that the city's true wealth did not lie around him, but behind, out into the forest—where the kingdom had lived in harmony with the natural world for centuries.

That was their greatest fortune.

Still, Benjie frowned, realizing something else as he looked back.

"Where's Gray?"

9:44 A.M.

"You have to keep going," Gray urged, glancing to his watch.

One minute . . .

Tyende had stopped only a few yards into the city. It was hard to say who halted first, the elderly tribesman or his ancient companion. As if responding to the same signal, they had both stopped.

Mbe dropped to his haunches, panting hard, his chest heaving, looking far older, as if he were fading before Gray's eyes. The large aardwolf settled to the floor, staring off toward the woods. Tyende lowered next to him, down to his knees. He draped an arm over his large companion.

"This is far enough," Tyende declared.

Gray sensed the tribesman was not referring to a distance measured in miles.

"You can't give up." Gray reached to him.

Tyende lifted an arm. Mbe growled, voicing what the tribesman likely felt. "It's not defeat. Not even surrender." He offered a small, content smile. "It's simply time."

"But—"

"My story is told. It is passed to you. That is enough."

Gray struggled with how to convince him.

Tyende glanced across the breadth of the dark city and removed his gold circlet. "Now is the time for kingdoms to come to an end." He returned his attention to the forest, following Mbe's long gaze. "And for mothers to let their children stand on their own, for better or worse."

Gray finally accepted that Tyende would not stir from here, but before he set off, he sought a reassurance. "The cure . . . could Kowalski share it with the world?"

Tyende glanced back one last time, his expression sad, as if Gray understood nothing. "Molimbo's people explained to me long ago. She is generous with her gifts, but they are brief. Once partaken, it fades quickly. While the miracle persists, the force behind it evaporates like water on a hot summer's day."

Gray took a hard breath.

So, no . . .

Tyende turned away, dismissing him with a raised hand. "You have all the answers you need."

Gray could wait no longer. He swung around and sprinted into the depths of the golden city. The countdown ticked in his head. He swore he could hear a distant whine of a plane engine, growing ever louder.

At the last second, he dove to the side, ducking into a home and sheltering behind a wall. And not a moment too soon.

The explosion struck when his knees touched the floor. The boom shook the ground, throwing him down hard. The span of a bridge cracked outside and collapsed in a tumble of gold blocks and dust. For the briefest moment, the entire kingdom flashed brighter, lit by that fiery burst. The city shone in all of its glory, polished by the blast, burning his eyes. Heat rushed like a gale through the city, searing his lungs.

Gray sprawled flat. He covered his head with his arms and shaded his face. He waited for the ground to stop shaking, for the furnace blast to subside. He then pushed to his feet and staggered toward the door. He leaned a palm on the frame. The gold remained surprisingly cool, further proof of the city's incorruptibility, withstanding even this.

He headed out again, concerned about another. *Tyende* . . .

Gray retraced his steps through the golden rubble. Ahead, limned against the light of a bright morning, he spotted the pair, still where he had left them. The blast had shattered the forest outside, stripping it away from the cliff, allowing the sky to shine on the city's face, in surely the first time in ages.

He hurried forward.

Tyende lay collapsed behind Mbe. The mountain of the aardwolf was curled around the tribesman's form, as if even in death, the beast sought to protect his friend. The large snowy body had become a wall between Tyende and the exit, sparing the dead man from seeing the destruction of his home.

Gray reached them, dropped to his knees, and placed a hand on the tribesman's shoulder, silently thanking him. As he did, Tyende stirred weakly. Whether a miracle or simply due to the sheltering love of a lifelong friend, the elder still breathed, though weakly.

"Don't move . . ." he urged the man.

Gray didn't hold out any hope that the tribesman would live much longer, but he wanted to make sure he didn't die alone.

Tyende's eyes opened. The old man found the strength to reach and pat Gray's hand, as if consoling him. "I . . . I'm surprised She didn't find you worthy," he said hoarsely. "I do . . ."

Gray felt a surge of guilt, of remorse.

A clatter rose behind him, along with an echo of voices. He glanced back. A flashlight bobbled through the darkness. Kowalski came into view, flanked by Benjie and Faraji.

Gray lifted an arm, guiding them to him, but he kept his other palm on Tyende. The old man wheezed softly. The others quickly joined them.

Benjie gasped at the tableau.

Faraji covered his face, as if refusing to accept it.

Kowalski merely shook his head and swore under his breath.

"Is there anything we can do?" Gray asked softly. "To make you more comfortable."

Tyende wet his lips, tried to speak, then tried again. "Let me . . . Help me see."

Gray understood and cradled the man up, leaning him against the wall. Tyende stared past Mbe's body to the valley beyond. The bright morning had already darkened, the sun clouded over by smoke. This gloom was no longer the solemnity of an ancient forest, but something far more malignant.

"I'm sorry," Gray whispered.

So much had been lost with nothing gained.

Tyende stared out at the destruction. His shoulders sagged slightly in grief, but his face remained stoic. "Sometimes it takes fire to clear a forest for new growth. Hope can even be found in flames."

"But—"

Tyende reached and patted Gray's hand again. "I said before . . . mothers can only warn and scold and teach for so long . . . then even their time ends. Like mine does now. Then *watoto* . . . *watoto* . . ."

As he faded, he clearly struggled to stay in the present, slipping into his native tongue with his eyes glazing over.

Faraji joined them, dropping to his knees. "*Watoto* . . . mean 'children.'"

Tyende stirred. "Children, yes, they must eventually stand . . . on their own . . . make their own mistakes." His gaze swung to the ruins. "Whether they gain *hekima* in time . . ."

Tyende shrugged sadly.

Gray turned to Faraji.

"Mean 'wisdom,' yes?"

Tyende touched the boy's knee in thanks. The elder's head swung toward another. He lifted a hand and weakly motioned Benjie closer. The biologist hurried and dropped next to Faraji.

Tyende tapped at Benjie's leg, then waved weakly at a bulge in the biologist's pocket. Benjie understood and shifted to free the *ndop* figure.

He lifted it toward Tyende.

A soft sigh of contentment wheezed from the old man. He found the strength to lift a trembling finger and run it over the features of William Sheppard, his old friend and teacher, clearly saying goodbye.

"The Mother . . ." Tyende whispered. "She only shares Her most precious gifts with the worthiest of us."

That certainly was William Sheppard.

Tyende's arm dropped leadenly, his voice going breathless. "*Ngedi mu ntey* . . . in *ngedi mu ntey* . . ."

His chin sank to his chest.

Time, at long last, had found the man.

Silence settled over the group.

After a few moments, Benjie lifted the carving of Sheppard in his hands. "Our lack of worthiness . . ." He gazed out at the destruction. "Maybe She was right."

Gray shook his head in defeat. Sheppard had been given the means to go home, to leave the valley cured. Afterward, the reverend had preserved his story, along with a possible path to salvation. He had protected it all in the *ngedi mu ntey*, in the precious Kuba Box. Just as Tyende had attested with his last words, honoring his friend in the end.

But we were not found worthy, even if Tyende might think so.

"We should go," Kowalski said. "We still need to meet that evac helicopter."

Gray nodded and started out, but Faraji remained on his knees and whispered a prayer over his fellow tribesman. Gray waited out of respect. Benjie used the time to resecure the *ndop* figurine into his pocket.

Gray suddenly reached out and grabbed the biologist's wrist. "Wait."

"What?"

Gray squeezed Benjie's arm hard. "*Ngedi mu ntey . . . in ngedi mu ntey.*"

Benjie frowned—then his eyes got huge with understanding.

"What?" Kowalski asked.

"Tyende's last words," Gray explained. "He wasn't telling us about Sheppard's gift to the world. Tyende was offering it to us."

A man who had found us worthy—even when the tree did not.

Kowalski's face scrunched. "Offering us what?"

"The answer." Benjie stared down with a measure of horror at the *ndop* still in his hands. He shoved it at Gray. "*Ngedi mu ntey in ngedi mu ntey.*"

Gray translated as he accepted the carving, "Kuba Box in Kuba Box." He stared across at the group, hoping he was right. "The Kuba keep their most precious tokens in such treasured boxes, but to preserve their most precious of all . . ."

"They might put a box inside another box," Benjie said. "Like a pair of Russian nesting dolls."

All eyes fixed on Gray.

He examined the figurine more closely. His fingers ran over the black wood, harvested from the roots of the mother tree. Then he finally spotted it: a silvery vein that circled under Sheppard's chin.

With a grimace of fear, Gray gripped the figurine's head and twisted hard. After three attempts, the top of the carving unscrewed, revealing it was as hollow as the trunk of the same tree.

Gray tilted the figure—and poured a fine powder into his palm.

Each grain glowed a bright silver.

Shining with the hope of salvation.

29

From the helm of his yacht, Nolan De Coster stared at the destruction he had wrought. It was one matter to consider it from a distance. It was another to see it up close.

He guided the sixty-foot vessel down the river past the ruins of the former mine. He gazed at the massive crater, which still smoldered. A new tributary split off from the river and drained into the smoky basin, slowly filling it, forming a toxic lake.

On the other side of the river, the jungle had been knocked flat, bulldozed by huge barges that had been blown into the dense forest. Their hulks would likely rust in place for centuries, serving as giant monuments to his power.

Most other men might be appalled at the level of destruction. He only felt a thrill, part pride, part awe.

This is my handiwork.

It was a crowning achievement, one that far outshone any centuries-old artifact. He stared across at the Abyssinian ceremonial headdress, adorned in gold and jewels. It rested next to him on the helm. He had absconded with the treasure as he abandoned his office and fled down the private stairs to the ATV. He'd had no trouble making it unmolested to the armored ship. With Ngoy's help, he had been able to quickly cast off and head downriver.

He stared behind him as he cleared the blast site.

He pictured the same level of destruction out in the mountains to the east.

While motoring away from the island, he had received confirmation of the successful bombing. He had also arranged for a helicopter to rendezvous another mile downriver, to airlift him to Cairo, then to his offices in Belgium.

There would be legal storms to weather after all of this, but he was a survivor. His billions would be a castle that no country or army could breach. He would use his wealth to rewrite history, to paint himself as a savior as his corporation funded hospitals throughout the Congo during the plague. Likewise, he would silence any detractors, bribe and blackmail and coerce his way to keep his stranglehold on this region.

He reached over and placed a palm atop the gold crown, knowing it was his birthright, as was all of Central Africa.

And soon the entire continent.

A shuffle of boots drew his attention from the wheel. He turned to the door of the wheelhouse as Ngoy appeared, freshly showered, looking far less terrified.

Ngoy pointed downriver. "How much longer until the helicopter—"

Nolan backed from the researcher, his heart choking his throat.

Ngoy read the terror in his face and ducked around with a flinch. As he did, he revealed what had quietly leaped up from the stern deck and landed behind the wheelhouse, trapping its prey.

The massive jungle cat bristled, a mountain of shimmering black fur. Even in the light of day, it looked more shadow than flesh. Out of that darkness, golden amber eyes glared coldly. White whiskers spiked from snarled lips. It didn't make a sound. The bared scimitars of its fangs were threat enough.

Ngoy screamed.

The cat struck out with a single paw. Claws slashed the man's head, ripping his face clean off, spinning him full around. Still, Ngoy screamed through torn flesh and bloody bone. The man crashed to the floor, writhing in agony.

The cat stalked over him, ignoring his wails.

The researcher was not the beast's primary target.

Nolan knew this.

For weeks, he had brutally tortured the cat during its captivity, earning its wrath. The altered beast must have lain in wait in one of the lower holds, possibly drawn by Nolan's scent that permeated the ship.

Nolan backed to the starboard side, toward an open window in the wheelhouse.

The cat paced him, toying, only now growling a note of fury.

Nolan turned and dove for the opening. Claws caught the back of his leg, ripped through linen and skin and meat. Still, he made it through the window. He tumbled and crashed two stories into the river. The dark waters swirled and frothed around his flailing limbs.

Panicked, he sputtered up and kicked toward shore. His torn leg burned underwater, but he did not relent.

Have to get hidden.

The yacht motored past him, the engine still engaged, but unmanned now—or nearly so. A glance back showed the cat leaning out the window. As claws dug into the sill, it raised its head, stretched its neck, and roared at the world.

In that moment, Nolan knew he was far from the king of this land, of these jungles. He kicked harder, praying for some measure of providence, even mercy. It was granted as he saw the yacht angle away from him, aiming for the far shore, carrying the beast with it.

He swam faster.

The forest rose higher ahead of him.

Nearly there.

A shatter of wood and a crunch of steel drew his attention across the river. The ship nosed hard into the far bank, driving deep into the jungle's edge. Once it came to a stop, a dark shadow leaped and vanished into its depths.

Nolan kicked the last distance to shore. He studied the river, searching for any attempt by the cat to swim to this side. So far, the jungle over there remained dark and impenetrable. He let out a sigh of relief as he reached the river-bank and kicked and crawled out of the water and sprawled flat in the mud. The recent floods had begun to recede, leaving tall slippery slopes stripped of vegetation.

Can't stop.

He dug his toes into the earth and fought his way up the steep bank. The slick mud resisted him. It was made all the more difficult as his legs began to tremor, rapidly weakening. His fingers dug hard, trying to claw for purchase. But his hands refused to cooperate. He thought it was panicked exhaustion—then remembered.

He twisted to stare at the tears in his leg, streaming blood, showing muscle.

Even the wound wasn't the issue.

His body continued to succumb to the poison in the cat's claws. Nolan's research team had identified it. A derivative of the succinylcholine, a drug used by anesthesiologists as a neuromuscular blocker. The compound paralyzed muscles, but it left one fully conscious and capable of feeling everything, including pain.

As his limbs grew progressively more leaden, he sagged into the mud. Fearing suffocation, he found the energy to roll onto his back. Unable to stop, he slid down to the water's edge.

The pain in his leg persisted. He felt hot blood running along his thigh and across his chilled calf. The paralysis made it harder to breathe, but he forced his ribs up and down.

Just have to wait it out.

The poison wasn't deadly on its own. Over time, an hour at best, it would fade.

He held out hope.

He shouldn't have.

He knew the Congo better than that.

His blood trailed through the water, pooled in the mud around him. It drew the jungle to him—ready to feast on the king of Africa.

First came the crabs.

30

On the third floor of the University of Kisangani's science building, Charlotte leaned over Frank, resting a hand on his shoulder.

Dr. Lisa Cummings flanked on one side, Benjie on the other.

They had gathered for the virologist's daily briefing in his makeshift biolab. The original facility on the fourth floor was still under reconstruction following the firebombing last month. Frank's new space was only one of countless research labs around the world currently working on recovery efforts.

"I think I'm beginning to understand how this virus works," Frank said. "At least in regard to a patient's neurological recovery."

Lisa leaned closer. "Show us."

The American doctor had been assisting Charlotte, along with a team of clinicians from around the world. It had been a little over a month since they had secured the counteractant to the stubborn *Omniviridae*—as the pathogen had come to be called, courtesy of Frank's original nickname for it. The virus still maintained a stubborn beachhead in the Congo. Cases continued to trickle in from outlying villages and towns, but at least the deluge had slowed.

Progress was being made.

Still, not much was understood regarding the *cure*.

"Look at this," Frank said.

On the screen, he brought up a giant virus that looked nearly identical to *Omniviridae*, at least in outward appearances. According to Frank, this new one was slightly larger and had twenty-two percent more genes. Otherwise, it was just as spiky as its malicious cousin. The new girus had been discovered encysted in the crystals that Benjie's group had brought out of the jungle.

Frank had been the first to revive it, which apparently wasn't all that unusual. Several years ago, a girus had been discovered in the Siberian permafrost. It had been frozen for thirty thousand years, yet once thawed, it came back to life.

Due to the historical context attesting to the powder's curative powers, Frank and Lisa had run a clinical trial among the worst afflicted at the hospital, those near to death. Miraculously, in less than a day, all the patients treated with the encysted virus had begun to revive. Since then, thousands had been treated, including Charlotte.

Afterward, the virus had been dubbed *Tyende kubicum*, named after the tribesman who had helped Benjie's group acquire the crystalline powder. If it wasn't for Tyende's century-long vigil, preserving such knowledge against a future threat, none of this would've been possible.

"Up until now," Frank said, "I had been focused on *Tyende's* DNA. Which continues to be a mystery. Not a single gene in that bugger is recognizable. I suspect it will take us decades before we can fully understand it—if we ever do."

"Then what did you learn?" Lisa asked. "What was your breakthrough?"

Frank pointed to the spikes crowning the virus. "At first, I thought these were identical to *Omniviridae's* spikes—those peptide strings that act like prions and knock out a person's higher cerebral functions."

"They're not?" Charlotte asked.

"Ah, but they *are*."

She frowned. "I don't understand."

"They're identical in *composition*—but not in *shape*! *Tyende's* spikes are actually mirror images of those sprouting from *Omniviridae*. They're cis and trans isomers of each other." He turned to the group. "That's why *Tyende* is so good at waking patients, treating their diminished neurological capacity. Its spikes bind to the *Omniviridae's* pathologic ones, like a key fitting a lock, neutralizing them until the body can flush them out."

"Fascinating," Benjie said.

"I still need to do more studies." Frank turned to Charlotte. He reached to her hand, still on his shoulder, and squeezed her fingers. "But recovering my laptop, with all the data from De Coster's research still on it, has proven to be a goldmine. The world wouldn't be as far along this recovery curve without it."

She smiled, feeling a blush of warmth. They had been spending countless hours together. He had remained at her bedside throughout her recovery.

Charlotte freed her hand and sought to change the subject. She turned to Benjie. "Um, what about your own studies? Into the mutations, the aberrations? I understand that incidences and encounters are still being reported."

He nodded, his expression serious. "They seem to be slowly abating. Ndaye and his eco-guards have collected a slew of specimens. So far, most appear to be mules, unable to reproduce, presenting as a single generational abnormality. But I doubt all of them are so compromised. Like those jackals we encountered who were guarding their pups. They had clearly bred successfully. But only time will tell for sure."

Lisa turned to the biologist. "What about the pilot program to crop dust the *Tyende* virus across the Congo? Could that help stem the tide, smother those last bastions of *Omniviridae* still smoldering in the jungle?"

Benjie shrugged. "We can't even begin to fathom what the *Tyende* virus is capable of. Like Dr. Whitaker said, it's a genetic puzzle box. Though I suspect the mother tree employed some form of epigenetic manipulation, to alter the virus's genetic expression as needed, turning it into a cure all."

"Like a viral version of a Swiss Army knife," Lisa said.

Benjie smiled, looking far more boyish again. "That sounds about right."

Frank checked his watch, clearly ready to wind things up. "Okay, I'll have to leave such mysteries to you all for a time. I have a flight to catch. But I'll be back in a couple of days."

Charlotte winced. "He knows you did everything you could. You know that, too, right?"

"We'll see."

The group dispersed, going their separate ways. Lisa accompanied Charlotte across the lawns and bright morning sunshine to reach the hospital. The entire second floor was dedicated to patients with the disease. They climbed up to the ward and prepared for another long day.

As Charlotte dressed in her PPE, she spotted Faraji past the glass partition. He was seated at a bedside, speaking animatedly, using his hands as much as his mouth. With so many patients from remote villages, many only spoke their native tongue. Add in doctors from around the world, and the hospital found itself in desperate need of a universal translator—and the young shaman-in-training certainly seemed to fit that bill. From talking with Faraji, it was clear he intended to carry on and preserve Woko Bosh's tribal lore, while absorbing and incorporating all he could about Western medicine.

Lisa pointed at the ward. "Looks like there are even more empty beds than yesterday."

Charlotte nodded. "Still, I'll be relieved when we can close this place down for good."

"We'll get there. Until then, don't forget to

savor your victories." Lisa motioned down the hall. "No matter how small they are."

Charlotte turned to see Disanka coming toward her. The woman had returned for her recheck—and not just her.

Charlotte hurried over, her arms out. "Let me see him."

With a huge smile, Disanka passed the baby to her.

Charlotte cradled his little form, his tiny legs battering her.

Disanka drew closer, placing a palm atop his tiny head. "Name him Woko."

Warmth swept through Charlotte at this revelation. "That's perfect . . . just perfect."

She pictured the shaman who had given his life to save them, who came such a long way with the Kuba Box. But more so, while Woko's treatment with the yellow powder might not have healed the child, it had bought the boy enough additional time to survive until a cure could be found.

If not for Woko, the child would not be alive.

Charlotte lifted the boy higher. As he stared down at her, he wiggled and burbled and blew snot bubbles. She smiled back.

Yes, this small victory is enough for anyone.

1:22 P.M.
Washington, D.C.

Gray sat in the waiting room. Nurses bustled behind the tall white desk. Behind them, black lettering graced the sleek wood paneling. It read MEDSTAR GEORGETOWN UNIVERSITY HOSPITAL. The specialized unit was dedicated to bone marrow and stem cell transplantation.

Kowalski was roomed down the hall, finishing his treatment, with his fiancée, Maria, in attendance. He had completed his two rounds of chemotherapy, which had knocked out his bone marrow. Today, they were restocking those depleted shafts with new stem cells. The apheresis team—the nurses and doctors who had collected those cells—had been going in and out of his private room.

"When is Seichan due back?" Painter asked from the seat next to him, drawing Gray's attention.

Gray straightened and cleared his throat. "Two days."

She had extended her visit in Hong Kong with little Jack by two weeks. The boy's grandmother had demanded more time with him, and she was not a woman to be refused. Still, Gray had never been separated from Seichan and his son for this long. His knee bobbed up and down, as if his very body were marking the time until their return.

"Is she still angry?" Painter asked.

"Pretty much."

Gray suspected that was part of the reason for her delayed return, as punishment. While she was happy he'd returned in one piece, she was still peeved to have missed out on all of the excitement.

He shifted his body, turning to Painter, ready to change the subject. "Has there been any sign of Nolan De Coster?"

Painter sighed. "Kat's been beating the bushes, rallying intelligence services around the globe. But it's like he's vanished off the face of the Earth."

After events in the Congo, De Coster's yacht had been found crashed and abandoned down the river. Only the jungle-ravaged body of Dr. Ngoy had been found aboard. Nolan himself remained missing. His corporation adamantly denied any knowledge of his whereabouts. But no one could be certain. He could've slunk off anywhere and be biding his time. Not that there would be much of a company to return to. Due to its CEO's crimes, De Coster Mining & Industry was being systematically dismantled, its assets sold off to cover the expenses of the ongoing global recovery efforts.

Additionally, the vast deposits of gold discovered in the mountains held the promise to finally end the DRC's cycle of colonialism. The wealth buried up there would fund the country's self-rule for decades, freeing it of the need to ever lean on the Chinese or any other government. In addition, all the archaeological attention and global interest ensured many eyes would be on that gold, helping to keep it protected.

As for the rest of the valley, it remained a cratered ruin. All the wonder hidden for millennia had vanished in one explosive moment. After the blast, a fire had spread throughout the valley, consuming everything. Gray and the others had barely escaped the flames to reach the rally point and the evac helicopter.

A month later, Gray still remained haunted. He struggled to find the hope in all that destruction, remembering Tyende's final words: *Sometimes it takes fire to clear a forest for new growth.* Even with the cure, Gray could not balance out all the death, the devastation, the displacement of countless people.

Mostly because it all could have been avoided. They'd had the cure all along, from the very beginning. Afterward, he had questioned Faraji. The boy had insisted that Woko Bosh knew nothing about the significance of the *ndop* carving, how it was actually a box within a box, a treasure hidden inside another.

None know, Faraji had assured him.

Apparently, it was a secret that Sheppard kept, shared only with Tyende, who remained behind in the valley to act as warden and caretaker. The reverend must have respected the tree, cherishing its secrets enough that he only wanted it shared with those who were deemed worthy enough to deserve it. In order to do so, one needed to make that sojourn, following the clues tied to the Kuba, before one could be judged.

And while the tree did not find us worthy— another did.

He pictured Tyende patting his hand, assuring Gray that he was honorable enough, entrusting him in the end with Sheppard's centuries-old secret. As Gray sat in the waiting room, he rubbed at that hand, wondering even now if that were true.

Am I worthy?

Painter noted his attention, and it clearly reminded him of another matter. "I heard from DARPA. Their latest plans for Monk's prosthesis are promising. He's been working with them, refining the schematics."

Gray smiled. "All so he doesn't have to keep blowing up his hand."

"He's a man on a mission."

"Like a dog with a bone." Gray inwardly winced at his choice of words, reminded that not all of the teams had returned from the jungles intact. He quickly swallowed and waved down the hall, shifting to another topic. "What are the chances that Kowalski's bone marrow transplant will put him into remission? The doctors have been more forthright with you. What are they saying?"

"Well, his oncologists are hopeful, certainly more than before. Whatever happened in the forest, in that glowing pool, it seemed to have improved his condition. Significantly so. His numbers are better across the board. It's why they rushed this procedure. To take advantage before he worsens again."

"So, he wasn't cured?" Gray asked.

Painter shrugged. "It's impossible to say. Batteries of blood tests showed no evidence of a curative virus, like the one being employed throughout the Congo. If anything was passed to Kowalski, it's gone."

Gray recalled Tyende's words: *She is generous with her gifts, but they are brief. Once partaken, they fade quickly.*

"We still don't understand that *Tyende* virus," Painter admitted. "It vanishes just as quickly in the patients treated in the Congo. It also seems to have no other curative power, no ability to extend life or longevity."

"At least, not this version," Gray said.

"Exactly. This *Tyende* strain seems tailor-made to only attack the *Omniviridae* virus. Nothing more. And once the task is complete, it dissipates. If there are any other miracles buried in its code, waiting to be released, it's beyond our scientific ability to obtain them."

But not beyond another's ability.

Gray pictured the mother tree. He knew it was just a figurehead. The true organism lay rooted far deeper—spread across a network both woody and fungal—a vast intelligence like no other.

Motion drew his attention down the hall. The slim figure of Maria Crandall appeared. She was fully gowned up, wearing a bonnet and mask. She waved a gloved hand toward them.

"If you want to visit," she called over to them, "they're finished."

Gray and Painter crossed to join her. Once they reached the door, she showed them how to don all the necessary isolation gear: gowns, masks, gloves.

"You should keep the visit short," she warned. "He's pretty wiped."

"Of course," Painter said.

Gray nodded his assurance.

Once decked out, they entered the hospital room. Isolation procedures were fully enforced due to the risk to the immunocompromised patient.

As Gray entered, he stumbled a step, shocked by Kowalski's current state. He hadn't seen the man since he had started chemo and radiation. Kowalski looked like a ghost of himself. His skin was ashen, with dark shadows under his eyes. His head was a smooth scalp.

Still, Kowalski filled the bed, looking as muscular and bulky as ever.

His eyes glared at the visitors, likely embarrassed to be seen in this state. Then again, that was his usual expression.

Gray revealed the gift hidden behind his back. He had it special-ordered. Though sealed in clear plastic to match isolation standards, there was no mistaking it.

Maria smiled, knowing Kowalski's obsession. "That's perfect."

It was a furry teddy bear—one that shouldered a tiny replica of Kowalski's lost Shuriken.

"No, that's stupid," the big man said. But before Gray could pull it away, Kowalski snatched it out of his hands. "But I can sell it on eBay."

"You know you're not going to do that," Maria scolded. "Though maybe you should. We're running out of shelf space at home."

He pulled the bear closer, settling it on the bed next to him. He patted its head but still looked disappointed with it.

"What's wrong?" Gray asked.

He turned, clearly wounded. "You could've got me the rifle, too."

6:20 P.M.
Spitskop Nature Preserve, South Africa

Tucker sat alone on the wooden porch of the sprawling, three-story home. The planks underfoot were whitewashed, matching the corbels and posts. Wide ceiling fans stirred the air but did little to diminish the heat of the dying afternoon.

To help with that, a cold bottle of beer sweated next to him.

The sun sat low on the horizon. Mirages still shimmered across the endless spread of savannah, dotted with clusters of acacias and bushwillows. Closer at hand, sprinklers hissed and swept a mist over a half acre of green buffalo grass. Elsewhere, the hum of grasshoppers sawing their legs droned on in an endless chorus.

Off in the distance, the Nkomo brothers prepped a tourist group for an evening safari, going over safety procedures. Christopher and Matthew were the only ones allowed guns in this corner of the game park. The trip was a photo hunt only. The brothers continually guarded these lands against poachers—and any competing tour outfits.

Tucker had invested in Luxury Safari Tours several years ago, making him a co-owner with the brothers. Since then, he had only returned to the park a handful of times, leaving the business and lands to the two men. Whenever Tucker sat anywhere for too long, he grew anxious, got antsy to move on. Still, he had enjoyed the *idea* of the place, a home where he was always welcome.

As he rocked in the chair, he felt a flicker of that wanderlust even now.

Not that he could travel anytime soon.

He had come to Spitskop to recuperate. His ankle remained in a boot splint, but he had removed the hundreds of stitches from his many wounds himself two weeks ago. The brothers had helped. Still, it had taken a painstaking hour. Most of the shrapnel was gone, but he suspected a few slivers remained. The hole in his cheek had left a puckered scar.

It was why he had waited until the late afternoon before commandeering the porch, like he did every day, when he could have the place to himself.

Don't want to frighten the guests.

While he enjoyed the sunset, he watched a cloud of dust working down the dirt road that led to this parcel. It moved slowly, drawing ever closer. He guessed it was a latecomer to the night's safari. That road led nowhere else but here.

He took a swig from the beer, then settled the bottle.

He waited.

A newer model Toyota Land Cruiser revealed itself, so dusty it was hard to determine the color. It passed by the turnoff that led to the Nkomo brothers and their open-air trucks. The SUV trundled over the cattle guard and crossed down the curve of the crushed granite driveway. It came to a stop at the foot of the porch.

Tucker considered going back inside.

But then the door popped open, and a familiar figure climbed out.

Frank lifted an arm toward him.

Tucker stopped his rocking, climbed to his feet, and thumped with his boot-splint to the porch rail. "Frank, what are you doing here? Why didn't you call?"

"Because you would've told me not to come." Frank circled to the rear of the Land Cruiser and popped the tailgate.

The door blocked Tucker's view. Frank vanished for a few breaths, then stepped back into sight. He kneed the tailgate closed and turned. In both arms, he hauled a plastic transport crate. He carried it toward the steps.

Tucker felt a surge of trepidation.

No . . .

Frank brought the crate up to the porch and lowered it to the whitewashed planks. As he bumped it down, a sharp, furious growl echoed out.

"I'm not ready," Tucker said. "I told you that."

Frank ignored him, bent down, and opened the crate door. "They removed him from a puppy mill in Missouri," he explained. "A real horror show. He was found curled next to his dead mother, the only one of his litter to survive."

Tucker shook his head, still refusing, but he couldn't stop himself from dropping to a knee. He stared into the shadowy crate. The three-month-old pup crouched at the back, haunches high, head low. Small dark eyes shone with fury.

Hackles shivered with warning. He was clearly a Belgian Malinois, with tawny fur and a black saddle over his back.

"Lackland tested him for their war dog program," Frank explained. "He failed. Judged him to be too feral, too savage, unredeemable."

The pup lunged and snapped at him, proving this point, then retreated again.

"I can see why," Tucker muttered.

Frank put his hands on his hips. "If anyone can tame him, teach him—"

Tucker stood and backed away. The pup slinked to the open crate door, looking ready to bolt, still growling at the world.

"You can train him," Frank insisted. "I know you can."

Tucker shook his head. "Not me."

Behind him, a nose pushed the screen door open.

Tucker pointed back. "He will."

Kane came thumping out, his front left leg still in its 3D-printed cast.

Frank had saved the dog's life back on the island, rushing Kane to the medical ward, using the meager supplies still there, doing mouth to mouth. Then the FARDC military had arrived, bringing in a med team. Kane was given the best care. The doctors even managed to salvage his leg.

Still, it remained unknown if Kane would ever fully recover.

If either of them would.

"You need this," Frank said. "You both do."

The pup growled, warning them to keep away. Kane thumped closer, rumbled deeply back, thunder behind his ribs. He stood tall, ears high, glaring sternly.

The pup retreated a step, then slowly lowered flat, driven down by that growl. He dropped his tiny muzzle on the planks, bowing before the true master here.

Kane glanced to Tucker.

He shrugged. "What do you think, buddy? You up to the challenge?"

Kane wagged his tail.

Tucker smiled.

Me, too.

AFTER

Molimbo stands at the edge of the stone ridge under a starlit night. A crescent moon hangs high. Bala keeps beside him, her fur cool, her eyes bright.

Behind him, the mass of the jungle croaks and twitters, hums and chirps. It breathes, as timeless as ever. Ahead of him, the dark valley is ash and blasted rock. Small fires light his former home, marking the encampments of those who came to pick and sift at the bones.

Ten hunters maintain this last vigil alongside Molimbo, five on each side, shadowed by their own companions.

The rest of the tribe waits in the forest. She had protected his people to the very end, casting a warning in the wind, that only their ears could hear. By now, the hunters had finished their songs, a chorus of grief and gratitude.

It took all night, and dawn beckoned.

It is time.

She is gone, but the tribe abides.

For one last purpose.

Molimbo grips the sewn leather satchel. The other ten hunters carry the same, draped from cords around their necks. Molimbo fingers open his sacred pouch.

The night is dark, but the pocket glows—where a large black seed rests at the bottom, entwined in a nest of shining silver fibers.

He draws it closed and hangs the satchel around his neck.

Without a word spoke, the ten hunters move silently into the forest and vanish with their aardwolves, heading in ten different directions.

Molimbo casts one last look across the ruins of the valley, then turns his back on it forever and goes another way. Bala follows, ever his shadow.

He is confident as he runs. It grows stronger with each step, like a sprig pushing toward the sun.

She is gone—but She will come again.

AUTHOR'S NOTE TO READERS: TRUTH OR FICTION

With the world spared another plague, let's lift up the hood and take a peek at the engine behind this story, to discern how much of this tale is based on steely facts and how much is gaseous fiction. This novel has delved into theories of viruses and evolution and looked into the future of the natural world—and our place in it. But before we venture into scientific explorations of what's to come, let's first look to the past, where often much of the future is written.

History of the Congo
In the notes at the start of the story, I elaborated on the atrocities committed upon the Congolese people throughout the waves of colonialism. I also mentioned one of the true heroes of that time: the Reverend William Sheppard, who was instrumental at shining a light on those brutalities, armed with little more than a Kodak box camera and his sheer determination. He was

indeed one of the first people to engage with the Kuba tribe (who are also referred to as Bakuba, which means "people of the throwing knife"). Though he had a difficult time converting any of them, they still revered him. Likewise, as depicted in this book, Sheppard protected the tribe against the Zappo Zap cannibals.

If you'd like to learn more about this time, about the Reverend Sheppard, I encourage you to check out these two books, which served as my two historical bibles for this story:

The Troubled Heart of Africa: A History of the Congo, by Robert Edgerton

Congo: The Epic History of a People, by David Van Reybrouck

Prester John and His Lost Kingdom

Shifting further into the past of Africa, history and mythology merge. I had always wanted to build a storyline around Prester John, this mythic figure. According to the fables surrounding him, he was descended from Balthazar, one of the trio of kings who had visited the Christ child in His manger. His kingdom was said to be one of astronomical wealth, with his legend tied to the Fountain of Youth, to the Ark of the Covenant, and to King Solomon's mine. For centuries, European rulers sent forth emissaries to seek him out, many of whom vanished into the jungle and never returned. Including Pope Alexander III's personal physician. It just goes to show the power of myth and story—unless it's all true.

Kuba People

This topic extends from the past to the present. The Kuba people still thrive in the Congo today. As mentioned above, they were indeed friends with the Reverend William Sheppard. Both in the past and today, the tribe's art remains respected around the world. From their elaborate carvings—like the *ngedi mu ntey* boxes and *ndop* figures—to their sophisticated work with raffia textiles. Even Picasso owed his cubist period to these people, studying an exhibit of Kuba art in Paris in 1907. So how could I not highlight such artistry in this book?

Pygmies

Another people featured in this novel have a long and fascinating history in the Congo. Today, the pygmy tribes are a disparate group, spread across central Africa, speaking several languages, but once they were *one* people, sharing an ancestral population going back 90,000 years. It wasn't until recent history—about 2,800 years ago—that wave after wave of invading farmers shattered this one tribe into many. Today, some tribes don't even know others exist. Likewise, anthropologists remain in the dark about much of these people's history. Geneticists still debate the reason for their short stature. Even the origins of pygmies remain unknown. So, who's to say if there isn't some lost tribe who preserves those secrets, who continue to be the forest's guardians?

But, for now, let's leave behind such historical mysteries and move forward to the present . . .

Congo of Today

After back-to-back brutal wars—the First and Second Congo Wars (from 1996 to 2003)—the DRC remains in a precarious state. Corruption runs rampant, placing the country at number 168 out of 198 on the "corruption perception index" index, as prepared by Transparency International. And though the country is one of the richest in natural resources, it still remains one of the poorest. Rebels, militias, and warlords plague large sections of the country. Poachers wreak havoc. But there remain many heroes who fight for the DRC's future, including members of the *Institut Congolais pour la Conservation de la Nature* (ICCN). These eco-guards—like Ndaye—struggle daily, in blood and strife, to protect those natural resources against far worse than just poachers. In a country teetering on the cusp, other nations—most notably of late, the Chinese—have sought to steal its riches, heralding a new era of colonialism that threatens to be just as brutal and devastating as those reported during William Sheppard's time. So, if this bit of fiction shines a brighter light on what's happening under the Congo's dark canopy, all the better.

On a side note, the tragic events of Lake Nyos in Cameroon described in this book—where 1,800 people were suffocated by a methane burst from that lake—truly happened back in 1986. Likewise, that same risk hangs over the heavily populated Lake Kivu, which straddles the border between the Democratic Republic of the Congo and Rwanda. There, millions would be killed if that lake ever exploded, which is a distinct possibility in the earthquake-prone region.

A Bit about Beasts and Bats

First, forgive a veterinarian-turned-author from indulging in his own creature creation. Certainly, many of the insects and animals featured in this story are of my own imagination. Still, I sought not to craft them in an entirely fanciful manner, but to borrow and steal from other species, while also adhering to basic behavior and biology. Though, even some of that behavior and biology may seem fantastical. Like ants who have empathy (they do!), or orange-tinted dwarf crocodiles who are evolving in real time while trapped underground (they are!). I also enjoyed shining a light on the monogamous nature of jackals, the temperament of hippos, and the existence of aardwolves.

I also devoted a large chunk of the book to bats and their strange biology, especially in regard to their unique ability to harbor viruses. I thought it might be of special interest during the time of COVID. All of the details concerning bats and viruses found in this book are true. Like how viruses are deeply entwined into a bat's unique immune system, how viruses tie into their ability to fly, how they contribute to the species' amazing longevity, even how viral DNA is baked into their genetics—and ours.

So, let's take a closer look at viruses in general. I've broken this next section into (hopefully) digestible parts.

Origin of Viruses

This novel discussed many of the current theories about the origins of viruses. Like if viruses can truly be considered *living* or are they simply self-replicating machines. That same debate dovetails into which came first—a sort of chicken and the egg scenario. Did viruses devolve from some other larger cell? Or did they come first and jump-start life on this planet—what's known as the Virus World Theory. I'll let virologists hash that out. Though, I lean toward the latter. Why? Simply because so many of our most important genes—from embryo development to immune function—come from viruses. Even the Arc gene, gained from viruses, is the foundation for our big brains. Without viruses, none of us would be around.

Search for Viruses

Frank's job, as described in this book, is vitally important. Yes, he helped saved Kane, but that's not what I mean. Seventy-five percent of all emerging diseases in the past century—Ebola, HIV, COVID-19—were passed to the human population from animals, known as zoonotic transmission. The Smithsonian's Global Health Program is just one organization that strives to search for the next pathogen that might trigger another pandemic. They employ many board-certified veterinarians and other specialists to collect data, to gather specimens from the field, all to create a database of potential threats.

What frightens many of the virologists I spoke

to—especially after COVID—is what they dub "Disease X." This is a theoretical disease pathogen capable of spreading rapidly, an organism that modern science has no preventative or cure against. How close was COVID to being that frightening Disease X? Let me just say that researching this novel during the time of COVID was not good for one's nerves. We mostly escaped what could have been far worse. Still, we need as many Franks out there as possible, so we're better prepared next time. And trust me, there *will* be a next time.

Giant Viruses

The first of these jumbo viruses was isolated from an amoeba in 1992. Due to its size, everyone thought it was a bacterium at first. It wasn't until 2003 that it was reclassified as a virus. Since then, many other giants have been discovered. That doesn't mean we understand them—not in the least. These viruses contain thousands of genes, most of them remain unknown. Like the Pandoravirus. Ninety percent of its 2,500 genes don't resemble anything else found on earth. Then there's the Yaravirus, an organism where *all* of its genes are alien. Such viruses are also strangely stubborn, even capable of coming back from the dead. One giant—*Mollivirus sibericum*—was discovered frozen in the Siberian permafrost. It was revived after 30,000 years of frozen hibernation. So, if we're searching for a Disease X, maybe we'd better pay particular attention to those giants.

Omnivirus

Again, forgive a veterinarian who spent too much time talking to virologists during a pandemic. Of course, I had to create my own Frankenvirus. The idea, though, came from before COVID. I had read about one giant virus's ability to protect itself by employing a CRISPR-like technique of gene editing. I also leaned on my own veterinary background and understanding of *Toxoplasma gondii*, how that protozoan alters the behavior of not only rodents, but also us. I was also intrigued by how a virus can trigger different manifestations, like how rabies can present in both a "furious" state or a "paralytic" form—which might sound familiar after reading this book. Likewise, with mad cow disease. It's caused by a nasty prion that triggers aggressive behavior in cows, but in humans, it presents with depression and loss of coordination. I also learned that one of the theories for the origins of prions is *viruses* themselves. Those bits of self-replicating chains of protein might indeed have been cast off from a virus.

So, I took all of these details to create the Omnivirus featured in this book. But considering everything above, maybe it truly is out there, waiting for Mother Nature to be fed up with us two-legged upstarts.

And speaking of Mother Nature . . .

Mother Nature—Green in Leaf and Red in Thorns

I had read the first book listed below (*The Hidden Life of Trees*) back when it first came out in 2016. I was fascinated by the revelations concerning the interconnectivity of a forest, and not just the trees, but also the underlying fungal network that joins it all together. I knew I always wanted to raise this topic in a novel—and this was my chance. I had tackled something similar in my older novel *Amazonia*, but with all the new research, I wanted to expand it even further. If you'd like to learn more about this intriguing and eye-opening topic, please check out these titles:

Hidden Life of Trees: What They Feel, How They Communicate—Discoveries from a Secret World, by Peter Wohlleben

Brilliant Green: The Surprising History and Science of Plant Intelligence, by Stefano Mancuso and Alessandra Viola

Finding the Mother Tree: Discovering the Wisdom of the Forest, by Suzanne Simard

Likewise, I've always been fascinated by the biology and evolutionary history of fungi and mushrooms, especially their role in the transition of life from sea to land. The oldest fungus was indeed found among fossils discovered in the Congo, dating back 810 million years. That organism is believed to have helped build the Earth's primordial soil, where the first plants would eventually take root. As to the oldest *living* fungus, that's indeed the honey mushroom (*Armillaria ostoyae*). It can be found many places, but the oldest is the patch in the Malheur National Forest of eastern Oregon. It's estimated to be 8,000 years old, covering 3.5 square miles, and weighing 35,000 tons—making it also the *largest* living organism.

Though the claim of being the *oldest* has a major competitor in the "Trembling Giant"—or Pando—of Utah. That stand of 40,000 interconnected clones of quaking aspen (*Populus tremuloides*) weighs 6,600 tons and may be as old as 80,000 years (though some believe it could be over a million years old).

Yet, no matter who wins that award, it's still a reminder that we humans are *very* young, and in our youth, often very ill-mannered when it comes to the stewardship of this planet.

Gadgets and Gizmos

This book is chock-full of all sorts of destructive weaponry—and one resilient Russian-made vehicle. The Shatun ATV 4X4 is worth looking up. I encourage you to watch videos online of its tough and nimble nature. I want one—just in case I'm ever trekking through a jungle (or a swamp, or a tough par 3 on a golf course).

As to weapons, the MOAB is a real bunker-busting bomb. The Massive Ordnance Air Blast, better known as the Mother of All Bombs, is indeed as strong as a small tactical nuclear weapon. The robotic dogs featured in this book—the Quad-legged Unmanned Ground Vehicles—are real. Though, I'll stick to the furry versions myself.

In regard to firearms, Gray's KelTec P50 handgun is real. But Kowalski's razor-disk-spitting Shuriken is of my own invention—though a prototype for something similar was put into production several years ago. Similarly, Kane's wireless bandolier that allowed Tucker to remotely drop small charges (flash-bangs, smoke bombs, and grenades) was my own creation. Because why should Tucker have all the fun?

And speaking of Kane . . .

Military Working Dogs and Their Handlers

I love Tucker and Kane. But how did this dynamic duo come to life? I first encountered this heroic pairing of soldier and war dog while on a USO tour to Iraq and Kuwait in the winter of 2010. Seeing these pairs' capabilities and recognizing their unique bonds, I wanted to try to capture and honor those relationships. To accomplish that, I spoke to veterinarians in the U.S. Veterinary Corps, interviewed handlers, met their dogs, and saw how these duos grew together to become a single fighting unit. I also vetted their stories with former and current handlers to be as accurate as possible. If you'd like to know more about war dogs and their handlers, I highly recommend two books by the author Maria Goodavage:

Soldier Dogs: The Untold Story of America's Canine Heroes
Top Dog: The Story of Marine Hero Lucca

Now, I expect to get a fair amount of hate mail following what happened to Kane. Why was I so cruel? I've featured Tucker and Kane's exploits through four novels, a novella, and a short story. After so long, I felt it disrespectful not to be as realistic as possible about the hardships endured by these brave four-legged soldiers. Though Kane's fate may wound many readers, I wanted to honor the sacrifice of military working dogs everywhere, those who have lost life and limb in service. Of course, this is not the last you'll see of Tucker and Kane. In fact, I need a new name for Kane's feral protégé. If you have any ideas, go to my website, send an email, and share your suggestions. There might even be a reward.

Okay, that's it. You may have noted a conspicuous absence from this novel, one former assassin-turned-ally. Fear not, Seichan will be returning from Hong Kong. Though she was sidelined in this book, she is about to be challenged like never before—as someone returns with a vengeance and has Sigma in their sights. So, rest up, gird those loins, and be ready for an adventure that changes everything—and I mean, *everything*.

RIGHTS AND ATTRIBUTIONS FOR THE ARTWORK IN THIS NOVEL

(image edited by author)
https://www.shutterstock.com/image
-vector/cross-thorns-black-white-simple
-vector-547120837

p. 171—Okapi
Drawn by author

p. 173—Message
Drawn by author

p. 177—Prester John Map
Public domain (image edited by author)

p. 180—1710 Map
Public domain—from the Historic Maps Collection, Princeton University Library (image edited by author)

p. 184—Virus Group
Obtained from a Creative Commons CCO 1.0 Universal Public Domain Dedication (image edited by author)

p. 185—Individual Virus
Obtained from a Creative Commons CCO 1.0 Universal Public Domain Dedication (image edited by author)

p. 211—Mycelium
Purchased with Enhanced License from Shutterstock
Royalty-free stock photo ID: 353791034 by Zita

p. 277—Genome Map
Purchased with Enhanced License from Shutterstock
Royalty-free stock photo ID: 1288865194 by Tartila
(image edited by author)
https://www.shutterstock.com/image-vector
/genomic-analysis-visualization-dna-genomes
-sequencing-1288865194

p. 311—Cross 2
Drawn by author

p. 314—Gravestone
Drawn by author

p. 317—Kuba Royal Pattern
Drawn by author

p. 327—Bats
Purchased with Enhanced License from Shutterstock
Royalty-free stock photo ID: 1669600384 by Marina Dekhnik
(image edited by author)
https://www.shutterstock.com/image
-vector/black-silhouette-flying-bats
-isolated-on-1669600384

p. 425—Tree and Roots
Purchased with Enhanced License from Shutterstock
Royalty-free stock photo ID: 1121523821 by entrophoto

(image edited by author)
https://www.shutterstock.com/image
-vector/tree-silhouette-on-white-background
-vector-1121523821

What's next for Sigma Force? From the African continent to the Australian one, Sigma Force is on the move to discover, contain, and resolve the world's next crisis . . . before it's too late.

An international research station off the coast of Australia explores a thriving zone of life in an otherwise dead sea. The area teems with strange bioluminescent corals that defy science—yet, the unique species might hold the key to saving oceans around the world. Still, early studies also reveal a life-altering danger, one that may far outweigh the benefits.

Before further investigation can commence, a massive quake shakes the region, igniting volcanic eruptions and triggering deadly tsunamis. Under the cover of this chaos, masked assailants attack the station, commandeering its personnel and resources. The incursion sets in motion a devastating chain of events that turns oceans toxic, corrupts coastlines, and threatens all life with a danger like no other.

Can Sigma Force stop what has been let loose— especially as an old adversary returns, hunting them and thwarting their every move?
For any hope of success, Commander Gray Pierce must find a key buried in the past, hidden deep in Aboriginal mythology. But what Sigma could discover is even more frightening, something lost for millennia—something that will shake the very foundations of humanity.

TIDES OF FIRE

Coming from William Morrow in Summer 2023

SIGMA FORCE NOVELS FROM
#1 *NEW YORK TIMES* BESTSELLING AUTHOR
JAMES ROLLINS

"[Rollins] is what you might end up with if
you tossed Michael Crichton and Dan Brown
into a particle accelerator together."
—*New York Times Book Review*

THE 6TH EXTINCTION
978-0-06-178569-6

THE BONE LABYRINTH
978-0-06-238165-1

THE SEVENTH PLAGUE
978-0-06-238169-9

THE DEMON CROWN
978-0-06-238174-3

CRUCIBLE
978-0-06-238179-8

THE LAST ODYSSEY
978-0-06-289292-8

"Nobody does this stuff better."
—Lee Child

JR3 0722